M000080989

kill

chain

DOMINIC MARTELL

db

DUNN BOOKS

Published by Dunn Books. First edition October 2020

This title is also available as a Dunn Books ebook.

This book is a work of fiction. Any references to historical events, real people, or real places, are used fictitiously. Other names, characters, places and events are products of the author's imagination. Any resemblance to actual events, places, or people—living or dead—is pure coincidence.

Library of Congress cataloguing-in-publication data is on file with the U.S. Copyright Office.

HARDCOVER: ISBN 978-1-951938-04-8
PAPERBACK: ISBN 978-1-951938-05-5
EBOOK: ISBN 978-1-951938-06-2

Designed by archiefergusondesign.com
Maps by Joe lemonnier

Manufactured in the United States of America

The essence of an intrusion is that the aggressor must develop a payload to breach a trusted boundary, establish a presence inside a trusted environment, and from that presence, take actions toward their objectives, be they moving laterally inside the environment or violating the confidentiality, integrity, or availability of a system in the environment. The intrusion kill chain is defined as reconnaissance, weaponization, delivery, exploitation, installation, command and control (C2), and actions on objectives.

ERIC M. HUTCHINS, MICHAEL J. CLOPPERT, ROHAN M. AMIN, PH.D.

2011. "Intelligence-Driven Computer Network Defense Informed by Analysis of Adversary Campaigns and Intrusion Kill Chains." Lockheed Martin Corporation, USA.

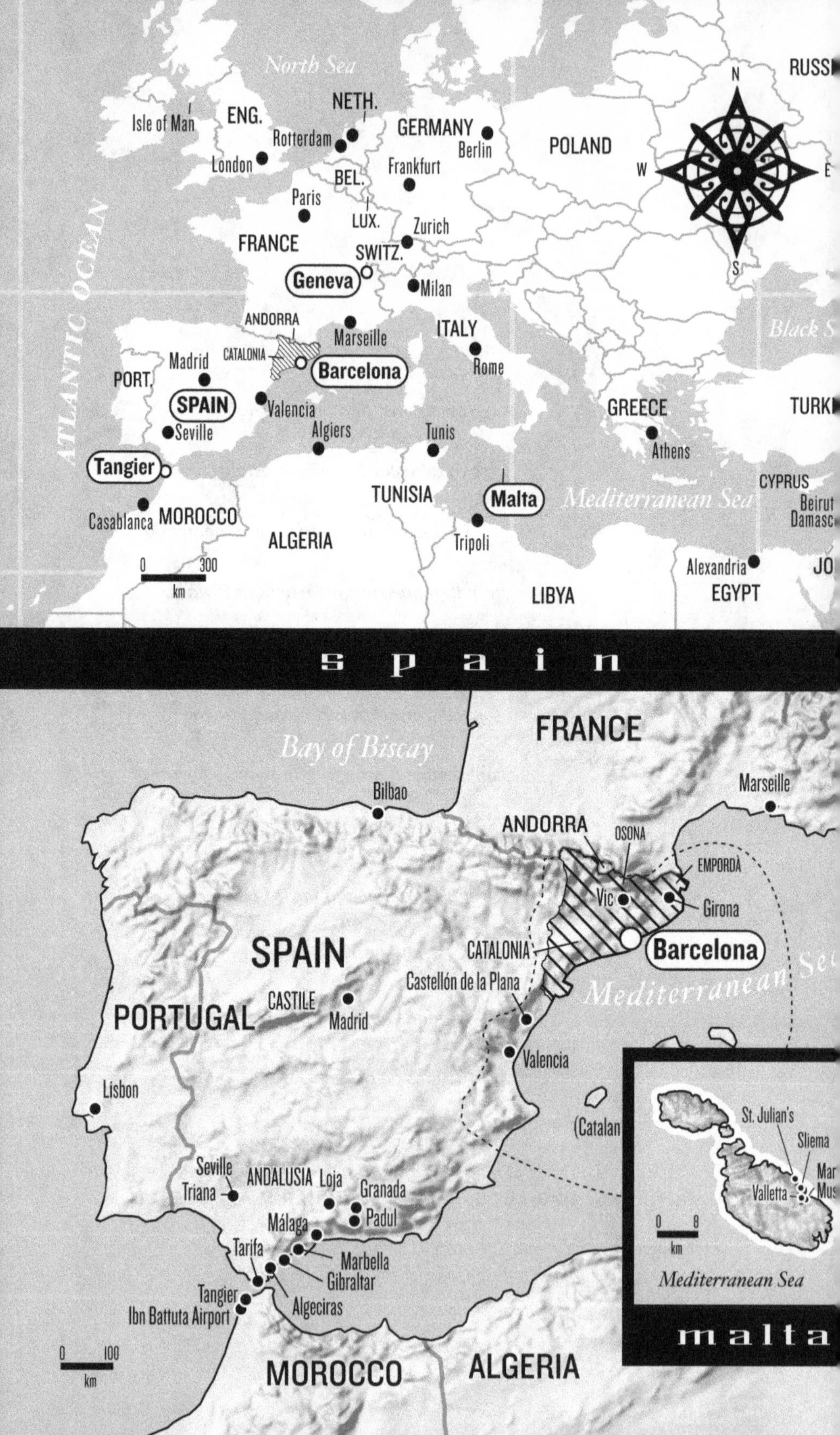
North Sea
Isle of Man
ENG.
NETH.
Rotterdam
GERMANY
Berlin
POLAND
RUSS
London
BEL.
Frankfurt
Paris
LUX.
Zurich
FRANCE
SWITZ.
Geneva
Milan
ATLANTIC OCEAN
ANDORRA
Marseille
ITALY
CATALONIA
Barcelona
Madrid
Rome
PORT.
SPAIN
Valencia
GREECE
TURK
Seville
Algiers
Tunis
Athens
Tangier
TUNISIA
Malta
CYPRUS
Mediterranean Sea
Beirut
Damasc
Casablanca
MOROCCO
ALGERIA
Tripoli
0
300
km
Alexandria
EGYPT
LIBYA
Black S
spain
FRANCE
Bay of Biscay
Bilbao
Marseille
ANDORRA
OSONA
EMPORDÀ
Vic
Girona
SPAIN
CATALONIA
Barcelona
Castellón de la Plana
Mediterranean Se
CASTILE
Madrid
PORTUGAL
Valencia
Lisbon
(Catalan
St. Julian's
Sliema
Valletta
Seville
Triana
ANDALUSIA
Loja
Granada
Padul
Málaga
Tarifa
Marbella
Gibraltar
Tangier
Ibn Battuta Airport
Algeciras
0
8
km
Mediterranean Sea
malta
0
100
km
MOROCCO
ALGERIA

Lake Geneva
Palais des Nations
MONTBRILLANT
LES PÂQUIS
Quai du Mont-Blanc
Jet d'Eau
Promenade du Lac
JONCTION
CHAMPEL
800
geneva
Bay of Tangier
Cap Malabata / Lighthouse
Hotel Continental
Ferry
Place Petit Socco
MEDINA
MARSHAN
Grand Socco
Port
Hotel El Minzah
Avenue Mohammed VI
Avenue Mohammed V
Avenue Moulay Youssef
MALABATA
CASABARATA
Place Jamia el Arbia
N1
Ibn Battuta Airport (3 km)
INDUSTRIAL ZONE
N2
BENI MAKADA
0
800
m
tangiers
GRÀCIA
Passeig de Sant Joan
Plaça de Tetuan
Avinguda Diagonal
Passeig de Gràcia
Via Laietana
Carrer de la Marina
Carrer de Muntaner
EIXAMPLE
Hospital Clínic de Barcelona
Carrer de Villarroel
Carrer de Comte d'Urgell
Parc de la Cuitadella
Zoo
Plaça de la Universitat
Les Rambles
GOTHIC QUARTER
Gran Via de les Corts Catalanes
Plaça dels Països Catalans
El Glaciar
EL RAVAL
Passeig de Colom
Carrer de Sants
Avinguda del Parallel
SANTS
Plaça d'Espanya
Barcelona Airport Hotel (7 km)
Port Vell
Mediterranean Sea
MONTJUÏC
300
m

kill

chain

1

When the buzzer on the street door sounds faintly, far away, Pascual barely notices, absorbed as he is in the slippery nuances of German inheritance law; what exactly is a *Pflichtteilsergänzungsanspruch?* The fact that the buzzer is normally controlled only by a button inside his flat fails to register. Even the whisper of a foot on the steps up to his rooftop terrace does not capture his attention until it is too late, though with reflection Pascual will realize that it was too late from the start. There was never a way to sidestep this tsunami; it is one more consequence of choices he made more than thirty years ago.

It is not until the document on his laptop abruptly and spontaneously closes, replaced by the shutdown screen, that Pascual realizes suddenly that something is very much amiss. Simultaneously his mobile murmurs on the desk, announcing the arrival of a text message. With the first stirring of dread he picks up the phone and opens the text. *Come join us on the terrace,* the message reads. *Bring your phone.*

Twenty years, he thinks. Twenty years of nothing and you thought you were safe. Pascual stares at the message, feeling for ways this could be innocuous and finding none. He passes a hand over his face, thinks briefly about the drop to the street from the window here in his study, decides that even if he could limp away into the night on a sprained ankle they would no doubt find him again before too long. He sits listening for a moment, hearing nothing but the usual sounds of a quiet street in a provincial Catalan town settling down for the night: distant television, blinds being cranked down over a bedroom window. Finally he pushes away from the desk.

He is not worried about homicidal attacks; no competent killer would bother to warn him. Pascual knows this must be another manifestation of his nemesis, the Stranger Who Knows His Name. The only question is what this one will want. He picks up his phone.

The walk to the door at the end of the corridor has never been so long. Pascual is thinking all the way: the message came in English, narrowing the range of possible antagonists. He has had dealings with the security services of half a dozen countries, in all of his languages. But that was in a different age. For twenty years no one has molested him; surely now he is obsolete, superannuated, yesterday's news, useless and forgotten. That, in any event, has been his ambition.

He unlocks the door and pulls it open, letting in a breath of cool night air. He stands looking across the landing at the two people making themselves at home on his terrace. The woman is in the armchair facing the door, legs crossed, a foot dangling in its sharp-toed boot, elbows resting on the arms of the chair, fingers loosely entwined. In the light from the streetlamps he can make her out as well as he could in the average cocktail bar, and affairs have been launched with less to go on. His impression is of blondish curls piled atop fashionably shaved temples, pale eyes, the slim body of a dancer or an athlete.

The man is sitting to his right, the lights behind him, and all Pascual could say is that if it came to fisticuffs the other would win. There is not much of a neck and a pair of massive shoulders in a black sport jacket over a black T-shirt. On the low table ringed by the three chairs stands a bottle of Lepanto, recognizable by its shape.

"I'm assuming you have some glasses in there," the woman says. If her English is not native, Pascual will need a larger sample to detect it. Her pronunciation makes her a Brit or someone who learned it there. "And I'm assuming you won't say no to a slightly better brandy than the one you usually drink."

Pascual stands looking at her, thinking of all the sharp remarks he might make, all of them futile. They know what he likes to drink; they are inside his computer and inside his home. Somebody has done their homework. He considers simply caving, meekly going to get the glasses and cutting to the chase, but he finds he would prefer to go through the motions, pointless though it may be. "What if I were to call the police?" he says.

She smiles. "We'd be gone by the time they got here. You'd have a lot of explaining to do. And we'd be back, sooner rather than later and slightly less polite. Why don't you just get the glasses and listen to what we have to offer you? You might like it."

"That I very much doubt," says Pascual. He stands for a moment contemplating the end of this stage of his life. Whatever the outcome of this little tête-à-tête, it almost certainly is going to mean another dislocation. A pity; he has been happy here.

He fetches three glasses from the kitchen. Sitting across from her as she leans to open the bottle, he studies the face. Europe's gene pool is scrambled enough that anyone could be anything at this point, but his first guess would not have been British; he would be inclined to say she was from somewhere east of the Elbe. Something about the cheekbones, perhaps. If she is past thirty it is not by much, and if she prefers women to men he would not be surprised. The hair perhaps. The black jersey and jeans hug a figure she does not mind flaunting. She pours and hands him a glass with two thick fingers of brandy in it. "You're working late tonight. Was that a last will and testament you were translating? My German's a little shaky, to be frank."

Pascual blinks a few times and says, "You can stop showing off. Hacking someone's computer isn't that much of a feat these days."

"Particularly when your security is so weak. You might wish to speak to someone at Traducciones Dragoman about their network. And you, you need to put a better password on your laptop."

"So you can close a program on my laptop. Hurrah. You can hack my door buzzer, too. Very good. What else can you do?"

The woman smiles as she pours a second glass and shoves it toward her companion. For herself she pours a scant centimeter and then caps the bottle and leans back in her chair, glass in hand. "Well, why don't you look at your bank balance there on your phone? I'll let that speak for itself."

"I don't do any banking on my phone."

"You do now."

Pascual returns her level stare for a full five seconds, then swipes to awaken his phone.

The woman says, "We downloaded your bank's app to your phone when you were out for a jog this afternoon. You probably didn't notice."

Pascual stares at the icon and then taps to open it. The woman says, "Enter your regular e-mail address. Your password is 'Rose1938', no spaces, Rose capitalized then lowercase, your original name and the year of your mother's birth. Not very secure, so you'll want to change to a stronger one right away. But look at your balance first."

Pascual does as he is told. He is curious as to what they judge his price to be. When he sees the figure *€102,385.32* he frowns and says, "Nice try. It can't be too hard to fake up a display like this."

"Oh, it's real. Dummy accounts designed to snare your data don't actually function. This one does. You could wire a few thousand to your wife's Banco Santander account, right here and now. Go ahead, you'll see. We transferred a hundred thousand euros to your account yesterday. The contract specifying the consulting services you are to provide a logistics firm in Rotterdam has been e-mailed to you. They are completely fictional, of course. But you have to tell the taxman something."

"A hundred thousand? By my standards that's a lot, but I have a feeling it's not much by yours. I'd say you're getting me cheap."

"Don't worry, that's just a retainer, good-faith money. The real payoff will come when you complete the job satisfactorily. Check your e-mail there."

Pascual just stares at her, feeling tentacles curling around his leg. Finally he looks at his phone. The e-mail app shows two new messages, one with the Rotterdam contract attached and another with an address he does not recognize and the subject line *Trust agreement*. Pascual opens it and reads, *Attached please find documents for your signature relating to the trust established as per our discussions of last week*. "What the hell is this?" he says.

"That's your payoff. You are the sole beneficiary and enforcer of a Cayman Islands STAR trust. The trust was established with assets consisting of one million euros. When you have completed the job, we will finalize the paperwork and you will have access to the money. Tax-free, with all the confidentiality the Cayman Islands are famous for. Yes, we're prepared to pay you one million euros to do this work for us."

Pascual blinks at her stupidly for a moment. "You're out of your mind."

"Not at all. We're confident you're the man we need."

Pascual stares into her pale eyes for a while, then shifts to the man. He is backlit but Pascual's eyes have adjusted enough to make out a reptile's face, heavy-lidded eyes absolutely impassive. Pascual looks back at the woman and says, "I've been out of the game, out of circulation, out of the way, for twenty years. What on earth do I have, what on earth could I do, that could possibly be worth a million euros to you?"

"Yourself. You and your very special talents."

"Spare me the bullshit. You can only want my memories or my connections. The memories I've suppressed, and the connections are all dead, in prison or long out to pasture."

"We don't want either of those things. We really do want your talents. You are highly qualified. And you are almost uniquely positioned to do what we need."

"I'm a freelance translator, not especially busy or ambitious, and consequently barely making ends meet, in a provincial backwater. I've had no involvement in or contact with any kind of intelligence or criminal operation, on either side, since before the towers in New York went down. My clandestine experience was acquired in a different world. I have worked hard to make myself useless and irrelevant, and if you think I'm not, I must question your judgment."

She concedes with the slightest of nods. "We're aware. Since you left Barcelona you've kept a very low profile. As for making yourself useless and irrelevant, publishing a tell-all book with a reporter from *El Mundo* is hardly the way to do that. I would say you're lucky the project never got off the ground."

"I wanted to do it. But they got to him. He had a career and a family to think of."

She looks amused for a moment, an eyebrow rising. "And you decided not to press the issue. I think that was wise. That's probably why you're still alive, which is slightly surprising, given the number of nasty people you shopped. You got away with it."

"Proving that I am, finally, really of no interest to anyone. At last."

She passes the glass of brandy beneath her fine long nose, her nostrils flaring slightly, but she does not drink. She says, "Which is precisely what makes you valuable."

"To the tune of a million euros? That's absurd."

"Believe me, it's not. Start with the fact that you've been out of circulation for twenty years and have been very careful to leave as small a footprint as possible. Do you know how unusual that makes you in the modern world? You have a very thin paper trail because the identity you were given when Mossad and the CIA were done with you was a sort of cut-rate minimum package, crafted the old way with forged papers and such, before everything was online, just enough to let you set up under your current name as a citizen of Spain and the European Union. What did you get, a DNI and a passport? There's no civil registry entry for Pascual March. They couldn't fake that. That must be why you never married Sara, though you call her your wife. You'd have had to produce your birth certificate. And your desire to live off the grid as far as possible means that you have a very light online presence as well. No social media accounts, and you never buy anything online. The flat here is in Sara's name, and you've never owned a car or joined any professional associations or borrowed any money. You have a credit card but you don't use it much. There's not much to get hold of if anyone gets interested in you. There was, in fact, just enough to establish you as the beneficiary of that trust. All they wanted was your identity documents and proof of residence, which we obtained quite easily."

Her casual mention of Sara sends a slow freeze through Pascual. He feels it is time to stiffen his spine a little. "I'm not going to do anything illegal."

She gestures with the hand holding the glass, the liquid swirling gently. "Your very existence is illegal. Here you are, living under a false identity, which you have used for more than twenty years now to shield yourself from outstanding criminal charges in the Federal Republic of Germany, among other places. Your conscience seems to have come to an accommodation with that."

"I was never formally charged with anything, in any country."

"The murder of Yossi Peled and his wife is still an open case. The shooter was identified and subsequently killed in Bulgaria, probably by the Israelis. The accomplice who rented the getaway car and delivered the weapon was never found. The people who debriefed you decided to be discreet about that, as part of their deal with you. But that was an informal and secret agreement between intelligence agencies. They couldn't make the case go away."

"Ah." Having been shown the carrot, Pascual has been waiting for the stick. "And you're willing to snitch. Or I suppose you'd say 'grass' in the UK."

"We really would rather not do that. We'd much rather you happily took the million euros and asked, 'How may I help you?'"

Pascual has been holding the glass of brandy, determined not to drink, but he finally buckles and takes a healthy slug. The Lepanto is considerably nicer than his usual tipple, but he feels it compromising him as it slides down his throat. He exhales and says, "I don't want your money, and I'll take my chances with the Germans. I've worked too hard to be nobody to give it up now."

The woman leans forward and sets her glass gently on the table. "I think you're being a little bit cavalier with regard to the prospect of a term in a German prison. Think of the effect on the woman you consider your wife. And that fine son you've raised here, in this pleasant town."

Here it is, the real stick. Pascual's heart has suddenly begun to beat harder. He locks eyes with the woman and says, "You bring them into this, I will call the police. Be assured of that."

Her look gone stony, she says, "They're already in it." Her eyes flick to her companion, and he taps at the phone in his hand. Pascual's mobile begins to vibrate.

There is a long stare-down between Pascual and the woman.

When he finally looks at his phone, two WhatsApp messages have appeared. The first is attached to a photo of Rafael grinning at the camera, the merest fringe of beard on his chin, a ring in his ear, a handsome devil and the person Pascual loves most on earth. The arm around his shoulders belongs to the woman taking the selfie, her head almost touching his, blond curls above shaved temples brushing Rafael's brown mop. Behind them is an Amsterdam streetscape, high narrow houses over a canal. "He's a charming fellow, your son," the woman says. "We had quite a pleasant chat. In other circumstances I might have let him take me to dinner, and who knows where that might have led? I have a feeling he's having a bit too much fun to make the most of his scholarship. But then you can say that about a lot of those Erasmus students."

"Leave him alone." Pascual has gone cold.

"We hope to. Very much. We really don't want to make his life difficult. Or your wife's, either."

Pascual takes the cue and looks at the second message. This one also has a photo, and the backdrop is unmistakable, the Alhambra riding high on its ridge behind Sara and the man taking the selfie, instantly recognizable despite the sunglasses as the man sitting to Pascual's right. In the photo he is grinning, looking harmless with his shaved head and three-day growth of beard. "She was quite flattered to be recognized," the woman says. "Even in Granada it seems flamenco singers are not exactly top-shelf celebrities."

Pascual closes the images and leans forward slowly to lay his phone on the table. "Who the hell are you?" he says.

The woman leans back in the chair and for the first time takes a sip of brandy. "You can call me Lina. And this is Felix."

"I didn't mean your names. As if you'd give me the real ones."

"You have to call us something. And our names are all you're going to get. That and a thorough briefing on what you're expected to do for that million euros. Look, Pascual. Focus on the positive here. We're about to make you a wealthy man. In exchange, all you have to do is give us a few weeks of your time and carry out a few simple operations."

"What kind of operations?"

"The kind you used to do thirty years ago. Call it logistics."

"Where?"

"In a few different places. All expenses paid, travel and first-class accommodations."

"I'm not going to facilitate any more murders. I'll throw myself under a train first."

"Dear me, we wouldn't want that. No, nothing so extreme. As I said, logistics in the service of an operation which has to be clandestine, for reasons which will become evident to you. For the benefit of parties you may or may not sympathize with, but who pose no direct threat to anything or anyone you hold dear. You have my word on that."

"Well, that's reassuring. Why me? Why go to all this trouble to recruit me? The world's full of people with similar abilities and fewer scruples. I have, after all, developed a few."

"You underrate your abilities. There aren't many people who can pass for a native speaker in six languages."

"Four at this point. My German and my Arabic are a little rusty."

"I'm sure you can polish them up fairly quickly. And as I said, you have an almost unique qualification besides the languages. We'll get to that. You'll be thoroughly briefed once we are assured of your wholehearted cooperation."

Pascual gives her a long hard stare. "Or a facsimile thereof, presumably."

"We'll settle for that if we have to. Look, try to think of it as a working vacation. And then you come home to the pleasant problem of administering your new fortune. We can recommend a good private banker if you wish."

"What I wish is that you would go away and leave me alone."

The woman who is calling herself Lina frowns at him, a playful sort of frown, accompanied by a pursing of the lips. She brings the glass to her lips again, pauses and says, "Fat chance."

Pascual sits nodding slowly, groping for escape routes but knowing all the time that there are none. They have given him the carrot and brandished the stick, and a big one it is. Ten minutes ago I was a happy man, he thinks.

Pascual's operational reactions have atrophied with time, but he feels a key one beginning to assert itself: rapid recognition of and concession to inevitability. He drains his glass, leans to set it on the table and sighs. "When do we start?" he says.

Pascual stands with his phone in his hand, watching the sky lighten above the rooftops to the east, a gentle dawn breeze stirring his hair. He has come stumbling onto the terrace, groggy after a scant hour of restless sleep, to find it deserted, the bottle of Lepanto and the empty glasses stark evidence that he did not dream the whole wretched business.

The conclusions Pascual reached in the dead of the night, sitting by himself after his visitors had departed, are very much present to him. He is in full-bore emergency mode this morning, and his finger is poised over his phone when he remembers his computer screen going blank, his phone humming on the desk. He takes a deep breath, his head clearing as he realizes that what he holds in his hands is for all practical purposes a direct conduit to the ear of his new employers. He tosses the phone onto a chair.

Moving slowly, Pascual takes the glasses and the bottle into the kitchen. He washes the glasses and without a second thought pours the rest of the expensive brandy down the drain. He rinses the bottle and runs water until the smell of the liquor is gone. He sets the bottle on the floor in a corner. He stands at a window, watching the lightening sky and thinking about the orders he has been given.

He goes into his study and taps at the keyboard to awaken his computer. It appears to be functional again this morning, the e-mail program operative with half a dozen unread messages, the German document still waiting for him to finish the translation. Pascual sits and sends an apologetic e-mail to the project manager at Traducciones Dragoman in Barcelona, pleading illness and asking for the German job to be reassigned. This will not do his standing with the agency any good, but he knows he may have done his last translation job in any event.

Pascual goes and stands under the shower, the water as hot as he can stand it, wishing he could stand there forever. Getting dressed, he thinks about Sara in Granada, far away. He picks up his phone to find that a text has arrived. It reads, *Good morning. There are trains to Barcelona Sants at 13:01, 13:10 and 13:55. Text when you are on the train. Exit station toward Països Catalans and wait for a call.*

Pascual ponders for a moment, then turns off his phone and tosses it onto the bed.

What would they expect me to say to her? Pascual asks himself, sitting on the terrace, phone in hand. He knows a working flamenco *cantaora* keeps late hours but judges the morning might be advanced enough that she might be on her feet. He taps her number into his phone.

"Hola, cariño," Sara answers on the third ring and Pascual's heart turns over. Their paths have diverged with the years and their

disparate passions, but she is still the mother of his child and the stoutest soul he has ever known. In a crisis his instinct is to fly to her, but that will have to wait.

"I hope I didn't wake you." Pascual knows that everything he says on this phone must be a performance for the benefit of a critical audience. "I imagine you were carousing till dawn in some low Gypsy den."

Sara's soft laugh comes over the line. "What ideas you have. In fact I was in bed by midnight and at the studio early this morning. We need three more tracks for this record, and Manolo and the producer are fighting over arrangements again."

"So I'm interrupting you at work. Apologies."

"No matter. They've gone off in a corner to wrestle over artistic principles, and I'm happy to let Manolo fight my side. The studio wants to make a pop tune out of the tango, with strings and a chorus, the usual nonsense, and Manolo and I are putting our foot down. I want to do real flamenco, and they want a Eurovision entrant. We'll probably compromise and give them a rumba. What's up with you?"

I have put the family in mortal danger, Pascual wants to say. He sticks to the script he has rehearsed. "I'm just calling to tell you I'll be going on a little jaunt soon. I've landed something like a real job."

"That doesn't sound like you. Are you quite well?"

"Completely sane. Just responding to incentives. Somebody offered me a lot of money, that's all."

"You're impervious to financial incentives, in my experience. Have you developed a gambling problem? Taken to drugs?"

Pascual laughs gently. "Without you here to keep me on the straight and narrow, what do you expect? No, really, it's just a plum job, that's all. A woman wants me to go around with her for a few weeks interpreting for her at business meetings. A chance to use all my languages, and a little change of scenery for a while. And a lot of money."

"A woman, I see. A young woman, by any chance?"

"Vida mía. You do me an injustice."

"I'm joking, *cariño*. I rejoice for you. Where are you going and how long will you be gone?"

"Both still somewhat up in the air. I meet with her later today for particulars."

"Keep me posted. And have fun, but not too much. Any word from our prodigal son?"

"Not recently. I assume he is absorbed in his studies."

"If he takes after his father, I doubt it very much. I miss you both madly. Listen, I have to go, I'm being summoned. Take care of yourself."

With a pang that nearly takes his breath away Pascual says goodbye. He rings off and stands staring at his phone, a leaden feeling in his stomach. He had long thought he was through lying, and here he has just told a string of lies to the best person he has ever known.

Pascual begins to believe the money is real when he whistles up 500 euros just like that from the cash machine outside the CaixaBank and the display shows his remaining balance to be *€101,885.32*. He trousers the banknotes with a guilty look over his shoulder and slinks across the street to the Bar Manel, his slightly down-at-heel local and second living room.

There are a few customers on the terrace, but the man Pascual is looking for is not there. He goes inside and spots him at a corner table, deep in conversation with two others, in their native Amazigh. Pascual nods as he passes and slides onto a stool at the end of the bar. The Chinese girl behind the bar greets him in her cheerful singsong, a musical Chinese-accented Castilian. "You have a bad face today. Don't you sleep?"

"I had bad dreams," says Pascual. "Give me a coffee with milk and one of those croissants."

Pascual devours his breakfast listening to conversations in Castilian, Arabic, Amazigh, Chinese, and the rustic Catalan of Osona. When he settled here in the heartland twenty years ago, he thought he would miss the cosmopolitan Babel of Barcelona, but Babel is everywhere now.

A slap on his shoulder rouses him from his thoughts. "We missed you on Saturday." The *tertulia* in the corner has broken up and Dris has come to join him at the bar, switching from Amazigh to the Catalan he speaks as well as Pascual. "We needed you to make even sides."

"I had a deadline to meet. I can't keep up with you young bucks anyway."

Dris laughs. In jeans and T-shirt, hair and complexion of a generically Mediterranean hue, he could pass for just about anything. A certain roughness of demeanor suggests a familiarity with hard labor and Spartan circumstances. In fact he was born in a destitute hamlet in the Rif and brought across the Strait as an infant. Pascual has known him since he was eight years old and plotting mischief with Rafael. "You don't have to keep up with us," says Dris. "All you have to do is stick a foot in when we try and dribble past. And you're good at that."

"That's the one talent we ancients have, being in the way. What's new with you? Any luck on the jobs front?"

Dris's smile goes away. "Not a thing. The slaughterhouses are laying people off, and the fellow at the garage hired a mechanic who came over from Girona. I could tell from the start he wasn't keen on me anyway. Who wants to hire a *moro* with a drug conviction on his record?"

"The record probably doesn't help. But you've got skills. Mechanics come and go. Something will open up."

"When? Thirty-three percent youth unemployment we've got in this country. What am I supposed to do? And they wonder why we want to go off and fight in Syria."

Pascual shakes his head. "I thought I'd talked you out of that."

Dris takes on a slightly shamefaced look. "Ah, don't worry. I know it's all horseshit. But I still don't have a job. I'm starting to think about going down to Barcelona to try my luck. But I don't know that I'll be any better off down there. Here at least my mother still feeds me."

"Let me propose something first." Pascual motions at the stool next to him, and with a curious look Dris sits. "Could you use five hundred euros? Just for starters. More as we go along. We can discuss terms. But five hundred as a retainer."

Dris's look shades to suspicion. "What do I have to do?"

Pascual drains his coffee, framing his pitch. "I've gotten myself in a bit of a jam, and I need help."

"Sure, anything I can do." Dris's expression goes very neutral and his voice goes soft. "Whose nose do I have to break?"

"Not that kind of help. I need somebody to take and deliver messages for me. By word of mouth. You never contact me by any electronic device, at least not any that can be traced to me. Any communication between us is face to face or through intermediaries. You leave a message here at the bar, for example. We can work out the procedures. There may be some travel involved. All expenses paid, of course. And you keep your mouth shut. And I mean shut tight. Not your best mates, not your mother. Anyone asks what you're up to, you tell them you've got a line on a job or whatever you want to tell them. But it has nothing to do with me. Understood?"

Dris blinks for a few seconds and then smiles. "You know, we wonder about you. The languages, the Arabic especially. Somebody said you used to be a spy."

"Something like that. I'll tell you the whole story someday. Now I just need to know if you're free to work for me for the next few weeks." Pascual reaches into his trouser pocket and pulls out the roll of fresh euros. Below the level of the bar he slaps it into Dris's hand. "Here's your retainer."

Dris glances at the banknotes and makes them disappear. "Suddenly I'm free," he says. "When do we start?"

"Now. Your first assignment is to lend me your phone."

Dris reaches into his pocket, but he is frowning. "For how long?"

"Long enough to make a couple of calls. I've got to talk to Sara and Rafael, and I can't use my phone, or theirs either. It's possible they're all being monitored."

"You're joking." Skepticism dawns on Dris's face.

"I wish I were. I'm not even going to call them directly. I don't want your number showing up in their call logs. I'm going to try to leave messages for them where they live and have them call you, not me. You'll take a message, the number of a safe phone where I can reach them, and a time."

Dris frowns, working it out. "Why don't you just go buy a prepaid phone?"

"Because since the Madrid attacks you have to link it to a DNI or a passport. And then it's not anonymous, and I still can't call them directly."

"There are ways to get around that. Give me a day or two and I can get you a phone."

"I don't have a day or two. As long as you don't go direct to their phones, this will do for now. We'll worry about safe phones later. And you'll need to go home and pack a bag. This afternoon you're getting on a train with me."

Dris's eyes are wide. "Where are we going?"

"Barcelona, to start with. After that, God only knows."

Pascual has known more than one Barcelona. His childhood Barcelona was straitlaced and somber, an occupied city with an Avenida del Generalísimo Francisco Franco slashing through it and gray-suited policemen looking down their noses at black-clad widows muttering in Catalan. The Barcelona into which the 13:10 delivers him is a world-class hipster mecca and tourist magnet overrun with emaciated buskers and peeling Nordics who've been in the sun too long. It is also a restive capital in a smoldering political crisis, its balconies draped with yellow-and-red striped flags.

Pascual is sometimes not sure which one he prefers; the old one at least had *El llanero solitario* on the telly, an indulgent *iaia* plying him with chocolate, and his mother, still young and beautiful if already sad, tucking him in at night.

On the train Pascual has time to chew nails and second-guess himself. Electronic surveillance is one thing and obviously a strength of the opposition, but the instructions for his arrival at Sants suggests they will have boots on the ground as well. Maybe just the charming couple who kept him up past his bedtime last night, maybe more; he has no way of knowing. Whatever the situation, he is aware that in twenty years whatever skills he may have had once have eroded.

He is also aware that the talent on his side is thin. The drug trade no doubt schooled Dris in certain basics of clandestine work, but Pascual has no idea if his two-year sentence at Castellón de la Plana was the result of bad luck or sloppy practice. At the very least he is hoping the lad can follow instructions.

So far, so good; Pascual comes up the escalator into the teeming station, casting casual looks about, without spotting him. Pascual orients himself and goes out onto the station's broad forecourt. He drifts toward the Plaça dels Països Catalans, scanning the crowd, and when he has nearly reached the street his phone begins to buzz.

"Go on across the bus lanes and look for a white Audi," Lina says in his ear. Pascual obeys, and here it is, parked at the curb along with a handful of others waiting to pick up arriving travelers. Felix is leaning against the bonnet with his arms crossed, glancing intermittently at Pascual but mostly scanning the space behind him. He grants Pascual the slightest nod and goes around to get in on the driver's side. Lina is in the back seat, putting away her phone and beckoning to Pascual. He gets in beside her, tossing his flight bag on the seat between them.

"You travel light," Lina says.

"Perhaps I'm in denial," Pascual says as the car slews away from the curb. "I'm hoping I'm not going to be on the road too long."

"A few weeks, probably. You'll be able to afford to expand your wardrobe. You'll need a nice suit or two."

"It's a costume drama, is it?"

"It is. And you've got the lead role."

Pascual shows his regard for proper business attire with a grimace. "What's on the agenda for today?"

"Today we brief you. Probably for the next few days. Then we turn you loose. We're not going to be looking over your shoulder the whole time. But we'll have ways of keeping you on the leash."

"I don't doubt it."

Nobody attempts any small talk as Felix pushes skillfully through traffic, down Tarragona to the Plaça d'Espanya and then out along the Gran Via away from the city center. Pascual's heart sinks as he recognizes the route to the airport. "Am I getting on a plane today?"

"Not today. Possibly next week, if you're a quick study."

Pascual stares out at a Barcelona he barely knows, the eruption of office and residential towers, shopping complexes and motorway interchanges that has encrusted the approaches to the airport at El Prat de Llobregat. Felix negotiates a roundabout and pulls up in front of a hypermodern structure with two blue-paneled wings attached to a red-paneled truncated cone pierced by an entrance; a sign announces the Barcelona Airport Hotel. Felix pulls into a car park and they get out.

"We've booked you a room," says Lina. "For a week, adjusted as need be. Shall we get you checked in?"

Inside the cone is a vast high-ceilinged lobby out of a science-fiction film, with views of the city projected on the arching walls, where a sleek honey blonde delivers a key card to Pascual with a perfunctory smile and points him in the proper direction. Felix has disappeared; when Pascual comes away from the desk, Lina smiles at him and says, "We've got a suite on the third floor. Why don't we meet there in, say, fifteen minutes?"

Pascual nods. "Send out a search party if I'm not there in twenty."

The window in his room has a splendid view of jetliners gliding in for a landing, the sea sparkling beyond the runways. Pascual is disoriented and overcome with foreboding. He pisses into a gleaming toilet and goes in search of his handlers' lair.

"Money laundering," says Pascual. "That's what you're talking about."

The suite has two bedrooms, each with its own bath, a kitchenette and this table by the window, bearing carafes of coffee and water, cups and glasses, notepads with pens, and a laptop computer. Here the only view from the window is of the sprawling result of a massive property bubble that has since burst.

Lina smiles. Today she is wearing a cool gray jacket over a black tee, discreet silvery earrings dangling. They make her look more feminine but no less Slavic. Pascual is still trying to get a reading on her accent. At her elbow Felix looks just as he did last night, imperturbable and brutish. "That's an uncharitable interpretation," says Lina. "Our principals prefer to think of it as preserving discretion."

"I see. Where does the money come from?"

"Activities that need not concern you. Above your pay grade, as the expression goes."

"Activities. Criminal activities, I'm assuming."

"That is often in the eye of the beholder. As you're no doubt aware."

"I'm aware that the conceit can provide a comfortable justification for a great deal of naked self-interest, yes."

"The only justification you need is that one million euros. Try to maintain focus."

Pascual senses this is not the time or place for philosophical disputation. "So I'm a mule, is that it? A smurf?"

"If you wish."

"And how much money are we talking about?"

"Well, ask yourself what kind of cut a mule usually gets, and that will give you an idea."

Pascual does the math. "That's a hell of a lot of cash. Is it in bales? Am I going to be driving lorries through frontier posts?"

"The world has moved on, Pascual." The merest hint of an amused look passes between Lina and Felix. "Cash is on its way out. In Sweden only about ten percent of transactions involve cash now. In China you can pay with a QR code in most places. Even in the heart of darkest Africa, in Somaliland, you can pay for most things on your phone. Cash will be extinct in a few years."

"Heavens. What's an honest crook to do?"

Pascual has been slumping on his chair in a passively aggressive way, determined to maintain a lofty detachment. Now Felix leans forward just a hair and says, "Look, buddy. You're being well paid for this. Now lose the attitude."

It is the first time Pascual has heard him speak, and to his surprise the words are delivered in a fair approximation of the Brooklynese he learned in his adolescence, with a slight overlay of something foreign. Pascual gives the stare-down a few seconds, recognizing an experienced intimidator, and says, "You've secured my cooperation. But not my affection."

Lina resumes. "Money's a fiction, as I'm sure you know. Money is whatever enough people agree to consider money. Once you've got an accounting system, money is nothing but a record of numbers. And numbers are easy to send around the world at the touch of a button."

"And one set of numbers looks much like another, which is the whole secret of money laundering."

"Correct. You can send a set of numbers flying around the world so fast it's impossible for the plods to keep up. All you need at the end is a bank account for it to land in. And there's the rub."

"Because a bank account has to have a name on it."

"Exactly. And everybody's got a Know Your Customer process now. Of course, the customer can be fictitious. But it has to be a convincing fiction. And that, finally, is where you come in."

"I'm the fictitious customer."

"That's right. You'll set up a series of holding companies, and then you'll provide them with bank accounts. And then at the proper time you will access the proper string of numbers and deposit dollars and euros into the accounts. That's a matter of a little basic computer literacy. We'll train you."

Pascual frowns across the table at her. "Hang on. If you could hack into my bank account, why can't you just sit down at your laptop there and set up these fake accounts yourself?"

Lina shakes her head. "The only hacking we did was of your phone. All we did was download your bank's app to it. Your account is of course perfectly real, and our payment to you was perfectly legitimate. And the accounts you set up will be perfectly real. As will the companies that own them. And best of all, the identity you'll be operating under will be real, too."

Pascual shakes his head, stares out the window, sighs. "Whose identity am I stealing?"

"Your own."

Slowly he turns back to look at her. "Now you've lost me."

Lina leans forward a little. "This is the best part, Pascual. This is why we chose you. You have something that's very rare. You have an unshakeable identity that is no longer your own."

As Pascual works on that, Lina reaches into a briefcase on the floor and pulls out a manila envelope. She slides it across the table to Pascual. Pascual undoes the clasp on the envelope and upends it to slide the contents out onto the tabletop. He picks up a passport with the burgundy cover of the European Union, imprinted with *UNJONI EWROPEA – MALTA*. He opens it and is confronted with his own photograph, staring at him glumly, the image taken two years ago, the last time he renewed his Spanish passport. He muses for a moment, wondering how they obtained his passport photo, then finally with a shock noticed the name printed next to the photograph: *Pascual Rose*. "You're crazy," he says.

"Not at all." Lina is shaking her head. "It's the perfect cover. It's an absolutely solid identity that will pass muster with any registered agent or bank compliance officer. It's rock-solid because it's real. You've got the documentation there to prove it."

Pascual reaches for a document labeled *CERTIFICACIÓN EN EXTRACTO DE ACTA DE NACIMIENTO* and stares at it stupidly for a moment before recognizing a certified copy of his own Spanish birth certificate, all the names he was given at birth laid out for the world to see. "I'm going to do this under my real name? That's insane."

"It's utterly logical. It's the perfect identity because it's real."

"Yes, and it's mine. That million euros won't do me much good in prison."

"You won't go to prison. If anyone ever gets interested in Pascual Rose and his financial activities, you'll have the perfect alibi. Your identity was stolen. And you'll be able to prove it."

"I can prove I stole my own identity? How does that help me?"

"You'll be able to show somebody else stole it. You'll be able to prove you were safe at home in your little town in Catalonia when the mysterious Pascual Rose was talking to lawyers in Panama and bankers in Geneva."

"How the hell will I do that?"

"We'll do it for you. You saw what we can do on your computer and your phone. We'll make sure there's a digital record of your presence in Catalonia throughout the period when Pascual Rose is active. Your phone's geolocation feature for one, because you'll leave your phone with us. We'll give you new ones for the job, along with a credit card for expenses in Pascual Rose's name. A few cash machine withdrawals, some purchases. All of that is easy to fake with a little cooperation from you. Throw in the occasional appearance at your local café, because you won't be on the road all the time, and if anyone ever questions you, you never left the country and you can prove it. No one will ever be able to prove you and the Pascual Rose who opened a bank account in Nicosia or Luxembourg are the same person."

Pascual blinks at that for a long moment. "If you can do all that, why can't you just set up a completely fake identity and hire some ambitious young crook to be that person? Why on earth take all this trouble and spend all this money to bother me? You said I was unique. What the hell is unique about me if you can tailor an identity to fit anybody?"

"That's a very intelligent question. And the answer is that until a couple of years ago, we could have done that. But things have changed. You heard about the Panama Papers scandal, no doubt."

"Of course. It wasn't exactly news to me."

"No. But it made enough noise that the politicians were finally moved to do something. It's gotten tougher to set up a shell company and funnel dirty money into it, at least in the type of country where you would want to keep your money, with nice stable banks and a high standard of living. The bankers are finally having to take their responsibilities seriously. There are new Know Your Customer requirements, new directives on identifying beneficial owners. They're developing tighter procedures for checking the bona fides of people who come inquiring about setting up corporations and trusts and bank accounts. They all use electronic identity verification now. They search the databases to see if your name pops us as a politically exposed person or a known felon. They can check credit history, police records, property ownership. Meanwhile, it's getting harder to construct a fictitious identity. Everyone leaves a digital track now. It's easy to forge a passport but a lot harder to alter or erase ten years of online activity. That's why you are such a valuable commodity. Your identity is split in two."

"What do you mean?"

"Pascual Rose's paper trail ends in the early nineties. We know he's real because he's in the Spanish civil registry and he left traces of his passage in New York, Paris, a couple of other places. There are records in Brooklyn in the late seventies and Paris in the eighties. But after 1992 there's nothing. He certainly has no online presence. Pascual Rose disappeared before everything was put on the computer. That means we have a blank slate for creating a digital record of his activity for the last twenty or more years, starting with the irrefutable fact of his existence. And that record will prove his bona fides to any bank on earth. And when he's done working for us, he can go back to being the blameless and inconspicuous Pascual March, with no one the wiser."

Pascual is shaking his head. "The Spanish police know all about me. Both of me. The Sûreté in Paris does, too. They know Pascual March was Pascual Rose. I was involved in a couple of fairly notorious homicide cases, in Barcelona and in Paris, twenty-some years ago, and I had to tell them all about myself. It's in their files. And if word gets out now that Pascual Rose is setting up dodgy bank accounts in the Cayman Islands, they're going to come looking for Pascual March."

"Well, first, there's no reason why word should 'get out,' as you put it. Bankers do not stay in business by publicizing the people who come and set up accounts with them. What they do have to do now is put you through a fairly rigorous Know Your Customer process. They call it 'onboarding' clients, and they insist the client be present. They ask for multiple IDs, and they'll verify them. Driver's licenses, passports, birth certificates. They'll compare your face with the face on the ID document and use biometrics to make sure it's actually you. That's where your actually being Pascual Rose is crucial. It's a lot harder than it used to be to fake up an identity. It's easier and more reliable to go with a real one. And Pascual Rose is lying there for the taking. As for those Spanish and French police files, it takes some searching to find them. You have to know where to look. I think your spook friends must have had a quiet word with the coppers and told them you were no concern of theirs. You're not flagged anywhere a bank compliance officer is going to look. And whatever you told the spooks when you turned yourself in never made it into any searchable record. There is no official record of Pascual Rose ever being involved in terrorist activities. You were too good for that. Pascual Rose is clean."

Pascual glares across the table at her. "But as you said, he hasn't done anything since 1992. Won't the bankers be a little curious about that?"

"Ah, but he has. He's been very active. But most of that activity has been in countries with fairly low standards of document authentication and cybersecurity."

"I see. Meaning you had no trouble faking the records."

"A little, but not much. And all of our fakery is rooted in the very real Pascual Rose. Trace it back, and you get eventually to those perfectly genuine Spanish documents."

"Impressive. And what am I supposed to have been doing all these years? What the hell was I doing in Malta?"

"What you were doing in Malta was mainly acquiring citizenship, which the Maltese generously allow people to simply buy, if they have enough money, with a minimal residency requirement. What you were doing elsewhere was what you've mostly done since you left Europe for good in the early nineties. You found a way to put your talents to use in the brave new post-communist world, when everything was suddenly for sale. You worked contacts, offered your services, ingratiated yourself with the up-and-coming men. You ran errands, brokered deals, took your cut. You spent time in Morocco, Jordan, Lebanon, Greece, Cyprus. Since 2007 you've been living in Dubai, making a perfectly legitimate living as a consultant for European investors in the Middle East. You've made a reasonable amount of money. It's not a bad life."

"I wish I could remember it."

"I'm sure you can fake up a few anecdotes to dine out on." A brief smile comes and goes. "So. First of all, you will pass muster when you are onboarded. And if—and this is a big if—if anyone ever decides that there's something fishy about the man who set up that foundation in Liechtenstein, you will be back in your little Catalan refuge and able to prove you never budged from it."

Pascual picks up his Maltese passport and stares at his photo. "Hang on. This has got to set off alarms. The same photo on two passports? They have them all in a big computer database now, don't they? They can't possibly miss the fact that you used the same photo."

"Well, we did and we didn't. You're right that the system is supposed to flag identical photos or even just the same face if it's used on different passports. But the technology's imperfect, and can be thwarted. When we borrowed your photo we ran it through a software tool that adds visual noise to alter the image slightly, just enough to fool the system."

A long minute passes while Pascual chews on all this. He finally nods, passes a hand over his face and says, "Wonderful. All very convenient. Except for one thing." He holds up his left hand, displaying thumb, index, middle finger and two stumps. "I came into the digital age missing two digits. I lost them in that affair that was hushed up in Paris. But it's something people tend to notice. And when the snoops from Interpol come calling, those bank compliance officers will remember it. And it's proof positive that Pascual Rose and Pascual March are the same man. The cops will believe this before they believe your cooked-up digital evidence."

"They might, if you were the only man in the world missing two fingers on his left hand."

Pascual blinks at her. "Oh, come on."

Lina merely smiles and looks at Felix. He jabs at the laptop for a few seconds and then spins it and shoves it toward Pascual. "Tell me what you see there," says Lina.

What Pascual sees is a man, captured in what appears to be a surveillance photograph, in grainy black and white, in a generic streetscape with cars and shop fronts, no legible signs to hint at the location. He is neither young nor old, not fair but not especially swarthy, mustachioed and carelessly barbered, as nondescript as the setting. He is looking out into the street, holding a cigarette to his lips with his left hand. "All right," says Pascual, "who's this, then?"

"Nobody you know. Notice anything?"

Pascual lets out an exasperated sigh. "It's just the way he's holding the cigarette."

"Scroll down."

Pascual scrolls to see a second photo, recognizably the same man, now talking with a mobile phone held to his ear. In this one his left hand is resting on the hood of a car, and the stumps where his little and ring fingers used to be are clearly visible. Pascual scrolls again to see a third shot, showing the man in what appears to be an airport concourse, striding along with a bag in his right hand and his left arm swinging forward, the maimed hand prominent. Pascual shoves the laptop away. "I repeat my question."

Felix reclaims the computer as Lina says, "Bassam Youssef. Syrian, forty-eight years of age. So, a little younger than you, but you've kept yourself in decent shape, and you could pass for a contemporary of his. No real resemblance, but you're the same physical type, brown hair and eyes, you could be from anywhere around the Mediterranean."

"Where are you going with this?"

"I'm just saying that if anyone gives a verbal description of you to a curious policeman, he could also be describing Bassam Youssef. Or vice versa."

Pascual nods. "And who is Bassam Youssef, really? What does he do?"

"He works for the Iranian Revolutionary Guards."

"Ah. In what capacity?"

"He does for them roughly what our fictional Pascual Rose does for his clients in Dubai. Makes deals. Negotiates things. Some of them not very nice, like bribes and ransoms. He's a little shadier than our Pascual. He is on some of those watch lists. That's why he had to steal Pascual Rose's identity to set up those holding companies for the IRG's business empire. That's if anyone starts probing, of course."

"I see." Pascual's brow furrows as he strives to see. "What a coincidence, about his fingers."

"No coincidence at all. We went looking for someone like him and we found him. In a war, what with firefights and explosions and whatnot, it turns out lots of people lose fingers. He lost his in a scrape in Aleppo, five years ago. He was with the Syrian Mukhabarat at the time. You know about the close links between the Syrian regime and Iran."

"Of course. So he's the fall guy, huh?"

"Only in case of need. He's the big red herring if anyone starts sniffing around your tracks. We can make it look like he's the one who resuscitated Pascual Rose. And that will send them off sniffing around the Iranians."

"And presumably the story would be that he chose me because of my injury. But how would he know about me?"

"It doesn't matter. He might have known you in Syria. He might have run into you in Dubai. He might have connections at the Sûreté. Who can say? Nobody will question it. They'll just wonder what the IRG is up to and that will absorb all their investigative resources for some time."

Pascual contemplates, meeting in turn the steady gazes of Lina and Felix. "Seems like a hell of a risk," he says. "And all on me."

"That's what the million euros are for," growls Felix.

Pascual nods. "All right. When do we get started?"

Lina says, "How does now sound? We've got a lot to cover. But there's no rush. It's a process and it can take some time. That's why you're committing for a few weeks or maybe months. Think of it as your job for a while."

Pascual is troubled by a faint echo of something he heard nearly forty years ago in Beirut, the PFLP recruiter leaning across the table to murmur, "It's not a vacation, *habibi*. It's going to be the hardest job you've ever had."

"Fair enough," says Pascual. "I'll try to think about the money."

5

Pascual is prepared for a veto and a shift to plan B if necessary, but when he tells Lina that he is going into the city for a late supper she merely says, “Fine. You don’t need our permission. You’re a big boy.” Perhaps reacting to the look of surprise on his face, she adds coolly, “If you’re planning to do a bunk, I must remind you of the cards we hold. We are working on the assumption that you are fully committed to the project.”

“Oh, yes.” Innocence is a look Pascual learned to simulate early in life. “I may not have many talents, but I can spot where my interest lies with the best of them.”

In the taxi he feels for his phone in his pocket by reflex before remembering that he purposely left it in his room. He knows they can track him with it; that would not especially concern him tonight, but he has read that a phone can be hacked to become an eavesdropping device, even when turned off, and that would be fatal. He has the taxi drop him at the foot of the Ramblas by Columbus on his pedestal and makes his way uphill through a scattering of late-evening idlers. The scruffy bottom end of the Ramblas was once his turf, and he has to suppress a pang of nostalgia for old haunts swept away by ruthless renewal. His life has been a series of episodes, with jarring discontinuities; his years of poverty in Barcelona were among his best.

The Glaciar is still there, tucked into a corner of the Plaça Reial under the arcade, a venerable institution with its marble bar and high timbered ceiling. Dris is leaning on the bar and surveying the female talent. In his day Pascual had his successes here, but now he is years past the median age. In any event, tonight he has more important things on his mind. "I thought you weren't coming," says Dris, dragging his gaze reluctantly away from a dark blonde in a very short dress.

"They kept me at it all evening. They've got a lot to teach me." Pascual orders a cognac and avoids looking at Dris.

"What are they training you for?"

"Larceny. Did they get back to you?"

Dris nods. "Sara says you can call her at her pension. But no later than eleven. They're touchy about that, she said."

"What about Rafa?"

"He gave me the names and mobile numbers of two girls he knows. He says if he's not with one he'll be with the other."

"I'm glad he's keeping busy."

"One is Elise and the other is Lotte." Dris sets his phone on the bar and shoves it toward Pascual. "I've entered the numbers in my contacts."

Pascual ignores the phone and pulls a beer mat toward him. "Do me a favor and just read the numbers out to me, will you?" Pascual produces a pen from his shirt pocket. "Then delete them."

"Why can't you just take my phone?"

"I'm in a state of high paranoia with these people. They could have someone following me, watching us right now, and I don't want them spotting you. I want to talk to Sara and Rafa on a nice, old-fashioned landline nobody's had time to tap. So just pretend you're looking for the number of the girl who's stood you up and read me those numbers if you would."

Pascual pretends to be drafting a poem on the beer mat, scowling at it as he writes down the numbers Dris dictates. When he is finished he slips the mat into a pocket. "Thanks. I'm off to pay my cousin a visit. I think he's the last person in Spain who has a landline. Try not to drool when you talk to the blonde."

Dris grins. "I don't need lessons from you, pop."

Pascual drains his *copa* and pushes away from the bar. "Listen, I don't know how the next few days are going to go. I think you can head home and wait to hear from me. If I don't get back there myself, I'll leave a message with Yu Yan at the bar. And the next time I see you I'll have more money for you."

Pascual leaves Dris edging toward the blonde and makes for the Liceu metro stop. Courtesy would require him to call and inquire whether his cousin Pere is receiving visitors this evening, but Pere seems to take vicarious pleasure in Pascual's bohemian existence and has taken him in at odd hours before. His wife is another story, but Pascual is prepared to withstand an icy reception. When he emerges from the Hospital Clínic stop he is on home turf; the placid treelined streets of the Eixample harbor his earliest memories. Pascual trudges up Villarroel and leans on the doorbell of the flat where his mother grew up.

Upstairs, Pere stands in the open doorway, gray and unfashionably mustachioed, belly straining at his belt, looking puzzled. "Pascual, what a surprise. Why didn't you let us know you were coming?"

"Apologies, cousin. Totally unforeseen. I just happened to be in the neighborhood, and I thought, how long has it been since I saw Pere and Sofia?"

Pere shoves the door closed and waves Pascual down the hall. "We're just having supper." He frowns. "Not sure if there's enough to go around, to be honest."

Pascual waves it off. "No need to feed me. Actually, I have a bit of an emergency. I've lost my phone, you see, and I need to make a couple of calls."

Pere looks unsurprised. "Left it on the train, did you?"

Pascual shrugs. "I don't know. Possibly somebody nicked it. Anyway, Sara's expecting me to call tonight and I thought I might just impose on you a little. I'll pay you for the call."

"No need."

"She's in Granada right now."

"Ah."

"Here, this ought to cover it." Pascual shoves a ten-euro note into Pere's hand. They have reached the kitchen, and Pascual leans in to see Pere's wife glaring at him from the table, laden with dishes, a *porró* full of wine and a half-consumed potato omelet. "*Hola,* Sofia. How goes it?"

"What on earth do you want?" Sofia was comely when young but has become something of a harpy with age. She has never taken to Pascual.

"Just stopping in to use the phone, thanks. How's everyone? The kids doing well?"

"What's wrong with your phone?" Eyes narrowed, knife and fork in hand, Sofia is not to be trifled with.

"Lost it, I'm afraid." Out of the corner of his eye Pascual sees Pere brandishing the banknote at his wife. "Won't be a minute." He turns to Pere. "Can I use the phone in the hall?"

Punching the number of the pension in Granada into the vintage Gondola telephone, Pascual hears an argument proceeding in hushed tones in the kitchen. Somewhat to his surprise the ancient instrument seems to function, and in two minutes he is talking to Sara. "What's all this nonsense, then?" she says. "What's wrong with our phones?"

"Our mobiles are being tapped. We have to assume anything we say is overheard. Until further notice."

There is a silence. Sara says, "What have you done?"

"I'm afraid I've gotten us all in trouble. What I told you on the phone this morning was not entirely true."

"What part of it was true, then?"

"The going off on a well-paid job. That part is true. The problem is that the job is clandestine and probably criminal."

"I thought you were done with that sort of thing." Sara's tone has gone cold.

"So did I. I would have told them to go to hell, but they showed me a couple of photos. Do you remember a man who took a selfie with you a few days ago?"

Another silence follows. "What about him?"

"If you ever see him again, run as fast as you can. They showed me a picture of Rafa, too."

When Sara speaks again, her voice is husky. *"Dios mío,* Pascual. Who are they?"

"I don't know. But they're paying me a million euros to do a job for them. And making it clear that you and Rafa are hostages if I refuse. So I'm inclined to say yes."

"Take it to the police. Now. Before it goes any further."

"They've anticipated that. The next thing that would happen would be that I lose you or Rafa."

There is a frozen silence. "They can't do that."

"They can, believe me. And they will. Listen, here's what you have to do. When are you done making this record?"

"Next week sometime, if all goes well."

"Fine. Carry on, as if nothing's wrong. For the moment nobody's in any danger. But when the time comes, you'll need to disappear."

"Disappear? *Querido,* I have a life. I have a career. What do you mean, disappear?"

"I mean drop out of sight, go to earth with the Gypsies, whatever."

"How long will I have to disappear for?"

"I don't know. Until I can find a way out of this. But you have to take this seriously. They have money, and they have power. They can control my computer and my phone. The only thing I can do for the moment is to go along. You and Rafa, at some point you're going to have to hide. Not yet. I'll get word to you."

"When? What are we talking about? A week from now? A month?"

"I don't know yet. As soon as I have a plan, you'll hear. In the meantime, anything we say on our regular phones is a performance. I am doing the job for them and telling you lies about it. You are swallowing them. I'll make sure Rafa gets the message. If you talk to Rafa about this, you can't go through your phones. We have to assume they'll be listening to anything that goes through our phones."

"How can they do that?"

"Technically, it's simple. All they need is sufficient resources. For the moment, you reach me via Dris, and you don't call him from your own phone. If you need to get a message to me, call Dris, but not on your phone. Use another one. Understand?"

Pascual is starting to think the connection has been lost when Sara finally says, "My God, Pascual. Twenty years. They have long memories, don't they?"

Pascual sighs into the phone. "Longer than you can imagine."

Rafa's gentle laugh coming over the wire make Pascual's heart turn over. *"Pare, què has fet?"*

"I've got us in a pickle, that's what I've done. I'm sorry."

"These are . . ." Pascual can hear the boy feeling for the right phrase. "These are old friends of yours from your outlaw days?"

"I don't know exactly who they are. But yes, directly or indirectly, they're connected to that period of my life." Pascual has told his son a sanitized version of his biography, never finding the right moment to give him the full horror story. An involvement in extremist politics and then a discreet collaboration with the authorities is the gist of it, and Pascual wonders if his son would be more ashamed of the terrorist or the turncoat if he knew the whole story. I will tell him everything, Pascual thinks, once we are clear of this. "You have to take this very seriously," he says. "These people are dangerous, take it from me."

"*Vale,* understood." After a pause the boy says, "What about you, are you in danger?"

"Not as long as I do what they say. Don't worry about me."

"I always worry about you. *Mamà* says you have the common sense of a headless chicken."

"She said that?" Pascual has to laugh. "What can I tell you? Your mother is a fine judge of people."

"You will contact what is known as a corporate service provider, or CSP." Today Lina is in business casual, white jeans and a camisole under a cashmere pullover, casual but no doubt pricey, an implicit reproach to Pascual in his limp cotton shirt and washed-out khakis. "Since the Panama scandal these outfits have had to tighten up their procedures a little, the ones that wanted to retain a shred of legitimacy, anyway. They'll verify your documentation electronically and scan all the databases to see if you pop up. And you will. But it will be the things we want to pop up."

"I'd better know what they are, then."

"It's all there in the folder. Your history since the middle nineties. That's your homework. Learn your cover story. Your legend, as the spooks call it. Memorize and elaborate. Create a whole narrative. Embellish, embroider. Make up all those anecdotes. Just make sure you don't come up with anything that can be disproved or that conflicts with some other part of the story. We'll rehearse you on it, of course."

"All right. Tell me more about these CSPs."

"They're firms that specialize in registering corporations. They usually deal with intermediaries for the owners of assets who want to conceal their ownership. For a little extra they also offer other services, like setting up bank accounts for your company. You are going to decline that offer and go on to set up the accounts yourself, because we want maximum dispersion of information."

"I see. Can I ask you what might be a stupid question?"

"Fire away."

"Can't you do all this online? Is it really necessary for me to fly around the world showing my passport to people in tropical countries? Surely we could do it sitting here at this table."

Lina cocks her head with a skeptical look. "Whose computer do you suggest we use?"

"Ah."

"Yes. You've seen what we can do. Any potential adversaries can do that, too. Anything we do online leaves a trail. Having you walk in with your passport, number one, minimizes the trail we leave, and number two, is faster. The KYC measures can be taken care of in a day or two after an in-person interview, and you have a day at the beach and a couple of nice dinners while waiting. I think you'll find it's really quite a nice gig."

Pascual lets that pass without comment. "Do you have one of these shops in mind, or am I supposed to go looking online, the way I'd choose a plumber or a podiatrist? Do they post star ratings from satisfied tax evaders?"

"Something like that, though a bit more covert. We've done some of the work for you. We took a look at a selection of them, and we've compiled a short list. These are the ones we feel are most likely to provide what we need with the necessary discretion." She slides a sheet of paper across the table. Pascual sees three names and addresses. The one at the top is *Empire Corporate Services (BVI) Limited*—with a post office box number below it followed by *Road Town, Tortola VG1110 British Virgin Islands*. "The woman we spoke to sounded quite charming. And they have a number of very solid clients, according to our research."

"That's a plus, I'm sure." Pascual peruses the list; the second entry is a firm on the Isle of Man and the third one in Luxembourg. "Is the geographic dispersion important?"

"Just diversifying. Regulatory attention and competence vary, and they can wax and wane. You don't want to put all your eggs in a basket that might be upset."

Pascual murmurs in agreement, pushing the paper away with his fingertips. "Tell me something. I'm going to have to give them the name of the ultimate beneficial owner, right?"

"That's correct."

"And who might that be?"

The corners of Lina's mouth tense slightly, the ghost of a smile. "That would be you."

"Me? I thought I was just the intermediary."

"Remember your priceless possession, that solid identity. Under this new regulatory regime, the CSP has to be sure it has good information on the UBO. And Pascual Rose will pass muster easily, with what we've set up. Now it's true, most tycoons will send a lawyer or some other flunky to set up the shell corporation, but it's certainly not unheard of for the beneficial owner to fly in and file the paperwork himself. Nobody will bat an eye. And it will be faster. We'll make sure you have all the documentation. Besides the beneficial owner, you'll need to provide the names of one shareholder and one director. Or you would, if you had any. Fortunately any CSP will give you the option of selecting nominee directors and shareholders. These are people who work for them, whose sole purpose is to conceal your identity. They are the directors of record but you run the company. It's quite a useful device."

"I can see that. Nominees it is, then."

"The good people at Empire will not disclose any of this information unless forced to by court order. Nobody's going to broadcast that Pascual Rose is the owner of a BVI corporation. Then you'll go to Geneva to open a bank account for the company in a nice safe Swiss bank. Repeat the process a couple of times, and when you're done we'll have several perfectly legitimate companies with Pascual Rose listed as the UBO, in case anyone ever gets interested. If they do, and if they ever connect him with you, you'll be able to prove you haven't been Pascual Rose since 1992. And it won't take them long to get onto the trail of the three-fingered Syrian."

Pascual is flashing on a vivid memory of being six years old and talked into mischief by older boys. He also remembers being the only one caught. "If I'm the beneficial owner," he says, "what's to stop me from making off with my ill-gotten gains the instant I've filled up those bank accounts?"

Lina smiles. "A very astute question. The answer is, there is going to be a time lag between your setting up the company and its becoming fully operational. The websites may brag that you can set up a company in two days, but that doesn't mean you'll be writing checks on that company account in two days. It means that with a little luck you can get the paperwork done. But then there are always bureaucratic delays, time for things to get recorded in registries, bank cards to be produced and posted, and so forth. In the meantime, you'll surrender all the relevant documentation to us, and you'll add a couple of signatories to the accounts. We'll provide you with the names and documentation. That's a less onerous process and can be done remotely. All this will happen before there's anything other than the initial deposit in the accounts. And once you've completed the transfer of money to the account, under our close supervision, you will cease being Pascual Rose and go back to being Pascual March. You'll have your million in the Cayman trust, and any attempt to exploit the Pascual Rose identity further will be, number one, difficult, as we'll have changed all the relevant passwords, and number two, dangerous, both with regard to law enforcement and with regard to, well, us, to be quite frank."

Pascual sits nodding for a moment. "You gave me your word that this enterprise doesn't threaten anything or anyone I hold dear. I'm not sure how you could know what I do or don't hold dear, but in any event you must see that the more confident of that I am, the more likely I am to devote myself to the enterprise. So humor me and set my mind at ease and, without naming any names, just tell me the general shape of this thing. What's the source of these funds you're so carefully cleansing?"

Sounding slightly exasperated, Lina says, "Pascual. There is so much dark money flowing around the world, all of it fungible, all of it from obscure sources, that in many cases we can't even say what the original source is. We've just found a way to tap into that. Be happy we're steering some of it your way."

Pascual smiles. "So you stole it. And somebody's not going to be happy about that. You don't think it might be to my advantage to know who that is? Who do I watch out for? Who makes me run for the hills?"

Lina sits tapping on the table with one long, lacquered magenta fingernail. Her face is perfectly blank. "If anyone shows up with evil intentions, I guarantee you won't recognize him." She raises one eyebrow. "And at that point it will be too late to do anything anyway." She rises from her chair and takes her glass to the sideboard. Pascual cannot help but notice her sleek form working in the jeans but finds himself unmoved. There is something arctic and sexless about this woman. Lina pours herself more mineral water, sips, turns and leans back against the sideboard. "The theft is taking place at a level so remote from you, nobody will ever associate you with it. The theft is taking place in a completely abstract, digital realm. When it is discovered, if it ever is, there will be no way to trace it to you."

"Except my name on all those accounts."

"We've been over that. We've got the perfect scapegoat all set up to take the fall."

"Wonderful. You're going to get some other poor three-fingered bastard killed, probably fairly gruesomely. And I'm supposed to feel cheerful about that."

"Don't waste any sympathy on him. Not on any of them. Who do you think we're dealing with? Our principals are one group of thugs. They have found a way to divert a massive amount of money from another group of thugs. We've been hired to cover their tracks, and we've devised an efficient and secure way to do it. And you're being paid a million euros to participate. You are causing no harm to any party or interest you need have the slightest concern for. For you it's easy money. I should think you'd be grateful."

Pascual blinks at her for a few seconds. "Well, then. I stand corrected. What could go wrong?"

Lina comes away from the sideboard, looking for the first time just the slightest bit irked. "Nothing," she says, "as long as you keep focus."

Normally when Pascual gets off the train from Barcelona it is with a sense of closure and relief, journey's end and the modest comforts of his flat an unhurried walk away. Today he comes out of the station and stands in front of it with a gnawing sense of pressing matters to attend to. Instead of making for the dull plebeian precincts across the river, he trudges uphill toward the Plaça Major.

The arcade enclosing the broad plaza is the heart of the old town; for decades the Snack has anchored its north side. It is the classic provincial Catalan tavern, with some history and a bit of attitude, and why it bears an English name nobody can say. Pascual figures the odds of finding Bernabé here are good. He makes his way through the tables on the terrace, nodding at an acquaintance or two as he does, and goes inside, all the way down the long narrow room with its stuccoed walls to the back, where Bernabé sits at a table with his laptop and his *café solo*.

"One moment," Bernabé says, without looking up. Pascual drops his flight bag on the floor and then makes for the *servicios*. There he takes out his phone and reaches up to set it on top of the toilet tank.

He uses the facilities, washes his hands, and returns to Bernabé's table. He sits opposite him and rubs his face wearily as the man's fingers fly over the keyboard.

Perched on his chair, Bernabé is roughly conical, the top of his head shining bald above a profuse black beard, sloping shoulders broadening into a thick torso. A waiter approaches and Pascual orders a *caña*. Bernabé concludes with a few emphatic jabs and finally looks at Pascual. "What's the matter, computer on the blink again?"

"No, the computer's working all too well." Pascual squares around to face him, elbows on the table. "The only problem is, I'm not the one controlling it."

Bernabé's eyes narrow. "Got hacked, did you?"

Pascual nods. "Very thoroughly. Computer and phone. By professionals."

"What did you do, click on something you shouldn't have?"

"No. This wasn't some random attack. They targeted me specifically. Apparently it wasn't too hard."

"I told you when I set everything up to be scrupulous with passwords."

"Yes. Apparently I wasn't scrupulous enough. But my assailants told me my employer's network wasn't very secure, either. It appears they have some serious technical resources on their side."

"What, you talked to them?"

"They dropped in for a late-night visit."

Bernabé blinks at him for a few seconds. "Sounds like this is not entirely a computer problem."

A small and bitter laugh escapes Pascual. "No. But the computer part of it is crucial. They can see what I'm doing on my computer, and they can manipulate it and shut it down whenever they want. They are obviously capable of tracking my location by phone, and for all I know they're listening to whatever I say when I have it on."

"They can listen even when it's off, with the right malware."

"That's why it's sitting in the bog right now instead of in my pocket."

"Pop the battery out."

"I almost did. But then I thought, if they're monitoring it, they can detect that. And I'd rather not make them suspicious."

"Throw the phone away. Get a new one. Have someone else get you a new one."

"It may come to that. But what I really want is a way to find out who they are. Is that possible?"

Bernabé frowns across the table. "I have the feeling there's a great deal you're not telling me."

"Listen, you really don't want to know about my problems. Take my word for that. All you need to know is that certain people want something from me, and they have established fairly complete control over my electronic life, which is to say my life as a functional person. So I don't have much choice but to comply. But if at all possible, I'd like to find out who they really are."

The size of Bernabé's eyes tells Pascual he has made an impression. "You can't go to the police?"

"In addition to the hack, there were some good old-fashioned threats. They are very effective. No, I can't go to the police. Not yet, anyway. What are the chances I, or rather someone with the required skills, might work backward from what has happened to me and find out who I'm dealing with?"

Pascual's beer arrives while Bernabé processes this, slumped and scowling on his chair. "I'd have to take a look at your system," he says finally.

Pascual drinks and sets the beer down. "I'm actually not sure I want to get you involved," he says. "For your safety, to begin with. I just want to know if it would be technically possible to look at how I was hacked and work back to the source. My understanding is that there are firms that specialize in computer security and computer crime. My intention is to hire one of those."

"It would be technically possible, yes. And yes, there are people that do the kind of thing you're talking about. But I think it would cost you a lot of money."

"I'm sure it would," says Pascual. He takes a drink of beer and sets the glass down. "That's actually not a problem."

Bernabé goes on blinking at him for a long time before saying, "I have heard some interesting rumors about you over the years. I never put much stock in them."

"You must tell me about them sometime. For now I'd appreciate some advice about a good security company I might employ. Money is no object. Somebody with an office not too far away, so I can walk in off the street and talk to them. I have a feeling the farther off the grid I stay with this, the better off I am."

"I think your instinct is sound," says Bernabé. He scowls at his laptop for a moment. "I heard a fellow give a talk at a conference I went to last year. Fernando Salera. He has a company called Tic Sec. He seemed to be the guru at whose feet everyone wanted to sit. He has a lot of high-level clients, they say."

"Where is he located?"

"Barcelona. Somewhere in Gràcia, I think."

"Perfect. Can you pull up an address for me?"

Bernabé goes to work. Pascual drinks his beer and listens to the comfortable murmur of people whose major worry is whether to bring one bottle of *vi negre* home for supper or two. Bernabé says, "His website only lists an e-mail contact. Not even a phone. Not surprising, really."

Pascual grimaces. "I could use someone else's e-mail, I suppose. I may be paranoid, but having seen these people take over my computer and my phone, I feel they own that whole space. Even sending out a cry for help online makes me nervous."

Bernabé ponders. "I could inquire for you, 'Inquiring on behalf of an associate,' that kind of thing. I can see if he'll meet with you."

Pascual gives it a long look and says, "I can't see how that could hurt. Tell him money's no object. That can't hurt, either."

"I'm assuming you don't want me to phone you when I get a response."

Pascual pushes away from the table. "Absolutely not. Will you be here tomorrow?"

"If I'm not at home I'm here," says Bernabé. "The cloak and dagger I leave to you."

When Pascual shows up at the soccer field, Dris looks surprised but says nothing. Pascual is greeted with backslaps and raillery, having missed the past couple of Saturdays, and he dearly wishes he had nothing more on his mind today than improving his dribble. Pascual came to athletic endeavor late in life but cherishes his weekly two hours of striving on the hard-packed earth of the field, testing his wind and taking wild flailing kicks at passing crosses. Once or twice a year he scores a goal.

During a break, he is gasping for breath, hands on his knees, when Dris edges over and says, "Don't tell me the job's off."

Pascual straightens up and manages to say, "It's still on. I've just completed my training, that's all. I get on a plane next week. As soon as my new wardrobe is ready."

"Your wardrobe?"

"They took me to a tailor to order a couple of suits. And to a salon to get this expensive haircut."

Dris sucks water from a plastic bottle. "I wondered about the haircut. Where does the plane go?"

"The British Virgin Islands."

Dris empties the bottle over his head and tosses it aside. "Where the hell is that?"

"In the Caribbean. Listen, I need you to get a message to Sara again. I'll write down the particulars."

"The Caribbean. Am I coming along?"

"Not this time. I won't need you."

"I've never been to the Caribbean."

"I'm just going for a couple of days to fill out some papers and come back."

"You might need someone to watch your back. You don't know what those two have in store for you."

"They won't be there. Look, my resources aren't infinite. When I get back, that's when I'll need you again, to make sure Sara and Rafa know what's going on."

Dris gives him a musing look, water trickling down the lines of his face, no doubt thinking of white sand beaches and tanned bodies in bikinis. "If you're sure."

Pascual slaps him on the shoulder. "I'm sure. Don't worry. I have a feeling that before this is all over you're going to earn that five hundred, and plenty more."

"You know where to find me," says Dris.

"Gràcia és un altre món," Pascual's grandmother was fond of saying. Gràcia is another world. Long after Pascual learned to discount the pronouncements of his elders, the effect of this one lingered, giving his rare ventures into the neighborhood a slightly haunted feel. The hillside town absorbed by the exploding Barcelona of the

late nineteenth century has managed to preserve a semblance of its village ambience with its narrow lanes and secluded squares even as the metropolis has crept ever further up the slopes around it.

It is not entirely untouched by mass tourism and the twenty-first century, Pascual reflects as he passes a tattoo parlor, a Syrian restaurant and a yoga studio, searching for an address. He finds it on a street just wide enough for a single file of cars and an old woman with a string bag full of produce plowing through a crew of bare-legged Scandinavian girls. He envisioned a flashy suite in an office tower on the Diagonal; instead he finds the name *Tic Sec* on a doorbell panel in a recessed doorway next to a pastry shop. Pascual pulls up in front, sweating in the heat, the computer bag beginning to weigh on his shoulder. Pascual pushes the button and a male voice says *"Sí?"* Pascual identifies himself.

"With regard to what?" The tinny little speaker radiates belligerent suspicion.

"To speak with Fernando Salera, please."

Nothing happens for a long minute. Pascual is about to jab at the button again when the door buzzer goes off. He pushes the door open and goes up a flight of stairs. At the top is a landing with a door standing open. Pascual goes through it into a corridor with two or three doors opening off it and halts, wondering if he has blundered. Shoved against the walls of the corridor are a bicycle, a large kite, an empty birdcage, a plaster reproduction of the Venus de Milo, a pair of swim fins, and a large brass water pipe straight from a Cairo café. A Catalan separatist flag hangs on the wall.

Pascual steps warily to the first doorway and sees he may be in the right place after all: here is a large room full of desks, each bearing several large computer screens and multiple keyboards, and two young men lounging on sleek black ergonomic chairs. One of them looks at Pascual and cocks a thumb toward the end of the corridor. "All the way back," he says.

At the end of the corridor a door stands open, and beyond it is an enclosed porch, with windows opening onto the interior of the block. Pascual stops in the doorway to stare, because the view is unexpectedly bucolic: tree branches waving in a gentle breeze, red tile roofs, neighboring terraces, a little secret haven in the heart of the city.

"Precioso, I know. Who are you?"

The source of the voice is a man sitting cross-legged on a sofa to the right, fingers flying over a laptop. He is thirtyish, swarthy, with stubbled cheeks and shoulder-length hair, barefoot in baggy shorts, a black T-shirt, and a multicolored kufi cap subjecting the flowing locks. He shoots Pascual an inquiring and not especially welcoming look.

"I'm Pascual. I believe you corresponded with my friend Bernabé yesterday."

The man stares; whatever he sees, it doesn't appear to reconcile him to Pascual's presence. "I thought you were going to call."

"Apologies. I thought my friend had made clear that the whole point of my visit was that I have to avoid phones. You're Fernando Salera?"

"I am. *Venga,* as long as you're here, make yourself comfortable." He waves at a wicker chair beside an open window and sets the laptop aside. "Sit," says Salera. "You look as if you could use a drink. I have Serranía spring water."

Pascual assumes this is a special treat and raises his eyebrows in appreciation. *"Gracias,* yes, that would go down well."

Salera rises and fetches a plastic bottle from a small refrigerator. Pascual takes the opportunity to scan Salera's workspace, the Persian carpet on the floor, the eccentric collection of chairs and couches, the abstract paintings in warm colors, the tables laden with monitors and keyboards, cables trailing off into a corner. Salera hands the bottle to Pascual and says, "So. First of all, anybody with legitimate security concerns would contact me normally, through my website or by phone if they've had previous dealings with my company. Your insistence on coming in person is completely unheard of and highly suspicious. The only reason I agreed to this was that your friend said money was no object, and I thought I might as well see if he was serious. So I assume that if you're here you have agreed to pay me the retainer of ten thousand euros I mentioned in my e-mail."

Pascual has barely had time to get the bottle open and down a gulp of what tastes to him like fairly ordinary water, if blessedly cool. He manages to swallow and says, "Of course." He sets the bottle on the floor, pulls a folded sheet of paper from his shirt pocket and hands it to Salera. "It will be paid by this woman, my *esposa de hecho*. I transferred the money to her account last night and she'll be looking out for your invoice."

"Why go through your wife?"

"Because I know the opposition can look at my bank transactions. A transfer to her account won't make them curious. A transfer to yours definitely would. She'll be your customer in the records, not me."

Salera peers at the paper and slips it into a pocket of his shorts. "What makes you think anybody would care if they knew you were engaging me?"

"The fact that they have threatened my family to force me to cooperate with them. They know I'm doing so reluctantly, and I'd just as soon they not know that I'm pushing back."

Salera gives Pascual a long, thoughtful stare. "So you're involved in some kind of criminal activity."

"Reluctantly. I'm being paid to assist in a large-scale money-laundering operation, with my participation assured by threats to my family. I have little choice but to cooperate."

Salera wanders back to the sofa and sits. "It seems to me this is a matter for the authorities. Why don't you go to the police?"

"Because I think my handlers are deadly serious about the threats to my wife and son. They've demonstrated that they know where to find them."

Salera frowns at that for a while. "Just what do you think I can do for you?"

"I'm hoping you can tell me who these people are. Make me secure if you can. When I have something to take to the authorities, I'll go to them."

Another long contemplative stare follows, the breeze coming in the open windows stirring Salera's locks. Finally Salera says, "I can't possibly get involved in anything criminal. My company's reputation depends on being on the right side of the law in all instances. I've built the best cybersecurity firm in Spain, with two offices here and one in Madrid, and I'm not going to jeopardize that to take sides in a dispute between criminals."

"If you want to bring in the authorities, I have no objection, as long as you can assure me that my handlers don't instantly become aware of it."

"We'll see about that. I'll need to know more about you, your background, your associates."

"I won't hide anything."

Salera looks unconvinced but finally nods, once. "*Vale*. Now, what do I have to work with?"

Pascual picks up the computer bag from the floor beside his chair and pulls out his laptop. "Here's the computer. I wasn't sure if you'd need physical access to it, or if you could do everything remotely."

"Oh, I'll definitely need to get into the machine." Salera places it on the couch beside him and folds his arms, settling in for a lecture. "That's the only way I can bypass the local operating system and look at memory and storage. Just having credentials to a machine doesn't get you through local and network firewalls. Even if there are no firewalls, using credentials to make a network connection to a compromised machine is still going to give you a compromised view. Really nasty malware can be extremely difficult to detect without bypassing the normal boot sequence. And you can't bypass the normal boot sequence without physical access to the machine."

Pascual nods sagely as if he had followed all that. "I've written down my passwords on a paper you'll find inside. Anything else you need, let me know. Anytime you need to communicate with me, you'll contact the man whose number is also written there, Dris by name. He'll get the message to me."

Salera sits for a long moment looking at Pascual. He says, "I never expected you to show up today. I thought you were probably just another crackpot. But if your wife comes through with the retainer, I'll see what I can do."

"That's all I ask," says Pascual.

Pascual has not crossed the Atlantic in nearly forty years and has forgotten how enormous a thing an ocean really is. When he lands in Miami he is in the dream state induced by air travel, dislocated in time and space, bemused. After making his way to the airport hotel he resists all urges to go out and explore the New World and finds a comfortably darkened bar where he watches a baseball game on television, struggling to remember the rules he was once taught on a playground in Brooklyn, until fatigue ambushes him and he staggers to his room.

The next day is spent in transit, aircraft and airports growing successively smaller until he finds himself on a throbbing turboprop lumbering low over a sparkling sea, green islands rising far and wide out of the blue, aiming for a runway that looks like a board laid down in the middle of a puddle. The heat assails him the moment he steps out of the plane. A taxi driven by a taciturn black man takes him along winding roads up and down hills into a fungal growth of buildings tucked into a crotch between steep green hills around a bay. Pascual pays off the taxi and stands in front of his hotel taking stock of Road Town, drowsy Caribbean cruise port and world capital of finance.

The hotel is large, modern and sterile, overlooking a photogenic harbor but surrounded by parking lots. Pascual checks in and stands on the shaded balcony outside his room wishing he was one of the pasty tourists roasting by the pool beneath him instead of an international criminal. He decides to leave the suit in the closet, making a quick read that in Road Town nobody is going to care much about business attire. Clad in white chinos, a batik shirt and cheap wraparound sunglasses, he ventures out into the sun, zippered leather portfolio in hand.

Away from the hotel there is a real town, with facades painted in luminescent colors and cars disputing possession of the narrow streets with cruise ship escapees. Pascual does not see a great deal of it, as the address given on the website of Empire Corporate Services proves to be a mere few hundred steps from the hotel up a sloping street. Pascual climbs a flight of stone steps skirting a lush garden to a porticoed white building with a sign announcing *Marlow House*. On the shaded veranda he hesitates for a moment, overcome with stage fright, staring at a little brass plate with the name of the firm on it before he pushes open a door and is greeted with a breath of arctic conditioned air.

"There are so many advantages to a BVI corporation," says the woman who introduced herself as Amparo; her English is lightly accented with Spanish but completely fluent. She is still well shy of forty, petite and dark of hair and eye, and Pascual wishes he could ask her to dinner instead of trying to pay attention to the stream of details she has so obviously mastered. "There's no required minimum capitalization. No financial statements are required, no yearly audits. If you're going to have annual meetings, they don't have to be here. You can hold them anywhere in the world. You're located in Malta, are you?" Amparo beams him a luminous smile.

Pascual's mouth hangs open for a moment before he says, "I don't spend much time there. I've been living in Dubai for the past few years."

"Oh, that must be fascinating. I've seen pictures. So futuristic."

"It's actually fairly dull. Unless you like expensive restaurants and exclusive clubs full of self-important blowhards. And at street level it's just another Arab town."

If Amparo is disappointed, she hides it nicely. Pascual's intention was to make himself more sympathetic, but if he has succeeded she is hiding that well, too. The smile is gone as she proceeds. "As for confidentiality, the beneficial owner of a company does not have to be made public, as long as the registered agent—that would be us—has documents to show the ultimate beneficial owner of the company."

"I am the beneficial owner."

She nods. "Very good. You will need to name one director and one shareholder. Of course, if you wish, for a little extra fee we can provide nominee directors and nominee shareholders for more privacy."

"I think that's the way I'd like to go, yes."

"Very good. Now, if you want even more confidentiality, you can use a BVI VISTA trust. That's a private trust company set up to administer a trust that owns the underlying company. This would allow you to manage the assets and the underlying company yourself while enjoying all the benefits of a trust." She pauses with an expectant look.

Pascual's head is beginning to spin, and Amparo's charm is beginning to wear off as he comes to terms with her role in this immense edifice of obfuscation for the benefit of the unscrupulous rich. He wants to shove away from the desk and flee out into the sunshine to find some brightly painted tavern with windows open to the street in which he can drink rum while watching the clouds over the sea. "I don't think that will be necessary, thanks."

"Very well. Now, we are required to carry out the Know Your Client procedures. We're going to need certain information." She pushes a sheet of paper across the desk. "Basically, a certified copy of a passport or other identification document, proof of address, which can be a utility bill, a bank statement, a reference letter, as long as it's written within the past three months. A few other documents."

Pascual scans the list, hoping Lina has provided everything on it, hoping the fakes are good, hoping he will not lose his nerve, hoping Fernando Salera is earning his retainer, hoping Dris is keeping his mouth shut. He pulls a folder from the portfolio and shoves it across the desk with his left hand. "All right. I think I have everything you need here."

Amparo takes the folder, her gaze lingering on the maimed hand, giving him a sympathetic grimace. "What happened to your hand?"

Pascual stares at the truncated fingers, at a loss. He has neglected to come up with a likely story. "I was careless with a power saw once," he says after a moment.

Amparo's grimace deepens. "I'm so sorry."

"It worked out for the best. I was forced to abandon my dream of becoming a concert pianist and went into finance instead."

She is looking at him uncertainly, trying to decide if he is serious. Pascual takes pity on her and smiles. "The music world is better for it, believe me."

In the 1980s Pascual spent a great deal of time like this, pretending to be a tourist in diverse locales while waiting for instructions, results or the clap on the shoulder that would mean arrest. Skulduggery, he found, often involved a great deal of downtime. At the moment he is pleasantly drunk, having spent the rest of the afternoon following his interview with Amparo drifting along the waterfront in search of his ideal tavern. He has found a number of them conveniently arrayed along a pier jutting out into the harbor, and if their charm is currently smothered under a horde of slovenly vacationers disgorged by the enormous sixteen-deck cruise ship looming over the end of the pier, the rum, at least, has lived up to its promise.

The sun is sinking toward the hills behind the bay, and with the easing of the heat and the anxiety, Pascual discovers he is hungry. He is standing with his hands in the pockets of his chinos, pondering the odds of finding a decent restaurant not jammed with drunks, when a female voice at his shoulder says, "Excuse me?"

He turns to see a woman of a certain age, not unattractive, with a shock of brown hair held back by shoved-up sunglasses and a pair of sleek brown legs rising from sandals to short white shorts. A capacious wicker bag draped over one shoulder, she is holding a mobile phone and training a hopeful gaze on Pascual. "I was wondering if I could ask you to take a picture for me. Of me, actually." She smiles, and Pascual's attention is drawn from the legs to a face that was beautiful twenty years ago and even now rewards a lingering glance. "It's just . . . It gets really old, taking selfies all the time."

When Pascual grasps what she wants, he takes his hands out of his pockets and turns to her. "Sure." She is American from her accent, possibly well on in her forties but still fit, nicely turned out but free of ostentatious jewelry and heavy makeup. She looks like some prosperous man's well-cared-for wife, and Pascual wonders where the man is.

"I just thought, the harbor is so pretty, I wanted a shot with that in the background, you know?" She is beckoning, maneuvering him into position. They are at the edge of the pier; across the harbor, warmly lit by the declining sun, are the green hills, dotted with villas. "Maybe here?"

She pokes at the phone and hands it to him, and he manages to produce a couple of nicely framed shots of her standing with a hand on the rail, beaming, Caribbean paradise spread out behind her. "Thank you so much," she says as he hands back the phone. "I'm Melissa, by the way." She sticks out her hand.

"Pascual."

"Are you on the boat?" She inclines her head in the direction of the nautical behemoth.

"Me? No." Pascual blinks at her stupidly. "I'm, uh . . . I'm here on business."

"Oh. Sorry." She grins. "I'm here because a girlfriend talked me into taking a cruise. 'You'll love it,' she said. And then she went and broke her ankle trying to dance on high heels the other night, so I'm pretty much on my own for the duration. Sorry, I thought you were one of us."

"No problem."

She waits for more than the brief smile Pascual gives her, but nothing comes. "Well." She stows the phone. "Thanks again. I will at least be able to prove I was here."

As she draws breath to take her leave, Pascual has a vision of the solitary evening ahead of him. "Actually, I was just thinking about finding a place to have dinner," he says. "Would you care to join me?"

She has the grace to look startled but not overly so; the smile she gives him is radiant. "Thanks, I'd love to."

Pascual's gaze sweeps the harbor. "I'm thinking if we can find a taxi we might even be able to get out of sight of the ship."

"That would be good," says Melissa. "It's a nice ship, but seeing what's two decks up is not exactly my idea of travel."

The taxi proves to be no problem, and after some consultation with the driver it whisks them about ten kilometers out along a winding coast road to a restaurant next to a marina, with palms all around, a canopy overhead, a gentle breeze off the sea and sunset tinting the clouds beyond a fleet of docked sailboats. "This is lovely," says Melissa, raising her Chablis. "Cheers."

Pascual duly touches glasses; in the taxi they were distracted by the views but he knows they have arrived at getting-to-know-you time, and he has not quite settled on who he is tonight. "So. What part of the States are you from?" he ventures.

"Kansas City. Once a cow town, always a cow town. Nice place, but it's good to get away once in a while. What about you?"

"I spent some time in New York."

"I thought so, from your accent. What about now?"

Pascual has not quite worked through the implications of sticking to his cover story versus making up anything he wants. Perhaps emboldened by the drinks, he says, "I mostly live in Switzerland now, in Zurich. But I travel a lot. I work for a hedge fund based in New York with offices all over the world. I was in Hong Kong last week."

"Wow, sounds exciting."

"You get tired of flying after a while, tired of hotels. What about you?"

Melissa performs an exaggerated shrug. "That is very much up in the air right now. I have just wrapped up a very messy and contentious divorce from a reasonably wealthy man, and while I probably will never have to work again, I know I will want to at some point. I worked in sales when I was younger, but I didn't much like it. So, ask me in six months. Right now I'm just having fun being single again."

"Congratulations."

"What about you? You have somebody to go home to in Zurich?"

Pascual takes his time answering, meeting her slightly wicked gaze. There is absolutely no doubt about what is on offer here, and he only has to decide if he wants to take it. His arrangement with Sara was settled long ago; the occasional dalliance need not threaten the bond that has endured repeated separations. He knows she has had her adventures, and he has had his.

"Nobody to speak of," he says. "The lifestyle doesn't encourage it."

"Sounds lonely."

Pascual smiles. "It has its compensations."

When Pascual wakes, it takes him a moment to remember where he is. There is a quiet hum of air conditioning in a dark room, a tangle of sheets, a crack of light beneath a door. His mouth is dry and his head weakly pulsing, but the glow in other regions of his body is ample compensation. Memory snaps back and he stretches out an arm to find the other side of the bed empty. He rises up propped on an elbow and finally connects the light beneath the bathroom door with the faint noises coming from behind it.

He sinks back on the pillow, reviewing the past hour or so. Not a lifetime highlight, he judges, but not bad for a tipsy middle-aged tryst. Gratifyingly, Melissa proved to be as appealing without clothes as with. Better, Pascual did not embarrass himself. All in all, he decides, almost enough to make this whole wretched trip worthwhile.

The door opens and Melissa emerges, illuminated by the light in the bathroom. She is dressed again, holding the wicker bag to her side. She starts a little when Pascual stirs, sitting up and leaning back against the headboard. She smiles and Pascual returns it. "Sorry. Didn't want to wake you," she says softly.

"Sneaking off, eh?"

"I was going to leave you a note." Melissa treads lightly to the armchair in the corner of the room and sets the bag on it, then comes to the bedside and sits. She runs a hand over Pascual's cheek, leans to kiss him lightly on the lips. "That was nice," she says. "But we both know it's a one-night stand, right?"

Pascual considers playing with her a little, pretending to make a scene, but decides that would be pushing the fun too far. "Of course," he says. "One of the best."

She kisses him again, a quick peck, and stands. "I think they'll still let me back on the ship. There's no curfew. So I think we'll just avoid the cold light of morning, OK?"

"OK. Thank you. Good luck and be happy."

"Thanks for a lovely evening. Lovely in every way." She rises, trailing fingertips across his cheek. "Sweet dreams." She goes to the chair, pauses to slip on her sandals, picks up the bag and makes for the door. With a wiggle of the fingers she is gone, closing the door softly behind her and leaving Pascual to contend with an onset of melancholy.

It is not until he has sat there musing for a few minutes that his eye falls on his portfolio, sitting on the chair in the corner. He focuses, reviews and is sure that he did not leave it there; he remembers setting it on the desk by the window.

Pascual frowns, remembering how Melissa emerged from the bathroom with the bag clutched to her side, a bag big enough to hide the modest-sized portfolio. With a feeling of dread he kicks free of the covers and walks slowly over to switch on the lamp on the desk. He picks up the portfolio and unzips it.

He quickly empties the contents onto the desk and sorts through them. Nothing seems to be missing; his Maltese passport is there, all the documents he showed Amparo and more, his return plane tickets to San Juan and beyond. He shoves it all back into the portfolio and switches off the light.

Pascual lies sleepless deep into the night. Finally he decides that the most plausible explanation is that Melissa was sent by Lina and Felix, a quality-control measure. With the resources they obviously have at their disposal, arranging a little honey trap to make sure he was following instructions would be a simple operation.

He senses there are other possible explanations, but he is far too tired to go down that road tonight.

Lina meets Pascual as arranged when he emerges from customs at El Prat and exchanges his phone for the one they issued him for the trip. “Here you are. We’ve taken it on a little jaunt to match what you told your wife. The meeting was in Frankfurt. You made two calls to restaurants there to reserve tables.”

Pascual pockets the phone. “I hope the food was good.”

“First class. Everything go well over there?”

Pascual has devoted a good portion of the return flight to serious thought about whether to bring up Melissa and has decided that for the moment the information is best kept in reserve. “Just fine. You want to see the documents?”

“We’ll take the whole folder, thanks. You should take a day or two, show yourself around town, have a drink with your pals, use your phone, before you go to Geneva.”

“All right. Do I have flight reservations?”

“You will when we give you the phone back. We’ll be in touch.”

“I can’t wait.”

Lina smiles. “You do sarcasm well. Call your wife. Tell her all about Frankfurt.”

▪ ▪ ▪ ▪

Guilt stirs in Pascual's stomach as he taps Sara's number into his phone. It is all very well to acknowledge the stresses imposed by diverging lives and talk about open relationships, but Pascual mourns the passing of the perfect intimacy he and Sara once had. The aftertaste of his dalliance in Road Town is sour for more than operational reasons. *"Vida mía,"* he says when she answers, meaning it.

"And what are you up to?" There is a note of uncertainty in her voice; Pascual is counting on her to remember that on these phones this must be a performance.

"I just got back from Germany. The first assignment of my new job. Two days of intensive negotiations with a roomful of investment bankers in Frankfurt. Had to get my German up to speed, bone up on all the terminology, *Doppelbesteuerungsabkommen* and all that."

"What?"

"Never mind. It was work, but I got paid well. You'd have been proud of me, behaving like a grown-up. I even put on a suit."

"Dear God. The things people will do for money."

"Every man has his price. How's the record going?"

"We're finished. Laid down the last track this morning. Manolo outdid himself, absolutely brilliant playing on the *bulería.*"

"Splendid. I look forward to hearing it. Listen, I ran into a friend of yours here. That Moroccan woman, I forget her name. She wanted to know if she can count on you for the festival next month. I told her you'd call her."

Sara hesitates only for a moment, processing the fiction. "Ah, yes. Najat. I did promise her I'd be there. I'll call her. Listen, I'm actually at lunch now, with some people. We'll talk more later, all right?"

"Perfect. *Adiós, guapa."*

"Ciao."

Pascual sits staring at the phone in his hand, full of admiration and regret.

Nothing has changed in the Bar Manel since the last time Pascual was here. Yu Yan rouses herself from a dream of far-off Qingtian as Pascual comes in, sliding off her stool behind the bar. "Where did you go? Long time I don't see you."

"I've only been gone for four days."

"Four days is long time. Every day you are here."

"I had business, in Barcelona."

"Ah, business. You make money?"

Pascual laughs. "Lots of money. For other people. Give me a *caña,* please."

Dris is at his corner table with his mates, making no sign he sees Pascual. Pascual drinks his beer and waits, watching the news in Catalan on TV3, the endless political crisis grinding on, Catalonia striving to square the circle of independence and Spain doubling down on denial. Eventually Dris detaches himself from his group and joins Pascual at the bar. "Have a nice vacation on your islands?"

"Splendid."

"And are there a lot of virgins there?"

"I don't think that's why they're called that. In any event I didn't meet much of anybody besides a shady lawyer or two. Any news here?"

"Your wife called."

"Not from her phone, I hope."

"No. She said to tell you she's going to go stay with some friends. She gave me a safe number where you can contact her."

A knot in Pascual's stomach eases. "Good. Have you heard from Rafa?"

Dris grins. "Rafa says you can reach him through Elise. You have the number."

"I'm glad he was able to settle on one. What about Salera?"

"He wants to talk to you. He gave me a number to call. You can use my phone."

"The good news is, I'm getting interested in this," says Fernando Salera in Pascual's ear. "The bad news is, I'm going to need more money. Ten thousand is not going to cover the work I'm doing on this. I've got two people working on it full time."

"My resources aren't infinite."

"Can you go another ten thousand?"

"I can do that. I'll transfer the money to my wife's account tonight. What is it buying me?"

"For a start, I've been able to determine how they got access to your computer. They hacked the Traducciones Dragoman network, probably through a phishing attack. I've spoken with the network administrator and told him the facts of life. I'll know more in a day or two. As for the phone, that was child's play. Mobile phones use a system called SS7. It was set up decades ago by telecommunications companies so they could route calls. But when they set it up, nobody anticipated the whole world having access to it. So the security is laughable. You can go online and get the software you need to hack a mobile. You might have downloaded an app that contained it, or they might have gotten to your phone through unsecured public Wi-Fi. If it wasn't one of those, they had to get physical control of your phone."

"While I was out for a jog, for example."

"For example. In any event, they are certainly capable of monitoring your calls and tracking you. It would be safest to meet face to face, well away from your phone. Can we set up a meet someplace where you're sure not to be watched?"

"I'm going to Geneva the day after tomorrow."

There is a pause, and Salera says, "Geneva, eh? Always wanted to see it. Supposed to be nice this time of year. Of course, I'll have to put the travel expenses on your account."

10

Long ago Pascual spent a couple of days in Geneva, on a lark with university pals from Paris. He remembers laughing in the spray from the Jet d'Eau, dancing in a nightclub, shouting in a girl's ear, furtive sex on a couch in somebody's cousin's flat. Claire, blond and freckled: what ever became of her?

Pascual hopes she made more of her life than he has. Here in the home of Calvinist severity he has opted for the sober gray suit, with an understated dark red tie. With the portfolio under his arm he looks entirely serious and uncomfortably out of place in the drift of idlers along the Promenade du Lac. He has an appointment with a banker in a quarter of an hour but would much prefer to go on gazing out across the sparkling lake on this fine summer day.

In the portfolio is a certified check for twenty-five thousand euros, made out to the recently established Regenta Holdings Ltd, a British Virgin Islands corporation. The check is drawn on the UBS account of Passau Novara & Co. AG, a company that Lina assured Pascual will withstand scrutiny when he deposits the check in the account he is here to open. Pascual consults his watch, heaves a sigh and turns away from the lake.

Swiss bank secrecy may be a thing of the past, but the banks are still here, everywhere Pascual turns. His image of dealing with Swiss banks has always involved a discreet private bank tucked down a side street, secretive functionaries murmuring about numbered accounts in thickly carpeted, oak-paneled offices, but there is to be no private bank, no numbered account for Regenta Holdings. All that would be superfluous, Lina explained; all that is needed is a corporate account in any reputable Swiss bank. The one Lina has chosen for him stands prominently on a quay beside the Rhone where it leaves the lake and undertakes its long meander to the sea. Pascual pushes in through big glass doors, and after inquiring is shown to a desk where he is greeted by a whippet-thin, sharp-featured young man named Étienne with a brisk manner, a receding hairline and an aggressive handshake. "Monsieur Rose. Enchanted. I understand you come to us from Dubai."

Alarm bells go off in Pascual's head as he sits, warily. "That's correct."

"I spent two years in our office there." Étienne's smile is a challenge. "I'm surprised we never ran into each other. One gets to know the expatriate community. We must have crossed paths at Barasti sometime, or Trilogy."

"I don't go in much for the nightlife." Pascual smiles. "And as I speak good Arabic, my social circle isn't entirely expatriates. I actually live in Old Dubai, near the creek. Quite unfashionable."

Étienne's face falls just a little as he sees that he is not going to be able to impress Pascual with his local knowledge. "Ah, very good. You are an old Dubai hand, then."

"If you wish," says Pascual, thankful for the time he put into studying websites catering to Dubai expats. He concedes Étienne a gracious nod. "It is a fascinating place, to be sure."

"I like this place," says Dris, raising his glass. "I could live here."

Pascual has to strain a little to hear him over the cheerful din of a crowded brasserie, tall windows opening onto a street lined with kebab joints and cocktail bars, a few early hookers taking the evening air. "I can see why," he says. "Where are you staying?"

"In a hostel, behind the train station up there. I ran into another Maghrebi who put me onto it. I had quite a good time last night, actually, with some girls we ran into in a club. You didn't tell me Switzerland was like this. I thought it was all rich bastards walking around with their noses in the air and you get arrested if you drop a cigarette butt. This I can handle. It is damned expensive, though. I'm burning through my cash."

"I gave you a thousand euros for this trip. Try to make them last."

They are in the Pâquis, Geneva's quarter of ill repute and easy virtue, a few streets and several income strata back from the lakeside quay where Pascual's four-star hotel lies, and this is Pascual's comfort zone as much as Dris's. Any lingering doubts Pascual may have had about Dris's organizational skills vanished upon his return from his appointment at the bank when he found the message light on his room phone blinking, the message consisting of the name of the brasserie and a time. Narrowly averting a possibly catastrophic mistake, Pascual first grabbed his mobile out of habit before remembering that the device is capable of eavesdropping, even when turned off, and tossed it onto the bed with a nervous spasm. On the walk from the hotel he took pains to look like an idle and rudderless tourist, making an effort to ascertain whether anybody in Geneva is tailing him. Pascual is still trying to process his encounter with the mysterious Melissa in the Virgin Islands. He considers the chances of her being a common thief quite small. There is a chance she was sent by Lina to keep him honest; that is the most parsimonious explanation. If somebody else is tracking him, it raises a good many questions to which he has no answers. In any event, time for caution; he tried a couple of classic maneuvers to shake a tail before slipping into the brasserie, taking a place at the bar, and waiting for Dris to approach him.

"Did you talk to Sara?"

Dris nods. "She's in Seville, with a friend. She gave me a number where you can reach her. Rafa's still in Amsterdam, and he says Elise's number is still good for him. He said to tell you he can be with you in six hours whenever you give the word."

"Good lad, but I don't want him anywhere near me right now. So what about Salera?"

"He's at the Hotel d'Allèves, not too far from here. He said to call him when you're ready to meet. I went and looked at it. It looks like a nice crib."

"I wonder how much they're charging him. It will go on my bill, I'm sure."

"He said you wouldn't mind the expense. A man has to work in comfort, he said."

Pascual sighs. "All right. Call him. Let's see what he's come up with."

▪ ▪ ▪ ▪

"To start with, I have phones for you." Fernando Salera pulls them out of a briefcase and slides them across the coffee table, four ordinary-looking smartphones in a clear plastic bag along with a folded sheet of paper. The coffee table bears glasses, cups and saucers, water bottles, two laptops, a smartphone and a spiral notebook covered with illegible notes. The table and the surrounding couch and chairs are in Salera's two-room suite in this unostentatiously upscale hotel tucked in a quiet tree-lined street a pleasant stroll removed from the Pâquis.

Salera has dressed up for the occasion, in jeans and a khaki shirt, socks lying nearby on the carpet should he want to venture out. "These are prepaid devices, purchased for cash and anonymous. They have been activated. You'll find the numbers on that sheet of paper. There is no link to any of you. They've all been supplied with an app that encrypts calls and text messages. Unless your adversaries are tipped somehow to the existence of these phones, there is no reason why they should ever be able to eavesdrop on anything said over these phones, and they won't be tracking your location through them. Now, if you think they might be visually observing you, they might notice or surmise that these are not your regular phones and take measures to break the encryption and capture these as well. You will have to decide how likely that is and act accordingly."

"Thank you." Pascual opens the bag and slides the phones and the paper out onto the tabletop. "So it's not paranoia to think they could be monitoring the phones of my wife and my son, as well as mine."

"Not at all," says Salera. "Once they had yours, they had all the numbers you had in your contacts. Add that to your calculations."

Pascual shoots a quick look at Dris, who shakes his head. "We've never talked on the phone, you and I. I'm in Rafa's phone, but would they examine all his contacts?"

"I don't know." Pascual turns back to Salera.

"The encryption I've given you will defeat the ordinary apps. But if these people have the resources they seem to have, they can break it eventually. So be discreet."

Pascual nods. "Dris, your next assignment will be to get two of these to Sara and Rafa."

Dris nods. "Rafa first? Amsterdam is just up the road from here, isn't it?"

Pascual shoots him a look. "All right, but you drop off the phone and then head south. If you and Rafa get to carousing, God knows when Sara will get her phone." Pascual turns to Salera. "So. Who are these people? Any clues?"

Salera leans back on the couch and scratches at the stubble on his neck. "Some. I talked to your service provider's security people and they gave me access to the network data. It's damn hard to attribute an attack, but it can be done. It's easy to identify the IP address of any computer that connects to yours, but there are ways to disguise that. They falsify the IP address; they go through proxy computers that they've taken over. So then you look at the data the hackers leave behind, you analyze comments, look at metadata. You consult other cybersecurity people, look at records of other investigations. There are lots of things to look at. It's a puzzle. You have to put the pieces together."

"And so far? Is a picture emerging?"

Salera smiles, but there is no humor in it. "The picture that is emerging is that the people who hacked you are very, very good."

"Oh, splendid."

"Don't worry. I'm better. They're covering their tracks pretty well, but the tracks are still there."

"And what do they indicate?"

"Well, for one thing, some of the metadata showed text that had been converted from Cyrillic to Latin characters."

In the ensuing silence Pascual exchanges a look with Dris, who is looking slightly puzzled, and then Salera, who is looking grim. "Wonderful," Pascual says. "Russians."

Salera shrugs. "Maybe. That could be faked like anything else. And even if it wasn't faked, it could be just residue from the route they took. It proves nothing."

Pascual leans back on his chair, passing a hand over his face. "I thought she looked Slavic. Him, too, very believable. God help us, I'm in the hands of the Russian mob."

"You're not in anybody's hands yet," says Salera. "So far it seems to me you're free to move about, come and go as you please. You could run away if you wish. Of course, you'd need to leave everything connected with your current life behind and be very careful in setting up a new one. I could help you with that."

"For another ten thousand euros?"

"Somewhat more than that, I'm afraid. This is taking up a considerable amount of my resources. You'll get an itemized invoice."

"Let me know when the meter gets to fifty thousand, would you? My resources are likely to be exhausted before yours are."

"As you wish. We're not there yet."

Pascual stares into the shadows high in a corner of the lamplit room. "In the Virgin Islands, there was a woman. A tourist, off a ship, or so she said. Very friendly. She wound up in my room. I caught her going through my papers. She might have been sent by my handlers to check up on me. Or she might have been a common thief. But if it was somebody else who sent her, how did they know I was going to be there? And how did she identify me?"

Salera's eyebrows rise just a tick. "I couldn't answer that. A leak somewhere in your handlers' setup?"

Pascual frowns at that for a moment. "So, what's next?"

Salera shrugs. "I'll keep trying to break the kill chain."

Pascual blinks at him, stupidly. "What?" Salera has been speaking Castilian but pronounced the phrase *kill chain* in English. "What's that, the kill chain?"

"It's a phrase borrowed from the military. It means the structure of an attack, from reconnaissance to the actions carried out on the objective. In cybersecurity we use the concept to analyze an intrusion and decide how to counter it at each stage. I've got some advanced analytics and I've got some good people working on this. We'll keep following the trail until I can tell you who hacked you and where they are. After that, it'll be up to you to decide what to do."

Pascual trades a look with Dris, who says, "Maybe then I get a couple of my old mates from Castellón and go have a talk with these people."

Pascual laughs once, softly. "Not if they're the Russian mafia you don't. If that's the case you take your severance pay and go home." He stands and goes to a window overlooking the street. "If that's the case, I think I'll just do what they tell me to do and hope I get away with it."

■ ■ ■ ■

The bright lights of the Pâquis are calling Dris. Pascual goes over the drill and then turns him loose. "Remember, tomorrow you're getting on a bus to Amsterdam. Don't get too drunk. Don't get rolled, and for God's sake don't get arrested."

"Me? I'm reformed. I'm only going into high-class joints tonight."

"And don't spend all your money. Have Rafa call me when he gets the phone, and then get to Seville as fast as you can."

"You can count on me, *jefe.*"

Pascual is dead tired by the time he reaches the Quai du Mont-Blanc and turns toward his hotel. The sun has gone down and the sky is going an impossibly pure deep blue over the shimmering lake. In the distance the western slopes of Mont Blanc are glowing gold. Pascual wishes he could enjoy the view.

In the hotel lobby a party is going on, or the dregs of one. The tail end of a wedding, Pascual guesses at a glance; a dozen or so people of diverse ages, the women in sleek dresses and elaborate hair, the men in suits with loosened ties and drooping mustaches, laughing and swaying, three sheets to the wind. Whatever language they are speaking, Pascual doesn't recognize it. Something from the Caucasus perhaps. They are blocking the way to the lift and Pascual edges around them.

"Oh, pardon, monsieur!" This girl in a tight satin dress speaks French, in any event; she apologizes for backing into Pascual as he passed. He gives her his most gracious smile, no offense taken, just a tired businessman heading for his room at the end of a trying day.

But now she is laughing, a hand over her mouth, and another girl, blond and ruby-lipped, is berating her for her clumsiness, trying to contain her own laughter. "Excuse her, *monsieur,* she's drunk."

Pascual murmurs something about how it happens to the best of us, striving to clear the throng, but now a man is squawking and flapping a hand at the girls, a manic look on his face, phone in hand, and suddenly the girls are embracing Pascual, one on each side of him, giggling, and the man is framing a shot of the three of them. "We'll make it up to you," says the blonde.

"It's your lucky day," the man says in French, taking the picture.

"Come have a drink with us," says the girl who bumped into him.

Pascual declines, and after assuring everyone he bears no ill will he manages to detach himself and make for the lifts.

In the quiet of the rising lift he feels a sudden chill. A wedding party is surely a lot of trouble to go to for the purpose, but if somebody needed a current photograph of the mysterious Pascual Rose badly enough, one has just been obtained.

11

This time it is Felix who meets Pascual in the café in Terminal 1 and takes delivery of the documents related to the spanking new Swiss bank account for Regenta Holdings Ltd, now holding twenty-five thousand euros. "Online banking set up? All passwords recorded?" says Felix, peering into the manila envelope. "Cards to be mailed to the post office box in Malta?"

"As discussed." Pascual gives him an indignant look. "What, you're afraid I'm going to run to the nearest cash machine and drain the account first chance I get?"

Felix responds with an utterly impassive look. "You would be surprised what people try to get away with."

Pascual makes a quick and somewhat impulsive decision. "Is that why you sent Melissa? To keep me honest?"

Felix freezes in the act of turning away. "Who's Melissa?"

"The woman in Road Town. She called herself Melissa."

The effect on Felix is quite satisfying. Pascual has been wondering what would dent his shell. Suddenly Felix's face is close to his. "You didn't tell us about a woman in Road Town."

"Because I assumed she was working for you."

"Talk. What happened?"

Pascual tells him. When he has finished Felix says, "Idiot. You fell for the oldest trick in the book."

"Maybe so. If you'd told me there might be opposition, I'd have been more careful."

"There's always potentially opposition. I thought you were supposed to be good at this."

"I guess you thought wrong. How did she know who I was?"

"Any number of ways. We're going to have to talk to Lina about this." Felix reaches inside his jacket for his phone.

"Can I go home first? I have to do laundry and feed the pets."

Felix taps at his phone and puts it to his ear, then snarls at Pascual. "We're paying you a lot of fucking money, friend. It's time you started taking the job seriously."

"Oh, I do," says Pascual. "Believe me, I do."

Pascual has no idea where Lina may be, but within a half hour he and Felix are talking with her via Skype from Felix's room at the airport hotel. Wherever she is, Lina looks sleek and unruffled, frowning at her screen as she listens to Pascual's tale. "American, you think," she says.

"That's what she sounded like to me. Midwest. If she wasn't, she was damn good with the accent."

"And she approached you on the street, out of the blue."

"On the pier, actually, but yes. She walked up and asked me to take a picture of her on her phone."

"So she had visually identified you somehow."

"Presumably. I wasn't wearing a name tag. I suppose she might have bribed somebody at the hotel desk to point me out, or something like that."

"Mm. Unlikely, I'd say." Lina blinks at the screen for a moment. "When we constructed Pascual Rose's online presence, the only photo we had was your current passport photo. That's in the CIR."

"CIR?"

"The Common Identity Repository, the EU's biometric database. If somebody was tipped off to Pascual Rose and could hack the CIR, they could find it. We hacked it. Somebody else could, too. What interests me is how they knew Pascual Rose was going to the British Virgin Islands."

At Pascual's side Felix says, "There are several ways to get his flight information. But they'd have to know to look for it. How did they get interested in Pascual Rose and where he was going?"

Felix and Lina commune in silence for a moment. The casual ease with which they seem to acquire information terrifies Pascual. He is thinking hard about the things he has to conceal from them when Lina says, "That's a discussion for you and me, Felix. Pascual, you're sure she took nothing?"

"Reasonably sure. Was anything missing from the company documents?"

Lina ignores the question. "So she was just there for the information. She wanted to know the name of the company Pascual Rose had just established. Tell me, did she by any chance take a picture of you?"

Pascual has to think for a moment. "At dinner she had the waiter take one on her phone, of the two of us. To remember the occasion, she said."

"Of course. So they now have a current photo."

"If you say so. Excuse me, but is it at all possible she was just a common thief? I imagine it could be a nice living preying on the type of man who slouches around the Caribbean setting up shell companies. At least some of them would carry a lot of cash. She gave me the treatment, then went through my things hoping to find a stash, but came up empty, nothing but a bunch of papers."

Next to Pascual, Felix vents a barely audible sigh. On the screen Lina shakes her head, the barest hint of a smile on her finely curved lips. "Possible? Of course it's possible. Tell me, when you were slouching around Europe setting up terrorist outrages, did you blithely opt for the least threatening interpretation of any unforeseen development? Or did you go on high alert?"

Pascual concedes with a tilt of the head. "Point taken. As long as we're on high alert, I should tell you that a couple of drunken girls collared me in the lobby of my hotel in Geneva and their friend snapped a picture of us."

Lina's eyebrows rise. "You don't say."

"These I think really were just girls partying. But the picture was a little odd. They were speaking some language I didn't recognize."

After a frozen moment Lina says, "A pity you didn't think to get a picture of them, maybe exchange addresses. Try to think faster next time."

"I promise. What next?"

Lina frowns at them via her computer far away. Finally she says, "Go home. Take a few days, show yourself around town, stick to the script. You've been to Milan this past week, did Felix fill you in?"

"Not yet."

"He will. You made some phone calls there as well. You know the drill. We'll be in touch."

"All right."

"And Pascual?"

"Yes?"

"On your next job, when a woman approaches you, run the other way, will you?"

"As fast as I can," says Pascual.

Pascual sits on his terrace in the cooling evening, listening to his neighbors quarrel over supper and wishing he had not flushed the Lepanto down the drain. Now that he has gone ahead and compromised himself anyway, it would be nice to have it.

When Fernando Salera's burner phone goes off on the low table in front of him, Pascual leaps out of his chair. He fumbles the phone onto the tiles, swears and finally manages to pick it up, glance at the number and answer the call. "So we can talk freely now?" says Sara in his ear.

Pascual sinks back onto his chair, the weight on his chest easing. "On these phones only. Don't, whatever you do, get this one mixed up with your regular phone."

"And where do these come from? Dris was not very communicative. Did you send him down here just to deliver the phone?"

"I did. These come from a man who is helping me get my life back. Where are you now?"

"I'm still in Triana, with Carmen. Where are you?"

"I'm at home. I talked to Rafa. He's got his phone. From now on this is how we communicate. If I call you on your regular phone, it's pure theater."

"Understood. How long is this going to go on?"

"I don't know. A few weeks, I think."

"And what should I be doing?"

"For the moment, nothing you wouldn't ordinarily do. There's a possibility nothing at all will happen except that I do what these people want and they pay me. But there's also a possibility I will call you and tell you to disappear until further notice. If that happens, it will mean something has gone very wrong and we are all in danger. And honestly, I don't know which is more likely."

Pascual sits and listens to nothing, phone at his ear. After a time Sara says, "If you do what they want, and they pay you, will you be able to live with yourself? Will you be able to look your son in the eye?"

"I will certainly not be able to look my son in the eye if they kill him because I refuse to cooperate. Or you."

There is a pause before Sara speaks again. "I understand that. Do what you need to do. But if I have to hide in a cave in order for you to preserve your integrity, I want you to know that I will do that. Without hesitation."

Pascual draws a sharp breath. All the reasons he loves this woman are suddenly vividly present to him, along with a keen awareness of all his failings. With a slightly thickened voice he says, "Understood. *Vida mía,* you have no idea how I long for you."

■ ■ ■ ■

Pascual comes awake in the dark, and it takes him a few seconds to identify the sound that woke him. This time the whisper of a step is not on the stairs outside but in the hallway, and the sound was the creak of the outside door swinging open. There is a soft click as it is carefully pushed shut.

Pascual is thinking about improvised weapons as the footsteps come softly down the hall; he will never make it to the window for the leap to the street. There is the little stone Buddha on the bedside table; skillfully handled, or merely with enough desperation, it will break a man's skull. Pascual reaches for it in the dark.

Out in the hall something falls to the floor with a thump. Light appears beneath the door. There is another quiet scrape of footsteps and then silence. Pascual swings his feet to the floor and sits on the side of the bed with the statuette in his hand, heart pounding.

The next sound he hears is the gentle plashing of a stream of urine falling into a toilet. Pascual sets down the statue, sighs, and puts his face in his hands. He sits like that while the intruder goes back up the hallway to the kitchen. Finally he rises and goes out into the hall. He walks past the familiar backpack lying where it was dropped and comes to a halt in the doorway to the kitchen, looking at his son.

Rafael looks up from the open refrigerator to grin at him. "*Pare*. Did I wake you? I'm sorry." In T-shirt and shorts, sandals, with hair hooked behind his ears and the brush of beard on his chin, he is the picture of slovenly youth and handsome devilry.

"What are you doing here?"

"I live here. Remember?" Rafael shuts the refrigerator door and steps toward him, arms open for the embrace.

"Aren't you supposed to be in Amsterdam?" Pascual grants his son a perfunctory embrace and then pushes past him. He opens a cabinet over the sink and hauls down the brandy. Not Lepanto, but the cheap stuff will have to do tonight.

"I told them I have a family emergency. Don't you have anything to eat?" Rafa has gone back to the fridge.

"There's some ham in there somewhere. Didn't Dris explain things to you?"

"Of course he did." Rafa extracts the ham and looks about for bread. "That was the truth about the family emergency, wasn't it?"

"It was. But you're not helping matters by coming home."

"You think I can let you be threatened by criminals and just sit there in Amsterdam doing chemistry problems?"

"You shouldn't be anywhere near home," Pascual says. "Whatever Dris told you, he failed to make clear the nature of the problem."

"Which is?" Rafa gives up on the day-old bread and stuffs a slice of ham into his mouth.

Pascual downs a slug of brandy. "The problem is, you and your mother are hostages. The threat to you is their strongest card. So the whole point is to remove you and your mother from their power. That means putting yourself where they can't find you. They located you in Amsterdam; they know you live here. You won't be safe, and I won't have any freedom of action until they don't know where you are. So your job is not to be here at my side with your fists up. Your job is to find a place to hide and find a way to get there without being tracked. Understood?"

Rafael chews, swallows, frowns at another slice of ham. "Understood. Except for one thing."

"What's that?"

"Why you? Why now? Why is this happening to our family?"

"That's a long story."

"When do I get it? I've asked *mamà* about it, several times. She always says it's your story to tell. What you've told me is a lot of folklore about being a political radical and having some brushes with the police. I have a feeling that's a little vague. *Mamà* has been completely frank about having been a junkie and a whore. I don't love her any the less for that. If anything, I love her more for coming clean. I'm waiting for you to do the same."

Pascual stares into his glass, ashamed, and then drains it. He slides the glass away down the countertop and looks up at somebody he has never seen before, a completely serious person challenging him to tell the truth. "Let's go sit down," says Pascual. "This could take a while."

“Nobody named Melissa appears in the passenger manifest of the ship that was docked in Road Town when you were there. Which is pretty much what we expected, of course. We could look for single women with her profile on the ship or otherwise entering the BVI at that time, but I’m not sure it would be cost-effective. She’s just a bit player, and whoever employs her, I’m fairly certain they were careful not to leave an obvious trail.”

Lina looks pale and a little worn today, perhaps from a hectic travel schedule. Apparently tired of the airport hotel, this time she and Felix have summoned Pascual to a flashy new hotel on Plaça d’Espanya, across from the old Arenas bullring now converted with Catalan efficiency into a shopping center. From the window of their suite he can look up the avenue to Montjuïc and remember Sunday excursions with his grandparents. “And the girls in Geneva?” he says.

“Not worth the trouble,” Lina says. “Nothing to go on there. As you say, they were probably just drunk. In any event we’ve other complications to worry about.”

Pascual turns from the window. “What kind of complications?”

“Somebody’s sniffing around our tracks. In cyberspace.”

Pascual tries hard to look uncomprehending. "How can you tell?"

"The technical details are probably beyond you. Suffice it to say someone's probing, discreetly, at our digital presence. Specifically the resources we deployed to keep tabs on you. Someone's interested not only in you, but in anyone who's keeping tabs on you."

Felix has been leaning back on his chair giving Pascual the reptile look. He says, "You wouldn't have dropped a hint somewhere by any chance? Told somebody about us? Asked for a little help?"

Pascual spreads his arms, a gesture of innocence. "Why? So I could be prevented from making a million dollars?"

Felix snorts gently and tosses things over to Lina with a look. She says, "You might just be curious. You might want to know who you're working for."

"I am and I do," says Pascual. "But I'm not stupid. I know where my best interests lie."

"I'm glad. I hope you never lose sight of that."

"Anyway, you can hear everything I say on the phone, right? You can read all my e-mails. You can even turn my phone into an eavesdropping device. Have you heard me calling for help?"

"I don't know that we would. There are lots of phones in the world. We certainly haven't been keeping twenty-four hour surveillance on you. We're trusting you to cooperate. Don't make us regret that."

Pascual waves a hand in dismissal. "You've got me by the balls, if you'll excuse my crudity. I'm not going to make trouble. Could these people sniffing around your tracks be law enforcement, by any chance? I've gotten the impression what we're doing is not entirely kosher."

"How perspicacious of you. Yes, it could be law enforcement. The point is, they seem to have gotten interested in us via you. Any ideas?"

Pascual shrugs. "My guess would be that my bank alerted the Vigilancia Aduanera when that hundred thousand euros plopped down into my account. That's quite a windfall for somebody like me. I'd be disappointed if it didn't get somebody's attention."

"That's certainly possible. But there's nothing illegal about a windfall. If anyone wants to speak to you about it, be ready to explain what you're doing for that company in Rotterdam."

Pascual nods slowly, thinking furiously. "All right. What's the next move?"

"I think the next move is, we send a minder along with you, discreetly. To look out for tipsy girls and loose women."

"And make sure I don't succumb to their charms."

"I would hope you wouldn't need a chaperone at this point to accomplish that. More to see if we can spot any opposition."

"Who is the opposition likely to be?"

Lina and Felix commune for a moment, expressionless. "The Vigilancia Aduanera, for example," says Lina. "Are you really that anxious to know? I would think a million euros would buy a fair amount of complacent ignorance."

Pascual gives in with a smile. "Oh, yes. Just idle speculation. Don't mind me. When is this next jaunt taking place?"

"Next week, say. We'll need a little time to set things up."

"And who's the minder going to be?"

"Well, I think Felix is free. Aren't you, Felix?"

"Nothing else on my calendar."

"And I might come along just for the fun of it," says Lina. "So you've got a few days to relax. Having a good time with your son, are you?"

Startled, Pascual manages to stifle the stupid question that rises to his lips. "Well, it was nice to see him. He just dropped down for a quick visit. He's supposed to be in Amsterdam, as you know."

"Yes. I don't believe the term is quite over. Is he playing hooky?"

"I suppose he is. He had some kind of drama with a girlfriend and needed to get away for a few days."

Lina smiled. "Ah, youth. Was this Elise or the other one?"

Now Pascual is chilled for a moment. "Elise, I believe," he says. "I'm afraid he is easily distracted from his studies."

"Well. No doubt he will settle to work eventually." Having none too subtly reminded Pascual of the iron grip she has on him, Lina grants him a smile. "I'm sure he's capable of focusing on essentials. Like his father."

"Oh, yes," says Pascual. "Locked in, one hundred percent."

"Go back to Amsterdam. Finish the term. There's nothing you can do to help me except act as if everything's normal. With any luck, that's all you'll ever have to do."

The shade and a sluggish breeze stirring the leaves of the plane trees provide a little relief from the heat. Pascual, his son and Dris are leaning on the parapet above the river that skirts the old town walls, currently a pathetic trickle.

Rafael isn't having any, Pascual can tell. The lad looks to Dris for support, but Dris merely shrugs. Rafa throws a pebble into the river and says, "How can I concentrate on my studies with this going on?"

"Exert yourself. That will be your contribution to the war effort. Carry on as if your work is all you're concerned about. The last thing we want to do is make these people think we're plotting something. We want them to believe that I'm cooperating fully and hiding the nature of this whole business from my wife and son."

Rafa gives him a keen look. "And why aren't you hiding it from us? Why go to the trouble of getting the secure phones, hiring your tech wizard? Why did you bother to sound the alarm in the first place? You could have done what they wanted and we would have been none the wiser."

"Two reasons. One of them I thought I explained the other night."

Pascual looks into Rafael's somber gaze and wonders if his full accounting of his past has lowered him in his son's estimation. "Yes," Rafa says. "You explained. And the second reason?"

"Very simple. I don't trust them."

"So what's your plan?"

"Number one, find out as much as I can. Number two, make sure you and your mother are safe. Or more precisely, that you can get to a safe place when I give the word."

"And three?"

"I don't know yet." Pascual turns to Dris. "This is where you come in. So far you've just run messages. At some point you may have to do more. Rent an apartment somewhere, where someone can hide. Pull up in a car and spirit somebody to safety. Things like that."

Dris nods. "Break somebody's nose?"

"You'd better hope it never gets to that point," says Pascual. "The whole idea is to avoid that. I just don't know how yet."

Leaves rustle, water trickles, cars go purring by. The temperature seems to have dropped a degree or two. Rafa trades a glance with Dris and says, "All right. I'll go back. Don't keep me in the dark."

Pascual nods. "That's why we have the secure phones."

"About anything."

"I promise."

Dris says, "Where are we off to next, you and I?"

Pascual squints into the light bouncing off the riverbed. "You, you're on leave for a few days. I'll have company on the next trip and I don't want you to be spotted. Use the time to think about what we'll need if things go wrong. A car, a bolt-hole. Things like that."

Dris nods. "Something to defend ourselves with?"

Pascual gives him a skeptical look. The last thing he wants to do is encourage recklessness, but he has vivid memories of things that would have gone better had he had the means to defend himself. "Can I trust your judgment? It's not a game."

"Of course."

"Then get whatever you think you may need."

"You're going home," says Lina in Pascual's ear.

"Home?" says Pascual. "I thought I was home."

"Your adopted home. Where you maintain that nice little pied-à-terre with the harbor view, the one you love so much."

"I'm afraid you've lost me."

"You're going to Malta."

"Ah. Yes, Malta. Such fond memories. Such nice people, to grant me a passport like that."

"Yes. In exchange for your ten thousand euro per year lease on the flat plus a two hundred fifty thousand euro investment and thirty thousand euro for what they discreetly call a contribution, don't forget. Have you in fact ever been there?"

"Never been near the place."

"Well, Pascual Rose has. He spent a few weeks there in 2013 to establish residency after the government initiated its passport selling scheme. Sadly, you'll have to stay in a hotel, because like a lot of naturalized Maltese you rent out the lovely pied-à-terre on Airbnb, and it's currently occupied. We'll fill you in on the details. Can you be in Barcelona tomorrow?"

"Let me check my calendar and get back to you," says Pascual.

There is a brief silence. "What a wit you are," says Lina. "Airport hotel again, room 329. Be there by eleven o'clock, prepared to fly out at three."

13

"I think what would best meet your needs would be a private exempt limited company," says the young woman with the exotic quasi-Asian looks, pale and delicate in a dark-gray dress. Her English is non-native but voluble, the accent slippery, her enthusiasm nearly breathless.

"I quite agree," says the fortyish rake whose shirt open over a hairy chest fails to carry the day over his thinning hair and double chin, fashionably stubbled though it may be. "The alternative would be a private limited company, which is more or less our standard offering, but for that you'd need at least two shareholders. If you're a one-man operation, the exempt is what you want. One director, one secretary, one shareholder, all natural persons, Bob's your uncle." This one is a Brit or a close facsimile, as everyone seems to be in this long-time Royal Navy anchorage.

The anchorage, or at least the patch of lambent sea lying just outside it, is visible way across the rooftops through the window of this upper-floor suite in a modern office building dwarfing its neighbors in a narrow street in St. Julian's, which Pascual has been assured is the happening district in Malta. The double-team approach has left Pascual slightly dazed. His energy was sapped by the walk from his hotel, the morning already hot when he stepped onto the road winding along the crooked seafront, the Mediterranean lapping at the rocks beneath it. The tortuous route and his misplaced confidence in his sense of direction left him sweating and slightly winded when he finally located the offices of SLM Group, a registered corporate services company employing, as far as Pascual can see, only these two amiable associates, who Pascual has been informed are called Nigel and Maya.

"There will just be some paperwork we have to attend to," says Maya, beaming as she taps at the computer keyboard in front of her. "We're required to register the beneficial owner. There is a fairly rigorous process to verify your identity."

Pascual feels a chill in the entrails at the thought that shoddy work on Lina and Felix's part could get him collared by a newly reformed and vigorous Maltese police force. "I should hope so," he ventures with what he hopes is an innocent smile.

"Oh, yes," says Nigel. "We're quite up to date with all that. EU membership has forced Malta to raise its standards. They pushed through quite a lot of financial and regulatory reforms."

"You would not believe how strict they are now," says Maya.

Pascual cannot resist a mild provocation. "Yes, I recall there was some controversy regarding, who was it? The prime minister's wife?"

Nigel takes this without blinking. "And nothing came of it. Guilt by association. The case was dropped. Look, any financial center is going to have a few dubious characters trying to get away with something. All the cases that have come to light, you know who they were? Foreign entities. Not Maltese."

"Bad apples," says Maya.

Nigel nods. "Absolutely. And we weed them out, as best we can. Why would we tolerate any kind of financial skulduggery? That would jeopardize our status as a financial center."

Maya pulls a sheet of paper from the printer on her desk and slides it across to Pascual. "Here's a list of the documentation we'll need. Now, since you hold a Maltese passport, things should go fairly smoothly. You have, of course, already been through the verification process in order to get the passport."

"Oh yes," says Pascual. "They were quite thorough."

Pascual likes places like Malta: strange, turbulent and ethnically jumbled, quintessentially Mediterranean, kind to the eye, warm, sun-washed yellows above glittering, restless blues. From Alexandria to Algiers, Ibiza to Naxos, he has enjoyed the bemusement of places where nothing is quite what he is accustomed to, where he is never far from the sea.

Released by Nigel and Maya after being assured that his documents will be prepared within twenty-four hours, Pascual ought to feel liberated and ready for an afternoon of idle rambling, but the prospect has been somewhat spoiled by being made mandatory. "Walk," Lina told him. "Make yourself visible. Be a tourist, dawdle and meander and gape at things. There's no better way to show up someone who's watching you."

"And I'm supposed to spot them?" Pascual asked. "That was never really a part of my skill set."

"You just walk. We'll do the spotting."

With this in mind, Pascual finds it difficult to play the vagabond with total conviction. He walks as instructed, through St. Julian's and Sliema, formerly separate towns now merged with Valletta into a single teeming warren of narrow streets with shuttered balconies, ponderous medieval portals cheek by jowl with glass-fronted storefronts, ranks of modern apartment buildings jammed together above palm-lined boulevards. As he walks he hears snatches of English, Italian, Greek, Swedish, Dutch, Polish, Russian, French, something unidentifiable from South Asia, and everywhere the mysterious local language, which sounds like a Sicilian trying to speak Arabic.

He takes the ferry from Sliema across the harbor to Valletta, grateful for the sea breeze and the vast bright expanse of sea and sky, trying to note all his fellow passengers without being too obvious, watching them all disperse as he lingers at the quay, pretending to take pictures on his phone. In Valletta he has a late but very pleasant lunch in a trattoria in the gloom of a narrow street overhung with ornately carved balconies. Afterwards he stands at the seawall at the tip of the peninsula watching boats play across the water and trying to be aware of who is around him. Finally he takes a taxi back to his hotel in Sliema, wanting nothing more than a long nap.

He is flat on his back on the bed, staring at the ceiling, when the hotel telephone on his bedside table rings. Go to hell, he thinks, having no appetite for a talk with anyone, least of all his handlers. He lets it ring long enough to establish his independence and then rolls wearily to reach for the phone, falling back on the pillow with the receiver to his ear. "Yes?"

"Mr. Pascual March?"

Pascual freezes. This is a woman's voice, but not Lina's. And who would ask for Pascual March? "I believe you have a wrong number," he says carefully.

"Let us try Pascual Rose, then," the woman says, and now the freeze goes all the way to Pascual's entrails.

This is not a native English speaker. Pascual rapidly assesses the accent; she pronounced 'March' like the English month and handled the English *r's* without difficulty, but the way she said 'Pascual' betrayed her. He says, *"Y usted, ¿quién es?"*

She switches to Spanish without missing a beat, confirming his guess. "I'm somebody you need to talk to."

"And why would that be?"

"Because your life depends on it."

Pascual swings his feet to the floor. He sits rubbing his face, briefly indulging the notion of throwing the phone into the corner and rushing downstairs to grab a taxi to the airport. "Explain," he says finally.

"I'll do that face to face. Are you alone?"

Careful, Pascual thinks. "And what's that to you?"

"Well, there is a woman who calls herself Lina who might be with you. Possibly a companion, too. I know they're in Malta. I don't want them to know we're talking. That's why I'm using the house phone instead of your mobile. Can I come up to your room?"

"What, you're here, at the hotel?"

"In the lobby. Can I come up?"

Pascual sits paralyzed, juggling astonishment, curiosity and alarm. In his ear the woman says, "Hello? Still there?"

"Still here. Look, I'm sure you'll understand my need for caution. There's a bar on the roof of this place. Can we meet there?"

There is a moment of silence. "I'd prefer to talk to you in private, but I can understand. Now, please understand my need for caution as well. Give me fifteen minutes before you get there, will you? I don't want any surprises. Look for a woman in a white skirt with her hair in a purple headband. If you don't see me, it means I don't like the setup."

Pascual has not liked anything about the setup since the whole thing started, but he knows a man in his position cannot pass up offers of information. "Fifteen minutes, *de acuerdo,"* he says.

A quarter of an hour later Pascual steps out of the elevator and pushes through a glass door onto the roof of the hotel. He sees the bar to his left under a canopy, two bartenders in black working briskly in front of a half-dozen drinkers on high stools, a scattering of tables shaded by umbrellas in the center of the space, and to his right smaller tables for couples lining the rail at the edge of the roof. Beyond that is the brilliant aquamarine sea.

Pascual stands for a moment scanning. There are only two women at the bar. One is hanging on the arm of the man next to her, a couple of sips away from toppling off the stool; the other is alone at the end of the bar, swiping at her phone. Neither of them has her hair in a purple band. Perhaps half of the tables in the middle are occupied by mixed parties. Pascual ambles slowly up the aisle between the tables, hands in his pockets, looking for a purple headband. He has gone a dozen or so paces when he stops abruptly, in shock.

“Hello,” says Lina. She and Felix are sitting at a table by the rail, drinks in front of them and to judge by the look on Lina’s face, not a care in the world.

All Pascual can come up with is, “What are you doing here?” He is thinking furiously: was the woman on the phone a confederate, merely a ruse to get him up onto the roof?

Lina says, “We had a feeling you would be up here sooner or later. Pull up a chair.” Moving slowly, Pascual takes a chair from a neighboring table, sweeping the rooftop with a look as he does so.

“Looking for someone?” says Felix as Pascual sits at the table.

“My friend from the Virgin Islands. Is she here, too?”

“Hoping to get lucky again, were you?” Felix has the smile of a nasty boy.

“Just wondering why you would pop up like this.”

“Because we need to talk to you,” says Lina. “And it’s always more pleasant to talk business over drinks, don’t you think?”

Pascual makes a vague noise of assent. A waitress has appeared and he orders a Negroni. “Were you shadowing me all day?” he says.

“Associates were,” says Lina. “That’s why we’re in Malta. We have resources here.”

“And what did your associates see?”

“Nothing alarming. They said it doesn’t appear anyone was tailing you. Of course, there are other ways of keeping tabs than by following you in the street. Did anyone approach you today? Ask for a selfie or snap your photo?”

Pascual opens his mouth to tell her about the woman on the phone, then shuts it abruptly.

"What?" says Lina.

"Nothing. A man on the ferry across the harbor asked me for a light. I told him I didn't smoke anymore."

"Yes, our people saw that. Probably inconsequential."

"They were on the ferry with me? They're good."

"Yes. All right, today it seems you didn't draw any undue attention. Things go well at SLM?"

"As far as I could tell. No alarm bells went off, no Interpol agents came bursting in. The passport seemed to pass inspection."

"Of course. It's perfectly genuine. As I said, we have resources here."

"The documents should be ready tomorrow."

"Splendid. You can fly on to Cyprus directly, then. I don't see any need to postpone setting up an account."

Pascual frowns at her. "Why Cyprus?"

"Why wouldn't you go to Cyprus?"

"I thought they'd had a banking crisis and been scolded by the EU because they were awash in dirty money from Russia. I thought we were going for respectability."

"Your information's a little out of date. This particular bank has just survived a money-laundering scandal and been given a clean bill of health. All of Cyprus has been given a clean bill of health, for that matter. They've cleaned up their anti–money laundering rules in response to pressure from the EU and the Americans, and put severe limits on dealing with shell companies. It's actually quite difficult to open a bank account in Cyprus now. There could be no better proof of Pascual Rose's legitimacy than to put the account there."

"If they're so clean now, how are we going to pull the wool over their eyes?"

Lina favors him with a faint smile. "No wool-pulling involved. You forget you have a well-established track record of business activities in Dubai and other places in the Middle East. The new directives that have come into force in Cyprus require a company to show proof of a physical presence or operations in its country of incorporation, and to divulge the beneficial owner. That excluded thousands of shell companies, most of them Russian. And the Russians have left in droves. But there is an exception for companies whose purpose is to hold intangible assets, such as financial instruments. And your holdings in Dubai fill the bill nicely. You're consolidating your financial empire by setting up a holding company. And with your ample documentation, the bankers will be happy to assist you."

Pascual shrugs. "All right, then. Am I going to have minders in Cyprus, too?"

"Why, do you think you would need them?"

"Well, if somebody's on to us, I'm the one at risk, right? It would be nice to know that if a couple of heavies try to shove me into a car slewing to the curb, somebody will be there to stop them."

Felix startles Pascual with a rumble of laughter. "If it gets to that point, it will be too late to do anything."

Lina says dryly, "The best we could do would be to get the plate number."

"Terrific."

Lina shakes her head. "Pascual, we haven't seen any signs here of any physical surveillance, and if anyone is tracking you, a quick hop to Cyprus tomorrow with a last-minute ticket purchase should catch them unawares. We're not really too concerned about people bundling you into a car. We're concerned about people sitting in a dark room looking at computer screens. The woman in the Virgin Islands may or may not have been associated with them. If she was, she obviously just wanted information."

Pascual's drink arrives and there is a lull in the conversation. Pascual stares out to sea, feeling out of his depth, hearing a voice saying in Spanish, "Because your life depends on it."

"If you're not worried, I'm not worried," he says finally.

"Excellent," says Lina. "There are several flights from here to Larnaca daily. You should have no problem getting a seat. I think Felix and I will steal away first thing in the morning and leave you to it. Tonight, we thought we might take you to a rather fine restaurant not too far from here, famed for its seafood."

Pascual likes a good feed as well as the next man, but the prospect of an evening in this company is not appealing. There is also his mysterious caller to look out for. He gropes for a way to decline but it occurs to him that it would be unwise to suggest he has any other plans. "Thank you," he says. "I was wondering what to do for dinner."

In the ensuing lapse in the conversation Pascual works on his drink, trying to look like a man anticipating a pleasant evening.

"Poor girl, she got stood up," says Felix, lounging on his chair, looking idly toward the bar.

Lina looks. "Who?"

"The one in the white skirt there. She came in, sat at the bar, took off her headband and combed her hair out, started looking at her phone. And now she's stalking out of here."

Pascual has the self-discipline to turn slowly to look over his shoulder toward the exit. All he sees is the back of a nicely shaped woman in a short white skirt, with a full head of chestnut hair, disappearing through the doorway.

The airliner's approach gives Pascual an opportunity to admire Larnaca, yet another sun-drenched town splayed out along a coast lapped by an azure sea, studded with high-rise hotels. Sadly, he will not get a chance to see it close up; all too soon the plane is thumping onto the runway south of the city and now he will have to fight his way out of the terminal into the heat and find a way to get fifty kilometers inland. There are not going to be any beaches or seaside breezes for Pascual on this jaunt.

The airport at Nicosia has been derelict since the Turkish air force punched holes in it in the summer of 1974, and if you want to go to Nicosia you have to fly to Larnaca and look at ground travel options. Pascual could afford better, but mostly because it is the first thing he finds, he winds up in a collective taxi with two Greek-speaking gentlemen sweating in sport jackets and a gloomy-looking youth of undetermined nationality in a Paris Saint-Germain jersey. Pascual's one indulgence is to slip the driver a little extra for the front seat.

Shooting along a fine four-lane motorway past rock-stubbled hills, Pascual recalls a long-ago marathon in a collective taxi from

Aleppo to Damascus, jammed between the East German fugitive he was escorting to the welcoming arms of Assad's Mukhabarat and a garrulous, snaggle-toothed old sheikh in a black-checked kaffiyeh. There are areas of his past he regards with nostalgia and others that evoke a queasy horror.

The Nicosia into which the taxi delivers him is an unprepossessing Greek city, hot and dusty, full of traffic racing past nondescript modern buildings. His hotel is a massive concrete honeycomb on a main boulevard; from the balcony of his seventh-floor room Pascual can look north to an older city with tiled roofs, domes and minarets. At some point it becomes Turkish: far away to the north, a gigantic flag with the crescent and star has been painted onto a mountainside. Pascual finds little charm in the view.

He retreats into the air conditioning and sits on the bed. There is a telephone on the bedside table, just as there was in Malta. Pascual stares at it, waiting for it to ring. He pulls out his phone, the one issued him by Lina, and sits holding it. After a time he sets it on the table, kicks off his shoes, and falls back onto the bed, arm over his eyes.

How did she know I was in Malta? Pascual has been working on this since he saw the white skirt disappearing through the door of the rooftop bar. There was no further approach in Malta, and Pascual assumes that his caller was scared off by the sight of Lina and Felix in the bar. He thinks it unlikely that she would be able to trail him to Cyprus, but then the fact that she knew enough to telephone Pascual March in a hotel room in Malta was wildly unlikely.

She knows about Lina, and she knows about Pascual March. What is the link? The one that jumps at Pascual is the one that everyone on the planet seems to share, the little slab of signal-spewing electronics that everyone carries. Pascual March's phone was hacked by Lina; there are calls and texts on it from Lina and from Felix, starting with *Come join us on the terrace*. Was Pascual March's phone hacked by someone else as well? Or was it Lina's phone that was hacked? Anyone monitoring Lina's phone would see the initial approach to somebody named Pascual March. And then, given sufficient curiosity, Pascual March's phone could be hacked as well.

But paths diverge. After the initial approach, Pascual March's mobile shows a fictitious record of travel arrangements and calls made on a spurious series of business trips in the service of a Dutch logistics firm. It was Pascual Rose in that room in Malta, and all of Pascual Rose's travel arrangements and business calls on this little world tour of tax havens have been made on the phone issued to him by Lina for that purpose. So how did the mysterious caller know that Pascual Rose was Pascual March?

That is not, perhaps, the best-kept secret, as Pascual himself pointed out to Lina. So, White Skirt has access to Spanish police records, or maybe just access to someone who remembers that nasty business with the fellow with two names, twenty or more years ago. And if she is tracking Lina's phone she will be able to track Pascual Rose, aka Pascual March.

Pascual swings his feet to the floor, mustering his energy for a foray out into what he hopes is the easing late afternoon heat. He picks up his phone and does a little searching, of the type a man with an evening to kill in an unfamiliar city might do, bringing up the map, clicking on tourist highlights, searching for watering holes and places to eat. If he is right, he is not just informing himself; he is announcing his agenda and leaving a trail.

A taxi takes him to Eleftheria Square and he finds the entrance to Ledra Street. Beneath canopies strung from the rooftops to shade it from the sun, Ledra Street shows signs of the same gentrification and homogenization that turned Barcelona's Ramblas from a gracefully aging dowager to a tarted-up floozy. Among shops with signs in Greek and English, Pascual passes a Starbucks next to a McDonald's. The street is long and straight, shooting north through the old city to the Green Line that has separated Greeks and Turks since the unpleasantness of 1974. Pascual stops short of the crossing to the Turkish zone and, failing utterly to find an atmospheric Greek taverna, backtracks to the Starbucks. Here he sits with an iced coffee and pretends to consult his phone, watching the street. People come and go, nobody lingers or gives him a glance. The only ones he sees more than once are a little knot of teenagers, boys and girls, drifting up and down, strutting, shoving, mocking, flirting.

The sunlight goes, streetlamps come on. Pascual locates an Armenian restaurant and has a decent meal, served by an earnestly accommodating woman who has no languages in common with him but manages to get him fed. He returns to his hotel and waits for the phone to ring; it never does.

"The Americans sent a Treasury official to read us the riot act," says Mr. Kourakis. "He told us to clean up our act or they would do to us what they did to the Latvians." Kourakis is chubby and balding, sweat beginning to stain his shirt despite the air conditioning in this spacious third-floor office in an ugly building in a tranquil modern quarter a long taxi ride from Pascual's hotel.

"What did they do to the Latvians?" Pascual admires Kourakis's glib idiomatic English but is beginning to tire of his volubility.

"They shot down one of their biggest banks, blew it out of the water. All they had to do was refuse to let it open a correspondent account in the U.S. Once they cut off the American money, the bank was history."

"Because of the Russians," says Christakis. He is gaunt and gloomy, a vulture to Kourakis's strutting pigeon. "The Americans make sanctions on Russia. And where do Russians wash their money? Latvia. And here." He stabs at the desk with a long bony finger.

"Until the guy from Treasury came and told us the facts of life." Kourakis grins. "And the government sat up and took notice. They saw what happened to the Latvians. Bang, overnight things changed. The Central Bank issued a directive, no more dealing with shell companies."

"And the Russians all go." Christakis gestures, a sweep of the hand. "Bye-bye, Russians."

"Not that they've actually left," says Kourakis. "There are thousands of Russians here. Walk down a street in Limassol and you'd think you were in Moscow. But all the shell companies had their accounts closed. Thousands of them. Now you have to prove you're a real business, with real assets and real activities. You gotta have a factory churning out widgets if you want to bank with us now. So that, I'm sorry to say, is why we have to put you through all this today." Kourakis finishes with a rueful look at the stack of papers on the desktop.

"I understand," says Pascual. "I have to say, I'm a little apprehensive. I don't have a factory and I don't make widgets."

Kourakis raises a hand, reassuring. "That was just a figure of speech. There are still plenty of legitimate uses for a holding company, and we're still allowed to do business with them. We just have to establish that there is a real functioning business behind it all, and the identity of the ultimate beneficial owner has to be recorded."

"I'm the beneficial owner," says Pascual. "And I think you'll find ample evidence of my business activities here." He taps on the accordion folder Lina presented him in Malta, full of faked documents that Pascual desperately hopes will look as convincing to two Cypriot bank officials as they did to his untrained eye.

"I'm sure there will be no problem," says Kourakis, his eye lingering for just a second on Pascual's maimed hand on the folder. "We had a look at what we could find online, and it looks like you've got quite a little empire there in Dubai."

Pascual nods, trying to look modest. "I've done very well. Well enough that my lawyer advised me it was time to consolidate, and put some assets into this structure."

"Very smart," says Christakis, nodding. "Many advantages."

"Yes." Kourakis pulls the folder across the desk toward him. "Now, it's going to take us some time to go through all this. What I would suggest is that you go get lunch. We've got a car, and I can have the driver drop you anywhere you want. He'll come back and pick you up when you're finished. We'll give all this a look-see and then there will be forms to fill out and that kind of nonsense. That will all go better after lunch."

"Very good." Pascual is already rising. "Well, till later then." Pascual is suddenly desperate to be gone, convinced that he has just deposited irrefutable proof of massive fraud with these two newly reformed and eagle-eyed guardians of financial probity.

"Just a second," says Kourakis, reaching for the phone. "I'll have the car pick you up in front." He rattles off some Greek into the phone and gives Pascual a thumbs-up. "The car will be there in two minutes. Mr. Christakis will take you down."

In the elevator Christakis is silent and avoids Pascual's eyes, whether because of his less fluent English or because he is already rehearsing the call to the financial authorities, Pascual cannot say. At the street door he shakes Pascual's hand and says, "See you later, then. Have a good lunch."

A black BMW X6 is waiting at the curb in front of the bank. The driver is wisely sheltering in a band of shade next to the building, smoking a cigarette; he comes to attention and tosses it away when Pascual approaches. He is squat and potbellied, with a head of tight curls going gray but mustache, thick brows and stubble on his cheeks still black. He does not look especially pleased to see Pascual. "You Mr. Rose?" he says, trilling the *R*.

"Uh, yes." Faced with this unexpected perquisite, Pascual has no idea what to do with it. "Can you take me to a good restaurant?"

The driver merely nods and steps to open the door to the back seat for Pascual, then goes around to get in behind the wheel. He seems to know where he is going, and Pascual supposes Kourakis must have given him instructions over the phone. As they pull away from the curb, Pascual flirts with the notion of telling him to forget about lunch and make speed for the airport in Larnaca, but he manages to quell the outbreak of nerves. He gives it a few seconds and says, “Where are we going?”

The driver seems to have exhausted his English in identifying Pascual. He tosses a few words of something that might or might not be Greek over his shoulder and concentrates on his driving, which is brisk and assertive. Pascual watches buildings, other vehicles and a few startled pedestrians flit by at close range. The quarter thins out, commercial blocks giving way to broader vistas, residential quarters with small apartment houses and a few villas, green space with an abundance of cedars, oaks and cypresses. They go squealing around a roundabout, and now they are on what looks like a highway heading out of town.

Pascual supposes Kourakis has worked the classic Levantine fiddle of steering Pascual to a restaurant owned by a cousin. He hopes the cousin is not in Larnaca or Limassol. “What’s the name of this restaurant?” he essays. In reply he gets another indecipherable growl.

The highway takes them past industrial parks, scattered knots of houses, patches of undeveloped ground baking in the sun, and puzzlement is beginning to give way to alarm. Pascual opens his mouth and draws breath, and then closes it when he fails to come up with anything effective to say.

In the front seat the driver is talking on his phone, steering with one hand. He laughs shortly and tosses the phone on the seat. Pascual’s hand slides inside his jacket and comes out with his phone. This is the one Lina gave him, the one she is presumably tracking, the one for that matter which ought to connect him with her with a single tap. If he is being kidnapped, he can at least broadcast it live. He swipes to wake the phone.

The driver slows and turns off the highway. After a couple of hundred meters they are in a residential neighborhood, villas with gardens on either side. It becomes just credible to Pascual that there could be a restaurant hereabouts. He sits with the phone in his hand, watching houses go by. They are large and prosperous-looking, bougainvillea and jasmine spilling over garden walls. The driver takes one more corner, slows and pulls through an open gate into a drive between two stone columns. He comes to a halt before a sizeable two-story white stucco villa with a portico at the side and a shaded porch. Over his shoulder he says, "OK."

Pascual says nothing. He is too busy noting his surroundings: the tall poplars visible over the roof of the house, the pleasant garden in front of it, the man behind the car closing the gate through which they have just driven, two more men coming through the garden toward the car.

And the driver, getting out of the car and saying something to the men in a language that is now, unmistakably, Russian.

15

Pascual climbs slowly out of the car, phone in hand. The driver is wandering away into the shade at the side of the villa lighting another cigarette, and there are three men converging on Pascual. None of them would pass muster with a casting director looking for Russian toughs. There are no tattoos, no broken noses and only one shaved head. But Pascual has enough experience with toughs and with Russians to know he is being presented with the genuine item. The physical authority and the Slavic physiognomy are unmistakable. "Peace," he says, raising his hands. "What's the word? *Mir.*"

The man on the right, a broad-in-the-beam brawler, makes a noise that might be a laugh. The one with the shaved head reaches out and plucks the phone from Pascual's hand. "No phone," he says.

"All right, no phone." Pascual watches it disappear into a shirt pocket. "Do I get it back later?"

The third man, so colorless as to be almost albino, with a mat of bleached-out hair and very pale gray eyes, takes Pascual by the arm and turns him toward the car. A shove leans him on it in position to be searched, and a couple of pairs of hands establish quickly and ruthlessly that he is not armed. "OK," says the egghead. "You come."

Pascual follows him up the front steps, the other two trailing. Inside it is cool. Past an entranceway a living room opens out, stretching all the way to the back of the house, where another garden is visible through glass doors. The walls are white, the floors are white, the long sofas are white, with scattered cushions in bright colors to relieve the arctic vista. There is artwork on the walls, abstracts that repel the eye. Hallways open on either side; a doorway in a partitioned-off dining area gives a glimpse of a kitchen. Pascual's guide takes him through the glass doors at the rear and out into the sun again.

Pascual's estimate of the value of the place goes up several notches when he sees the half acre of garden spreading out, the poplars shading paths bordered by lavender, thyme and sage, the swimming pool sparkling in the sun. Someone in Russia is doing well, and probably not by doing good. Beyond the swimming pool is a terrace shaded by a pergola with a riot of bougainvillea forming a roof; this appears to be Pascual's destination. A man and a woman are seated in the shade under the pergola around a low table holding glasses and bottles. Pascual's guide steps aside as they reach it, motioning for him to proceed.

"Well, here he is. You must be our friend Pascual."

The man is young, no more than thirty, fit, tanned and nicely groomed. He wears a dark-gray tee with the manufacturer's logo on the breast and black shorts, hugging a slim athletic build. He looks like a hotshot tennis player ready to take on all comers at the country club.

Pascual notes all this with a glance and then does a full-voltage double take as his eyes light on the woman, because he has seen her before. "Hello, Pascual," says Melissa, giving him a cool smile. Today she is wearing a white robe, possibly over a bathing suit, as her hair is wet, held back by the sunglasses on top of her head, her feet in sandals.

Somebody pulls a chair scraping across the tiles and nudges Pascual's legs with it. Pascual is staring idiotically at Melissa. He manages to sit. He says, "Kansas City, huh?"

"I did live there," she says. "For three years. For a cow town it's not a bad place." She turns to the youth and to Pascual's astonishment lets loose a stream of fluent Russian. Pascual does not speak it but has heard it enough to recognize native ability. The youth answers in Russian and Melissa turns back to Pascual. "So," she says. "I think maybe introductions are in order. I'm Tatiana, and this is Konstantin."

Pascual blinks at them. "Tatiana. OK, give me a second. This is all moving kind of fast for me."

"No hurry. Would you like something to drink?"

Dazed, being offered drinks two minutes after steeling himself for enhanced interrogation, Pascual just sits for a moment openmouthed. On the table are various types of liquor, vodka prominent among them, mixers, an ice bucket, a bottle of wine in a clay cooler, a carafe of water. "I think maybe just water, thanks."

Melissa pours and hands him a glass. "Very wise. On a hot day like today, you don't want to drink too much alcohol, get all woozy."

"No," he ventures after a restorative gulp. "That's a recipe for a headache."

"Maybe worse than a headache," says Konstantin. His English is accented but fluent, the international English that everyone from

Shanghai to Buenos Aires speaks these days. "You maybe want to take a swim after lunch. And you don't want to be drunk. This fellow I know, he drowned in his swimming pool, day just like today. Hot day, he had few drinks, he went in the pool, his wife found him facedown, one hour later. Passed out and drowned. Poor guy." The look on the lad's face is completely blank.

Pascual pauses with the glass at his lips. "Well, I wasn't planning on swimming."

"That's a good idea. It would be big problem for everybody, have to pull you out of the pool, call the ambulance, talk to police. Explain to everybody what happened. That would be very embarrassing for us."

The country club tennis whiz is gone, replaced by a contract killer with eyes thirty years older than the rest of his face. Pascual locks eyes with him for a long moment, and the ice water is not the only thing causing this chill in his insides. He turns to the woman who seduced him a hemisphere away and says, "OK, Melissa. Sorry, Tatiana, why am I here?"

Konstantin answers. "You're here because I want to know who the hell I paid hundred thousand euros to, and for what. You mind explaining that to me?"

Pascual carefully sets the glass down on the table. "If you're referring to the hundred thousand euros that was deposited into my bank account, that was done without my knowledge. And the people who did it certainly didn't mention you."

"And who was that?"

Pascual takes a moment to think, because he can see that the choices he makes in the next few seconds are going to determine a great deal, including whether he lives out the day. "If you really want to talk to them, here's what you do. You take my phone from your man over there, and you bring up my contacts and hit the first name on the list. She'll pick up and you can ask her what the hell is going on. You may not even have to do that, because she might be listening already. I'm pretty sure she can turn it into a listening device when she wants to. If you want our talk to be private, you should have your man go for a walk somewhere."

Konstantin blinks once or twice and then calls to the man with the shaved head, who has been lurking somewhere behind Pascual. He starts, pulls Pascual's phone out of his shirt pocket, listens to Konstantin's instructions, and then wanders away down a path with it. "So who we talking about?" Konstantin says.

"I could tell you the names they gave me, but that wouldn't be worth much. They came and made me an offer I couldn't refuse. The money just showed up in my bank account. They didn't say where it came from."

"Well, it came out of my pocket." Konstantin is giving Pascual the stare again. "I didn't like that."

"I can see why. But I'd say you should take it up with them."

"Oh, sure, I'll do that. Thanks for the advice. Only problem is, I don't know who they are."

"I don't either. Like I said, they showed up at my house one night and said, 'Here's a hundred thousand euros, and by the way we know where your family is. And here's what we want you to do for us.'"

Konstantin stares, tapping one finger on the arm of his chair. "Register companies and open bank accounts."

"That's right."

"And why do they need all these companies?"

"Well, they told me it was to hide a great deal of money one group of criminals was stealing from another. They didn't name names or go into details."

Konstantin's eyes narrow. "And why did they choose you?"

"Because I'm the perfect fall guy. I have two identities and an identifying mark that no one is likely to fake." Pascual holds up his left hand, then cocks a thumb at Tatiana. "Between her and the guys at the bank here, you seem to be pretty much on top of things. If you knew enough to send her to the Virgin Islands, why can't you figure out who they are?"

"You think they put their names on everything? When I sent Tatiana to Virgin Islands, all I knew was, somebody paid this guy, Pascual March, a hundred thousand euros from a bank account that belongs to a company I own. And I only found that out because I decided to make, what do you call it, an audit, because I find out the guy that ran the company was stealing my money. Embezzle, is that the word? And I see this Pascual March got paid one hundred thousand euros from that account. Except it was funny, because the guy got killed, and the payment happened after the guy was dead. So who made payment?"

"They call themselves Lina and Felix. They seem to be pretty good at manipulating people and pretty good with computers. Maybe they even killed the guy."

"No, that was me."

"Ah." Pascual swallows. "I see."

"So then I look, who is this Pascual March? I have guys who are pretty good, too. And they tell me, this guy, his passport photo is almost the same as a guy named Pascual Rose, and he's a hotshot guy in Dubai, and he just made plane reservation to go to the Virgin Islands next week. So I send Tatiana."

Tatiana says, "And I used my Midwestern gal charm on the clerk at your hotel to get him to point you out to me."

Pascual raises his hands in surrender. "I didn't want any of this. I didn't know about you, I didn't know where the money was coming from, I didn't know anything. All I knew was, they offered me money and threatened my family if I didn't cooperate. What would you have done?"

"Maybe same thing you did. Not my problem. This is your problem. The question is, what are you going to do?"

"Look, I was conscripted into this. You want your hundred thousand euros back? I'll do what I can. I've spent a lot of it, on expenses. You want it all back, then you're going to have to go after them."

"And how do I do that? I don't know who they are."

Pascual sees where this is heading. He can see his choices spelled out clearly, all of them bad. Suddenly he could use a drink, a big iced slug of good Russian vodka. It may not help his judgment, but then good judgment is only really useful when there are good choices available. He drains his water glass and reaches for the nearest bottle. "Fine. You want me to help you get your money back. I'll help you do that."

Konstantin laughs. "You are not a very smart kind of crook, are you, Mr. Pascual?"

"Not much of a crook at all, to be honest."

"Funny. Look, a hundred thousand euros for me is . . . what do you say? Chicken food. Small change. I don't give a shit about hundred thousand euros. You told me these people are stealing a lot of money, right? A lot more than a hundred thousand?"

"Considerably more, I was led to understand."

"Excellent. And who are they stealing it from?"

"That they didn't say."

"Well, they're maybe gonna try to steal it from me. If they do that, they gonna have a problem. *You* gonna have a big problem. But I don't think that's what they're doing. I think they used my bank just to make people think I'm the one doing the stealing. And I don't like that. That could make big problem for me. What I think is, they're gonna steal it from somebody else. And I like that. I like it because they are doing all the work. Once it's stolen, all I need to do is take it from them." Konstantin leans forward and jabs a finger at Pascual. "And to help me do that, I have you."

"Yes," says Pascual, pouring himself a stiff one. "For that you have me."

16

"So, no mishaps? No stern-faced EU regulators flashing badges at you, no gangsters hustling you into cars at the curb?" Lina takes delivery of the folder with the documentation for the freshly opened Cypriot bank account of the newly activated Maltese corporation, Pascual sliding it across the table to her. The generalized hubbub of the airport concourse around them cocoons them from curious ears. "Everything go well?" One raised eyebrow betrays what looks to Pascual like supercilious amusement.

Pascual shrugs. He has devoted the past day and a half to thinking through his position, weighing this against that, threat against threat, risk against reward. One school of thought says that his first loyalty is to the people who are paying him a million euros, and that the only sane course of action is full disclosure and an emergency session to plot defensive measures against a breach of security by top-level international brigands. Another says that no obligation can be construed to anyone who includes threats to his family in their toolkit, and that being able to call on Russian muscle might be a crucial asset at a critical moment. It may come down to which side's expectations are easier to fulfill when push comes to shove, and it is too early to say. For Pascual the deciding factor is who is going to be harder to lie to, and he is fairly sure that with all their resources, that will be Lina and Felix. "Tell me," Pascual says, "What good is all your spyware if you don't even know who I had lunch with on Thursday? I thought you were able to track me wherever I go. You can even turn my phone into a listening device, if I'm not mistaken."

The supercilious look vanishes. "Why would we do that? Until you give us a reason not to, we have decided to trust you. We can of course go back and look at your data and see where you've been. As for eavesdropping, if you're worried about it you can always remove the battery from your phone. Of course, we would find the lack of a signal very suspicious and would ask for an accounting." She assumes an exasperated expression. "Look, we have better things to do than monitor you constantly. Now, who did you have lunch with?"

"You know a young fellow named Konstantin? From Yekaterinburg? He didn't give me a last name. You can probably figure it out. There can't be too many young guys from Yekaterinburg who have the money to maintain a mansion and an extensive posse in Nicosia. He has a place in Limassol, too, he said. He seems to be doing very well for himself."

Lina has gone absolutely still. "Talk," she says finally.

"He detected your payment to me. The hundred thousand euros. You went through his bank to make it look as if he was behind me, didn't you? Well, he happened to sniff it out, and he got curious. He was the one who put the lady onto me in the Virgin Islands. She was there in Nicosia, too."

Pascual senses a brain working furiously behind the marble exterior. "All right, cut to the chase. What did they say?"

"Mostly they asked a lot of questions. They wanted to know who I was working for. They wanted to know who your target was. Most of all, they wanted me to help them get in on the fun. They want a piece of the action."

"And what did you tell them?"

"What do you think I told them? I told them I'd be happy to help."

Seconds go by as Lina processes all this with a complete absence of affect. "I suppose you had to," she says.

"It was that or wind up at the bottom of the swimming pool. But they're like you. They know how to motivate a man. They offered to cut me in on it. It was agreed I would do nothing for the present except feed them information, passwords, account numbers and so forth, to help them drain these accounts I'm setting up, when the time comes. I am now their mole in this operation. I'm to advise them when the time is ripe for them to strike."

Frowning very slightly, Lina leafs quickly through the contents of the folder. "I see. Well, I'd say you handled a difficult situation about as well as you could. Thank you for the full report. This is going to call for a reassessment, of course."

"That does seem wise."

"You've earned a little break, I'd say." She shoves his regular phone across to him. "Go home, play your role, tell your friends about your trip to Finland, relax for a few days. The Isle of Man and Luxembourg were to be next on the agenda, but in the light of this development we'll have to reconsider everything." For a moment the mask slips, the ice cracks, the composure wavers, as Lina expels what sounds like an exasperated breath. She steadies and says, "We had already decided it's a good idea anyway to take a little time and watch the phosphorescence in our wake. There are still indications somebody's interested in what we're doing in cyberspace. It won't be too long, don't worry. We won't keep you hanging."

Pascual waves, an airy gesture of indifference. "Don't hurry on my account. There is one thing I feel I've earned."

"What would that be?"

"The full story. About who I'm helping to rip off. Who are you stealing from?"

"You don't think that could be dangerous knowledge?"

"I think on the whole ignorance is probably more dangerous. I may not be a full partner in this enterprise, but I think I've shown I'm a loyal employee. How about a little respect?"

Lina takes time to think about it, securing the folder and shoving it into the briefcase she lifts from beside her chair. "I'm not going to give you a name. That would be in violation of every principle of operational security, even if we can trust you completely. I will tell you that our target can afford to lose what we're arranging to take from him, and he certainly didn't acquire it honestly in the first place. I can't say he won't miss it, but he's not going to find his financial position too terribly damaged. So your conscience needn't be too troubled on that score. We're not stealing from widows and orphans."

Pascual takes a shot in the dark. "Is he by any chance Russian?"

Lina does not blink. "He's a very wealthy man. And a slice of it is going to the poor, in the form of your million euros, among other things. So try to think of yourself as Robin Hood. It may help you get through this."

Pascual laughs a laugh of quiet desperation. "I'll do that. That seems preferable to thinking of myself as a pickpocket with his hand inside a Cossack's cloak."

Pascual waits. The sun has gone down, the heat dissipated; the neighbors have put the children to bed and turned on the telly. Here on Pascual's terrace with a new moon rising above the rooftops and vintage Clash just audible in some nearby fan's bedroom it is possible to imagine that nothing has changed in the past month, that Lina and Felix never sat here and the Virgin Islands and Cyprus were nothing but a fever dream.

But Pascual waits, because he knows it was all real. And he knows that after a week of silence on all fronts, it is just about time for somebody, whether Lina or Fernando Salera or a woman in a white skirt or possibly even a Russian gorilla, to rattle his cage again. He raises the glass of cheap brandy to his lips.

He nearly drops it as the buzz of the doorbell startles him. He swallows, freezes and wonders: Ignasi, meandering by, looking for a late-night chess game? Encarna, the widow downstairs, with another transparent pretext to lure him in and woo him? Or is this the rattling of the cage? Pascual rises, goes to the edge of the terrace and looks down into the street.

The woman at the door has made it easy for him; she has put on the purple headband, though under the streetlights the color could be just about anything. She looks up as he leans into her peripheral vision and he gazes into her large dark eyes for a long moment. "Pascual?" she finally says.

"Momento." Pascual goes to the landing and reaches inside the door to his flat to press the button. The buzzer goes, the handle turns, the door at the bottom of the stairs swings open. Pascual waits until her eyes rise to find him at the top of the stairs, then goes and resumes his seat on the terrace, listening as she climbs the stairs. When she reaches the landing she orients herself, spots him and turns, surveying. "Splendid," she says. "Your own little rooftop bar."

"Smaller than the one in Malta."

"And more private." She is scanning still, looking at his neighbors' windows, the surrounding rooftops and nearby balconies. "I hope." She takes a step toward him. Tonight the pleasant shape is in jeans, the only white the white of her clogs, painted toenails showing; a figure-hugging top leaves her arms bare except for a bracelet on the right one and a watch on the left. A cloth bag hangs over one shoulder. The mane of hair kept off her forehead by the headband looks as if it would be a rich chestnut in full sunlight. Even in the half-light she is not hard to look at, the type of woman who will turn a head or two as she passes.

"We could move inside," says Pascual. "But it would be much warmer. The only people in a position to eavesdrop are the people in the flat directly behind me, and as you can see, their windows are closed and their air conditioning is running. Across the way there, they'd have to turn off the television to hear anything. My mobile's inside, and unless somebody's got a directional microphone on one of these rooftops, I imagine we can speak freely if we keep it under a shout. Have a seat."

"Very well." She lowers herself onto the chair opposite Pascual, setting the bag on the tiles. "Can I trouble you for a glass of water? It's quite warm tonight."

"I can do better than water if you want."

"Tonic or just mineral water with a little ice would be lovely if you have it."

She is certainly a native Spanish speaker, but not a Catalan; she could easily be a Madrileña. Pascual stands. "That I think I can do." He goes inside and pours her a glass of *agua con gas* from a bottle in the fridge. When he brings it to her she has taken the headband off and is running fingers through her hair. She stuffs the headband into her bag. "That has served its purpose, I suppose. Too hot for it tonight."

"Was it the sight of Lina and Felix that made you shed it in Malta?"

"No. I had never seen them, had no idea what they looked like. I was tracking the location of her phone, on mine. I nearly had a heart attack when I realized she was right on top of me. I almost bolted, but I decided to strip off the headband and wait to see what happened. You I recognized from your passport photo. And when you joined them, you confirmed my guess. There weren't a lot of other likely candidates. My only worry was that you might side with them and blow the whistle on me."

Pascual polishes off the last of his brandy and frowns at the glass. He would dearly like another one, but he would have to make another trip to the kitchen, and he knows sobriety is in his best interest tonight. He leans to set the glass on the table. "So. You have the advantage of me. You know all about me, and I have no idea who on earth you might be, except you are probably not collecting for Cáritas. Are you Vigilancia Aduanera? Centro Nacional de Inteligencia? Seguridad Nacional? Or some agency I've never heard of?"

She drinks, swallows, cradles the glass in her lap. "None of the above. I'm with nobody. I'm a freelance, an amateur, a gadfly. I'm here in no official capacity. All I am, really, is a concerned citizen."

"You'll excuse me, but I find that hard to believe. You identified Pascual March with Pascual Rose and tracked him down in Malta. You knew who was running him and you were tracking them on your phone. That's a talented amateur."

"You'd be amazed at what your phone betrays."

"Less and less so every day."

"But I confess I had a little help."

"All right, humor me. Who are you?"

She sips water and sends him a cool look over the glass, the rim of it just caressing her lower lip. "My name is Artemisa Pereda," she says. "My father was Benedicto Pereda."

Pascual sits dumbly returning her gaze until he realizes the name is supposed to mean something to him. "Forgive me," he says. "I don't know who that is."

"You don't read the scandal sheets? You don't follow hushed-up security fiascos, corrupt political deals, fugitive spies? That surprises me, given your background."

"I have devoted a good deal of effort to removing myself from that world and keeping it at a distance. You're going to have to start at the beginning."

"Very well." She sets the glass on the table and settles back in the chair, crossing her legs. My father enjoyed a certain notoriety some years ago but had been out of the news for a decade or so. He was by turns a businessman, a political fixer and a spy. He infiltrated terror groups for the Policía Nacional and laundered money for crooked ministers. He set up Swiss bank accounts for African dictators and recruited mercenaries to overthrow them. He sold rockets to rebels in Chechnya and blood diamonds to gangsters in Italy. He delivered ransom money to kidnappers in Colombia and helped a Serbian gangster escape from prison in France. He was given a medal by King Juan Carlos and was on Interpol's Most Wanted List for three years. He even faked his own death once, to evade arrest in Singapore. He had what you might call a colorful career."

Pascual has known others whose careers were said to be colorful and learned to be wary of them. "It sounds as if he kept busy. It also sounds as if his loyalties were pretty much up for auction."

"That is certainly true. The one loyalty he had that never wavered was to me. He was probably not a very good man. But he was my father."

Pascual acknowledges that with a nod. "What happened to him?"

"Nobody knows. One evening last spring he got into his Porsche in Rome and drove off to meet a man who was supposed to have a business proposition for him. That's what he told his current girlfriend, anyway. He never came back, and the following day his car was found in the hills near a stretch of road known to be a prime spot for picking up prostitutes. There was blood on the seat that the DNA said was his. He has never shown up, alive or dead. The Carabinieri say he was probably lured into an ambush by a prostitute and robbed. But his phone was left on the passenger seat, and that's a quick grab for a thief. Of course there is a vocal minority that claims he faked his own death again. That's what the mistress thinks. She's convinced he ditched her for another woman."

"And what do you think?"

"I know he's dead."

"How?"

"When he faked his death in Singapore, he got word to me. 'Don't worry, I'm all right and I'll be in touch.' That came in a letter, using a code only the two of us knew, mailed from Australia, God knows how. This time, there's been no message. Nothing. And the blood was his, if the Carabinieri forensic science lab is to be believed. Some fool said he could have cut himself to set the scene, but my father was quite squeamish, couldn't stand to have blood drawn. I can't see him doing that. And there was a lot of blood. I think he really is dead, and I think he was killed so he couldn't tell anyone what he'd been doing for the six weeks or so before his death." Her voice has sunk to a husky purr, and the look in the dark eyes says the grieving is done and the reckoning is coming.

Pascual says, "And what had he been doing?"

The merest hint of a smile plays on her lips. "More or less what you've been doing for the past few weeks."

Pascual has been expecting something along these lines. He decides perhaps he will permit himself another drink. He stands and says, "You've gained my full attention. Do you know who killed him?"

"Well, it wasn't your friends in Malta. I don't think they get their hands dirty very much at their level. But I would bet they signed off on it."

Pascual frowns down at her, hands in his pockets. "And why have you gone to all the trouble of tracking me down and warning me?"

She stiffens a little. "First, because while my father may have been a scoundrel himself, he did not raise me to be one. So basic humanity compels me to try to prevent your death. But secondly, you are my best hope of finding out who these people are and what they are up to. In order to bring them to justice if possible."

"And if not?"

A few seconds go by before she says, "Let's not get ahead of ourselves." The voice has gone husky again.

Pascual makes for the kitchen, deep in thought. He pours himself another tot of the cheap stuff and returns to the terrace and sits.

"How do I know you're telling me the truth? How do I know for sure who you are, for that matter?"

The woman reaches into her bag and pulls out a pocketbook. She unzips it and extracts from it a passport and an identity card with an embedded chip, also bearing her photo. She hands them to Pascual.

The Spanish passport attests that she is *Artemisa María Pereda Fernández*. The card certifies her as a member of the *Ilustre Colegio de Abogados de Madrid*. Pascual hands them back. "Artemisa."

"The goddess of the hunt. Wild, indomitable and chaste. My father knew his mythology, and he knew what he wanted his daughter to be. My mother had little to say about it, as was usually the case in their marriage, which didn't last long."

"And so you became a lawyer. Accepting for the moment that you are who you say you are, how do I know you're telling me the truth about all this?"

"You don't. Even the documents could be faked, of course. Do you have a convincing alternative explanation for my presence? Are you willing to bet your life that yours is true?"

By way of response Pascual shrugs. "You seem to have an impressive array of resources at your disposal already. How does a lawyer from Madrid track the mobile phone of an international criminal and find out the life history of an ex-terrorist?"

"As I said, my father's phone was left in his car. It was returned to me with his other effects in Rome. And my father still had some friends left in the right circles. They have been very generous with technical help."

"And you were able to identify this woman who calls herself Lina from his phone?"

"Not directly. It took time and a lot of patient sifting. My father lived on his phone. He made a couple of dozen calls a day. Most of them were inconsequential. But in among all the chaff we saw a series of calls and texts to and from a number that was registered in Russia, in the name of a company incorporated in Cyprus."

"What a surprise."

She registers the sarcasm with a lift of the chin. "The texts didn't tell us much except that my father had met the owner of the number face to face in Rome, twice. And then he embarked on a series of trips to various places around Europe. Luxembourg, the Channel Islands, Liechtenstein. All closely following exchanges of calls with that number."

"There does seem to be a familiar pattern."

"Yes. He was dancing to the tune from the phone registered in Russia. The company is an obvious shell, and we were unable to get access to the phone's data. Whatever encryption she's using, it's state of the art. But we have been able to track its movements the old-fashioned way, by multilateration. And we were able to look at when and where my father talked to that phone and then search flight records, hotel records and so forth. And we were able to correlate his calls to the phone number with the movements of a certain Selena Baran, traveling on a Kazakh passport."

"Selena. Lina. She appears to have dropped a syllable."

"Yes. We couldn't get access to the passport photo, so we had no idea what she looked like. But we could keep an eye out for the name, and we did manage to tap into the Russian phone provider's data, so we could look out for the next instance of that number being used. After my father's death it went quiet for a long time."

"And then the next time it popped up, she was talking to me."

Artemisa nods. "That's right. And you were very well known to the people who were helping me."

"I've probably met some of them."

"They didn't say. But they gave me your history."

"And you decided to save me."

This draws a smile, though it is not a particularly warm one. "That may be a side benefit. My principal concern is to find out who had my father killed and what they're up to."

Pascual sits listening to the faint breathy murmur of a placid summer night in a town where nothing much happens, envying his neighbors in their untroubled sleep. The moon has cleared the corner of the roof. Pascual says, "And how do you intend to proceed?"

"That depends on you."

She leaves it at that, and Pascual turns his glass this way and that, admiring the rich amber of the *conyac*. "What do you need from me?"

"Whatever you can give me. Who, what, when, where. Why, if that's available. How much did they offer you for your cooperation?"

"A million euros, in a Cayman Islands trust."

Her eyebrows rise slightly. "And what have they given you by way of a pretext for your activities?"

"I've been told I'm facilitating the laundering of a great deal of money stolen by one criminal group from another."

"That is probably true. They haven't named any names, I suppose."

"No. There are indications that Russians are involved."

"That doesn't surprise me. There are Russians involved in just about any criminal undertaking anywhere, these days. What indications?"

Pascual takes a sip of brandy to give himself time to think. How much does he trust this woman? Even if she is to be trusted, where do his interests lie? There is still the school of thought that says a million euros in a Cayman Islands trust trumps all other concerns, but that school has been weakened by the tale of Benedicto Pereda's sticky end. With two distinct factions already competing for his loyalty, Pascual foresees nothing but increased complications. And yet Artemisa's tale of filial loyalty rings truer than anything either of the other factions has come up with. "I was hijacked in Nicosia by a gang of Russians," he says.

"And how had they gotten onto you?"

"The up-front money Lina paid me came from a Russian account. No doubt to throw investigators off the track. But the owner of the account happened to notice it. He got very interested in me and managed to find out I was coming to Cyprus. Apparently he has his own computer wizards. So I was invited to lunch to explain myself. I promised to help him siphon off whatever she diverts from wherever she's diverting it."

Artemisa's eyebrows rise. "At which point you will be in an extremely uncomfortable position."

"It's not exactly a featherbed right now. But yes, my life has just gotten more complicated. And now here you are."

"To complicate things further."

Pascual drinks, contemplates the remaining centimeter of brandy, throws caution to the wind and drains the glass. He leans to set it down and meets Artemisa's intense gaze. "Actually, you may have simplified them. If I'm ticketed for the same destination as your father, it does have a certain clarifying effect. Concentrates the mind, as somebody said. The question now becomes, not 'Can I possibly get away with my life as well as a payout from at least one side,' but rather, 'How can I possibly get away with my life?' Which should be a simpler problem to solve. Oh, and the lives of my wife and son as well. Throw that into the mix, because Lina made clear that those are the stakes."

Artemisa ponders, frowning slightly. "If it helps at all, I doubt very much that the Cayman Islands trust is real."

"Possibly not. I'm fairly certain the threat to my family is. They also made clear they would be happy to shop me to prosecutors in Germany for a murder I abetted thirty-five years ago."

"So your position is . . . delicate."

"That's one way to put it. Let me ask you this. Is there any reason why I shouldn't at this point simply contact the authorities and throw myself on the mercy of the court? I confess that the thought of that million euros has been clouding my thinking. I have allowed it to weaken a long-standing resolution to live a blameless life, or as close as I can come to it. I see now that they succeeded in corrupting me, again. So, why shouldn't I go to the police, tonight?"

"If you think you can do so without endangering your wife and son, that would be a possible course of action. If, of course, you're not worried about those German prosecutors. But let me give you a few things to consider."

"Other than the ethical considerations?"

"There are always others. First, what police are you talking about? There are some serious questions of jurisdiction here. We are talking about an international criminal conspiracy spanning continents, and

I don't think the local Mossos *comisaría* has much experience with those. The CNP might be a better bet, but that is likely to take you deep into a bureaucratic labyrinth. Interpol might be the most logical choice given the international nature of the thing, but Interpol brings its own jurisdictional tangles. In any event, going to the authorities brings one huge risk. It makes what you are doing discoverable to your antagonists. A police investigation is a leaky vessel."

"So what do you suggest?"

She takes her time in answering. "The people who are helping me are, after all, at most one removed from the legitimate authorities, however you define them. And they are much better at discretion. Given the nature of this operation, the resources your antagonists obviously command, the pressure they can bring to bear on you, I would say that you're better off relying on my unofficial contacts with the darker corners of the Spanish security services. For the moment. Before we can take action against them we have to know a lot more about them."

It is Pascual's turn to muse, staring past her at the rising moon. He has no reason to trust Artemisa Pereda except that of all the people who have dropped into his life recently she is the only one who has not threatened him. She could be a consummate liar pursuing nothing but her own agenda; Pascual knows from bitter experience that a woman's physical attractions can mask a heart as black as coal. But Pascual also knows that his choices are limited and allies are precious. He can feel the cheap brandy starting to take hold, lightening his head and threatening his judgment. Perhaps only because of that, he says, "*De acuerdo*. I put myself in your hands."

18

Pascual has not seen Enrique Campos in ten years and is not certain he will recognize him. He has seen what the onset of middle age can do, and when last sighted Campos was showing signs of nearing, if not the cliff edge, at least the start of the long slope down. In addition, Pascual knows a man's habits can change over time and thus there is no guarantee that ten years on he will still take his late-morning coffee in the same bar halfway up a tree-shaded side street off the Passeig de Gràcia, an easy ramble from the Barcelona office of the national newspaper for which Campos has toiled since he first became interested in Pascual March, ex-terrorist and reputed government informant.

Sometimes, however, men hold true to form. Pascual spots Campos halfway down the long zinc bar, coffee at his elbow, thumb working rapidly at his mobile phone. The beard is gray, the glasses fashionably updated and the midsection considerably augmented, but the man is unmistakably the same. Pascual heaves to a meter away and waits for him to look up. When he fails to do so, Pascual says, "In the old days it would have been *El País, La Vanguardia* and *ABC,* the competition, all spread out and taking up far more than your share of bar space. Now you just look like any other office drone desperate for a hookup on Tinder."

Campos looks up and freezes, and a look of wonder slowly illumines his face. "*Hostia*. You're still alive."

"For the next few days, anyway. How are you?" Pascual extends his hand.

Campos hangs onto it as if he requires proof of Pascual's solidity. "Oh, splendid. The boy's out of work, the girl's in love with a hopeless ne'er-do-well and the wife's mother is moving in with us all. Tinder's no good to me until I have a room of my own. Where have you been keeping yourself?"

"In the provinces. I don't get to town much. Still with the paper?"

Campos shrugs. "What else am I going to do? If we'd produced that bestseller, I might have been able to retire early, but I was shown the error of my ways."

"Me, too. Probably for the best, really. It gave me twenty years of unmolested seclusion." Pascual flags down the barman and orders a coffee of his own.

Campos has interpreted the use of the preterit in the last remark and is peering at Pascual. "Am I to understand that the twenty years have come to an end?"

"Abruptly. Listen, I took a chance on finding you here instead of calling you at the office because I don't want anyone to know I'm talking to you. And I'm talking to you not because I want to revive the book project but because I need information and you have lots of it, or ways of getting it, anyway. Quid pro quo as before, but we're not talking about a book. The most you'll get out of it is maybe a lead on a story, and I can't promise that. *¿Vale?*"

Campos gapes for a moment but finally nods. "*Vale*. What kind of information?"

"The kind I should be able to get by myself in this marvelous information age, except that I can't be detected gathering it in the usual fashion, meaning through a device like that one in your hand. I've been tracked down and shanghaied."

"Shanghaied?"

"Forcibly recruited, by a combination of threats and enticements, to participate in a massive criminal operation. And meanwhile thoroughly hacked and electronically surveilled. I'm firmly attached to a digital tether, and if I'm going to cut myself loose I'm going to have to go low-tech for a while."

Campos has gone into conspiratorial mode, leaning a little closer. "I'm not sure I totally follow, but if I can help, I'm happy to. What do you need to know?"

Pascual's coffee arrives and he takes time to doctor it before answering. "What can you tell me about Benedicto Pereda?"

The eyes behind the spectacles widen. "*Dios mío*. Don't tell me you have anything to do with that scoundrel."

"Not a thing. But I'd like to know a hell of a lot more about him."

"So would we all. He's disappeared again, hasn't he?"

"So they say. Do you buy it?"

"All I know is what got written at the time. He was supposedly kidnapped, in Rome, I believe. His car was found with bloodstains in it, but there was no sign of him. The consensus is, he's faked his own death again to avoid prosecution or worse."

"What was he involved in when he disappeared? Any rumors?"

Campos shakes his head. "Not that I've heard. Could have been anything. He was a criminal entrepreneur, a dealer in everything from antipersonnel mines to tax-free Swiss accounts. What's your connection?"

"I met his daughter recently."

"His daughter? I didn't know he had a daughter."

"That's who she claimed to be. Can you confirm that? So many people have told me so many lies, I take nothing for granted anymore."

Campos frowns at his phone. "Let's just see what bubbles to the surface here." He goes to work with the dexterity of an adolescent. After a few seconds he says, "Artemisa by name?"

"That's what she said."

Campos belabors the phone for a few seconds longer and then with a satisfied grunt turns it toward Pascual. "Is this her?" Pascual sees a series of screenshots coughed up by a search engine to the prompt *Artemisa Pereda,* and the face is undoubtedly that of the woman who sat on his terrace the previous evening.

"That's her."

"It says here she's a lawyer in Madrid."

"That's what she told me. She also told me she's convinced her father's dead."

Campos gives him a sharp look. "How can she be sure?"

"The blood was his, and he hasn't gotten in touch. She wants to find out who killed him and what he was up to. She claims to have contacts in the security services who are helping her."

"And why was she talking to you?"

"Because it looks as if the people who recruited Benedicto Pereda are the same ones who recruited me."

"Hostia." Campos draws back a few centimeters, as if afraid of

contagion. “You told me once you were in a business nobody was allowed to retire from. And here I thought you’d succeeded.”

“So did I. You’ll forgive me if I don’t give you the whole story now. If I manage to extract myself from this, you’ll get it. I give you my word. But first I’d be grateful if you could find out whatever you can about what Benedicto Pereda was involved in just before his death. Or steer me to someone who might know.”

“He’s a little bit yesterday’s news, but I can try.”

“And don’t tell a soul you’ve seen me. This little chat never happened, you know the drill. Anything you learn, don’t transmit it electronically. I’ll give you the number of a bar where they will take a message for me. Ask for a Chinese girl named Yu Yan. Just tell her you want to see me and leave a time and place to meet when you have something to tell me. Whatever you learn, don’t put anything online. Write it down on an old-fashioned piece of paper.”

Campos has begun to look a little skeptical. “You wouldn’t be suffering from just a touch of paranoia, would you?”

“Is that what you thought when I told you my story twenty years ago?”

Campos’s look goes somber. “No. Forgive me, one forgets. If anyone has the right to be paranoid, friend, it’s you.”

The Bar Estudiantil has anchored one end of the Plaça de la Universitat as long as Pascual can remember, a stronghold of cheap eats, cheerful if inconsistent service and squalid toilets. He was never enrolled in the university whose somber facade dominates the Gran

Via side of the plaza, but academic credentials were not required to chat up a pretty girl with an armload of books, and Pascual has fond memories of the place.

Dris is sitting by himself at an umbrella-shaded table on the terrace beneath the palms. He looks bored, perhaps because there are no pretty girls in range, with or without books. Pascual strolls past him, making brief eye contact, and goes into the air-conditioned interior, where he sits at the bar and orders a *plato combinado,* the classic *butifarra* with beans, for old times' sake. He is halfway through the meal when Dris slumps onto the stool beside him, his back to the bar. "Nobody on your tail, as far as I can tell," says Dris. "But the square's full of people. Somebody could be waiting to pick you up when you leave."

Pascual shrugs. "As long as nobody's snapping a picture of us right now, I'm not too concerned. What did I do this morning?"

"You went down the Ramblas to the Cafè de l'Òpera and had a couple of coffees. Then you went through to the Plaça Reial and sat and talked to a sweet blonde from Denmark."

"You don't say. How did I do?"

Dris grins. "You didn't get a mobile number, but if you're down at the beach at the end of the Barceloneta tonight around midnight, she may be there with a couple of friends."

"Sounds promising. I may send you in my stead."

"I was going to suggest that. After that you went off into the Raval and looked at sunglasses in a Chinese shop. Then you came here and had lunch." Dris turns to set Pascual's phone on the bar. "In case anybody asks."

Pascual shoves it back toward him. "Keep the phone. Give it back to me tonight. Do something else I might do this afternoon."

Dris makes it disappear and looks gloomily out at the sunlit plaza. "When's the next trip out of the country? I could use a change of scene."

"Soon," says Pascual, scooping up the last of his *judías blancas*. "I think that's what the meeting today is about. I don't know if I'll need you to come along on this one. But sooner or later I will. I have a feeling things are about to get complicated."

"Actually, we're not especially concerned about the Russians," says Lina, smoothly brushing a blond forelock out of her eyes with long sharp-nailed fingers. "They're not a serious threat."

Pascual shoots her a startled look. "Not to you, maybe." He has only just settled onto his chair in this ground-floor meeting room at the airport hotel, having miscalculated the time required for a taxi to shove through afternoon traffic to El Prat de Llobregat. Lina and Felix are on a flying visit today, with a getaway flight to catch in two hours' time, and Pascual's tardiness has them in a peevish humor. "You're not the one they know how to find."

"That can be fixed. Everything can be fixed. What were the arrangements for communicating with your new friends?"

"There is a Japanese restaurant on the Diagonal, owned by a Russian, it turns out. I am to report there when I have something to hand over. I'm to make paper copies or put things on a flash drive. Account numbers, passwords, whatever. They want access to any accounts I set up."

"Yes, they want you to save them the work of cracking your passwords. They just see a chance for an easy score here. And we'll let them have one. We're willing to write off the initial deposit and maybe a paltry million or two as a decoy. Then we'll raise the alarm, chastise the bank for its weak security, change the account numbers and make sure the new passwords are unbreakable. Once we're satisfied the accounts are secured, we'll be ready to move to the next phase."

"Which is?"

"What do you think? Actually filling the accounts."

Pascual frowns. "But what happens when the Russians see that nothing significant is going into those accounts? I have a feeling they'll demand explanations. And they'll come straight to Pascual March for those."

"Unless you take defensive measures, yes. We can help you disappear if you like. We can even change the beneficiary of the Cayman Islands trust. To whomever you want to be next."

Pascual sits calmly returning Lina's impassive gaze, feeling his prospects contract. He has a feeling he knows what Lina means by "disappear." For the moment, however, he has no choice but to play the loyal employee. "That's very generous of you," he says. "So. Where am I going next?"

"I think Luxembourg next, for one-stop shopping. It's a good place to set up a company, and there are lots of banks. And then I think possibly one or two more trips after that. In addition to the accounts we're willing to let them know about, we're going to need one or two more they don't know about, just in case things don't go as planned. This is going to extend your period of employment a little."

Pascual quails at the thought. "Do I get overtime?"

"You're on salary. You're still getting a million euros for a few weeks' work. I should think that would be sufficient. We're talking about one or two more little jaunts, that's all."

"Someplace where there are no Russians," says Pascual. "If possible."

Lina smiles. "Difficult," she says. "These days, that's very difficult."

In Gràcia the tourists are beginning to look haggard, worn down by the heat and driven by hunger to peer uncertainly at the menus posted on restaurant walls. Pascual shoulders his way through the throng, deep in thought. He leans on the doorbell for Tic Sec and announces himself to the tinny voice that answers. Climbing the stairs, he flags for a moment, unbearably weary, before pressing on to the landing.

The corridor is empty but for the bric-a-brac, and Pascual hesitates, wondering if he should call out. Halfway down, Salera steps out of a doorway and says, "Ah. Just the man I want to talk to. Did you get my message?"

"No, I just happened to be passing and thought I'd see how things stand. What's the news?"

"Come back to my office." Salera leads him back to the terrace at the rear. "I left you a voice mail on the secure phone."

"I left it at home today. My employers were in town and summoned me to a meeting."

"Really? Were they here to discuss the terms of your will, by any chance?"

"My will?"

"Have a seat." Salera waves him to the wicker chair and sits on the sofa. "I'm assuming you were careful and made sure not to lead anyone to my door."

"As careful as I know how. I used the old wheeze of ducking down one Metro entrance and up the next at Plaça Espanya before grabbing a taxi."

"Let's hope it worked. Your employers are starting to worry me."

"They worried me from the start. What's this about my will?"

Salera jabs at the laptop on the table in front of him before answering. "We've been spending a good deal of time on your case, and finding some interesting things. Looking for traces of Pascual Rose in cyberspace, we turned up an interesting entry in a public registry maintained by the Maltese Ministry of Justice, which keeps a record of deeds, registered debts, things like that. And wills. And it turns out, you seem to have filed a sealed will with a Maltese civil court." Salera smiles at Pascual. "Do you recall doing that?"

For a long moment Pascual says nothing, feeling a chill seep through him. "No. Can't say I do. Interesting. Tell me, who did I make my beneficiary?"

"Ah. There you're asking too much. The registry doesn't contain the will itself, only the fact that it exists. The court will have a copy, and possibly the notary. But under Maltese law, the contents of a will cannot be disclosed, and a copy of the will cannot be obtained until the testator dies. If it was drafted on a computer in the notary's office and his security is lax, I might be able to break in and read it." Salera smiles again. "But that would be criminal. If you really want to know, I'd talk to the notary. I can give you his name and contact information."

Pascual nods. "It would be interesting to know who impersonated me. Presumably even in Malta you have to have a real person and a couple of witnesses to draw up a will."

"Unless they did it all by electronic sleight of hand, by hacking into the registry and the court archives. Not out of the realm of possibility."

"But it would be even more interesting to know who the beneficiary is."

Salera is frowning now, leaning forward, intense. "No doubt. But to me what jumps out is just the fact that they created a will for you. What does that say to you?"

Pascual begins to laugh, gently, shaking soundlessly in his chair. "Nothing I didn't know already. It means I'm disposable."

"I think it may be a little more urgent than that."

"Yes." Pascual nods. "It means they have plans for my disposal."

Salera nods. "I confess to you that I am out of my depth in this matter. Not technically, you understand. I am confident that in a matter of weeks, if not days, I will be able to identify the source of this intrusion. Names and locations. But normally at that point there is a nice reassuring policeman I can hand things over to. All I do is gather intelligence, and when I deliver it I am confident that it is going to a legitimate authority. In this case I have been hired by a man who admits he is involved in criminal activity. I took the case because you convinced me you were being coerced, and because I was curious. And because you could pay, of course. Now I find I'm reaching the limit of my comfort zone. When it comes to wills made out without the knowledge of the supposed testator, with Russian gangsters involved, it's time to call in the nice reassuring policemen."

Pascual has no argument to offer. He remembers Artemisa Pereda saying, "A police investigation is a leaky vessel," and he remembers Lina saying of his wife and son, "They're already in it." He decides a small fib is in order. "As it happens, I am already in touch with the authorities, via an intermediary. Elements of one of the Spanish security services are aware of my situation, and I have been advised to let them handle matters."

Salera gives him a long appraising look, and Pascual can see him trying to decide if he can believe this. The deciding factor becomes apparent when Salera says, "Very well. Then I'm afraid we need to discuss your account." He reaches for the laptop on the table in front of him and turns it toward Pascual. "Here is an itemized invoice of the hours we've devoted to your case. You've run through your retainer, and I'm afraid I'm going to have to ask you for another ten thousand euros."

"Luxembourg," says Pascual into his secure phone. "They are sending me to Luxembourg to set up another account. They're not going to try to fool the Russians. They plan to let them have a nibble, then cut them off."

"I wish them luck with that." Artemisa's voice is flat, conveying skepticism. "But then all they need is a smoke screen, to give them time to move the money around. Some of the accounts my father opened have already been emptied and closed. They are rubbing out their tracks as they go."

"And the money is to go into the accounts I'm opening. But where is it in the meantime?"

"That's an interesting question, isn't it? It's also interesting that they are willing to toss millions to the Russians just to throw them off the track. What does that say about the amount of money at stake?"

Pascual knows the question is rhetorical. He also knows that tracks are not the only things that are getting rubbed out in this process. "I spoke with my security guru. He tells me they filed a will for me, in Malta."

Seconds pass, and Pascual can read Artemisa's mind as it works. "Who is the beneficiary?" she says.

"I asked the same question. The will is sealed."

"Fascinating," she says after another pause. "Keep me informed."

"Soon," says Pascual. "It's not going to go on forever. As long as I'm useful to them, there's no danger. When they tell me, 'Thank you very much, you've done a fine job, here's your severance pay,' that's when things will get serious." Here on the riverside esplanade under the plane trees Pascual is just a man on a solitary walk with a phone to his ear. If anyone is watching him with particular interest, there is no way of telling which phone it may be.

"And what do we do then?" In Pascual's ear Sara's voice is subdued.

"What you and Rafa do is go to earth. Together or separately, but you have to disappear until I give the all clear. Have you made arrangements?"

"Yes. You remember Soledad? She's running an organic farm just south of Granada now. She said I can stay there, as long as I need to. I've talked with Rafa about it. If he can't make it down to Granada, he knows who to go to in the Camargue. Sometimes it's useful to be a Gypsy. And what about you, what will you do?"

"I'm still working that out. I've got people helping me. We're tracing the hackers, trying to identify the people who are running me."

"So you've alerted the authorities. You've got the law on your side."

Pascual ambles a few paces in silence, the breeze off the river stirring the leaves above him. "Not exactly. At one remove, maybe. It's delicate, Sara. My handlers are alert for any sign I'm trying to put one over on them. If they think I've blown the whistle, they won't be happy. But yes, that's the goal. Bring the law in at some point."

Sara goes silent long enough for Pascual to reach the bridge at the end of the esplanade. Ahead are the lights of the boulevard, the inviting sight of the terrace of the Bar Manel a couple of hundred meters down, the terrace crowded on a summer evening. Pascual's heart sinks as he contemplates another evening alone. "*Vida mía.* I miss you. I can't tell you how much."

"Come to me, then. Or let me come to you."

"Not now. But when this is over, I want to live with you again. Just for a time, as long as we can bear it."

Sara's laughter sounds in his ear, lightening his heart. "As long as we can bear it, *de acuerdo.*"

"Wherever you want. Granada, Seville. Madrid, even."

"Now I know you're serious. I won't make you live in Madrid, I promise."

"I would do it for you."

"All I want you to do for me is live. Wherever it may be. Just stay alive."

"That's the plan," says Pascual. "Believe me, that's plan A, B and C."

It is all beginning to blend together, as it did in the old days. When Pascual was crisscrossing Europe in the 1980s, running messages, cash, arms and killers from one squalid safe house to another, he would sometimes wake in the night and be unable for a moment to remember what city lay outside the shabby hotel room he found himself in.

The room in which he awakens from a brief and restless nap is anything but shabby, but it still takes Pascual a moment before he remembers that if he rises, goes to the window and parts the curtains, he will see the Place d'Armes in Luxembourg below. Very faintly through the thick double panes of glass he can hear the not unpleasant murmur of a public square becoming lively as the lights come on and evening cools the pavement.

He is sick of it all already, the endless parleying and paperwork, the glib lies and stock assurances, the jargon and the jovial insincere business bonhomie. Over the past three days he has succeeded in establishing a Luxembourg public limited company and opening an account for it at the Luxembourg branch of a highly respectable Dutch bank, pending approval of the KYC/AML compliance officer, which he has been assured will be a routine matter. He has an early morning flight to Barcelona via Zurich tomorrow and no idea how to kill another empty evening except to brood: to go through it all once more, the shapes and permutations of potential disaster and how to evade it. He has his secure phone with him, but his last conversation with Sara was constrained, with nothing much to say until they know if their family has a future. Pascual exerts himself and manages to stand up.

He treats himself to a shower and a change of clothes and then masochistically checks his bank balance on his phone. He is rapidly running down the hundred thousand euros he was staked to; between Salera's exorbitant invoices and Dris's walking-around money he is less than twenty thousand euros. He puts on a jacket and descends to the lobby.

It is a boutique hotel, and in the small lobby with three or four idlers in armchairs Pascual instantly feels conspicuous, a guilty reaction to the lie he has been living. He drifts toward the doorway to the quiet cocktail bar where he spent too much time and money the previous evening and is seized with a sudden need to be as far as possible from these prosperous complacent precincts. He wheels and makes for the exit to the square.

Pascual walks, hands jammed into his pockets, shouldering through crowds, scowling at the good people of Luxembourg as he goes. He finds a taxi stand behind the cathedral and tells the driver to take him to the main railway station. Decades ago, in the innocent years before he sold his soul to the devil, Pascual passed through Luxembourg on a holiday ramble. His recollection is of a sleepier place, with fewer office towers; the Grand Duchy seems to have done well out of finance. He recalls finding cheap food and amiable company in the streets near the station.

The taxi wheels onto a road skirting a deep gorge and then turns onto a bridge crossing it. Past the bridge is a long straight boulevard and at the end of it a broad forecourt beneath a clock tower and the grand facade of the main railway station. Pascual pays off the driver and ducks up a narrow street, looking for his youth.

He is certainly closer here to the lower socioeconomic status of his youth; there are restaurants with exotic names, hotels of the type that cluster a half dozen to the block, occupying the upper floors of bars, and the inevitable signs touting *NIGHT CLUB* and *STRIP TEASE*. Pascual turns up his nose at a *BRASSERIE DISCOTHEQUE* and laughs at an establishment that claims on its awning to be at the same time a *BRASSERIE, PIZZERIA, RESTAURANT* and, should dinner make one drowsy, *HOTEL*. He opts for a mere *RESTAURANT LOUNGE BAR* because it offers a large window with a view of the street. Inside, it is cheerful enough with an early evening crowd and sufficiently down at heel to suggest he will not pay too much for his beer.

The window allows him to spot his two pursuers as they confer briefly on the pavement. It takes him only a second to peg them as two of the idlers in the hotel lobby he left ten minutes ago and another two or three to work out that they must have grabbed the next taxi in the rank. The time they take to come through the door and make for his table is devoted to judging that they are probably not Russian gangsters and look much more like policemen.

One is tall and robust, young by Pascual's standards, with brown hair cut to military standards and a sport jacket over a T-shirt; the other is even older than Pascual and of unimpressive stature, hair gone gray where it is not gone altogether and a mustache signaling a stubborn adherence to the aesthetic of his youth. His suit could stand to be pressed.

"Pascual Rose," he says as they reach his table, putting an end to any hopes Pascual may have had of mistaken identity. He says it with certainty and a hint of a German accent. His hair may be gray, but his eyes are an ageless, icy Teutonic blue. He and his companion pull out chairs without being asked and sit, the old one across from Pascual and the young one to his left.

Pascual looks at them in turn, thinking fast and to no particular effect. Who is on to him now? He wonders how so many outsiders got invited to this party. "That's right," he says, knowing a bluff would be useless. "And you are?"

The old one nods at the younger. *"Das ist Ralf Weisen. Ich bin Joachim Wirth."*

Pascual's German is a little rusty, but he welcomes the chance to exercise it. The names mean nothing to him. Slipping easily into their language he says, "And what agency might you be with?"

Wirth smiles. "What makes you think we are with an agency? Maybe we just want to make you a business proposition."

"Then you would have approached me at the hotel. You wouldn't have bothered to play 'follow that taxi.' But then maybe you just did that for fun."

"Not that much fun when you make it so easy. But we're a lot less likely to be overheard in this din than at the hotel."

Pascual glances over his shoulder. The din seems to have abated just a touch since the Germans walked in, with a few looks coming their way. "You're making some of these people nervous. You're going to make them even more nervous when you show me your credentials."

Wirth laughs. "You want a little card that says 'Counter-Terrorist Squad'? Our credentials are what we know. And we know quite a bit about you, Herr Rose."

Pascual nods. In truth he is suddenly feeling the chill in the entrails, the mouth gone dry, the uptick in the heartbeat, thinking about an open murder case in the Federal Republic. The arrival of the waiter to take the Germans' order grants him precious time to think. "Let me ask you this," he says. "Which Pascual Rose do you think you know about? The one who lives in Dubai and works in finance, or the one who disappeared in 1992?"

This time it is Weisen, the young one, who answers. "Both of them. We're quite up to date on you." He has honed the copper's flat stare to a razor edge.

Still looking almost genial, Wirth says, "'Finance' sounds nice and respectable. I congratulate you. So, two Pascual Roses. I suppose you're going to tell me they're two different people."

Pascual makes a show of contending with inner conflict, grimacing, giving a slow shake of the head, finally sighing. "I am. You may be surprised to know that the current Pascual Rose is an assumed identity. It was created to enable me to carry out certain operations. I am told the original Pascual Rose is dead." Pascual is flying by the seat of his pants, having judged that charges for false documents and whatever else he may be guilty of will be both easier to evade and less onerous than that thirty-five-year-old rap for accessory to murder.

Weisen and Wirth exchange a look, and now Weisen is amused as well. "We are quite anxious to discuss those certain operations with you, actually. But first, please do tell us who you really are." He can hardly contain his mirth.

Pascual draws out the sullen look, the cornered man forced to come clean. "My name is Bassam Youssef. I am Syrian."

That freezes them for a moment and gets rid of the smiles, at least; they trade another look and Wirth says, "How interesting. I suppose you would be willing to have your biometric data taken, for comparison with Pascual Rose's?"

"On what grounds?" says Pascual, knowing as he says it that the game is up. "Am I charged with a crime?"

"Traveling on a false passport is a crime. If you are, as you say, a Syrian national traveling on a Maltese passport in another man's name, then we can certainly arrange to charge you with a crime."

Pascual drums his fingers on the table, holding Wirth's gaze, trying desperately to look unconcerned. "And if I am Pascual Rose, traveling on my own legally obtained Maltese passport, what concern is that of yours?"

Wirth leans a little closer, eyes narrowing. "In that case, there is a thirty-five-year-old murder case I would like very much to discuss with you."

The beer arrives for the German cops and Pascual thinks briefly about knocking their glasses into their laps and sprinting for the door. He toys with his own glass, running through less desperate options. "My name is Pascual March," he says finally. "It was legally changed under an agreement concluded among Mossad, the CIA and the Spanish Ministry of the Interior in 1992."

"Ah, we know all about Pascual March," says Wirth. "My agency was a reluctant party to that agreement. We were persuaded, against the better judgment of some of us, that the value of the intelligence gained by your defection justified it."

Pascual remembers weeks spent in an Israeli cell, aware that the outcome of protracted disputes among hard-faced professionals would determine his fate. "Your agency being what, the BND?"

"You remember how we protested, do you? I took it quite personally. I was adamant that you should not be excused from the consequences of your participation in the murder of Yossi Peled and his wife."

Here it is, the gravest legal threat and the heaviest weight on Pascual's conscience. He has lived for years with the fear that these embers would flare up. Pascual runs through the things he might say: All I did was deliver the weapon and rent the car, I did not know who the target was, I was told they would be military personnel, I considered myself to be at war. He was forced to admit to himself long ago that he had known all along that it would be a murder in cold blood, whoever the target was. He says quietly, "I am not in a position to question your judgment."

Wirth stiffens, just perceptibly. Whatever he was expecting to hear, apparently this was not it. His expression hardens again and he says, "I knew Yossi Peled, and I wanted you very badly. They had two young daughters, did you know?"

Pascual shakes his head, in silence. Around them the din has resumed. Pascual has hit a wall; he has no way to calculate what this rabbit out of a hat is going to mean to his prospects, in any dimension. He is already thinking that in a German prison he might at least be out of the reach of Russian gangsters and vengeful cybercriminals. He reaches inside his jacket and pulls out his phone. He knows that the odds are that no one is currently listening to this conversation; he knows that even if someone is, it is unlikely that they can make out much of the conversation with the ambient noise. Nonetheless he leans to set the phone on the floor under his table. He says, "What do you propose to do?"

Wirth trades a look with Weisen, easing back in his chair. "That depends entirely on you," he says.

Pascual has heard this line before. Impatient, he says, "Make your pitch."

The look that passes between the two Germans this time tells Pascual they were not expecting things to go quite so well. Wirth looks at him and says, "Those operations you mentioned. We want to know who you're working for now."

The flood of relief nearly knocks Pascual off his chair. Is that all, he wants to say. He sees that this is not nemesis come knocking, but merely something he is very familiar with: another intelligence operation. He takes a deep drink of beer and heaves a great sigh. "That makes two of us," he says.

Wirth does not take this well. "You're not in a position to make jokes."

"It's not a joke. I was conscripted into this by the classic carrot-and-stick method. You will appreciate the irony that part of the stick was the threat of criminal prosecution in Germany."

Wirth shows his appreciation by the barest hint of a smile. "And who was in a position to threaten this?"

"I don't know who they are. All I could give you at this point would be a physical description of a man and a woman. The carrot was one million euros in a Cayman Islands trust. The names they gave me are of course false. They began with a total electronic blitzkrieg, taking control of my digital existence. They can monitor my movements and possibly my conversations at all times. They were the ones who revived Pascual Rose and gave him a history for the last twenty-odd years. I have reason to believe they intend him to be entirely disposable. So my loyalty to this operation is exactly zero. But their hold on me is, until further notice, quite firm."

Wirth gives this a long thoughtful frown. "So. They threatened you with me, in essence. You know what that means? That means they're not the ones who own you. That means I am the one who owns you. As of now, you belong to me." He sits back and looks at Weisen. "Ralf, I believe we've acquired an informant."

Two hours later Pascual has had all the beer and conversation he can stand, most of it here in Wirth and Weisen's hotel room, getting outside a room-service dinner and trying to organize his thoughts under the withering stares and belligerent questions of two professional skeptics. "Of course it's all about terrorism," says Wirth. He looks a little the worse for wear, his tie loosened and the hair at his temples askew. "Why else would they come to you? That's your area of expertise."

Pascual sighs. "I explained that. Because of the dual identity. The question is how they knew about that. It's not exactly a secret, but you would have to move in the right circles. That's why I think they have intelligence contacts, at some level, several removes maybe. And I don't think it's about terrorism. I think it's all about the money. I think that much is true. It's a heist, nothing more."

Wirth and Weisen trade another of their looks. Weisen says, "And you've never met any other operatives, besides this Lina and Felix. What about in Malta? They told you they had assets there. You didn't see any of them?"

Pascual shakes his head. "They told me I was followed all day.

I didn't spot anybody. Maybe they were lying, I don't know. That's what they told me." He shrugs, remembering a woman in a white skirt going through a doorway. Pascual has realized two things during this interview: one, that resistance is useless, and two, that information is a priceless commodity, to be surrendered when necessary but never to be volunteered.

"And in Cyprus," says Wirth. "The Russians. Could you identify photographs?"

"Probably. The names I was given mean nothing to you?"

"It's not my area of expertise." Wirth stands and goes to the window. He moves the curtain aside and looks out for a few seconds, then turns. "I do terrorism. I've been doing it for forty years. When Pascual Rose cropped up again, triggering alarms, they came to me. I thought, 'Ah, it's finally happened. He's reverted to form. He's back in the game, he couldn't stay out of it.' And here we are. I thought you were probably working for the Iranians now, via your Syrian connections. Now you tell me it's all about Russian gangsters."

"There is a nexus there," says Weisen. "Russian gangsters and terror. Certainly Russians and Syrians."

Wirth nods. "No doubt." He sighs, coming away from the window. "We're going to have to consult with some people back in Berlin. I would love to haul you back there with us, but that would probably put an end to the whole thing, and I want the people farther up the tree." He comes to rest in front of Pascual's chair and frowns down at him. "You return home tomorrow? We will give you a number in Madrid to contact. When you do so we will give you further instructions for communicating with us, meeting if necessary. If you fail to contact the number in Madrid you will instantly be considered a fugitive and extradition proceedings will begin for the murder of Yossi Peled. Never forget. You belong to me now. You are my informant, and you will faithfully inform me of anything I wish to know, or you will find yourself standing before a judge in the Federal Republic of Germany. Have I made myself clear?"

Pascual has never reacted well to authority asserting itself; it is one of his weaknesses. In the present circumstances he manages to nod. "Very clear, yes, thank you."

Pascual has checked in for his Swiss Airlines flight to Zurich and is slumped on a seat in the waiting area, gazing unfocused at the scuffed toes of his shoes and contemplating the minefield his life has become when Lina plops down beside him and says, "You look like you could use a cup of coffee."

Pascual leaps out of his skin but has sufficient discipline not to cry out. After the first shock he manages to produce a smile. "I didn't expect to see you here," he says, pleased to find he can speak.

Lina is sleek and groomed, as cool and superior as always, her fade freshly barbered, dressed in black from head to the toes of her spike heels. From the height of her superior self-possession she looks down her nose and says, "I told you I'd meet you at the airport as usual. I just didn't say which one."

Pascual is thinking fast. What are the odds she was listening in on his fatally compromised phone just at the moment when Wirth approached him last night? Slim, he has already judged, but the possibility that that is what explains her presence this morning is supremely alarming. The Germans took the idea that the phone was bugged seriously enough to make sure it was in another room when they conducted their discussions. "I suppose you want the paperwork," Pascual says, reaching for the portfolio at his feet.

"As usual. Anything to report? No unusual activity in the vicinity? No rustling in the bushes, no approaches by sinister females?"

"You're the only sinister female I've seen this week." Pascual is rooting in the portfolio, frantically wondering if this is a test. He decides that if she does know about the Germans, there is nothing useful he can do and he will find out soon enough. He extracts the bundle of documents related to his new Luxembourg business empire and hands it to Lina. "There you go. The bank cards will be sent to the post office box in Malta."

"Very good." Lina slips the folder into her bag. "You will need to report to the Russians now, won't you?"

"I suppose so."

"Give them everything. Everything from the accounts you've set up so far. Passwords, everything. We'll let them get a million or two and then we'll discover it. We'll be very indignant with the banks about their security and threaten to move the accounts, and they'll be very apologetic and give us new numbers and make everything secure again. The Russians will have had their fun and we won't be out very much money, and the accounts will still be there. Don't worry, we'll take care of it. You've done your part."

"It must be nice to be able to write off a million or two like that."

"Cost of doing business. Who was that you spent the evening with at the Sofitel last night?"

Pascual takes his time zipping up the portfolio and placing it on the floor by his feet. He rapidly judges that she is going on the location data alone. He suspects that if Lina knew about the Germans he would be dead already. With great dignity he crosses his legs and smoothes a trouser leg. He turns to Lina and says as casually as he can, "She told me her name was Sylvie. I didn't ask for identification."

Lina raises an eyebrow. "You are incorrigible, aren't you? Did this one go through your things as well?"

Pascual shakes his head. "They were safe in my room, back at my hotel. I do learn from experience."

"Shame on you. What would your son think?" Lina holds out her hand. "I'll take the phone. Your regular one is in your mailbox at your flat. You didn't budge from home this time. You put a nice dinner at that new bistro in the Rambla de l'Hospital on your credit card last night, if anybody asks. Oh, and check your e-mail. The agency wants to know if you're accepting work again. You might as well, you know. There's going to be some downtime and it will give you something to do, as well as establishing that you were at home and working as usual during this period, if it ever comes to an investigation." Pascual hands Lina the work phone and she stands. "We'll be in touch," she says. "I think we're close to wrapping this up."

"I am pleased to hear it," Pascual says, though the words fill him with dread.

The Diagonal slashes across Barcelona straight as a laser beam, separating the hoity-toity neighborhoods in the Collserola foothills from the humbler quarters sprawling down toward the sea, eight lanes of traffic keeping the plebes at bay. To Pascual it has always represented the Barcelona that secretly wants to be Frankfurt, lined with office towers sporting corporate logos in neon. Tonight he is slouching along the pavement in search of a Japanese restaurant where the elite take their sushi and seaweed.

He finds it just shy of the Plaça Macià, where the traffic veers off to tear down Urgell. The entrance is discreet considering its reputed price level, an awning with a few golden kanji characters on it and the name of the joint in modest Roman characters below it. Pascual is hoping he will be admitted in his sport jacket and freshly shined shoes.

Inside he confers briefly with a hostess who is as Japanese as he is and who informs him with just the slightest touch of haughtiness that he may proceed directly to the bar. Here he perches on a stool and gawks at the extravagant interior decoration, the space lit an eerie blue by a video aquarium occupying an entire wall, cruising electronic fish distracting the diners from their fare. The barman looks Slavic, and Pascual judges he may be just the man he needs to talk to. He has no idea what kind of cocktail the initiated might order in a tarted-up clip joint in Japan and meekly requests a dose of the first whiskey his eye alights on behind the bar. When the barman delivers it, Pascual says in Castilian, "Is Vasily Andreyevich here tonight? I bring greetings from his cousin Yuri." This is the formula Pascual was rehearsed on in Cyprus, and he exerts himself not to look too self-conscious as he mouths it.

The barman replies without hesitation in flawless Catalan. "At the table in the back. But you have to clear it with the head waiter first." He juts his chin in the direction of a distinctly Japanese-looking man in a dark suit who is casting a critical eye on the work of the chefs at the sushi bar, feverishly chopping hunks of fish.

Sheepishly, Pascual thanks the barman and pays for the drink, tipping generously. He grabs his glass and approaches the head waiter, who looks like Toshiro Mifune with a stomachache. He repeats the nonsense about cousin Yuri, managing only to deepen the man's scowl. "What is your name?" the samurai growls in Castilian. Pascual gives his first name, and after looking him up and down, the man saunters off toward the rear of the place, hands clasped behind his back.

Pascual makes out a semicircular booth with two men and two women in it. The men are middle-aged, the women considerably younger. The head waiter leans over to speak to the heavier of the two men and everyone in the booth looks at Pascual. He resists the urge to give them a cheery wave. The fat man says something and the waiter beckons to Pascual.

Walking down the room in the submarine ambience, Pascual feels like a diver in an old-fashioned weighted suit, cautiously approaching a submerged wreck. He reaches the booth and addresses the fat man, who has thick jowls, thicker eyebrows, and a single tuft of hair on the top of his head. "Vasily Andreyevich?"

"Call me Sancho," the man replies in Castilian. "Here everybody calls me that." He slaps his ample belly. "Because of the *panza.*" He looses a peal of ragged laughter and looks at his companions, who duly feign amusement, the women with more enthusiasm than the man. One is a blonde, past her prime but nicely turned out in a low-cut yellow dress, and the other is pale and raven-haired, a serious looker with a sultry smoldering gaze. "And you are Pascual," Sancho says. "Sit." He flaps a hand at the seat opposite him. The men are at the ends of the semicircle, hemming the women in, and the second man has to scoot a little to make room for Pascual. This one has a fine head of white hair, an impeccable gray suit, and the seamed face of a prison-camp trusty. Pascual thanks him and in return gets a look that says, Don't get too comfortable, mate.

"I present to you my friends. This is Elena, that is Mia," says Sancho, waving at the blonde and the dark one in turn. "Elena was beautiful once, can you believe that?" He reaches out to pinch her cheek, which she endures without flinching. Sancho says, "And Mia, she is just beginning to be beautiful, don't you think?"

Pascual meets Mia's sullen stare and says, "She doesn't need me to tell her that."

Sancho barks out a laugh. "No, that's true. She belongs to that one next to you, but she is too young for him. He is Grigory, who everyone calls The Viper, I don't know why." He laughs again, but nobody joins him. Elena shoots a nervous look at Grigory, and Mia merely smolders further, looking at the video wall, where a shark is currently sweeping in an arc toward the camera.

Sancho says, "I have been waiting for you, Pascual. My friend in Cyprus told me you have something to deliver."

Pascual nods and pulls an envelope from inside his jacket. "I have something that will interest him." He hands it across the table. "I think he will find here everything he needs in order to proceed."

Sancho opens the envelope and pulls out the single sheet of paper it contains. He unfolds it, runs an eye over it and then replaces it and stuffs the envelope inside his jacket. He grins. "Luxembourg, eh? I had to leave Luxembourg in a hurry once. I wonder if they are still looking for me."

"I don't know about that," says Pascual. "But they still frighten wayward children with tales of your exploits."

Sancho cackles with laughter again and Pascual is ashamed of his sycophancy. He has no desire to spend the evening in this company and hopes to be dismissed shortly. He takes a pull on his Scotch. "And how is your wife?" says Sancho. "The beautiful Sara Muñoz."

Pascual freezes with the glass in his hand. He blinks a few times and says, "You know my wife?"

"Not personally, I regret to say. But I certainly know of her. The great Sara Muñoz, the *cantaora*. Eh, Elena? One of your favorites, no?"

Elena's face lights up. "I adore her. Sara Muñoz is your wife?"

Pascual sets his glass down gently. His heart is suddenly pounding. "She is indeed. I am surprised that you have heard of her."

Sancho claps a heavy hand on Elena's arm. "Since we came here Elena has become quite interested in flamenco."

"Such a wonderful music," says Elena. "I fell in love with it immediately. I have even taken lessons in the dance."

"You should see her," says Sancho. "Stamping around on those heels, clicking those castanets. Not very convincing as a Gypsy, but it keeps her happy."

Elena rolls her eyes and says, "Is your wife here in Barcelona?"

Pascual manages a weak smile. "Not at the moment. She spends a great deal of time in Madrid and in Andalucía. She has just finished making a recording, in fact, in Granada. I am lucky if I get to spend three months a year with my wife."

Sancho laughs and says, "Some men would consider it lucky only to have to spend three months with their wife."

A distasteful rasping sound to Pascual's left proves to be Grigory, joining in the laughter for the first time. Mia is looking at him with contempt. Sancho says, "Your wife is appearing at the festival in Jerez this winter, is she not? We will have to go and see her. Perhaps you can introduce us."

"Oh yes, that would be wonderful." Elena's enthusiasm appears genuine, but when Pascual's eyes find Sancho's again, all he sees there is the unwavering stare of a man who knows he has just successfully delivered a message.

Then abruptly the look softens and Sancho smiles and raises his glass. "My cousin Yuri will be very grateful for this information. We are in your debt. The next time you go to Andalucía you must call on us. I have a restaurant in Marbella. El Pirata it's called." His belly shakes as he laughs. "But they didn't put my picture on the sign. They said that would frighten people away. So instead there's a fellow with a big black beard and a patch over one eye. The fellow who runs the place is called Leonid. Tell him Sancho sent you and he'll take care of you."

Pascual dips his head in gratitude. "I look forward to it," he says, stifling his self-loathing.

Joachim Wirth's injunction to report to a German spy nest in Madrid is unequivocal, but the mechanics of obeying it are problematic. Pascual's own phone will certainly betray him; if Lina and Felix do not actually listen in on the call they will certainly be able to look at the call log and wonder. There is the secure phone issued him by Salera, but Pascual's instinct is to restrict that to the narrowest circle possible. He has no idea what Pandora's box he might be opening by using it to call a front number for the Bundesnachrichtendienst. He knows of a nice safe landline up Villarroel in Barcelona, but the thought of contending once again with Pere's wariness and Sofia's open contempt depresses him. He opts in the end for the Bar Manel, leaving his phone at home. "I have a favor to ask you," he says to Yu Yan, raising his voice to be heard above the pleasant tumult of an early evening crowd.

"Everyone asks me favors," she says, giving him a rueful look. "Who does favors for me?"

"Do this one for me and I am your servant forever."

This makes her giggle at least, but customers are shouting orders at her and it is several minutes before she has the leisure to drift back and lean on the bar in front of him, giving him a skeptical look. "No credit," she says. "You drink, you pay."

"Not that kind of favor. I've lost my phone and I need to make a call to Madrid. Let me use the bar phone and I'll pay you for the call."

She frowns at him for a while, but in the end she beckons, and Pascual follows her to the cash register, where she reaches under the bar and comes up with the phone. She sets it down and says, "You pay me two euros."

Pascual coughs up the coins and pulls the phone toward him. Wirth insisted he memorize the number before leaving the hotel room, sound tradecraft no doubt, and Pascual mutters the numbers in German as he dials. The phone rings three times at the other end and a man's voice says, *"Dígame"* in impeccable Spanish.

Hoping he has not misdialed or misremembered, Pascual repeats the formula Wirth rehearsed him in, in German. "I'm calling with regard to the Carabanchel property."

There is a short silence, and Pascual wonders what he is going to do if he has botched the call. *"Einen Moment,"* says the voice at the other end, to Pascual's relief. He waits for perhaps thirty seconds, and the voice resumes in German.

"Is this your personal number?"

"No. They will take messages for me here."

"Very good. You are in Barcelona?"

"Not too far from it. A small town in Catalonia."

"Good. You are to go to Barcelona next Tuesday. You will go to the offices of Inmobiliaria Bosch at 189 Muntaner. You have an appointment with Herr Becker at twelve noon."

"Hang on, can you repeat that, please?" Pascual nips a pen from a can by the register and scrabbles for a beer mat. The voice patiently repeats the instructions, adding, "If you do not appear at this appointment, we will be forced to begin proceedings."

"I'll be there." A click sounds in his ear.

Pascual hangs up, finishes jotting and replaces the pen. Yu Yan is peering at him. "You said Madrid. You call Germany? Now you have to pay me two more euro."

"No, no, that was Madrid. They have Germans there, too."

Looking distinctly unconvinced, Yu Yan puts the phone back beneath the bar. She freezes for a moment as her eye falls on something and she says, "Ah, I forget." She brings up a piece of paper with a note scrawled on it and hands it across the bar. "A man called for you yesterday. He left this message."

Pascual takes the note and reads in Yu Yan's somewhat clumsy hand: *FOR PASCUAL – CAMPOS MUST TALK TO YOU – CAFÉ 11:00 ANY MORNING.*

"You've been keeping very interesting company," says Campos. Behind the lenses of his spectacles his eyes are wide. "I am becoming more and more interested in Artemisa Pereda."

Pascual has found that his interest in the subject has been somewhat eclipsed by other developments in recent days, but Campos's message was enough to draw him back to Barcelona on the early train. "Tell me."

"In the first place, she's not only a lawyer, but quite a well-connected one, it seems. She's with López Olmos, which you may have heard of."

"Sorry, who is López Olmos?"

"Not who, what. It's a very well-connected law firm in Madrid."

"I've never had enough money to be well-informed about law firms."

"Well, this one's been in the news quite a bit. You surely must have followed our absorbing royal scandals these past few years."

"If being vaguely aware of them qualifies as following, yes."

Campos shakes his head in wonder. "You truly are a hermit, aren't you?"

"Not especially saintly, I'm afraid."

"Well, the various royal layabouts and delinquents who have been caught stuffing money into their royal pockets have all been advised by López Olmos. That's about as prestigious as it gets for a law firm, and I imagine it's also fairly lucrative. So you seem to be moving in exalted circles all of a sudden."

"The royal family hasn't come up in our discussions. At the moment she seems to be concerned chiefly with what happened to her father."

"Yes. It turns out she has requested an indefinite leave of absence from the firm, according to my well-placed source. It is assumed she is distraught over her father's death."

"She doesn't seem distraught to me. She seems . . . formidable."

"I'm sure she is. Her ex-husband no doubt regrets provoking her."

"Ah. I wondered if there were any men in her life besides her father. She doesn't exactly repel the eye."

"Well, she managed to snare a high-flying executive at BBVA. She turfed him out a couple of years ago and got a very nice settlement. It seems he got caught dallying with some stray blonde he picked up in Ibiza."

"I did not get the impression she is of a forgiving nature."

"No. I learned a few other interesting things about her as well."

Campos turns a sip of coffee into a dramatic pause and Pascual grows impatient. "Go on."

"She has been linked with certain figures who are most politely described as being associated with the extreme right."

"You don't say. That does surprise me, though I'm not sure why it should. I suppose because she is fairly presentable, and I tend to expect people on the right to slaver and screech."

Campos gives him a wry look. "Where have you been? Some of our most beautiful people are out there, *de derechas*. In any event, our Artemisa has been associated with some prominent figures at the right end of the spectrum."

"Associated how? I've been associated with some truly ghastly people in my life, so I try not to hold associations against people until I know more."

"Associated as in, one of her clients is Juan Pablo Villafranca, the man behind the Covadonga League."

"Don't know it, I'm afraid."

"You really should be better informed. The Covadonga League is an anti-Muslim organization, formed a few years ago to turn back the Muslim tide, as they see it. We haven't had a lot of that sort of thing in Spain, not compared to other countries, but now we're catching up fast. Villafranca's an old-fashioned *latifundista,* or the closest thing left to one. He owns a lot of olive trees down in Andalucía, and besides running the Covadonga League, he's a big bankroller of Vox, our up-and-coming populist party. And your Artemisa's his lawyer."

Pascual shrugs. "Lawyers often have shady clients."

"Indeed. They don't always attend meetings convened by their clients with extremist political figures, though. Artemisa was spotted at a little conclave Villafranca held in Madrid a few months ago with some of the more rabid Islamophobes on the political scene, including Menéndez Ortega, that Guardia Civil colonel who was cashiered for compiling illegal dossiers on left-wing politicians. Not a very savory crowd."

"No. Interesting, but I'm not sure it has anything to do with her father's death."

"Perhaps not. But Menéndez Ortega was reputed to be involved in some of Benedicto Pereda's intrigues."

"Is that so?" Pascual considers. "Well, I will have to ask her about that when I see her next."

Campos leans closer to Pascual. "And when do I get the story?"

"When it's over." Pascual drains his coffee and shoves the cup away. "If I'm still alive."

Muntaner is a street Pascual knows well. As a footloose boy just starting to push the boundaries of his world, he once started walking uphill on Muntaner to see where it went, like Burton and Speke in search of the source of the Nile. Hours later, exhausted, he came stumbling home having discovered nothing more exotic than Sant Gervasi.

Nearly fifty years on, he finds Inmobiliaria Bosch not far from his boyhood home, in a modern building with lots of glass squeezed between two dignified old stone facades. The agency has a street-level storefront, displaying photos of available flats and houses in its window. Inside, there is a pretty receptionist examining her nails. When he asks for Mr. Becker she snaps to attention and punches a number into the phone on her desk. After a brief consultation she leads him past a couple of desks where people with phones to their ears appear to be doing real work and into a rear office where he finds himself face to face with a thin man he has never seen before and Joachim Wirth.

"Very punctual," says Wirth. "I commend you. Sit down. This is Herr Becker."

Pascual shakes hands with the thin man, who has a shaved skull above angular features, partly masked by a goatee and mustache. "At your service," says Becker. "We are grateful for your cooperation."

"The pleasure is all mine," says Pascual with a straight face. He turns to Wirth. "So, they decided to let you keep me?"

"Before we begin," says Wirth, holding up a hand. "Please take a look at this." He hands Pascual a sheet of paper. On it is written, *Give me your mobile phone*. Pascual hands the paper back. "Good thinking. Can't be too careful. Fortunately, I have already given the matter some thought. The phone is currently sitting on the bar in a restaurant two streets away. That is, if nobody has turned it in to the barman or walked off with it. I will go and inquire when we have finished here."

Wirth is irked, Pascual can see. "We need to examine that phone. If they installed spyware on it, as you claim, we can track it back and begin to investigate who they are."

"Thereby alerting them to the fact that you are on to them."

"Thereby making use of the only concrete evidence we have."

Pascual shakes his head. "I'm not going to risk being exposed that way. They have demonstrated to my satisfaction that they control the airwaves as long as I'm using my own personal phone or the one they give me when I travel. Even taking out the battery will make them suspicious. They have explicitly said so. My recommendation would be that you set up some secure way for me to communicate with you and wait until I have some concrete evidence to give you."

Wirth's look hardens. "Your recommendations will be taken into account, certainly. But remember that you are my informant, and not the reverse."

"I am quite aware of that. I'm also aware that I am under virtually constant observation, at least potentially. So I am determined to proceed with care."

Wirth glowers; Becker clears his throat and says to Wirth, "I can understand our friend's concern. It would be good to have the phone at some point, and perhaps your technical people can arrange a way to mask any examinations they might make. But for the moment, let's discuss what other measures we might take." To Pascual he says, "As you note, my colleague Wirth remains on this case because of his familiarity with your background. But it appears this is less a matter for the BND than for the agency I represent, the BKA."

Pascual takes a second to sort out the letters. "The Bundeskriminalamt."

Becker nods. "The Federal Office of Criminal Investigation. My area of expertise is money laundering. And it seems that is what we are dealing with here."

"So I have been led to believe."

"We are wondering in fact if this is not another tentacle of the so-called Global Laundromat, the main conduit for dirty money coming out of Russia. You are no doubt familiar with the scandals involving banks in the Baltic area, Moldova, Cyprus, even our own Deutsche Bank."

"Superficially."

Wirth leans in. "We've been able to identify the Russians you met in Nicosia. From the description you gave us of the people and their location. This Konstantin Popov appears to be a rising star. He won some nasty fights in Yekaterinburg and elsewhere, culminating in a couple of murders in Cyprus that saw off a Georgian gang that has aspirations there. He is reputedly quite smart and quite ruthless."

"I did find him persuasive, yes."

Becker says, "So in the first instance, what we need from you is the data on all the companies and accounts you have set up."

Pascual says, "I'll give you what I'm giving the Russians, which is what my employers are willing to let the Russians have."

Wirth frowns. "If they're letting the Russians have it, it means it's not going to help us that much."

"You'll have the account numbers and the beneficial owner, which is me to begin with. The plan is to dispose of me and have ownership pass to them by way of a will they've filed for me in Malta. If that's not enough for you to start with, I don't know what would be."

Wirth and Becker stare at him for a moment. "How do you know about the will?" says Wirth.

Upon consideration Pascual has decided it is best to be discreet about Fernando Salera. "I found it recorded in a Maltese government database. I suspected something along those lines and went looking for it. Do you see the position I'm in?"

Becker frowns and says, "Delicate, to be sure. When are you supposed to meet with your employers next?"

"Undetermined. They generally summon me by text message and give me instructions orally. They have kept me fairly busy for a month now. I would not be surprised if they sent me on another mission next week."

Becker and Wirth trade a look. Becker says, "The timing is tight. We'll have to assemble a team, talk to the prosecutors, talk to the Spanish."

"I can have people here tomorrow," growls Wirth.

"There's no point in bringing people in until we've laid the legal groundwork." Becker turns to Pascual. "We'll need you to sign an agreement regarding the terms of your cooperation. You can of course consult a lawyer if you wish. A quick trip to Germany would be ideal, but if that's not feasible we can fly in someone from the Prosecutor General's office. At some point you are probably going to have to wear a wire. There are risks to you, of course, but in return we may be prepared to resolve your legal issues in the Federal Republic."

Pascual sits listening, astonished, the phrase "a leaky vessel" sounding distinctly in his inner ear. He looks at Wirth and sees that the old BND man is as dismayed as he is, though no doubt for different reasons. "Whatever you say," says Pascual blandly.

"What a relief," says Pascual, taking his phone as the barman hands it to him with a superior smile. "I'm an idiot. I can't believe I walked away and left it."

"Happens all the time," says the barman. "As expensive as these gadgets are, you think people would be more careful with them."

"I will be now, that's for sure. *Moltes gracies.*"

Trudging down Muntaner, exhausted from his session with the Germans, head spinning from a new raft of instructions to follow and another layer of deception to maintain, Pascual thinks to check for messages. A text from Lina is waiting for him. It reads, *Stand by for instructions, travel next week.*

Perhaps to ensure that Pascual shows up on time, Lina and Felix have scheduled today's meet at a mid-range business hotel just up the street from Sants station. A sunny terrace with table and chairs just outside the room keeps drawing Pascual's eye, but Lina and Felix have set up at the desk, where laptops can be plugged in and street noises kept out. "Morocco," says Lina. "Ever been there?"

Startled, Pascual jerks his gaze back to Lina's pale features. "No. But I understand that Pascual Rose has. The fake one, that is."

"Indeed. In 2004, I believe we said. He set up a trading company to export frozen seafood. Sadly it never did much business, but there it is in the company registry, where we inserted it."

"Let me guess. He's going to reactivate it and turn it into a holding company."

One finely microbladed eyebrow rises. "That's a very good guess. Actually you're going to acquire a shelf company, one with a track record and a bank account, and some convenient operating losses that will get turned into tax benefits for the seller. You'll remember we said this is a backup, an insurance policy. A cache the Russians won't find out about. So actually you'll merely be acting as an agent in this case, arranging the purchase of this company by a Swiss holding company. Your name will not appear in the registry at all. The Russians won't have any way of knowing you're involved in its purchase."

Pascual muses. "A Swiss company. The mysterious Passau Novara again?"

"Nothing mysterious about it. It's a perfectly legitimate holding company. And it's interested in exploring opportunities in Morocco. Hence this purchase. One reason you're going to Morocco is that things can happen fast there. The company's there for the taking and their standards of due diligence are still not quite what they would be in the Channel Islands or London. And palms can be greased if necessary to make things go smoothly. So we can get this taken care of in a few days and then move on to the final stage."

That phrase has a sinister ring to Pascual, but he merely nods. "Morocco. The Arabic is quite different from Levantine there. Never could make much of it. But in my experience most of them speak French."

"And these days, probably English," Lina says. "I'm sure you'll find a way to make yourself understood."

"No doubt. Where money is involved, people are inclined to make that extra effort."

Pascual has never been a workaholic or anything close to it, but he is finding that in his present circumstances there is nothing like a tedious job of work for taking his mind off darker matters.

Since his supposed recovery from his fictional illness, Traducciones Dragoman has obligingly sent him a raft of it. Today he is translating a set of Syrian civil status documents bearing numerous inscrutable handwritten entries, and he is fast developing a headache. When his phone buzzes, he picks it up and then realizes it is not this one that is producing the noise, but rather Salera's secure phone sitting on the corner of the desk. He grabs it and sees Artemisa's number above a text reading simply, *Waiting in the street*.

Pascual puts on shoes and descends. A silver Audi sits at the curb a few meters from his door, Artemisa behind the wheel. Pascual strolls casually to the passenger side and gets in. "Did I miss something? I wasn't expecting you."

She smiles as she puts the car in gear and pulls away from the curb. "If you're not expecting me, nobody else can be, either."

"That seems like a sound approach. I met with our friends again yesterday."

"So I surmised. I was alerted that Lina's phone had sprung back into action. What's the news?"

"They're sending me to Tangier on Monday. To buy a company."

"Interesting." Artemisa reaches the corner and points to the right. "This will take us out of town, won't it?"

"It will. Are we going anywhere in particular?"

"Just going for a drive. Touring your pleasant little corner of Catalonia. I must say, I'm seeing a lot of separatist flags hanging on balconies. Finished with the Spanish state, are you?"

"I think that's the general consensus around here. Are we going to argue politics?"

"Not if you don't want to." Artemisa steers down the old medieval road to Barcelona, now a placid two-lane blacktop lined by plane trees. "Why Morocco?"

"According to Lina, because they're not especially scrupulous about the paperwork, and they're bribable. She's going to try to keep this one off the Russians' radar."

"They know about the Russians?"

"Yes. But they say the Russians don't worry them. They'll let them have a few million and then shut the door. But they're making contingency plans anyway. They're arranging for me to buy a shelf company, acting for a Swiss company. My name won't go in the registry, so the Russians won't know about it. That's the theory, anyway."

"That might work. Is this the same Swiss company that's been writing the checks to seed the accounts you've opened? Passau Novara?"

"Yes."

"I thought so. We looked into the company. It's owned by a Russian holding company, curiously enough."

"More Russians?"

"Or the same ones. Was it really an accident the Russians in Cyprus got onto you?"

Pascual starts, then stares at her. "You're making my head spin."

"Don't worry, there are smarter people than you and I working on this. When do you leave for Tangier?"

"On Monday."

"Where are you staying?"

"They've booked me into one of the chain hotels, I believe. I was hoping for something with some local color, but I don't think that's high on their list of priorities."

"No, too bad. They should have booked you at El Minzah. You expect to see Sydney Greenstreet around every corner in that place. What's this company you're supposed to buy?"

"It's an import-export company that has apparently fallen on hard times since the death of its founder. The heirs are anxious to unload it, and my principals should be able to pick it up cheap. They've completed much of the process online, and all I have to do is show up and give the lawyers some documents. And then I will open a number of bank accounts for it, at both local and international banks. At some point I will be instructed how to fill these accounts with stolen money."

"Perhaps it's time to think about what happens when you bail out."

"Let me add a complication. I spent some time with a couple of German federal agents the other day."

"You don't say. How did they find you?"

"Somebody detected the resurrection of Pascual Rose in cyberspace. An old BND man who has wanted to see me behind bars since the mid-eighties tracked me down in Luxembourg. I told him about Lina and Felix. The next time I saw him, in Barcelona, he was with a BKA copper who wants me to put on a wire and build a criminal case against Lina and Felix for the federal prosecutors. They think it's all a sequel to the Russian Laundromat of a few years ago."

Artemisa drives for a while, frowning at the landscape as the road rises and dips. "That I doubt. The methodology is different. And whatever my father was up to, it didn't have anything to do with the

Moldovans or the Latvians. We still don't know who was behind it. We don't know who Lina and Felix are or who's behind them, and most importantly we don't know where the money is coming from. Somebody's pulling off an enormous heist, and we don't know who's getting robbed." She takes a bend smoothly, shifting and steering with skill. "Are you going to cooperate with the Germans?"

"Is there a reason why I shouldn't?"

"Not necessarily. If you want to wind up on the right side of the law, you have to bring the law in at some point. But you need to be very careful about how you do it, if you're right about your family being vulnerable. How sure are you that you can put them out of reach of Lina and Felix?"

"I'm not sure of anything. The Germans have me by the throat. They can nail me for a killing back in the eighties. They want to fly me to Germany to meet with prosecutors and formalize a collaboration agreement, all kinds of formalities. What they want is an airtight legal case. I have a feeling that throwing in with the Germans will start a lot of cumbersome machinery going, and I don't see how Lina and Felix can miss detecting that."

"I'd say your feelings are accurate. But you're the one at risk, so if you think the Germans are the best bet to protect you and your family, I'm not going to tell you not to do it. Your choice would seem to be, do you let the Germans wire you up and run you as an informant, or do you trust my fellows to figure this thing out while you play along with Lina?"

"That would seem to be the case."

"Can you put the Germans off for a while?"

Pascual watches the placid Osona pastures go by, green hills in the distance. He laughs gently. "They've waited thirty-five years. They can wait a few weeks longer."

"No more than that. This thing is not going to go on forever. In fact I think we're getting to the final reel." She vents what sounds a little like a sigh. "I've just been in Italy."

Pascual shoots a look at her profile. "Following leads?"

"Not really. Talking to the carabinieri, though, yes." She looks briefly at Pascual. "It seems my father's body has been found."

Pascual just sits with his mouth open for a moment. "Where?"

"Near Rome. Not too far from where his car was found."

Pascual looks for signs of distress and finds none. "I'm sorry."

"So am I. I would almost rather it had not been found."

"It must have been . . ." Pascual gropes for something not too explicit.

"Yes. It was badly decomposed, of course. But that's not the worst of it."

Pascual is not sure he wants to hear the worst. After a moment Artemisa says, "He was dismembered. His remains were stuffed into a trash bag and thrown in an illegal dump. He was, it appears, very expertly dissected shortly after being killed."

Pascual winces. At least it was after, he thinks, but manages not to say. "How was he killed?"

"He was shot at close range, in the head, three times. He was identified by his teeth, which were intact, unlike the skull. This was confirmed by DNA. One does not like to dwell on what the forensic procedures must have involved after all these months."

"No. I'm sorry, this must be very painful."

"It is, at least, final. I thought you should know."

"In case I need further convincing?"

"In case you are still tempted by that million euros they promised you."

"Not since I found out that Pascual Rose's last will and testament has been filed in Malta."

"Dios mío. How do you know that?"

"I hired my own cybersecurity expert. He's expensive, but he seems to be able to sniff things out. Here's a thought. Did your father leave a will?"

"Yes. He prepared it years ago, and it was perfectly legitimate. What little he had, he left to me. That's not how they did it with him. He was never the beneficial owner, only an agent. That made the process of setting them up a little more complicated, but there was no problem with succession. But if Pascual Rose had no will, that would be a convenient device for them. It would be interesting to know who the beneficiary is. In any event, you are getting close to the end."

"Apparently."

"Then it might be time to think about getting your family out of harm's way. Do you have a plan?"

Pascual quails at the thought. "I do. How good it is, I suppose we'll find out."

"Make it as good as you can. And move fast. My father disappeared five days after he returned from the last trip he made."

"Five days."

"Less than a week. That's what you'll have left when you complete the last task they give you."

▪ ▪ ▪ ▪

"Tuesday," says Joachim Wirth in Pascual's ear. "At the real estate office on Muntaner again."

Around Pascual the happy uproar of a bar full of topers getting outside their *aperitiu* swells, providing perfect cover for plotting with intelligence agents. Appeased by the ten-euro note Pascual slid across the bar, Yu Yan has stopped shooting him dirty looks as she pours drinks. Pascual plugs his free ear with a finger. "Just what's going to happen?"

"You're going to be briefed, that's what. We thought about flying you to Berlin for a lightning visit, just an overnighter, but given the extent to which they seem to be able to track you, it was decided it was more secure to bring everyone here. They're flying in the whole team. The lawyer from the prosecutor's office, a couple of investigators from Becker's squad, the technical wizards. You'll be interrogated, detailed statements taken. You'll sign an agreement and you'll be issued a secure phone and instructed in communication protocols. They'll train you about wearing the wire when it comes to that. Be prompt and be prepared for a long day."

Pascual has a vision of half a dozen crack agents of the Bundesrepublik in a cramped office, trading uneasy glances and checking their watches as it becomes apparent they have been stood up. "I'll be there," he says, "Unless they're sitting on top of me. In that case I won't." He hangs up smartly and pushes the phone across the bar to Yu Yan.

"No more," she says, putting it back under the bar. "They see you use the phone, now everybody wants to use it."

"I think that's the last time," Pascual says. "I'm getting a new phone tomorrow. Pour me another *caña,* would you please?" Pascual turns to look for Dris and finds the youth has read his mind, drifting to the bar to join him. "What's the news? The phones have gone silent."

"It's happening. On Monday I fly out to Tangier."

"Tangier? My Tangier?"

"The one in your ancestral homeland. Ever been there?"

"Once. I have a couple of uncles there. And a sweet girl cousin." Dris's look goes far away for a moment, then he shakes his head. "But she's married now, sad to say."

"Well, then you won't have any distractions. You're coming with me, and you'll need your wits about you."

Dris nods, focused now. "And what am I going to have to do?"

"Maybe shadow me, make sure I'm not stabbed in the back or shot in the face. Or I might send you back to Spain to watch over Sara and Rafa, make sure they're out of the way and safe. At some point I'm going to have to give them the signal to go underground. I don't know when. I don't know how I'll know when it's time. I think I'll have a few days' warning. I hope so, anyway. I think we're getting close to the end. Actually, I don't have any idea how things are going to go, and I'm scared out of my wits."

Dris gives him a long look and then reaches out to slap him on the shoulder. "Don't worry, *jefe*. I'm with you."

"Book your flight tonight. I'm going on the morning flight with Iberia. If you get there Monday night, that will do. Get yourself a hotel room and wait to hear from me. Did you ever get hold of that thing we mentioned? For protection?"

Dris shakes his head. "It's tough here. I used to have a contact, but he's back in Castellón."

"No matter. We're more likely to need it in Tangier. Do you think you could get hold of one there?"

Dris gives a little whiff of laughter. "In Tangier? Easy. With enough money."

"A car would be a good idea as well, if you can rent one. I can let you have another thousand. I'm running low myself. I'll get it to you tomorrow."

"Tangier," says Dris, his gaze drifting away again. "My grandfather always told me it was the wickedest city on earth."

Pascual's memories of his dark years underground are dominated by night trains, dreary coach journeys, station buffets and backstreet hostels, piss in the gutters and bugs in the bed. His current trials, he reflects as he stands at the window of his hotel room, have at least elevated him to a better class of venue for his depredations. From this air-conditioned and amply padded cell twelve stories up, isolated from the heat and noise of the city, he can see the glittering Bay of Tangier beneath him; in the hazy distance across the water, startlingly close, the rugged coast of Spain.

The hotel is shiny and sterile like upscale hotels everywhere, designed to keep guests safe from contact with local peculiarities and irritants. After a day spent contending with these, Pascual is finding that there is something to be said for this approach, if one can stifle the guilt. A shower, a short nap and a change of clothes has him facing the coming evening with, if not optimism, at least resignation.

The short flight from Barcelona and an exorbitantly priced taxi ride from the airport had him at the hotel before lunchtime. The *cabinet d'avocats* where his meeting with Maître Chaouki Larbi was scheduled proved to be a short taxi ride into the old European quarter just outside the medina, where wrought-iron balconies and walls tinted blue or ochre recall towns elsewhere around the Mediterranean. Pascual spent some time long ago in Algiers, and he finds echoes of it here, along with elusive notes of Córdoba, Málaga, Marseille.

In his lofty chamber with whirring ceiling fans and high windows, straight out of *Pépé le Moko,* Larbi was smoothly Francophone and fully briefed. There is only the formality of certain fees to be paid, customary understandings to be observed, and the company registration for Malabata Holding, S.A.R.L. will be transferred; if Monsieur cares to return on Wednesday all should be in order and an invoice will be prepared.

Pascual wants something strong and cold to drink; he wants to talk to his wife and son. His last conversation with Sara was unsatisfactory; he could feel her impatience spiking, skepticism beginning to outweigh anxiety. He has not talked with Rafael in a week and trusts the boy is doing nothing more foolish than neglecting his studies for drink and dalliance.

Most of all Pascual wants everything to be over. He remembers being a small boy, on the eve of some critical showdown between Barça and the archenemy from Madrid, asking his grandfather who would win. Maybe us and maybe them, the old man told him; we'll know tomorrow. Pascual remembers a sleepless night, the uncertainty worse than the thought of losing.

Maybe us and maybe them. Maybe we will all be safe and maybe we will all be dead in five days. Pascual takes his secure phone from the desk. He wants badly to hear from Dris. Now that he is on the ground, his preparations strike him as ludicrously inadequate, one petty street tough versus a team of professional malefactors. He is mad to be here, mad not to have thrown himself on the mercy of the Germans, mad to put his fate in the hands of a politically connected lawyer from Madrid.

Perhaps it is not too late. Could the BND have assets in Tangier? Pascual quashes that thought and comes away from the window, aware that he will go genuinely mad if he stays here in this room. He puts on his jacket and slips the phone into a pocket. He has spotted at least one bar in the hotel, and he can think of no reason why he should not drink himself to sleep tonight.

He opts for the one on the roof, despite uncomfortable memories of the last time he had cocktails with a view of the sea, and with half a gin and tonic inside him, a breeze ruffling his hair and the westering sun gilding the slopes of Cap Malabata, Pascual is beginning to recover his equanimity. The key will be to remain in close touch with Salera and with Artemisa. When either of them has something concrete he can take to the authorities, whether the Germans or Artemisa's shadowy colleagues, then it will be time to send Sara and Rafa into hiding and make his own escape.

It would be good to know if Dris has touched down. Pascual pulls the secure phone from his pocket and thumbs it into action. He sees no missed calls, no texts waiting. He is contemplating whether to try to contact Dris when he is startled by a woman's voice saying, "No need to reach out, we knew you were here."

Pascual gapes up at Lina, struck dumb and with the bottom falling out of his stomach. She pulls up at his table, sleek and feline in black boots, jeans and jacket, with her superior smile. Felix is a couple of paces behind, glowering, a pit bull trotting behind a panther. "What the hell are you doing here?" Pascual manages to say.

I ought to have known, he thinks. Of course they could pop up anywhere, at any time. He is keenly aware that he is sitting here with his top-secret secure phone in his hand.

"Didn't we mention we would be joining you here? Careless of us. May we?" Lina sinks gracefully onto the chair opposite Pascual and Felix plops down to his left. "We are moving into the final phase," says Lina. "We thought it best to proceed here directly to wrap things up. Who were you trying to reach just now, if I may ask? I remind you that the phone we issued you should not be compromised by using it to communicate with anyone outside the scope of this operation."

Pascual slips the phone out of sight. "I was going to see what I could find out about restaurants in the vicinity. I am told I must not leave Tangier without sampling a *tagine.*"

"Leave it to us. We were hoping to enjoy your company at dinner again. If it's *tagine* you want, there is a small place in Avenue Moulay Youssef I can recommend."

Pascual nods with a sinking heart, trying to appear pleased. "You do get around, don't you? I take it this is not your first time in Tangier?"

She flicks a glance at Felix, stone-faced on his chair. "We've done one or two things here. How did it go with Maître Larbi today?"

"Fine, as far as I could tell. I got the impression he'll just add the bribes onto the invoice."

"That's generally how it's done. When will the documentation be ready?"

"Wednesday, he claimed."

"Good. You have a little time to relax and enjoy Tangier before the last step, then."

"Which is?" Pascual says, fighting an onset of dread.

"The key to the treasure chest," Lina says. "Your last and most important performance. We are waiting to hear from our correspondent. Then there will be an onboarding procedure for Pascual Rose to go through, including a short teleconference, and you'll have completed the work you were hired for. But tonight we relax. Ah, here's our waiter."

As Lina issues a complicated cocktail order in decent French, Pascual looks at Felix and meets a cold reptilian stare, unblinking.

Pascual closes the door of his room and throws the bolt. He peels off his jacket, drops it on a chair and flings himself onto the bed, exhausted. The *tagine* rumbles in his gut. It was as good as advertised, but Pascual's appreciation was hampered by the need to remain civil while Lina orchestrated a caricature of a congenial dinner among colleagues, talking ceaselessly for two hours and revealing absolutely nothing, holding forth on everything from Moroccan cooking to Thai sex tourism. Pascual has to admire her professionalism.

He rolls, stirs, rises to use the bathroom. He returns to the bedroom and pulls his secure phone from under the mattress where he stuffed it in a panic upon returning to his room in the brief hiatus between drinks and dinner, terrified at how close he had come to betraying everything. A call from Dris in the presence of Lina and Felix would have been disastrous. Pascual curses himself as a fool for not anticipating their appearance. He awakens the phone and sees two text messages waiting.

One is from Dris: *In Tangier. Have car. Waiting for orders*. Pascual's tension eases a little. He texts back: *Soon. Stand by*. The second text is from Artemisa: *In Tangier. Call me*.

Astonished, Pascual stares at it for a few seconds. The whole world is descending on Tangier. He reaches to punch *Call* but freezes. The phone given him by Lina and Felix is in his jacket pocket hanging on the chair, and it is almost certainly primed to capture any words he might speak. He sits for a moment thinking and then hits *Reply* and taps out a text: *Lina and Felix here at hotel. Where are you?*

He sends the message and then goes to pour himself a glass of water. When he has drunk it, he stands at the window for a minute, watching lights in the port far below. When he picks up the phone again, Artemisa's answer is already there: *Hotel Continental. Must talk. If and only if you can evade L & F, come here*.

Pascual checks the time. Despite the interminable dinner the night is young, not yet ten o'clock. Pascual sighs and begins to tap out a message to Dris.

Evading Lina and Felix ought to be easy, but Pascual has developed a superstitious dread of their omniscience. With his secure phone in his pocket and Lina's poisoned one plugged into a charger in his room, he takes the elevator down to the lobby. There he hides in an armchair in a corner, pretending to look at his phone but watching people. After a few minutes he takes a deep breath, puts the phone away, stands, takes a last look around and strides briskly out into the night.

He waves off a doorman offering him a taxi and walks fast, leaving the bright lights of the hotel entrance behind. The hotel lies on a huge roundabout with traffic sweeping around it at high speed. Beyond that is a vast plaza in front of the main train station, a hulking modern construction with twin towers flanking a broad entrance. Pascual manages to cross to the plaza without being run over and is immediately assailed by a youth offering him hashish in three languages. Pascual shakes him off and keeps walking. He gains the station entrance and goes inside. Here it is sparsely populated because of the hour. Pascual drifts, scans the area idly, finally heaves to in front of the departure board and pretends to study it, fending off more touts. The fourth or fifth one is Dris, who instead of offering him *kif* murmurs, "In a minute, go out the side door to your left and wait on the pavement like you're looking for a taxi."

Pascual strives to look bewildered as he makes his way to the exit. Outside there is a curb where cars are lined up to retrieve arriving passengers. Pascual finds a clear space and in seconds a battered white Renault is swerving over, Dris at the wheel.

"I don't think you brought anyone with you, but I'm not a professional," he says as he pulls away into traffic. "If you did, let's hope this throws them."

"Nice set of wheels," Pascual says. "Where'd you get it?"

"My uncle has a friend who has a garage. He's always got a car or two around that he'll rent out. Where are we going?"

"Hotel Continental. You know it?"

"Everyone knows it. You picked a good place to lose anyone who might be following."

The Hotel Continental proves to be in the medina, perched like a fortress on the heights above the harbor, reached by a series of cobbled switchbacks after a sweep along the seafront boulevard. Dris stops abruptly at the gate to an enclosed forecourt and says, "Here you are. Shall I wait? Or you could call me when you want to be picked up."

Pascual considers. "Why don't you come up with me? I think it's time you two met."

Dris nods and pulls into the forecourt. He eases the car into a vacant space and they get out. Pascual stands looking up at a whitewashed facade, windows with horseshoe arches, a balustraded terrace. He pulls out his phone and taps to call Artemisa.

"You're here?"

"Just outside."

"You're sure you're clear of the wicked witch and her lap dog?"

"I don't think we were followed. I left their phone at the hotel. If they're tracking it, they'll think I've gone to bed."

"Who's we?"

"My bodyguard. I'll introduce you."

There is a brief silence, and she says, "*Vale*. Come inside and find your way to room 137, then. It'll be through the lobby, up the stairs to your right."

Inside there is a reception desk just as in any other hotel, though this one is out of the *Arabian Nights;* Pascual saunters past it as if he owns the place, nodding at the clerk, who nods back. He gives Dris the eye but says nothing. Pascual leads Dris up the stairs. They wander a little before finding the right room; the place is full of Moorish arches and secluded nooks. Pascual finds room 137 and knocks.

Artemisa opens and beckons them in. Tonight she is in casual mode, in jeans, a denim shirt over a tube top, hair flying free, another European tourist looking for a party. Her eyes narrow a little as she sizes up Dris. "Who's this, then?" She shuts the door behind them.

"I present to you my friend and protector, Dris. His help has been invaluable."

Artemisa does not look entirely sold on Dris but grants him a wary nod. She turns to Pascual. "You look like hell."

"I spent the evening pretending to enjoy myself."

"Have a drink." She points at a table where a liter of water and three glasses stand. "If you want something stronger we can have it sent up."

"Perhaps later." Pascual collapses on a chair. The room is lamplit, shadows in the corners, with a double bed, two armchairs, a wardrobe with a mirror on the door. Dris makes his way to the window, parts the curtains with a finger to look out, then turns and leans against the wall, hands in his pockets.

Artemisa says, "Is your companion fully informed of what we are dealing with?"

Pascual says, "If you mean, is he to be trusted, I would say absolutely, yes."

Artemisa and Dris trade a look. Dris's face is completely blank. "Very well," says Artemisa. "We'll trust him." She picks up her phone and taps at it. "I want you to meet someone." She puts the phone to her ear, waits and says softly in English, "He's here." She swipes and sets the phone on the desk. "He'll be here in a moment. He's in the room next door."

Pascual is not sure how many more surprises he can take today. "Who is it?"

Artemisa smiles. "He's the man who knows where the money is coming from."

Three soft knocks sound on the door. Artemisa hurries to open it and a man comes in from the hall. He is small in stature, almost frail, fiftyish, wearing a brown suit only a shade darker than his skin, with a dark red tie. He is balding, the remaining hair slicked straight back, and he affects a neatly trimmed mustache. He has eyes like black marbles, glinting in the lamplight. He nods at Artemisa and then stiffens, looking at Pascual and Dris in turn. Artemisa shuts the door behind him. In English she says, "So. I present to you Pascual. And . . . Dris."

The man's hand is thin and bony but the grip is firm. "I am Najib." He looks at Dris uncertainly.

Dris grins and says, "No speak English. *As-salaam aleikum.*"

Najib bows slightly. *"Wa aleikum as-salaam."*

"And I don't speak Arabic, so English it will have to be," says Artemisa. "Take the other chair," she says, a hand on Najib's elbow. "I can sit on the bed."

Najib shrugs. "As you wish." He accepts the glass of water Artemisa pours him and sits daintily, feet together, looking uncertainly from her to Pascual and back.

Artemisa perches on the side of the bed and says to Pascual, "Najib has just come up from Casablanca on the train. I persuaded him he should come and talk to you."

Pascual looks at Najib. "You live in Casablanca?"

He shakes his head. "I live nowhere. I was in Libya, then I go to Italy. I study in Italy, many years ago. But now they will not accept me. So I leave. My daughter is in Egypt and my son in Dubai. I have one brother in Casablanca. I live in any place where someone give me a bed." His English is carefully enunciated, the English of a man who learned it from books, and imperfectly.

"And where is your home?"

"My home is Libya. The poor massacred country."

"Not the only one, sadly."

"No. But the only one that is my home."

Artemisa intervenes. "Tell Pascual what your job was."

Najib nods. "I work for the Libyan Investment Authority. For many years. I was . . ." He looks at Artemisa. *"Contabile?"*

"Accountant."

"Yes, accountant. I was accountant for the Investment Authority. This is . . ." He gropes for the words. "Sovereign wealth fund, for Libya." He looks at Artemisa and she nods. "Until they dismiss me."

"And why did they dismiss you?"

"Because the thieves tell them to."

Pascual sits waiting for the punch line. "Big pots of money attract thieves," he says finally. "So, your superiors were stealing from the fund?"

Najib shakes his head. "Not my superiors. The thieves at the National Bank."

Artemisa leans in. "You have to understand the situation. As you know, Libya is in chaos, divided between factions. But everyone depends on the oil money, and the National Oil Corporation still controls that. You remember, Haftar tried to sell oil in the east, and the UN prohibited it. He tried to establish his own oil company, his own national bank. But the international powers, including the big oil companies, support the NOC and the central bank in Tripoli. So the oil money still goes there. But that is also where much of it is stolen. Everyone steals, all the militias, all the politicians. Everybody takes a small piece. But Najib found out about one very large piece."

Najib nods. "They should send the money to us. Every year. But since two years, the money is less. Much less. When the money did not come, I go to the bank and ask questions. And they tell me lies. So I ask more questions. I have a friend at the bank, and he help me." He shakes his head. "My friend was very brave man. They tell him to not ask questions, and he continue to ask."

Pascual can see where this is going. Najib raises haunted eyes to him and says, "They kill him. They say militia kill him, in the street. But one day before, he call me and tell me he find out about one very big thief. And then they kill him."

Pascual waits for more, but Najib is gazing moodily into his glass. "How big is this thief? How much has he stolen?"

"I think about . . ." Najib frowns, getting the numbers right in an unfamiliar language. ". . . twenty-two billion."

Pascual blinks. "Billion. Twenty-two billion dollars."

"I think. More or less." Najib waggles his hand.

Pascual trades a look with Artemisa. She says, "Yes. They're not stealing from some Russian oligarch. They're stealing from a failed state too dysfunctional to keep its national wealth from disappearing."

Pascual sags back on his chair. Suddenly he wants that stronger drink. "So," he says. "Who is this very big thief?"

Najib shrugs. "My friend did not tell me his name. Only the man who send the money."

Artemisa says, "The bank official who authorized the transfers is known. But who ordered him, pressured him, paid him to do this, that is the question. There are several suspects, and each has his connections to external actors. There is the faction of the Saudis, the Emirates and the Egyptians. There is the government in Tripoli, supported by the United Nations, with Turkey and Qatar behind them. And there is ISIS."

"Dear God."

"Yes, that's a nice thought, isn't it? The Islamic State with twenty-two billion dollars to spend. My contacts in Spain are trying to trace all the connections, to identify the organizer of this. There is always the possibility it is merely a criminal group. There are Russians who are capable of something like this."

Pascual shakes his head, stunned. "Evidence," he says. "What evidence do you have?"

Najib says, "My friend send me everything, in e-mail. He send it on the day they kill him." He frowns and corrects himself. *"Killed* him. He know there are many thieves, too many thieves. But the biggest thieves, he did not know who was it. He only know where the money . . . went." Celebrating his grammatical triumph, he takes a drink and makes them wait. Pascual and Artemisa trade a look, and Pascual sees an odd glow of anticipation in Artemisa's eyes.

Najib resumes. "He send me the information about banks, with numbers of accounts, all the numbers. Two hundred million here, eighty million there, one billion dollars in this bank, two billion in that one. Since two years they are sending the money from the Central Bank to these accounts. All of them companies in Qubrus—sorry, Cyprus—in Dubai, in Cayman Islands, in Malta, here, in Luxembourg. More than twenty billion dollar. Twenty billion dollar that should belong to Libyan people. When Haftar or another militia steal, the money at least it goes to people in Libya. This money, it goes to Italy, to Andorra, to Liechtenstein, to a corporation we don't know who owns it. More than one corporation."

"And most of them now inactive, their bank accounts closed," says Artemisa.

Pascual frowns. "So where is the money now?"

"Well, that's the question, isn't it? Wherever they have put it, waiting for you to provide them with a whole new layer of anonymous accounts to receive it. My colleagues are working on getting access to the records of the accounts my father set up, but it's not easy."

Pascual turns to Najib. "How did you find all this out?"

"I ask too many questions. I ask my director, I ask the president, what about this money? They tell me, we will find out. I wait, and then they come and tell me, nobody knows about this money, better you don't ask questions. Better maybe you go away from Libya. So they dismiss me."

"At least they didn't kill you," says Pascual.

Najib nods. "I know if I make problem, they kill me. So I don't make problem. I leave. I go to Italy. But in Italy I continue to ask questions. Only very . . ." He puts a finger to his lips.

"Discreetly," Pascual suggests. "I'd say you are a very brave man."

Najib shrugs. "My friend was very brave man. Me, I don't make problem and I leave."

Artemisa says, "But you continued to ask questions. You found out about my father."

Najib nods. "I found out one man in Genève, who was in Libya before. With the United Nations. He was adviser at the Central Bank, and he know about the thieves. That is why he leave Libya, they dismiss him like they dismiss me. He help me very much. Together we find who establish these companies. Same one for all companies. "

Pascual takes a wild guess. "Benedicto Pereda."

"Yes. And then I find out he is dead."

Artemisa's eyes are locked with Pascual's. "A dangerous position, to be the man who establishes these companies."

Pascual takes a great gulp of water. "I get it. Believe me, I get it. How did you two get together?"

"There was a lot of information online about my father. Najib read he had a daughter, and he searched for me."

Najib says, "I want to know what information she have. Maybe nothing, or maybe she work with her father. Maybe she could help me, maybe she is a criminal. Maybe she is in danger."

"He contacted me through the Colegio de Abogados, the what do you call it, the bar association, in Madrid. I decided you should talk to him."

Pascual looks from one to the other, the frail little man on the chair and the head-turning female on the bed. They are both gazing expectantly at him. He looks at Dris, who has been leaning on the wall forgotten. "So," he says finally. "What are we going to do?"

Artemisa says, "I think the only answer to that question right now is that we need to keep you alive. I can have you at Ibn Battuta Airport in half an hour. Do you have your passport with you?"

The thought stuns Pascual. He could bail out right now, ditch everything and flee to the waiting arms of the Germans, the Spanish, whoever will have him. Tonight he could go to bed in a different country. "Of course," he says.

"Then all you have to do is say yes, let's go."

Pascual drains his water glass and sets it on the bedside table. He looks at Najib and he looks at Artemisa. "Who do we go to?" he says.

Artemisa raises an eyebrow. "That's a very good question. What's the proper jurisdiction? It is a crime for the Libyans to prosecute, but I don't think that's going to happen. So who do we report this crime to? One of the international bodies that deals with financial crime? FinCEN in the U.S., or the UN Office on Drugs and Crime? Interpol, perhaps, or the Guardia di Finanza in Italy, since there is already a criminal case there. Whatever we do, it will be only the beginning of a very slow process. And you, and Najib, will need to be protected."

"And my family."

"Yes. Perhaps it's time to put their safety in the hands of professionals."

Pascual looks at it for a moment longer. Safe harbor, put it in the hands of the professionals. Let them find a place to bury him and

Sara and Rafael where they will be safe as long as they renounce the lives they have built and never stir out of hiding again. "What do Lina and Felix do if I disappear?"

"I think probably they also vanish immediately."

"And become very hard to track down."

"Do you have an alternative?"

"Let my computer wizard find out who they are. He claims to be close."

"He can do that even after you're safe, can't he?"

Pascual shrugs. "Maybe. What happens to the money?"

"Not your concern. Investigators will track it down."

As easy as that, Pascual thinks. "Lina said tonight that there is one step left. An onboarding procedure for the final operation, by teleconference. She said it was the key to unlock the treasure chest. She also said it would be my last and best performance."

Artemisa peers at Pascual for a long moment. "Why here? Why do it in Tangier? They could do a teleconference anywhere."

"I got the impression they were in a hurry. They want to be ready to move the instant the paperwork for the last bank account comes through."

"Or to make you disappear. That would be easier here than in Spain."

"That's a cheerful thought."

Artemisa blinks at Najib. "Here's another cheerful thought. Could they know about you? I hope I haven't made a mistake by bringing you here."

Najib shrugs. "If they know about me, they will go to Casablanca. I did not tell my brother I was coming here."

Artemisa frowns at things a while longer and turns to Pascual. "I can't tell you what to do. I'll take you to the airport right now if you want."

Pascual meets Najib's melancholy gaze. He looks at Dris and says in Castilian, "The question is, do I give up and leave right now, or stay here and try to get enough evidence to put somebody in jail?"

Dris shrugs. "Go or stay, I'll have your back."

Pascual takes a deep breath. He looks at Artemisa and cocks his head toward Najib. "Take him," he says. "He's the one who needs to be kept safe. Me, I need to stay and unlock that treasure chest. When we know where the money is, we'll go to whoever you think we should go to."

"You won't have much time."

"Five days."

"I would guess less. The fact that they are here in Tangier indicates to me that they want it to end here."

Pascual rises from the chair, creaking, feeling a hundred years old. "Well, then," he says. "I will have to work fast, won't I?"

Pascual scans the lobby as he crosses it, seeing nobody but a few late-night idlers paying him no attention. He pulls up at the lifts and punches the button, footsore and weary, hardly able to stand. He closes his eyes and sways a little on his feet. "That's a good way to lose your wallet, wandering around Tangier at night," growls a voice at his elbow.

Pascual jerks to attention to see Felix giving him the basilisk look, a meter away. For a panicked moment he wonders how long the bastard has been following him, and then he realizes he must have just emerged from the bar. "I wanted to see the ocean," he says. "There's a beach down at the end of the street." He lifts a foot, showing Felix the sand on his shoes and the cuffs of his trousers.

Felix makes a soft dismissive noise. "You should take your phone when you go out. What if we need to contact you?"

"You really have nothing better to do than monitor my phone? I was told to relax and enjoy Tangier."

"When this meeting is set up, we'll need to contact you at short notice. Wherever you are. So take the phone."

"OK, boss. You got it."

"You run around without the phone, it makes me wonder if you're doing something you don't want us to see. Or seeing someone."

"Her name was Aziza," says Pascual. "Or so she claimed." The lift arrives and Pascual boards, turning his back on Felix.

On the way up Felix gives Pascual a pitying look, shaking his head. "On the beach? That really is insane. Forget your wallet, you're lucky you didn't get your throat cut."

Pascual favors him with a smile. "That's why we come to Tangier, friend. To live dangerously."

In his room Pascual sheds his jacket and shoes and collapses on the bed. He will never be able to sleep; the balloon has gone up and there are plans to make, perils to anticipate, wits to be collected. He quails at the thought. A gentle buzz penetrates the mental fog. This must be the secure phone, in his jacket pocket. Pascual rolls, leaps to answer it. A text has arrived from Salera: *Call me*.

Pascual shoots a superstitious look at Lina's phone, still plugged into the charger. Can it hear him? Pascual disconnects it, stands thinking for a moment, and then takes it into the bathroom. He lays it on the sink, starts the shower going and returns to the bedroom. He picks up the secure phone and hits *Call*.

Salera answers immediately. "This is positive," he says. "I wasn't sure I'd be hearing from you."

"What a reassuring thing to hear. Any particular reason?"

"The quality of your opposition, mainly. You have been hacked by some very serious people."

"I could have told you that. Who are they?"

"I can't give you names. But I can tell you who they're working for, or at least whose tools they're using. Have you ever heard of Stuxnet?"

"It rings a bell. Some kind of virus?"

"A top-of-the-line virus. Stuxnet is the worm that took out the Iranians' nuclear program in 2010. It infected the computer systems that controlled their centrifuges, took them over and basically ordered them to shake themselves to death. It was a brilliant coup and the first major cyberwar attack. And who was behind it?"

"How should I know? The yanquis, presumably."

"Good guess, but it was a joint effort. Stuxnet was the product of a collaboration between the U.S. and Israel."

"Israel."

"That's right. The Israelis have a crack cyberwar unit, world-class."

"And that's who hacked me?"

"I can't say that. What I can say is, to spare you the technical details, that the people who hacked you share a good many tricks and leave some of the same tracks as the people who did Stuxnet. I don't know if it's the yanquis or the Jews or somebody who learned from them, but they're good and they've got a firm hold on you."

"Can you do anything to loosen it?"

What sounds like a soft laugh comes through the ether. "I can't do anything about your hacked phone. I can possibly attribute the attack on your computer with a little more precision in a day or two. At that point I can support you if you choose to go to the authorities. What are your intentions?"

An excellent question, Pascual thinks. He strives to concentrate. "I've been given to believe that they need my cooperation for one more onboarding operation. After that I think I will be expendable, and I only need to decide what authority is the right one to go to."

"Pick one. You're in Tangier?"

"How is it my movements are public knowledge? Does the world know every time I go to the toilet?"

"You think I can't track the phone I gave you? When is this onboarding operation supposed to take place?"

"Any day. They're waiting for some deal to be completed."

"And there's a physical meeting involved? Are they there with you?"

"Yes. At the same hotel. Keeping a close watch on me."

"That doesn't sound ideal. You want my advice?"

"Of course."

"Start thinking about how you're going to get out of Tangier."

Pascual rises early, emerging from a restless, dream-ridden sleep. A Tangerine dawn is making the Strait glow outside Pascual's window, impossibly beautiful in luminous shades of rose and aquamarine. He stands looking longingly at Andalusia in the distance, so close and so painfully remote. He sits on the bed, thinks for a time, then awakens his secure phone and taps out a text to Dris.

He showers, dresses, slips his secure phone into one pocket and Lina's into another. He descends to the hotel lobby and wanders until he finds a newsstand, where he purchases yesterday's *Le Monde*. He tucks it under his arm and saunters out into the searing cacophony of a Tangier morning. A doorman produces a taxi and Pascual tells the driver to take him to the Petit Socco.

The Petit Socco is a wide place at the confluence of two streets in the heart of the medina, overlooked by the balconies of cheap pensions and ringed with café terraces. Here is the Tangier that once drew the seedier type of European and American artist like moths to a flame, overlaid now with satellite dishes and shops peddling tourist tat. Pascual selects a café and makes his way through the crowded terrace into the interior. Here there is less light and fewer people. There is a counter, mirrors on the wall, a few wooden tables, only two of them occupied. Pascual sits at a table in the rear, orders a mint tea from the boy behind the bar, and devotes himself in turn to the newspaper and to watching to see who comes in.

When Dris enters, he sits two tables away and ignores Pascual to jab at his phone. Pascual feels his secure phone buzz in his pocket and extracts it. Dris's text reads, *Nobody obvious with you. Back door past toilets.* Pascual texts back, *OK*. He puts away his secure phone, folds up the newspaper with Lina's phone inside it. He stands, leaving the paper on the table. Dris calls to him: "*Monsieur,* have you finished with the newspaper?"

"Ah, yes. It's yours if you want it." Pascual scoops the paper from the table and hands it to Dris with a smile. Then he makes for the toilets down a passage in the rear. At the end of the passage is a door open to the street. Pascual ducks out into the foot traffic and makes for the Hotel Continental.

"Stuxnet." Artemisa pronounces it carefully, avoiding the Spanish tendency to insert a vowel before the *s*. "That's the Israelis."

"And the Americans," says Pascual. "It was a joint effort, my fellow says."

Artemisa shakes her head. This morning she is in business casual, blazer and slacks, a professional woman with places to go and things to do. Her hair is still wet from a shower and her suitcase lies open on the bed. "You think Lina and Felix are yanquis? That seems improbable to me. On the other hand, the Israelis have a significant intelligence presence around the Mediterranean, in Malta for one. And in Morocco."

"Here?"

She nods. "The Moroccan Jewish community is old and deeply rooted. And not entirely gone."

"The Israelis are stealing Libya's oil money?"

"They're laundering it, at least. I'd bet anything on it. Whose idea it was to steal it, who knows? An operation like this, it could be rogue. Intelligence agencies have been known to find ways to supplement their budgets. Or it could be professional courtesy, one agency lending another its expertise. Here's the question: Who wants Libya's oil money and has Israeli friends?"

"Who wouldn't want Libya's oil money?"

She concedes with a nod. "So look at the friends, eh? One of my colleagues in Madrid has been working on my father's connections. However my father got involved in this, it didn't come out of nowhere. And ask yourself the same question: Who picked you, and why? Who knew about Pascual Rose?"

"Well, my first approach was to the Americans. But yes, the Israelis took possession of me. There was an old spy named Dan who spent a lot of time with me. But I doubt he's still alive."

"He'd have friends and colleagues who are still there. I'd bet that's the connection in your case. As for my father, my colleague and I believe it was from another direction."

"What's that?"

"When my father was selling arms to the Chechens in the nineties, he worked closely with an intermediary named Khalid Hussein. And he was a very interesting fellow. He ran his operations out of Beirut, but he was actually a Saudi. And it was determined that he had close ties to one branch of the royal family."

"A Saudi. That is interesting."

"Yes. He seems in fact to be quite close to the fellow who's currently on the throne. And consequently, probably, to his very active and forward-thinking son. And he met with my father a couple of weeks before my father went off on the first of his missions."

Pascual wanders to the window. The curtain has been pulled aside and he has a splendid view of the port and the headland beyond. "The Saudis? Working with the Israelis?"

"They have been cooperating for years. They are united by a fear of Iran, of course. Lina told you the scapegoat is a Syrian in Iranian employ, no? I think that was probably the truth. If things fall apart, they want the blame to fall on Iran."

Pascual stands thinking, watching a ferry trailing a curving white wake as it rounds the breakwater, heading for Spain. "Why would the Saudis want to steal Libya's oil money? Don't they have enough of their own?"

"You would think so. I'm just speculating, but the Saudi regime doesn't seem like the world's most stable or confident polity to me. Everything they have they owe to oil, and now this young upstart wants to diversify the economy and move it away from oil. I can't imagine that everyone's happy with that. Any real shift will have political consequences, and politics is a zero-sum game in a place like that. If the prince is serious, he's going to have to allow real competitive markets and independent centers of power. That's going to make winners and losers. And he's going to have to compensate the losers unless he wants big trouble. So this could be a bone to throw to somebody who's losing out in the new Saudi economy. Or it could be the losers themselves behind it, taking their compensation into their own hands. Or, for that matter, it could be the prince's own private insurance policy. If things go wrong and the new Saudi economy comes crashing down, he'll still have a steady stream of good old-fashioned oil revenue to feather his nest."

Pascual tries to read the calm look in those dark eyes. "If it is the Saudis who are behind this, and if we can prove it, what happens when we expose it?"

"I would imagine that heads will roll. Literally. The strongest faction in Riyadh will come out on top and blame everything on the losers. Just as with the Khashoggi killing. Exposure may not bring down the people behind it, but the world will have a little more evidence of their corruption. We have to take what we can get."

Pascual nods a few times, slowly. "They won't be very happy with us, will they?"

"No. That's why you need to step very carefully for the next few days."

"I plan to. Where's Najib this morning?"

"In his room. He's taking the train back to Casablanca this afternoon. I couldn't persuade him to fly out to Madrid with me. He says he is tired of running. I am hoping he will keep a low profile until somebody is ready for him to testify."

"You're leaving today?"

"This afternoon." Artemisa hesitates before saying, "You could come with me."

Pascual turns back to the window. "Then who will find out where the money is?"

"I know where the money is."

Pascual wheels, startled, to see Artemisa smiling. She says, "I've heard from my colleagues in Madrid this morning. They got access to the statements for three of the accounts my father set up. They were able to see where the payments from those accounts went."

"And?"

"They went to a firm in New York that has a very specialized niche. What do you know about cryptocurrency?"

Pascual gapes at her for a moment. "Cryptocurrency? Bitcoin?"

"Among others. You're familiar with the concept?"

"As familiar as I am with Einstein's general theory of relativity. I am aware that it exists."

"Well, you should try to educate yourself a little, because that's where they've parked the money. This firm in New York brokers large cryptocurrency transactions. Transactions too big for the exchanges that most people use."

"They converted twenty-two billion dollars into cryptocurrency?"

"So it seems. And I'd bet that this last step Lina told you about is to convert it back into something the Saudis are more comfortable with. Dollars, euros, gold. And this firm in New York will have an onboarding procedure. That's what they need you for."

Pascual considers that, holding Artemisa's unblinking gaze. "And so that's why I can't leave yet."

Artemisa frowns, goes to the bed, pulls the suitcase toward her. "You are either very brave or very foolish," she says. "Where's your minder today?"

"Dris? Taking my phone for a walk, in case they're tracking it."

"They could have visual surveillance. Is he a trained operative?"

"No, just a delinquent with the usual low cunning."

"And you trust him."

"I've known him for practically all of his life. He and my son grew up together."

"So he's an amateur." Artemisa stands with arms crossed, frowning. "Well, he's in it now. Let's hope he's a talented amateur."

"The phone's in the car. It rang a couple of times," Dris says as they approach the Renault, two wheels up on the pavement in a narrow street just outside the medina. "I ignored it. They didn't leave a voice mail."

"Lina, no doubt," says Pascual. "Just checking up on me, I hope. I'll probably get a scolding. So, what did I do this morning?"

Dris puts a hand on his arm to halt him a few steps from the car. "You spent an hour or so at the Grand Socco, just watching people. You wandered through the medina enough to be sure nobody was tailing you, at least not very close. You decided not to buy a brass tray, a water pipe, or a Berber rug."

"Wise decision. Thanks."

"You were just a tourist. And if there was any surveillance to see who was carrying the phone, I didn't see it. But I'm not a professional."

"I trust your judgment. My guess is they're relying on electronic surveillance. It seems to be their modus operandi. But I'm told they have resources here, so let's go on being careful. You can take me back to the hotel now, and then I shouldn't need you anymore today.

I plan to just take refuge in the air conditioning and complain about the locals to anyone who will listen."

Dris laughs, with just a hint of an edge. "Try not to do it too loudly when the help is around, will you? They have enough to endure without having to listen to your insults."

In his room Pascual sets Lina's phone on the bedside table and then picks up the remote control and turns on the television. His interest in Moroccan television is limited to seeing whether it works; when he has settled on a French soap opera subtitled in Arabic he tosses the remote on the bed, takes his secure phone into the bathroom and shuts the door. He taps in Salera's number, expecting to get voice mail, but the man himself answers after three rings. "Cryptocurrency," says Pascual. "They've turned twenty billion dollars into cryptocurrency, and now they want to turn it back. What do I do?"

There is a brief silence. Then Salera laughs. "Cryptocurrency? That's the last thing I would do with twenty billion dollars. That sounds like a good way to turn it into ten billion dollars."

"Nonetheless that seems to be what they've done. And they need me to pass an identity test in order to convert it to real money."

"Fiat money is the term. And if I had twenty billion in crypto, I'd want to convert it to fiat as fast as I could. But then I'm a skeptic. Fascinating. How did you discover this?"

"Somebody got access to the accounts at the other end and saw that the stolen money had gone to a firm in New York that arranges big cryptocurrency transactions. Will they use the same firm to turn it back to fiat? And how can I get evidence of all this to take to the authorities? I don't understand how the whole thing works. Educate me."

What might be a sigh is faintly audible in Pascual's ear. "All right, let's say you have a lot of stolen dollars. And you want to launder this money by converting it into cryptocurrency. So you set up an account on a cryptocurrency exchange and purchase the currency of your choice. Now, are these funds adequately laundered by this process? Is their provenance obscured?"

"From the way you pose the question, I'm guessing no."

"Very good. The whole point of the blockchain technology that underlies cryptocurrency is that it is in theory perfectly auditable. Anyone with the necessary expertise can trace the history of a coin from its creation to the end of time. So at first glance, cryptocurrency is not a very good vehicle for laundering money. If some Somali pirate or Albanian white slaver gets tripped up and arrested, and their crypto addresses revealed, all the people they've transacted with can be traced. It's now a liability to own any coins descended from those accounts. You've heard of blood diamonds? Now we have blood coins."

"Twenty-two billion worth."

"Yes. Now, as you might imagine, some very sharp minds have applied themselves to this. With some fairly sophisticated cryptography, a way was found to make sending coins secure and genuinely anonymous. There are platforms that are auditable, but only with user permission. It's now impossible to tell how you acquired the coin without breaking the cryptography."

"Perfect for money laundering."

"Yes. Especially after you take your coins to an exchange meant for trading one cryptocurrency for another, between platforms that were not designed to interact programmatically. You convert your blood coins to something else, and now someone else has your blood coins and what you have is essentially untraceable. You trade it out to a second wallet address that you own, and there you are."

"So now you have a lot of clean bitcoin or whatever. How do you make it into dollars?"

"Well, that could be problematic. Especially if you have a lot. And twenty-two billion is an enormous amount, unprecedented. The largest bitcoin transaction I'm aware of was worth about a hundred million dollars. So I'd guess they're going to take their time with this, so as not to upset the market and attract attention. And even at that, they're going to find it difficult. The main crypto exchanges were designed for people at the consumer level. There's not enough liquidity to handle big transactions. If you've got a whole lot of crypto and you want to turn it back into fiat, you have to go to an intermediary set up to handle large amounts. That would be this firm in New York. It matches big buyers with big suppliers, and the rates are negotiated instead of bot-traded. The broker takes a cut, of course. But at the end you have dollars or euros or whatever in a nice safe traditional bank account. Provided you can pass the verification process. If it's a legitimate firm, they will have some kind of process, probably similar to the one a bank would use."

Pascual is silent for a moment, phone to his ear, mind racing. "Evidence," he says. "At the end, they will have their dollars and euros. What will we have? Is there any way you can track these transactions?"

"If I have the addresses. Every cryptocurrency transaction and every crypto wallet has an address, a long string of characters that identifies it uniquely. If I have that, I can track the money. To actually access the money, you need the address and also a private key, which is also a long string of characters. But if all you want to do is track it, you can do that with the address. You just put it into a search engine online and you can see where it goes."

Pascual thinks for a moment, eyes squeezed shut. "How would a person obtain those addresses?"

"Well," says Salera after a pause. "They would have to give them to you. Are they likely to do that?"

"Doubtful," says Pascual. "Very doubtful."

Stress and a restless night are catching up with Pascual, and he dozes off in his chair on the terrace of the hotel, in a shaded spot near the pool where a French girl in a scant bikini is ostentatiously dipping a toe in the water for the delectation of a pair of middle-aged Frenchmen. He is awakened by the buzzing of Lina's phone in his shirt pocket. He fumbles it and manages to answer just as Felix walks into his field of vision with a phone to his ear.

"So it does work," says Felix, putting away his phone and pulling up in front of Pascual. "We thought maybe you'd forgotten to charge it."

"Oh, it works." Pascual shoves it back in the pocket. "Sorry, I meant to return your calls. I had the ringtone volume turned down low and didn't hear it. Possibly because of the music in the café where I sat for a while. What's new?"

Felix greets Pascual's flippancy with his usual granite obduracy.

"Why do you think we gave you that thing? You're supposed to answer it when we try to contact you."

"Sorry, I didn't think anything important was going to happen for a day or two. I've been in tourist mode. When's the big meeting happening?"

"This afternoon. Four o'clock, in Lina's suite. You're to be ready with all your documents."

"And how's this going to work? Who am I talking to?"

"Who do you think? The person in charge of the onboarding procedure. There will be a VoIP connection. You'll have to scan and transmit your documents, then show them to the camera. You'll speak to the examiner and show him your hand."

"Ah, yes. My unique identifier." Pascual peruses the stumps of his missing fingers. "I'm glad it's finally proving useful."

Felix is not amused. "Try to be serious. Shave and comb your hair if you can manage that. It's a business meeting. Dress accordingly."

"Absolutely. You can count on me." Pascual flashes a smile at Felix and gets nothing in return but a baleful glare. He drops the smile and says, "Look, Felix. I'm as committed to this as you are. As you are fond of reminding me, I'm getting a million euros. I just don't respond well when people try to intimidate me. So give the leg-breaker act a rest, will you?"

There is a brief stare-down, Pascual doing his best to look unmoved. Felix voices a barely audible noise of contempt and says, "This afternoon. Be there at 3:45. Room 339. Don't make me come looking for you."

▪ ▪ ▪ ▪

"It's time." Pascual stands in the bathroom of his hotel suite, phone to his ear. In the mirror over the sink he sees a man in middle age, gaunt and gray, eyes wide with stress. He turns away. "Time for you to go."

"Dios mío," says Sara. "Just like that, eh?"

"Just like that. Completely serious, *vida mía*. You have to go to Soledad's farm, and you have to go now. Immediately, you hear me?"

"I hear you. When will I see you?"

"In a few days. I'll contact you when I'm done here. Just go. Leave your regular phone. Don't book anything online. Get a ride or pay cash at the station."

"Soledad will come and get me. What about Rafa?"

"I'll call him in a moment."

"Can I talk to him?"

"As long as you use these phones. I'll let you know when it's over."

"And if we don't hear from you?"

Pascual laughs gently. "Then you'll read about me in the papers." He rings off and brings up his son's number. Rafael makes Pascual wait but answers just before the call goes to voice mail. "Time to go," Pascual says. "Now, today, immediately."

"Pare, no fotis. What, drop everything and go?"

"That's it. Right now. Be somewhere else tonight. And don't leave tracks. Throw away your regular phone."

"Throw it away? It's got all my photos, everything."

"They can track it. Leave it with somebody or mail it home. You have cash?"

"I've got enough to get me to Granada. Can they track me if I use my bank card?"

"I wouldn't bet they can't. Use it as little as possible."

"Vale. What about you, *pare?* Are you going to be all right?"

The note in his son's voice robs Pascual of breath for a moment. "I'll be all right. Go take care of your mother." He rings off and punches in Salera's number. When he answers, Pascual says, "It's happening. This afternoon. I'm to present documents and go through a procedure to prove I'm who the documents say I am."

In his ear Salera says, "And that you are alive and not a faked image. It's called proof of liveness. The procedure can be automated, but it sounds as if your lot are being especially careful. I would, too, with so much money involved."

"So supposing I pass, what happens then?"

"They will start cashing out their crypto and putting it into the accounts you've set up."

"And they won't need me anymore."

"I imagine your usefulness will cease the moment the onboarding is deemed complete. I would do my best to be on your way to somewhere else at that moment."

Pascual stands massaging his aching brow. Through the door he can hear keening Arab music on the television out in the bedroom. "They need me up until that moment. That gives me leverage. How do I use it?"

"Well," says Salera. "I can think of one or two things. But you would need a good deal of nerve."

Pascual stands at the window of his room, looking far out across the shimmering Strait of Gibraltar at a country he hopes to see again, probing at the plans he has made and searching for things he has forgotten, overlooked, miscalculated, bungled. Finally he turns on the television and goes back into the bathroom jabbing at his secure phone. "I need you to buy something for me," he says when Dris answers. "And get it to me somehow here at the hotel, within the hour."

"This should take no more than half an hour," Lina says, looking relaxed and casual on her chair, legs crossed and scarlet nails clicking faintly as she taps them idly on the desktop. A few centimeters from her hand sits a laptop, up and running, with a mouse attached. Pascual Rose's identity documents lie in a neat stack next to a scanner connected to the laptop by a cable. Felix sits opposite Lina, looking as usual as if someone has just stepped on his toe.

Their suite is a notch up from Pascual's, larger and with a balcony overlooking the hotel gardens, with this sitting room and a small alcove with a bar in addition to the two bedrooms. Coffee and pastries are laid out on a sideboard. "Whatever it takes," says Pascual. "I'm not doing anything else today."

Lina says, "It's a slightly more rigorous procedure than the one a lot of banks have adopted, where you do it all by phone. Take a picture of your documents, send it, confirm the data once it's extracted, then take a selfie and let their facial recognition technology carry out the liveness verification. Since there's a lot at stake, our correspondents are insisting we go a little farther. They want to make sure you're who you say you are by actually talking to you. Hence the Skype setup. We'll be logging in in a moment."

Pascual nods. "All perfectly reasonable. And I'm supposed to give them a cheery wave with my left hand as well, I understand."

Lina concedes him a cool smile. "Merely raising it into camera range will do, I imagine. We've already scanned and sent your documents, but they'll want you to hold them up as well, all part of the process, designed with multiple confirming factors. They are very thorough."

"I should hope so. There's a lot of money at stake. Can I ask a question?"

"Of course."

"What happens if I refuse to cooperate?"

For a long frozen moment nobody moves or says anything. Pascual sits staring at Lina as calmly as he can. Finally Lina blinks once and says, "Now why on earth would you do that?"

Pascual shrugs. "Well, for one thing, I might try to extract a guarantee of my safety. And my family's. Because it seems to me that once we're done with this little masquerade here, I'm completely disposable as far as you're concerned."

Lina's eyes flick to Felix and back. "Pascual. We have shown you the documentation for your compensation. That trust in the Cayman Islands is real. Once we're done with this little masquerade, as you put it, we're prepared to sit here and walk you through the final steps to take possession of it. And after that you're a free man and you need never see or hear from us again. We'll put you on a flight to Barcelona this afternoon."

Pascual nods again, assuming an expression of humble gratitude. "And you might be perfectly sincere and fully intending to honor your commitments. But you'll forgive me, given what I've seen of the way you operate, if I don't trust you for an instant."

Clickety click, click, click, go Lina's nails on the desktop. "What sort of a guarantee do you have in mind?" Her face has gone utterly expressionless.

Pascual draws a deep breath. "I want the address of your cryptocurrency wallet. Any and all wallets. That will make it possible, eventually, to track all the cryptocurrency transactions you've carried out, from the first purchase of crypto until now. You probably put the crypto through a mixer, so I'll need the initial addresses you used when you first converted it. You shouldn't have any objection to that. Nobody can make off with the money without the private keys, but with enough time and resources the transactions associated with that wallet can be traced back to you. With the wallet address stored safely I have a guarantee. I can set up the classic 'in case of my death' scenario. In case anything happens to me, or to my wife and son, I can arrange for the address to be transmitted to the proper authorities, say FinCEN in the U.S. or maybe the FATF. And they can trace the transactions. But if nobody ever threatens us, it will just be our little secret."

For a time nobody says anything and the only sound in the room is the gentle purr of the air conditioning. Lina and Felix commune silently for a moment and then Lina looks back at Pascual. "You seem to be very well informed."

"Call it an educated guess. Where else were you going to park all that money?"

Lina's eyes narrow. "How much money do you think we are talking about, Pascual?"

Just in time Pascual remembers he is not supposed to know the figure. "Enough to justify all this. Enough to pay me a million euros and all these expenses. I may be a technophobe, but I'm capable of learning. You think I haven't been working night and day to educate myself about these matters? After a while it was obvious. Wherever this money came from originally, with your skillset, the natural choice for you was to change it into crypto to launder it."

Again Lina's eyes flick to Felix and back. Her chin rises a few degrees. "Well, heavens. Well done. If it's really an educated guess, hats off to you. But if we thought you had help in getting to that conclusion, that would very seriously piss us off, Pascual."

Pascual sees no need to respond to that. "The address. I'll need all the addresses. When I have that, we can commence this onboarding procedure."

To Pascual's left, Felix stirs for the first time. "You're not in a position to bargain, asshole. You hold up your end of the deal, or you'll regret it."

Pascual turns slowly to face him. "What, you're going to beat me up? Prop me up in front of the camera with a bloody nose and missing teeth? With a gun to my head? I wonder how that will go over."

Felix does what Pascual least expects: he smiles. Slowly he reaches for a cell phone in front of him. He picks it up, swipes, taps, puts it to his ear. Seconds go by and he says, "Stand by." He looks at Pascual and says, "You stop this bullshit and do what you were hired to do. Or I give the word, and your boy dies. Your choice."

Pascual's stomach drops away into free fall. Here it is, the test. What are the chances Felix is not bluffing, that something went wrong, that Rafa was too slow, that Felix's web is too wide, his resources too great, that Pascual has blundered and is about to gamble away the life of his son? He heaves a great sigh. "Good luck finding him," he says.

Felix hesitates for only a second, but it is enough to give Pascual hope he has made the right choice. Felix puts the phone to his ear and says, "The boy. Go." He thumbs the call off, sets down the phone and gives Pascual the reptile look.

Pascual feels a great calm settling over him. Whatever the outcome, the dice have gone tumbling down the table and all that remains is to settle the bets. He turns to Lina and says, "I'll need that address. I will give you an e-mail address to send it to. When I receive word that it is authentic and allows the transactions to be tracked, then we can start the onboarding process."

Slowly, Lina's face regains its animation, and she almost smiles. "Dear me, Pascual. You haven't been very straightforward with us, have you?"

"That's pretty rich, coming from you."

With a little toss of the chin Lina says, "You can't possibly expect me to e-mail the addresses to anyone. That would be absurdly insecure. We'd abort the whole operation and start all over again with another mule before we'd do that. And you can imagine what that would mean for you personally. If you don't believe we can reach your wife and son, you will admit that we have you here and now."

"All right, then." Pascual reaches into his shirt pocket and pulls out a USB thumb drive. He tosses it onto the desk. "Put it on there. I'll wait."

The thumb drive lies on the desk as three people trade looks for what seems like a long time. The look Felix gives Pascual is blistering. At length Lina says, "Pascual, would you mind stepping out onto the balcony for a moment? Felix and I would like to discuss this briefly."

Pascual gives her a gracious nod as he stands. He gives Felix only a glance as he passes, striving to look unruffled. He slides open the door to the balcony and steps out into the heat, closing the door behind him.

He looks down at the hotel grounds three stories below him, the tops of palm trees waving in a gentle breeze, the swimming pool directly beneath him, the terrace with tables and chairs beside it. A couple of early swimmers are in the pool. A few idlers are on the terrace. Pascual leans on the railing and watches the play of sunlight on the water in the pool, trying to keep a stirring of dread at bay. He turns and through the glass sees Lina and Felix conferring, Lina cool as always, unperturbed, Felix scowling, hunched forward. They fall silent and Lina turns to look at Pascual and gestures for him to come back in.

"Sit down," she tells him as she picks up her phone from the desktop. Her fingertips dance over the screen and she puts it to her ear. "Hello, Max. I'm afraid we've run into a little delay here. Can we reschedule for say, an hour from now?" She listens, smiles, says, "Thank you so much, and sorry for the inconvenience." She sets the phone down and looks at Pascual. "All right. We'll give you the address."

"So we have an agreement?"

"Of course."

"Then you can call off the dogs."

Felix says, "Ha. So, not quite so confident, maybe?"

Pascual turns to him. "Confident enough to call your bluff. Are we going to sit here and wait until your hit team reports back to you that they can't find him? Or let's say they do find him. You really think I'll cooperate if you kill my son? At that point suicidal violence becomes my preferred option. Look, you need me, and I've agreed to cooperate. All I want is a little insurance. So let's just save everyone the trouble and keep things amicable, why don't we?"

Felix grunts with disdain. Lina says, "I think that's an excellent point. We'll call off the dogs." She turns to Pascual and gives him an arctic smile. "Just as soon as you complete the onboarding procedure. Now, shall we proceed?"

Desperately hoping he is not missing some fatal point, Pascual concedes with a wave of thehand. Lina pulls the laptop and mouse toward her. "Very good. You'll need to be patient for a moment." She pecks at the keyboard, frowning faintly. "I must say, you are a quick study if you picked up all this by yourself."

"Of course he didn't," says Felix. "He's sold us out. I say we strip-search him for a wire."

Pascual spreads his arms. "I'll hold still." Felix glowers and Pascual says, "Oh dear, have I called another bluff?"

"Boys," says Lina. "Let's keep it civil." She maneuvers the mouse, types some more and then swings the computer screen toward Pascual. "Here. See for yourself."

On the screen Pascual sees a QR code and jumble of data beneath the heading *Wallet Home*. There are columns labeled *Transactions, Send, Receive* and *Import/Export*. Lines below that show *Total Transactions, Total Received, Total Sent* and *Final Balance,* all followed by strings of digits. He says, "All right. I see it. Now interpret it. Tell me what I'm seeing."

"It's not that hard." Lina points. "What you are probably interested in is this. The balance. This wallet contains this many of this particular coin."

"And how much is this particular coin worth in money I can understand? Say, dollars?"

"I believe today one is going for around eight thousand dollars."

The figure on the screen is in the thousands. Mental arithmetic has never been Pascual's forte, but a mild effort is sufficient in this case to show him that there is nowhere near twenty billion dollars here. "And how many wallets do you have?" he says.

"What makes you think we have more than one?"

"Again I'm guessing from the size of this operation. You have to be stealing billions to make all this worthwhile."

Lina looks almost amused, but the rapid tapping of her fingernail on the desktop betrays her. "Who's coaching you, Pascual?"

"Wouldn't you like to know? Maybe I'm just smarter than you thought. I want all the wallet addresses. May I?"

Before Lina can respond, Pascual reaches for the mouse and moves the cursor to an icon labeled *Wallets*. He clicks and the screen changes. "Oh, my," Pascual says, looking at a list of names arrayed beneath the heading *Wallets*. "What is that? About . . . I count seventeen wallets there." He shoves the laptop back toward Lina. "I want all the addresses."

Lina's face has gone blank again. Pascual merely blinks at her, trying not to let her see how hard he is thinking. She looks once at Felix, but he keeps his gaze steady on her. She looks back at him, and with great satisfaction Pascual notes a tremor of annoyance in the marble features. When the clicking of Lina's fingernail stops, Pascual senses he has won. "All right," she says. She picks up Pascual's thumb drive. "I'll export the addresses as a CSV file. I'll put it on your drive here. Why don't you pour yourself a cup of coffee? This will take a few minutes." She plugs the drive into the USB port of the laptop.

Pascual has a feeling that coffee will only exacerbate the shaky state of his stomach, but he has no better way to pass the time. He shoves away from the table, and avoiding Felix's eyes, goes to the sideboard. He fills a cup with ink-black coffee and goes to stand at the door to the balcony, looking out at the lazily waving palm fronds in the garden. Behind him he can hear the clicking of Lina's fingers on the keyboard. Felix murmurs something in a language Pascual cannot quite make out, but Lina makes no response. At length she says, "All right, here you are."

Pascual goes back to the desk and sets down the coffee cup. Lina is holding the USB drive up to him. "Show me," he says. "Put it in the machine and show me what's on the drive."

Felix makes an exasperated noise, almost a growl, but Lina merely shrugs slightly and complies. She plugs in the drive, shifts the mouse around on its pad, and clicks a few times. The screen shows a directory with one file labeled *Wallets*. Lina opens it and Pascual sees a list that looks just like the one he saw on her computer. "Satisfied?" Lina says.

"Yes, thanks."

Lina closes the directory and extracts the USB drive. She hands it to Pascual. "Now," she says, "do you think we might get on with our business? We've kept some very busy people in New York waiting long enough."

Pascual nods. "Of course. One moment, if you will." He turns and walks deliberately to the balcony door. He pulls it open and steps out into the sunshine. Behind him he hears Felix shove away from the desk. Pascual steps to the balcony rail and spots Dris three stories below, at the corner of the garden. Pascual whistles once and without waiting flicks the thumb drive out over the rail. He watches it sail three stories down to land at Dris's feet and then turns to see Felix storming across the room toward the balcony.

Pascual heaves the sliding door shut with a boom, bringing Felix up short. This slows him only for the scant seconds it takes him to claw at the handle and tear it open, but Pascual hopes it will allow Dris to duck out of sight. Felix charges out onto the balcony like a bull out of the *puerta de toriles* and dashes to the rail. He glares down at upturned faces of sunbathers, swimmers and one distracted gardener.

"Clumsy of me," says Pascual. "I think it went in the pool."

Pascual barely has time to bring his hands up before Felix grabs him by the collar and the hair and hauls him back inside the room, Pascual clipping the edge of the door painfully with his shoulder as they go. Felix propels him across the room to fetch up against the wall. "Bastard," he barks. As Pascual regains his balance, Felix advances slowly, arms away from his sides with the look of a man intent on doing damage.

"Felix." Lina has not moved from her chair. She has presided over the whole thing with the air of a not especially engaged nanny watching two toddlers squabble. But Felix halts at the sound of her voice. Lina says something to him, softly, in a language that to Pascual sounds like Hebrew.

Felix straightens up, takes a breath and points at Pascual. "You'll pay," he says. "I promise you, you'll pay."

Pascual has no doubt he will. But he also knows that for the moment he has won. "Those people in New York are waiting," he says. "And you messed up my hair."

Felix turns and strides to the desk, where he snatches up his phone and jabs at it. Pascual runs his hands over his hair, straightens his jacket, and turns to Lina. "Ready when you are," he says.

Lina shakes her head once, slowly, the faintest of smiles on her lips. "We appear to have underestimated you, Pascual."

Pascual walks slowly to the desk and resumes his seat. Felix is growling into the phone in Hebrew. Pascual says, "I have my insurance, which is all I wanted. I'm happy to help you complete this process now, and I look forward to being left alone with my money after that."

Lina grants him a graceful nod. "Very well. Let's see if they're ready in New York."

"My name is Pascual Rose. I am a citizen of Malta with residences in Valletta and Dubai. This is my Maltese passport." Pascual holds the document up to the screen, then picks up another. "Here is my bill for electrical service at my Maltese residence for the month of June of this year."On the laptop screen a bespectacled gnomish bald man in New York nods once. "Very good, thank you." He hesitates for a moment, mouth open. "If you don't mind, we are advised that you bear a certain distinguishing physical characteristic. Could you please display that?"

"Certainly." Pascual raises his maimed left hand for the camera, rotates it back and forth. "Nothing up my sleeve," he says, drawing a brief humorless chuckle from New York.

"Thank you." The gnome looks off-camera uncertainly for a moment, nods and then looks back at Pascual. "That will conclude our procedure today. We just need to review all the data as per the process, but I don't anticipate any problems. You should receive notification of approval by e-mail within twenty-four hours."

Lina pulls the laptop toward her. "Thank you, Max. Much appreciated, and we'll be standing by."

There is some concluding small talk via VoIP while Pascual shoves away from the desk. Felix is still smoldering, sitting with his phone in his hand, watching Pascual's every move. Pascual grins at him. "What's eating you? You got what you want. I got what I want. Everybody's happy, right?"

Felix says, "We'll find him."

"Maybe you will. But he won't have the thumb drive anymore."

"There's no expiration date on this. If anything gets out, even ten years from now, we come for you."

Pascual assumes a look of innocence. "You don't trust me? That's funny. Look, Felix. You know how the game is played. We all want an edge. You leaned on me, I found a way to lean on you. That's all. It's stable. It's an equilibrium. So chill."

Lina shoves the laptop away and says, "Pascual's right. He's just restored a little balance, that's all. It's not in his interest to betray anything. He'll get his money and then he'll be implicated, too. We will be one happy family, united in a cheerful criminal conspiracy."

"It brings a tear to the eye, just thinking about it," Pascual says. "Speaking of the money, what do I have to do to take possession of it?"

"We'll give you the documents and the passwords," says Lina. "We can do that this afternoon if you want. There will be just a couple of phone calls to make to set things in motion."

"All right. So, I have an open reservation on Iberia. Can I book the flight now? Am I really done?" He reaches for his passport on the desk.

"You're done." Lina neatly scoops the passport out of his reach just as his fingertips approach it. "We'll make the flight arrangements." She shoves his passport into her portfolio. "We thought it would be nice to fly out together, after a last celebratory dinner tonight. Not a *tagine* this time. We thought we'd move upscale a little and take you to the best French restaurant in Tangier."

Pascual sits with his hand outstretched on the desktop. "If you don't mind, I think I'd rather make my own arrangements. No offense, you understand. Just a desire for a little solitary decompression."

Lina zips the portfolio shut. "We'll handle things," she says. "We've got a contact at the airport who can pull strings for us. But he'll need to see the passports. Will an early flight tomorrow suit you? We can have you home by mid-afternoon."

Pascual slowly sits upright. He looks from Lina to Felix and back again. "Whatever you say." He stands and makes for the door. "I'll be in my room if you need me."

▪ ▪ ▪ ▪

Out in the hallway Pascual resists the urge to run. He forces himself to stroll, hands in his pockets, expecting any second to hear the door open behind him. His heart has accelerated and sweat creeps at his hairline. Pascual knows his usefulness has come to an end, and he doubts he will be granted five hours, let alone five days. The confiscation of the passport was an unmistakable sign. Felix's rush to the phone was another; the enemy has assets close by. Now Pascual wishes he had not left his secure phone in his room; it allowed him to call Felix's bluff on being searched, but it means he has to go back and retrieve it. If not for that he would abandon everything and take to his heels.

He takes the lift to the floor above his and then walks down one flight in the stairwell. He stands with his ear to the door for a long moment, hearing nothing, before he pulls it open a crack and looks to see an empty hallway. He musters his courage and walks swiftly to his room, pulling out his key card. He has a bad moment as he enters the room, thinking how easy it would be for people with Lina's capabilities to defeat the lock on a hotel room door and admit a man to sit quietly in the armchair waiting for the occupant to return. Heart pounding, Pascual scans quickly, seeing nobody. He stares at the half-open door to the bathroom, listening hard for the breathing of a man with a knife or a garrotte or a silenced pistol.

Get a hold of yourself, Pascual thinks. They would not have had time to set it up, not quite. In any event that is not their style. The danger will be later, after the triumphant dinner or on the way to the airport. Lina will want a chance to gloat. He takes Lina's phone out of his pocket and drops it on the bedside table, then stoops to pull his secure phone from beneath the pillow. He awakens it and sees he has missed a call from Artemisa. His finger is poised to return her call when he pauses, thinking perhaps it is more urgent to vacate the room. He stands for a moment assessing: how much can he take with him? Pack a change of clothes? Leave it all and run?

The phone in his hand vibrates. Startled, Pascual swipes. A text message from Dris appears: *Get out. They're coming for you.*

Pascual wastes a few seconds in frozen panic and then moves. In the corridor he breaks into a run. As he reaches the door to the stairwell he hears a bell chime, announcing the arrival of the lift. He goes down two flights, making a lot of noise, before he thinks to stop and tear off his shoes. His stockinged feet make much less noise on the concrete steps, and when he has gone down two more floors he is able to hear a door come open above him. He halts and listens, panting a little. Someone comes into the stairwell and takes three quick steps. Pascual holds his breath. For a long moment nobody moves. The steps recede and a door slams.

At the bottom of the stairs Pascual puts on his shoes and carefully cracks a door marked *Sortie*. Outside is a stretch of pavement. Pascual slips out, pulling his phone from his pocket, looking about wildly for assassins. He does not even notice the battered white Renault parked across the street until Dris honks at him.

"I knew you weren't going to come out the front," says Dris. "That left the side exit or the one to the swimming pool, and I knew you wouldn't risk parading past all those people." He muscles the car around a corner onto the seafront boulevard, the tires squealing.

"You're a genius," says Pascual.

"Just experience. I've had to slip out the back a few times in my life. You want the gadget back?"

"No, keep it for the moment. You may be the one who has to deliver it. Who was coming for me?"

"*La poli,* I think. You're lucky I spotted them. I went back into the hotel after you threw me the gadget and ditched the shades and grabbed the cap and jacket I'd hidden in the shitter next to the bar. Then I just sat in the corner of the lobby and watched for a while, pretending to look at my phone. These two blokes who looked like coppers came in from the street and met up with one who came out of the lift. I couldn't hear much of what they were saying, but one thing I did hear was your room number. That's when I sent you the text."

"Police? Are you sure?"

"That's what they looked like to me. You learn to smell them. Somebody grassed on you."

"That makes no sense." Pascual shakes his head. The car is not the only thing moving too fast for him. "Where are we going?"

"Wherever you want. I can take you to the airport directly if you want."

"They took my passport. I'm not flying anywhere today."

Dris steers smoothly past a scooter laden with cartons of eggs. "I'd say you're in trouble, *jefe*. What are you going to do without a passport?"

"I don't know. I need to talk to Artemisa."

"Who?"

"The woman who was at the Hotel Continental. She tried to call me." Pascual wrestles his phone out of his pocket and punches her number.

Artemisa answers straight away. "Where are you?"

"In a car, near the port. Where are you?"

"At the Spanish consulate. Najib's been arrested."

Pascual can hear the strain in Artemisa's voice. "Sûreté nationale, according to the credentials they flashed at me. National police. On some ridiculous pretext, an immigration violation. They came for him at the hotel. We had just checked out, and I was going to go to the station with him in the taxi. But it's worse than that."

"What do you mean?"

"They refused to tell me where they were taking him. I spent a couple of hours making phone calls and going around to police stations. When I finally got someone to admit they'd had him, I was told he'd been turned over to the DST."

"What's that?"

"The Direction de la Surveillance du Territoire, the domestic intelligence agency."

"Why would they want him?"

"My God, Pascual, why do you think? Because the Saudis, or the Israelis, or somebody they own, told them to grab him. It's the coverup, in high gear. They'll be looking for you, too."

"They already are. They just missed me at the hotel. But what can the Moroccans arrest me for?"

"Well, according to people here at the consulate, there's an Interpol Red Notice out for you. Issued at the request of Germany. You're wanted as an accessory to murder."

Pascual manages a bitter laugh. "I guess I should have gone to that meeting. Should I come to the consulate? Would they protect me?"

"You mean keep you from being arrested? They can't. It may be the Germans who want you, but the arrest will be made by the Moroccan police. If they have a legitimate warrant, the consulate will have to turn you over. And then the DST can come for you, too."

"And I can't even prove who I am. Lina took my passport."

"Then I'd say the consulate's a bad bet until I can get some help from Madrid. I've got all I can handle trying to save Najib's life. The only hope is to make noise, get some international attention, get somebody to intervene. Can you go somewhere and lie low for a day or so?"

"One moment." Pascual lowers the phone and says to Dris, "Can you hide me for a day or two?"

Dris shrugs. "I can hide you for ten years if you want. You want to hide in Tangier, you go to Beni Makada."

"I'm still in Tangier," says Pascual into his phone. "Looking for a way out."

Pascual stands on a rooftop, where lines hung with washing jostle for space with satellite dishes, potted plants, plastic tubs and a couple of dovecotes. Sprawling away beneath him is Beni Makada, poor and restless like countless other *quartiers populaires* Pascual has seen from Aleppo to Algiers, four- and five-story tenements above streets jammed with narrow shops flogging mobile phones, stacks of shoes, glittering arrays of jewelry, dresses on mannequins, onions in bins, kebabs on spits. Dris ushered him up four flights of concrete steps to get here, after stashing the Renault in an alley barely wide enough to allow them to exit the car. Dris's uncle, aunt and assorted cousins are reportedly somewhere in the building beneath him. Pascual has no idea what Dris told them; all he knows is that food and tea appeared shortly after their arrival, brought by a wide-eyed girl of ten or so.

Salera says, "Why can't you just fly?"

"Lina confiscated my passport. And the Moroccan police are looking for me because of a German appeal to Interpol."

"*Joder.* You've got problems, friend."

"Tell me about it. I've also got the wallet addresses for the cryptocurrency transactions."

There is a brief silence. "Incredible. How did you manage that?"

"I used the leverage we talked about. It didn't make them happy. I think they were counting on a quick repossession before I could pass off the flash drive, but I found a way to get rid of it right away."

"Who's got it?"

"A friend. It will get back to Spain one way or another."

"If you can get to a computer, you can send the file to me."

"And what will you do with it?"

"What do you think? Take it to the authorities. The FATF, probably. This is an enormous theft, if what you've said is true. To be able to trace it will be a huge victory. Send me that file."

Pascual takes a deep breath. "That would be the responsible thing to do, no doubt, from the point of view of public service. But then I won't have my insurance."

"What do you mean?"

"I told Lina the file won't be released unless something happens to me or my family. If it's published, I lose my leverage and there's nothing to stop them from carrying out their threats. Then we have to live in fear forever."

"I take your point. Where are your wife and son now?"

"My wife is with friends near Granada and my son is somewhere along Route Nationale 7 in France, hitchhiking south to join my wife. How long are they going to have to stay in hiding?"

"Until Lina, or whatever her real name is, and all her accomplices are in custody."

"And how likely is that?"

"That depends on the effectiveness of the prosecution. There will be jurisdictional questions, no doubt. But the case is there. I'm pretty close to being able to tell you who's doing the hacking. There's a short list of suspects, all members or veterans of Unit 8200."

"What's that?"

"The Israeli cyberwar unit. The best on the planet. This is an Israeli operation. I can say that with some confidence now."

"They're working for the Saudis."

"You're not serious."

"I am. I'm going to put you in touch with a woman named Artemisa Pereda. She knows all about this. You two need to put the case together and blow the whistle. Blow it until you run out of breath. With any luck, I'll be back in Spain in a day or two and able to help."

"We'll need those wallet addresses."

"You'll get them once I'm sure nobody's going to come after me. They've committed at least one murder to cover this up. Haul in the killers, expose the paymasters, and I'll help you make the case against them in court. Until then, I'm keeping my insurance."

Pascual waits, watching boys kicking a soccer ball in the narrow street below, while Salera muses. Finally Salera says, *"Vale.* I hope you know what you're doing. *Suerte."*

Pascual sits bemused on a stool, cradling a glass of tea, listening to the dissonant murmur drifting up from the streets. The evening prayer call has come and gone, and the quarter is subsiding, exhausted by the heat and tumult of the day. Dris gestures at the jumble of rooftops stretching away into the dusk, fading into a scattered constellation of lights that diffuses in turn into the indigo abyss over the sea. "This is where hill people from the Rif, like my uncle, came to seek their fortunes. The ones that didn't try to swim the Strait, anyway. When my uncle moved here the roads weren't even paved. Now they have nice streets and sidewalks, but they still have forty percent youth unemployment. Lots of guys like this one." Dris reaches out to give a playful slap on the back of the head of the youth sitting next to him. Dark and intense, he was introduced to Pascual as cousin Slimane.

"Yo y todos mis amigos," says Slimane. His Castilian is a little stiffer than Dris's, but it is better than Dris's French. "I'm lucky. At least I have my father's shop. Not much of a career, but it's something to do. Most of my friends, they have nothing. If they're not selling *kif*

they're getting brainwashed at the mosque. Beni Makada sent more jihadis to Syria than any other place in Morocco. A lot of them didn't come back."

Dris says, "I suppose that's one way to deal with unemployment."

Pascual has nothing against hopeless Moroccan youths but no attention to spare for their plight. After assuring Sara and Rafael that everything will be over in a few days, he has spent the evening thinking of all the ways he could be proved wrong.

His phone buzzes in his pocket, Artemisa's number on the screen. "Give me some good news," says Pascual.

"Najib's dead."

Pascual stands and walks slowly to the edge of the roof, fetching up against the wall. "No."

"A suicide in his cell. That's the story they're selling." This is a new Artemisa, tense and breathless. "Me, I'm at the airport, about to get on a flight to Madrid. Just after I cleared customs my contact at the consulate called me to say the Sûreté was there, asking about me. If I get on this flight it will be a miracle."

"You must have made too much noise."

"No doubt. You need to get out of Morocco, however you can. Nobody's going to help you here. I have to go now, they're boarding. Good luck. Call me if you need help. I'll do what I can."

Pascual stands with the phone in his hand, waiting for the beating of his heart to subside. He turns to see Dris and Slimane staring at him. "Bad news?" says Dris.

"Fatal." Pascual puts his phone away. "The deaths have begun."

"Who?"

"A man I talked to last night. He was arrested this morning and now he's dead."

In the silence Pascual resumes his seat. Slimane says, "We've heard that one before. Shot while escaping?"

"A suicide in his cell."

"Another classic. Are you next?"

"I think that's the plan. How am I going to get back to Spain? I have no passport."

Dris and Slimane exchange a look. At length Dris shrugs. Slimane turns to Pascual. "How much money do you have?"

"In cash? A few dirhams and maybe fifty euros. I have a bank card, but my account's getting low. Maybe four or five hundred left."

Dris says, "I've got about three hundred euros."

Slimane shrugs. "It might be enough. There are different price levels. According to risk, of course."

Pascual says, "What are we talking about?"

Dris turns to him in the gloom, and Pascual can just make out the white of his teeth as he grins. "Well, what's the shortest route home? You can see it from here. Or you could, in the daytime."

Pascual stares. "You're serious."

"Why not? People do it all the time. Most of them don't drown. I say we go across the water."

Pascual has to laugh. "It seems to me I hear about a lot of them who do."

Slimane says, "You just don't hear about the ones who make it. I've got friends who've done it three or four times."

Pascual sighs. "Well, I can't say I have a better idea. What are we talking about, one of those leaky ten-meter *pateras* with a hundred people on board?"

Slimane shrugs. "Top shelf would be a *narcolancha,* a rigid-hulled inflatable with two or three 250-horsepower motors. The dealers use them to run *kif* across the Strait. You'll get across in thirty minutes, and your chances of arriving are excellent. They know how to dodge the patrol boats, or they pay them off. But that will cost you three or four thousand euros."

"So we're not going first class," says Pascual. "What does economy look like?"

"Well, there will be a range of options. The Strait is the narrowest point. People have done it in kayaks. Or inflatables. You can row a boat across, or sail one if you know how. If you don't have a boat, your best option is going to be an old fisherman from one of the villages along the cape. They'll take you across for five or six hundred euros. But you need to know someone."

"And who do you know?" says Dris.

"I know a man who buys fish for a restaurant here in Tangier. He asked me once if I had ever wanted to go to Spain. I told him no. He said if I ever did, let him know."

Dris and Pascual confer silently, peering at each other through the gloom. "*Vale,*" says Pascual, turning back to Slimane. "If you don't want to go to Spain, I certainly do."

Pascual wakes from a doze as the car slows and the hum of asphalt beneath the tires is replaced by the crackling of gravel. *"Llegamos,"* says Slimane, in the passenger seat in front of him. Pascual looks out the windshield and sees headlights sweeping over a high bank crowned with brush, a rough track descending through trees. When last he was conscious they were on a highway east of Tangier, mountains to the right and land sloping down to the sea on their left, the sun sinking behind them and the coast of Spain glowing in the sunset far off across the water.

In the front seat Dris and Slimane are muttering back and forth in Amazigh, with an edge of tension. Pascual opens his mouth to ask where they are, then closes it. The answer would mean nothing to him. Somewhere on the coast of Africa, about to plunge into the sea. Pascual wishes he could nap through the whole thing. He has been suppressing a feeling of dread since Dris came up the stairs onto the rooftop in Beni Makada two hours ago with the word that it was time to go.

"Joder," Dris swears as the car jounces over ruts. Sticking with

Castilian, he says to his cousin, "You're going to have to drive this thing back up. If you take the car back to Abu Hassan with a cracked oil pan, that's your problem."

"I'll have him send you the bill. Look, I think we're here."

The track has leveled off and the vista opened out, the trees left behind. Dris brakes as they come onto an open space at the foot of a steep slope, black sea feathering onto white sand a hundred meters away. A light flashes twice at the foot of the slope ahead of them. "There he is," says Slimane.

Dris drives for another twenty meters and stops. He switches off the engine and they get out. The only noise is the wash of the waves onto the beach. The light flashes once more and footsteps sound on the rocky ground. Pascual discerns two figures, maybe three, at the foot of the slope. Slimane steps forward and a conversation in Amazigh ensues. Dris reaches into the car for his flight bag and the five-liter bottle of water Pascual hopes will be sufficient to provision them.

A stiff breeze is sweeping in off the sea. Pascual turns up the collar of his jacket and pulls it tighter around him, fervently grateful for the moth-eaten sweater Dris produced from somewhere for him to wear under the jacket. Pascual has a feeling that his feet are not going to be the only part of him to turn cold. He turns to look out to sea. The night is dark with no moon; it is all he can do to distinguish sea from sky and land. The beach sweeps in a graceful kilometer-long arc from the jagged headland above them to another distant one. About fifty meters out he can see a boat, long and low, riding gently on the waves. Closer at hand Pascual can just make out a group of figures at the foot of the rocks, standing about a black shape drawn up on the sand.

Slimane is trudging back toward them over the scree. "You want to look at the boat?"

Dris beckons to Pascual and leads him down onto the beach. As they approach, the group at the foot of the rocks takes shape: four men gathered around a small inflatable raft, pulled up onto the beach. The four men are silhouettes, entirely black from head to toe against the faintly gleaming rocks, and as he nears them and makes out the whites of their eyes Pascual realizes they are Africans.

"Now that's service," says Dris. "They've even provided transport out to the boat. You won't have to get your feet wet." He peers through the darkness at the craft riding at anchor. "Looks solid enough. It's got a motor."

"That should get you across," says Slimane. He walks back up the beach toward the men who flashed the light.

Pascual nods at the Africans. Guessing at a likely language, he says, *"Bonsoir."*

A couple of the men mutter a greeting in return. "Two more?" one of them says. "We're already full."

Pascual can see someone moving on the boat, bending over the motor. He judges the craft to be at least ten meters long. It looks ample to carry six men. He shrugs and turns away to follow Dris back up the beach to where Slimane is in consultation with the two men who appear to be running the show. As they approach, Slimane says something in Amazigh to Dris, who turns to Pascual. "It's time to pay."

Pascual reaches inside his jacket and pulls out the roll of banknotes he and Dris put together in the afternoon, the dregs of Pascual's hundred-thousand-euro stake. "How much does he want?"

"As agreed, six hundred euros."

"I can't see a thing." Dris activates the flashlight app on his phone and holds it so Pascual can see to count out the notes, shielding it from view with his body. He takes the money, douses the light, and walks to hand it to Slimane. Pascual stuffs the remaining banknotes, maybe enough for breakfast and bus fare if they make it to Spain, back into his pocket.

Dris says, "So, are we ready for this?"

Pascual squares around to face him. "I suppose I am. You don't have to be. You can get back in the car with Slimane and go back to Tangier. You can fly home tomorrow on the return half of your plane ticket as if none of this ever happened."

"What, and let you have all the fun? Forget it." Dris's teeth flash in the dark.

Pascual squeezes his arm. *"Gracies, noi."*

The man with the light flashes it briefly on the notes as Slimane hands over the money and growls something inaudible. He raises the light and flashes it three times, and a second later the motor rumbles to life on the boat offshore. Slimane comes to join them and says, "That's it, then. *Bon voyage."*

Dris embraces him, clapping him on the back. There is an exchange in Amazigh, then Dris hands him the keys to the car. "Take the car back to Abu Hassan, tell your father thanks for everything. We'll be all right. I'll call you when we get to Tarifa."

Slimane extends his hand to Pascual. "Good luck."

Pascual follows Dris down to where the raft is beached. As they approach, one of the Africans leans down to rummage in the bottom and tosses two life jackets to them. "Can you swim?"

"Well enough," says Dris. "I won't drown."

Another man says, "More important, can you row?" He lifts a short paddle from the bottom of the raft.

Dris casts a look out to the boat and laughs. "Considering the distance we have to cover, I think I can manage." He leans down to place the water bottle and his bag in the raft, next to a six-pack of one-liter bottles already there.

Nobody else laughs. The Africans have already donned their life jackets. Two of them grasp handles on the side of the raft and pull it into the light surf, then jump aboard.

"I guess we'll be getting our feet wet after all," says Dris, wading into the water. Pascual has managed to get his life jacket on and cinched tight, and he stoops to take off his shoes and socks and roll up his trouser legs, seeing no reason to spoil his fine leather brogues. The Africans and Dris have all boarded by the time Pascual manages to flop aboard the tossing craft, soaked to the waist and gasping from the shock of the water. The thing is just big enough for six, and there is a great deal of jostling and some swearing as people settle in place. Pascual realizes that what he thought was the bow, drawn up on the sand, was actually the stern; the four Africans have taken the positions in the bow. The Africans have deployed the four paddles and sit with them poised over the side; Pascual wonders what they are waiting for. Alarmingly, the boat ahead of them is underway, turning slowly to head out to sea. *"Allons-y,"* he says. Why are they not paddling furiously in pursuit of the boat?

The penny does not drop until the tow line snaps taut, jerking the raft enough that Pascual nearly falls backward over the stern, saved by Dris's strong grip. He steadies and adjusts to the motion of the craft as the boat tows them slowly out toward the open sea.

Dris and Pascual slowly turn to look at one another. "You don't think . . ." says Pascual.

Dris makes no answer. The wind hits them in the face as they clear the headland. Dris begins to swear, slowly and quietly, first in Amazigh, then Catalan, finally in Castilian. "The thieves," he says. *"Chorizos, cabrones, capullos."* The raft rises and falls on a swell, the Africans beginning to experiment with the paddles, trying to steady the craft. Pascual can see nothing; he might as well be immersed in a vast tank of ink. He is already chilled by the wind.

Abruptly the sound of the boat engine is cut off, and the raft ceases to move forward. A voice comes from the darkness ahead, yelling something Pascual fails to understand. One of the Africans is leaning over the bow of the raft, hauling in the suddenly slack towline. The one in front of Pascual twists around and thrusts a paddle at Dris. "Here," he says. "You think you can manage? We'll see how you do. Now you row. Straight ahead, for Spain."

Suffering has never been part of Pascual's skill set. He has known people who exult in it, from his bullheaded cousin Jordi, pressing the pace obnoxiously on hikes in the Empordà, to the dead-ender Palestinian thugs in the Yemeni training camps, embracing masochistic endurance rituals in the hopes it will help them kill more Jews. It has always seemed more reasonable to Pascual to avoid suffering whenever possible.

Where not possible, he struggles. Here in the middle of the Strait of Gibraltar in the middle of the night, with hypothermia slowly sapping the warmth from his core, hands blistering from the endless paddling, neck chafed raw by the life jacket, stomach in agony, Pascual is close to giving in to a despair as black as the night around him. It would be easy to simply lean back and let himself go into the dark welcoming waves; he has heard that drowning is not a bad way to go.

"Courage," says Dris, his voice ragged. "Don't give up. One hundred more strokes."

"Vale." Somehow Pascual finds the strength to pull the paddle

through another stroke. Very quickly after being cast adrift, a rough democracy crystallized on the raft as six men realized that without cooperation they would not survive the night, much less reach Spain. With four paddles among six men, a system was worked out for sharing the work: paddle five hundred strokes and then pass the paddle to the man behind you, forward if you are at the stern. They take turns counting aloud. Five hundred seemed an impossible number to Pascual at the start; now he has lost count of how many turns he has taken. Now the next man's five hundred strokes are all too short a time for exhausted muscles to recover.

"À gauche, plus à gauche." At the bow Laurent shouts back over his shoulder. The Africans are Laurent, Seydou, René and Ibrahim, all Francophones, three from Senegal and one from Ivory Coast. The introductions were Dris's idea, an attempt to build camaraderie with a group that was obviously dismayed at having two more passengers appear at the last minute to add weight and take away space.

"How much farther, do you think?" Pascual knows the question is a mark of his inadequacy, his desperate need for a reason to live. He can see intermittently, as the raft rises and falls on the swell, faint lights far ahead of them. They have drawn no closer for hours.

Dris says, "It's about fifteen kilometers from where we left to Tarifa. People have swum it."

Pascual finds this hysterically funny but lacks the wherewithal to laugh. "I would almost prefer to swim. How much farther?"

Seydou twists to growl at him over his shoulder. "Save your breath for paddling. You'll know it when we get there."

"We have gone at least halfway," says Dris.

René cries out. *"Merde,* you made me lose count." He slumps sideways, his paddle trailing in the water. The raft yaws, dips and rises again.

"Rest for five minutes," says Laurent. "Don't lose that paddle."

René pulls in the paddle. "Is there more water?" Dris leans to hand him the five-liter bottle, considerably lighter than it was several hours ago. For a time nobody speaks and there is only the vast hollow sighing of wind and sea and, just audible beneath it, the sound of six men panting.

"Those lights are moving to the left," says Seydou. "Where is this current taking us?"

"East," says Laurent. "Toward Sicily."

"Toward the wider part of the Strait," says Dris. "We can't afford to rest too long."

Ibrahim says, "There's more wind. The waves are getting bigger."

"There's a storm coming in from the Atlantic," says Seydou. "I can smell it. They smell just like this in Dakar."

There is silence for a moment as six men contemplate the image of their vessel in a full-blown Atlantic gale. Laurent says, "Then we'd better get back to work."

"I can see the coast," says Laurent.

Nobody responds. Nobody has the energy to do anything but paddle. Even René and Seydou are paddling with their hands, clawing desperately over the side, as the raft soars and plunges on the swell surging in from the Atlantic. It has become clear to every man on the raft that there will be no more resting if they want to reach shore before the full force of the storm crushes them. To their right the eastern sky is lightening, dawn approaching; to their left is the abyss: a sky blacker than night above an ocean, all the more terrifying now that there is light to see it, waves beginning to show whitecaps.

Pascual has taken refuge in a trancelike state, eyes closed, in which he can contemplate his physical agony with detachment at each stroke of the paddle. Pull, straining against the water: here is the sting of his lacerated hands on the shaft of the paddle, here is the groaning protest of the depleted muscles of arms, back, shoulders, core. Lean forward and do it again: here is the pain. The pain is your life now, and it will never stop.

It seems I can suffer after all, Pascual thinks, if there is no choice.

"Donne-moi ça!" Seydou twists to rip the paddle from Pascual's hands. Pascual would be grateful for the respite if he were not ashamed. He grants himself a few seconds of rest before he begins paddling with his hand, knowing it is futile and pathetic.

"Not much farther," gasps Dris, digging at the heaving sea with his paddle. "Hang on a little longer and get ready to swim."

Swim? That was not in the contract. In delirium Pascual wonders where he can lodge a protest. Again he wants to laugh but finds the effort too much. He claws at the water, putting what concentration he can muster into coordinating with Seydou's paddle strokes.

Just as Pascual has decided that lapsing into a blissful coma would be preferable to any further striving, he becomes aware of a new sound beneath the howl of the wind. He squints into the spray, and as the raft rises on the crest of a wave, he sees that this rumble he is hearing is the noise of surf breaking on a shore that is, amazingly, at a distance that can be measured in meters rather than kilometers.

Hundreds of them, to be sure, but with this immense surge now sweeping them in toward land, they go fast. In the growing light Pascual is startled to see how close they are to land, after all that. He has spent the night dreaming of welcoming white sand beaches and seaside amenities, stumbling from the raft to the nearest bar; surely those lights he saw in the distance must mean civilization? But now he sees only barren hills rising from the surf, a desolate coast.

Laurent screams something at the top of his lungs. The paddlers stop all at once, and everyone looks to see where he is pointing. *"Hostia puta,"* says Dris, and the awe in his voice chills Pascual.

A line of jagged rocks juts up from the surf like black teeth in a rabid maw. The swell is carrying them toward a gigantic shredder. There is a moment of frozen horror and then Seydou screams, "Jump!" and rolls over the side of the raft into the sea. He disappears for a moment and bobs back up, thrashing, three meters astern, wild-eyed and spewing water. "Jump! You're going to die!"

That is all René needs to join him, making the raft lurch as he shoves off with his feet and falls backward into the waves. Laurent and Ibrahim stare back in horror, paddles suspended. The raft surges on toward the churn of water through the sawtooth reef.

Dris shoots his arm out to the right. *"Là-bas, à droite!* There's a gap. Row! Row hard, to the right!" He digs into the sea with his paddle. Laurent and Ibrahim snap back to action and Pascual grabs the paddle Seydou jettisoned; for a moment they all flail at random, rhythm lost. Then Dris twists to shove his paddle over the stern, using it as a rudder, slewing the raft to the right. Pascual has the sense to help, pulling back with the paddle till the nose of the craft comes around. Then he begins to paddle like hell. Dris screams out the count. *"Un, deux, trois . . ."*

They are in a race to make the gap before the wave carries them onto the rocks. The raft is lighter minus two men, and the prospect of being drawn over those rocks like cheese over a grater is pumping adrenaline into their veins. Pascual takes one look at the reef, coming closer at a terrifying rate, then closes his eyes and bends to his work. He digs at the water in a frenzy, to the point of complete muscle failure, and when he collapses and looks to his left he sees that they have lost: there, a few feet away in a raging surf, are the rocks that are going to cut them to pieces, and there is no gap in sight.

"Row!" Dris screams, and Pascual pulls the paddle through twice more before there is a tremendous jolt, the raft tips, and Pascual gets a last poignant glimpse of the rosy eastern sky as he begins to pitch over the side into the foam.

He is hauled back by a hand on his collar, and instead of capsizing, the raft miraculously rights itself and thuds into a cauldron of white water. Pascual is on his back on the bottom of the raft and Dris is on top of him; the raft is yawing and pitching with incredible violence and water is cascading down on them.

For a moment Pascual is underwater with no air in his lungs and he panics, lashing out. Then his face is clear and he can take in a great gasping breath, but he is stunned as the raft slams down onto rocks, dealing him a painful blow on the shoulder. A surge of water carries the raft free, and then suddenly it is over; they are bobbing in shallow water, buffeted by waves, and Dris is slipping over the side.

Pascual manages to pull himself up to a sitting position. Dris is hauling on the raft by the handle at the side, pulling it toward a rocky beach a few meters away. Laurent and Ibrahim are nowhere to be seen. Pascual winces as he maneuvers to tumble off the raft and then cries out as he bangs a knee on a rock. Fervently glad he troubled to put his shoes back on during the night, he steps gingerly over an ankle-breaking seafloor, face screwed up in pain, hanging onto the side of the raft, until it beaches itself and there is only a narrow band of rocks to cross before a strip of sand.

Pascual pitches forward onto the sand and lies with his eyes closed for what seems a long time. He becomes aware of voices behind him in the surf and he rolls to see Dris and Laurent pulling a dark limp body through the froth.

Pascual watches in dumb exhaustion as Dris and Laurent drag Ibrahim onto the beach. The way Ibrahim's arm drops onto the sand when Dris releases it tells Pascual all he needs to know. Dris stands for a time looking out to sea, hands shielding his face from the wind-driven rain that has finally caught them. There is no sign of René or Seydou. Dris comes stumbling back to sink onto the sand beside Pascual. At the water's edge Laurent weeps as rain lashes him, bending over Ibrahim, who is done with weeping forever.

"We were lucky," says Dris.

Having left Laurent behind to wait for René and Seydou to wash up on shore, Pascual is forced to concede that the outcome could have been worse, but in his present state of numb exhaustion, what he feels is some distance from a warm feeling of good fortune. "You saved my life," he says. "Thank you."

Dris makes no reply. Rain drums on the roof above them and wind whistles through gaping orifices that once held doors and windows. In a pelting rain he and Dris staggered two hundred meters up a barren slope to a gravel road that took them around a point to this cluster of abandoned buildings, a round tower on a promontory and a couple of long stone structures, one of them roofless, with the look of old military barracks. In the corner farthest from the door Dris has managed to light a fire with his cigarette lighter, with collected trash for kindling and the last remnants of wood ripped from window frames for fuel. It might be enough to stop Pascual's shivering, but it will die out before anything like comfort is in sight.

Pascual is grateful to be on dry land but would be happier if that entailed being dry. "What now?" he says.

"When the rain stops, we walk. Let's see where we are." Dris reaches inside his jacket and pulls out a clear plastic bag, zip-sealed at the top. Pascual is startled to see their two mobile phones and the USB drive inside, along with a few banknotes and Dris's passport. For twelve hours he has thought of nothing but survival, and now here is life with all its complications clamoring for attention.

"You were well prepared," he says.

"Not well enough," says Dris. "If I'd known what swindlers Slimane's pals were I'd have shot them and taken the boat. But I think all this stayed dry, so that's something." He hands Pascual his phone. "You want the gadget?"

"Not yet. Keep it until I know what the hell I'm going to do with it." Pascual's fingers are trembling and he does not even try to turn on his phone. Dris jabs at his, waits, curses and says, "No signal. Where the hell are we?"

Pascual lets his head droop forward onto his knees. He wishes he could go to sleep. Dris says, "We can't be too far from Algeciras. That current pushed us a long way east. I say we try and get to a road and see if we can't call a taxi to come out from Algeciras to get us. But I'm not going anywhere until the rain stops. Meanwhile, take off your socks and your shirt and let's see if we can't dry them out a bit. You're better off naked than sitting there in wet clothes. *Cago en Déu,* what I wouldn't give for a towel and a blanket right now."

■ ■ ■ ■

A helicopter is hovering over the rocks where Pascual and his shipmates made landfall. "They won't find anything but bodies," says the farmer, jutting his grizzled chin at the spectacle as he steers carefully up the track. "Nobody goes onto those rocks and survives."

Pascual can barely understand his thick Andalusian dialect, replete with dropped *s*'s and elided *d*'s. Dris roused Pascual from an uneasy doze when the farmer came chugging up the track in an old Renault open-bed pickup from a scattering of buildings now visible a few hundred meters further along the coast.

The rain has abated and the wind dropped as the storm blows itself out. Jammed between Dris and the farmer, Pascual has stopped shivering, but he can feel his weakened immune system preparing itself to succumb to whatever biohazards may be wafting about his nostrils. Dris appears to be none the worse for wear, a little bedraggled but believable in the role they are trying to sell to the farmer, of two foolish hikers who set out to walk to Tarifa along the coastal path without checking the weather forecast. "You're lucky it caught you before you'd gone very far," the farmer says. "There's no shelter all the way to Tarifa once you get around the point."

"Next time we'll take the bus," says Dris. "If you could just drop us on the highway, we'd be grateful. We can call a taxi from Algeciras."

The old man shrugs. "I'm going to town to buy paint. Where do you want me to drop you?"

With only a second's hesitation Dris says, "We're staying at a hotel near the bus station."

In half an hour they are in Algeciras, in front of the bus station, babbling thanks and waving as the truck pulls away from the curb. Traffic zooms around a roundabout, palms wave in the breeze;

through a gateway they can see buses drawn up in bays and on the opposite side of the roundabout a pair of taxis sit idle at the entrance to a train station. Mere hours ago they were thrashing for their lives in the surf. Pascual sways a little on his feet and Dris steadies him with a hand on his arm. "All right?"

"All right. Listen, I can't afford to pay you anymore. But I could put a ticket on a credit card and you could jump on a train over there, or fly home from Málaga."

"Is it over? Is your problem solved?"

"Not yet."

"Then why would I go home? I didn't sign on to leave you standing on a street in Algeciras looking like a drowned rat." He casts a look around, scanning the roundabout and the streets feeding into it. "Another thing I didn't sign on for is to get you scooped up by the police. I'd bet good money that old bastard is talking to them right now."

Pascual is dimly aware that fatigue, cold and hunger are making him stupid. "You think so?"

"He didn't believe that story we fed him for a moment. Would you?"

"I suppose not. But I think the police may be my best option at this point."

"Let's walk." Dris steers Pascual by the elbow. They skirt the roundabout and go up the first street beyond the railway station. The sun has come out and Pascual is beginning to revive a little. At the first corner they find a bar with tables on the sidewalk and sit, still damp but no longer dripping. The waiter who eventually saunters out of the bar scowls but takes their order. Pascual takes out his phone and powers it up. He sees he has missed a call from Artemisa but he has other priorities. He taps on Sara's number. He has a signal but the call still fails. He tries again. Finally it goes through and miraculously Sara says, "Where are you?"

At the sound of her voice Pascual nearly breaks down. When he can control his voice he says, "In Algeciras. We're safe. Is Rafa there?"

"Not yet. He called from Valencia last night. He says with luck he'll be here today." Sara's voice is fading out. "When will we see you?"

"I don't know. Today, tomorrow maybe. We'll get there as soon as we can."

Sara's voice is faint. "I can barely hear you. The signal's weak up here . . ." The call drops and Pascual puts the phone away.

When their coffee and a couple of *bocadillos de jamón* arrive Dris says, "Don't be too anxious to talk to the police. What does your mystery lady say?"

Pascual remembers the call from Artemisa. He returns it and she answers immediately. "Where are you?"

"In Algeciras."

"Are you in a safe place? Can you stay there?"

Pascual has recovered sufficiently to produce a puff of laughter. "Safe compared to what? I'm hoping to get picked up by the Guardia Civil."

"No. Don't let that happen. Go join your wife and son."

"Why? How could I be better off at this point than safe in a cell, waiting for the Germans to come and pick me up?"

"The Israelis will get to you before the Germans do."

"The Israelis? You're joking."

"Not at all. Listen, there were three hard cases from the CNI waiting for me when I got off the plane in Madrid. They had me up all night answering questions."

"Why?"

"Somebody in Israel put a word in the ear of somebody here. The colleagues who have been helping me got an earful as well. I was instructed to cease and desist at once, to stop impeding an ongoing operation of the security services."

Pascual is dumbfounded. "What, the Spanish are in on it, too?"

"I think it's just professional courtesy. There have been very good relations between our services and the Israelis for a long time. I would guess someone in Jerusalem called someone in Madrid and said, Listen, friend, we've got something going in Tangier, and a gadfly lawyer and a couple of disreputable ex-officers of your service are trying to blow the whistle on it. Can you help us?"

"Good God, they can cover it up at this late date?"

"They can certainly try. I've been gagged, on national security grounds, and it's still possible I'll be arrested. And I'd bet you they're working on their own version of events, which they'll put out at the first opportunity."

"So what do we do?"

"You get to a safe place and wait. I've got other allies, other people I can appeal to. Things are going to move very fast now, I think."

The faster the better if it gets me to a hot shower and a warm bed, Pascual thinks. "What about you? Are you in danger?"

"I think we can assume that anyone who knows about this is in danger. So the implication of that is, tell everybody. When they realize they can't kill everybody who knows about it, we'll be safe."

As Pascual is putting his phone away Dris says, "There they are. What did I tell you?"

Pascual looks down the street and sees a Guardia Civil patrol car pulling in through the gateway of the bus station.

"Looking for us, you think?"

"I'd bet on it."

Pascual sighs. "I'm not sure we could have gotten on a bus or a train anyway. How much money do you have left?"

Dris points at his change lying on the table. "What you see here. I've got the bank card but there's next to nothing left on it. What about you?"

"I've got the credit card they gave me. The only problem is, they are almost certainly monitoring it. Using it means leaving tracks."

Dris turns his head to look toward the bus station. "I'd say we have ten to fifteen minutes here. When they don't see us there or at the railway station, they'll come straight here."

Pascual nods. "There's one thing I could do with the credit card."

"What's that?"

"If we can find a bank, I could get a cash advance on the credit card. And then when the police have given up on us we could go back there to the railway station and I could use the card to reserve two train tickets to Barcelona. And then we walk across the street with our cash and buy a couple of seats on the bus to Granada."

Dris looks at it for a couple of seconds and smiles. "That could work."

■ ■ ■ ■

"It's not working," says Pascual, staring in dismay at the screen of the cash machine set into the facade of the bank, which is flashing *Tarjeta anulada*. He turns to Dris. "The card has been canceled."

Dris blinks a few times. "What now?"

Pascual takes a deep breath. He can feel the coils tightening around his chest. "They'll be able to see the location where we tried the transaction. So now we get the hell out of Algeciras." None too soon, Pascual thinks; he has yet to detect any particular charm in the place. They are in a labyrinth of narrow pedestrian streets near the gigantic port that makes Algeciras one of Europe's prime entry points for narcotics. On the walk from the bus station Pascual began to limp, his unsuitable shoes beginning to blister his sodden feet. Pascual is aware of the pathetic figure he must be cutting, the dapper sport jacket ruined, his face unshaved, hair in greasy strands. Soon he will begin to smell.

They head downhill, past shops mostly shuttered for the siesta. "I could steal a car," Dris murmurs.

"Let's try not to commit too many outrages," says Pascual. "I think our best course is to call someone in Granada and see if they can come and rescue us."

"How fast can they get here? Granada's a long way away."

Pascual has no answer. They emerge onto a busy seafront boulevard and Pascual instantly feels exposed. For lack of an alternative they proceed along the pavement, aware of cars sweeping by. Signs point the way to the ferry terminal; beyond several lanes of traffic they can see cranes in the port, and in the distance far across the bay the famous Rock lies black against the sky. "There's somebody who might help us a lot closer at hand," says Pascual, "if we can give him a good enough story."

"Pascual," says Pascual into his phone, enunciating with care. "Tell Leonid I am a friend of Sancho's."

At the other end there is silence, and Pascual suddenly sees his desperate ploy for what it is, utter foolishness. Finding a number for El Pirata in Marbella was child's play, but so far he has been unable to get the woman who answered his call even to admit to the existence of someone named Leonid, much less put him on the line. Pascual is on the point of ending the call when the woman says, "And who is Sancho?"

Pascual is about to say, "Sancho Panza, who the hell do you think," but he stops himself. "Vasily Andreyevich," he says, making it sound as ominous as he knows how. "Sancho Panza because of the *panza*. Now let me talk to Leonid."

Only a couple of seconds go by before the woman says, *"Momento."*

Pascual stands in a recessed doorway with a finger in his ear while Dris leans on the wall, listlessly thumbing his phone. They are a couple of streets back from the seafront, in a quiet, charmless quarter. "Who are you?" says a voice in Pascual's ear.

"My name is Pascual. Are you Leonid?"

"What do you want?"

The tone is not encouraging but Pascual perseveres. "Sancho told me to talk to you if I ever needed anything. I'm in Algeciras and I need a ride."

"This is not a fucking taxi stand."

The voice is deep and rough around the edges, the Castilian fluent but accented. Pascual says, "I'm aware of that. I need a ride because the police are looking for me and I'm out of money and friends."

"That's your problem. I've not been told about anybody named Pascual."

Pascual takes a calming breath and says, "If you can call Sancho you can ask him about me. I'll wait."

This brings no response. Pascual is about to hurl his phone at the pavement when the voice says, "Wait, then," and the call ends.

Dris gives him a questioning look over his shoulder. Pascual says, "He'll get back to me. Do we have enough money for more coffee?"

They take refuge in a Moroccan restaurant in an arcade along the boulevard, squeezed between a travel agency and a two-star hotel. Dris carries on a desultory conversation in Arabic with the proprietor, who seems unconcerned by their dishevelment, while Pascual broods over a glass of tea. He has already written off the Sancho ploy and is wondering if they can stow away on a ferry or a container ship or a lorry full of bricks. His phone buzzes and he nearly knocks the glass over while tearing it out of his pocket. "I need your exact location," says Leonid.

■ ■ ■ ■

It happens fast, in the time it takes to nurse a second glass of tea. Marbella is a scant eighty kilometers up the road, but Pascual guesses that a Russian crime lord with a base in Marbella and an interest in international shipping will have assets in Algeciras. The bearded specimen who gets out of the Mercedes at the curb and scans the terrace of the restaurant with a professional eye wears a black T-shirt that looks sprayed on over a set of weight-room muscles. With his fair complexion and eyes of subzero blue he looks as if he were born somewhere north of the Black Sea. He gives Pascual a head-to-toe scan as he approaches.

Pascual is already pushing away from the table. "Kolya?"

Kolya merely nods and shifts his attention to Dris, recognizing a fellow hard case. They exchange the slightest of nods and Kolya leads them to the Mercedes. Pulling away from the curb he says, "You need anything? Doctor? Clothes? Something to drink?"

Pascual says, "All of the above, but no emergency. For now, just get us off the radar. We have to get to Barcelona eventually, but a night in a warm bed would do us good."

And that is it for the conversation; small talk is not part of the job and Kolya knows his job. He manhandles the Mercedes through portside traffic and onto a highway that swings away from the sea. Pascual watches the hills go by and fights sleep as he tries to think two moves ahead. He knows he has swapped one set of problems for another and hopes he has won the exchange.

Eventually sleep wins, and when Pascual is awakened by the slowing of the car he finds they have entered the nightmare wonderland of the Costa del Sol. Here mass tourism, vice, graft and money laundering have spurred fifty years of breakneck development and smothered a hundred kilometers of sun-blessed coastline under concrete. Pascual watches a Burger King go by, followed by an Irish pub. On the right is the sea, palms line the road, and high-rise apartment buildings climb the slopes on their left. Pascual trades a look with Dris. They discussed alternatives while waiting for Kolya: split up or stick together, reveal their true destination or play it close to the vest, ask for transport only or hold out for shelter. Dris could probably handle a night of sleeping rough but Pascual does not have the stomach for it. It was decided to see if Russian hospitality will stretch to a night's lodging, a shower and laundry service.

In this case Russian hospitality does better than that. The house they are taken to is somewhere past Marbella in a nameless region of the sprawl, on a winding street climbing away from the sea, comfortably above the hurly-burly of the main drag and comfortably separated from the villas on either side. White stucco and red tile roof, steps going up from a locked street-level gate, with a terrace overlooking a small garden full of jasmine and hibiscus and a view of the sea. The man who descends to the gate at Kolya's honk to admit them shows them to their rooms at the end of a tiled hall. He is Latin American, possibly Colombian, short, dark and brisk in his movements and speech. "Put your clothes outside the door and I'll wash them. There are robes in the closets. Do you need a doctor?"

"My feet are blistered, that's all. Some antiseptic and some bandages would be good."

"I'll bring them to your room. When you're ready, you'll find drinks in the dining room. I can prepare supper whenever you wish."

The shower is heaven. Pascual is in a daze, astonished to be alive. He remembers Laurent weeping on the beach. Was that only this morning? He waits for a sharp pang of survivor's guilt to pass. When he has dried himself and dealt with the blisters on his feet, he must contend with the question of whether he needs sleep or food more urgently. He opts for food and puts on the plush robe and slippers he finds in the closet.

He finds Dris on a chaise longue on the terrace, in a robe that matches his and with a bottle of beer in his hand. "Don't we make a cute couple," Pascual says.

"At least we're dry." Dris takes a pull on the beer. "What are they going to charge us for all this?"

Pascual pulls over a chair. "In theory, they owe me. I'm just cashing in a favor." He shoots a look in the direction of the kitchen, where he can hear the Colombian banging pots. "But that's a good question. The only thing I'm confident of is that they won't give us up. That would go against the code. But it might be wise to slip out first thing in the morning."

The Colombian comes out of the kitchen and announces that a meal will be served in half an hour. Pascual declines a drink and retreats to his bedroom. Reclining on the bed, he calls Artemisa. "Any news?"

"I've talked with a friend in the office of the Secretary of State for Security. He says to lie low while he does a little probing. The lid is being screwed down because the Israelis are selling it as a counter-terror operation. Maybe it's a rogue operation, or semi-rogue, a case of outsourcing with a discreet wink from the higher-ups. Or maybe it's a Mossad operation all the way. Fear of Iran makes strange bedfellows, and the whole thing could be a way to get Libya's oil before Iran does. You know the Iranians have to be looking for a way around the sanctions, and they would love to get their hands on a revenue stream like that. Whatever it is, it goes high enough that somebody over there got our agencies to agree to keep it quiet. It's bound to fail. But for the moment you have to keep your head down. Are you in a safe place?"

"Almost. Call it temporary shelter."

Pascual signs off and calls Sara. "Tomorrow," he says. "I'll be with you tomorrow."

"I hope so." Sara sounds subdued, perhaps merely from boredom at this point. "Then you can explain to Rafa and me how this is all going to end."

"He's there, is he?"

"He's here. He decided to take the bus from Valencia. He was tired of thumbing rides."

"How did he pay for it?"

"I don't know, Pascual. What does it matter?"

"They can monitor the activity on his bank card. I explained that to you."

"I don't know what he did. He's here, that's all I know. José Antonio picked him up in Granada."

Pascual sighs. "It's probably all right. I'll explain everything when I get there. Tomorrow."

The Colombian knocks on the door of his room. When Pascual opens it, the man hands him a neatly folded pile of clothes with a pair of shoes on top. "They got these for you," he says. "If you're being hunted, you'll want to get rid of the clothes you came in. The jacket was ruined anyway."

Pascual sorts through the pile: his own underwear and socks, freshly laundered; jeans, a cotton sport shirt, a light windbreaker, more or less in his size. The shoes are trainers, easy on his bandaged feet. He dresses and emerges from his room to find supper laid out in the combined living and dining area: garbanzos and chorizo, a green salad, bread and cheese, a bottle of *tinto*. Dris is already tucking in, outfitted in fresh clothes.

They have shoved their plates away when footsteps come up from the street and the front door opens. Three men enter. For a moment Pascual thinks he is back in Cyprus; these could be the same toughs that welcomed him there. On closer inspection he realizes they are only stamped by the same die, generic Slavic bad boys, thick-necked, short-haired and no doubt short-tempered to boot. They lock eyes instantly with Dris and again there is the mutual recognition, half tribute and half animosity, of members of the streetfighter class. The alpha male comes in last, the oldest and hairiest, with a slightly grayed pompadour and Brezhnev-class eyebrows. From the look of him he will also have the shortest temper. *"Buenas tardes,"* he growls, and Pascual recognizes the voice.

He stands and extends his hand. "Leonid?"

Leonid ignores his hand. The other two toughs casually gravitate to the living area and drape themselves on the furniture, positioned to keep anybody who might panic from making it to the terrace or the street door. Leonid takes a seat at the head of the table. "All well? Food and lodging satisfactory?"

Pascual nods. "Completely. We thank you."

Leonid grunts once, has a brief stare-down with Dris, and turns back to Pascual. "Why are the police looking for you?"

An excellent question, Pascual thinks; he hopes he has come up with the right answer. To a criminal organization a man being sought by the police is always a liability. "Because I know who stole twenty-two billion dollars."

Leonid stares without blinking while Pascual sweats out the silence. "Where is the twenty-two billion dollars?" says Leonid.

Pascual manages a smile that he hopes looks confident. "That's a little complicated," he says. "Some of it is going to go into accounts that Sancho and his pals in Cyprus will be able to access, thanks to me. I'm hoping that's earned me a night's lodging."

Leonid grunts again, softly. "Sancho is grateful. He told us to take good care of you. But he also asked a question."

"What's that?"

"What happens if the police catch you?"

"That would be unfortunate. But only for me. What am I going to tell them about you, or Sancho, or his pals in Cyprus? It's the source of the twenty-two billion they'll be interested in."

Leonid stares at Pascual for a long time. He grunts one final time, casts another look at Dris, and then pushes away from the table. He stands and looks down at Pascual. "You are in a very interesting position."

"You could call it that."

Leonid looks at his men in the living area and says, "Make our guests comfortable. Perhaps they would like a game of cards." He pauses, a thought striking him. "Perhaps you would like some more interesting company? Female company? You've had a rough time. You could probably use some physical therapy. It's easily arranged."

Pascual raises a hand. "Thank you, no. I am a happily married man."

Leonid raises one impressive eyebrow. "I don't see what that has to do with it, but as you wish. The young man?"

Dris shakes his head. "Very kind, but I could use a sound night's sleep."

Leonid shrugs. "Very well." He makes for the door. Over his shoulder he says, "The house is yours. You can stay here as long as you want."

Pascual says, "Very kind, thank you. But I think we'll be pushing on tomorrow."

Leonid pulls open the door but pauses and turns. "Whatever you wish. Sleep well."

Sleeping well is something Pascual hopes to achieve again someday, but he fears it will not be tonight, despite his crippling fatigue. He has managed to strip to his underwear in preparation for collapsing on the bed when his phone goes off. The number showing is Salera's. Pascual considers ignoring the call but decides the stakes are too high to risk it. "Are you still in Morocco?" says Salera.

"No, we managed to cross the Strait. We're back on Spanish soil and drying out."

"I congratulate you. If you were still in Morocco, you would probably be in jail."

"Or worse."

"Not much worse than a Moroccan jail, I hear, but I take your point. Would you like to know who you're up against? I can give you names now."

"What, real names?"

"The ones on their official records, anyway. It wasn't easy to get this. We were able to work back from some of the hackers' code to the particular team involved and then with input from your lawyer friend we managed to correlate phone data with travel vouchers and so forth and come up with some photos, which she identified."

"You amaze me. Who are they?"

"The woman who calls herself Lina appears to be Tamar Ulitskaya. She's quite likely an actual Unit 8200 member. And we think your friend Felix is Pavel Landau, an ex-Mossad officer who left the service three years ago. They're both Israelis of Russian origin."

Pascual repeats the names. "Well, then. Thank you. I'll know what to call them the next time I see them."

"I think if I were you I would try to avoid that. You're in a position to thwart the heist of the century, and they can't be too happy about that."

"No. I'm hoping to become invisible while somebody else does the thwarting."

After a silence Salera says, "You may not have that luxury. I have a feeling you're going to be in this up to the eyes, right up to the end."

Pascual comes awake deep in the night with somebody's hand over his mouth. When he is conscious enough to panic he hears Dris's soft whisper next to his ear. *"Tranquilo."* Pascual lets his heartbeat subside, then nods slightly. Dris removes his hand and breathes, "We're leaving. Move slowly."

Pascual rises, bedsprings creaking madly beneath him. The room is pitch black with the metal blinds cranked down over the window, but a patch of floor is suddenly lit by Dris's phone, guiding Pascual to the chair where he draped his clothes. "Get dressed in the bathroom, shoes and all," Dris whispers.

Pascual obeys. Made stupid by fatigue, he is happy to have Dris make the decisions. They had no chance to confer after Leonid left; passing up the game of cards, Pascual collapsed into bed, hoping the morning would bring a clear head and a chance to plot tactics.

When he comes out of the bathroom, Dris flashes the light once; he is at the door of the room, listening. Pascual wonders how Dris made it into his room without rousing anyone; the lad displays unsuspected talents at every turn. Now he comes toward Pascual on light feet and steers him gently with a hand on his arm into the walk-in closet opposite the window. He gently slides the folding doors almost shut, leans close and says, "Don't move until I tell you." Pascual nods. Dris steps to the window, grasps the strap that will raise the blinds, and after a brief pause hauls down on it with rapid strokes.

The blinds make a terrific racket coming up, as things become visible in the light from the streetlamps outside. The blinds slam into their housing at the top and Dris twists the handle and tears open the twin casement windows. Footsteps are coming rapidly down the hall. Dris jumps back from the window and squeezes in beside Pascual in the closet. Pascual hears the door to the room slam against the wall and a muttered curse in Russian. The man comes into sight as he rushes to the window and leans out. The second man appears on the walk outside and they exchange a few words. The man outside dashes away to the right and the man inside rushes back out of the room. Dris grips Pascual's arm. A few seconds go by and the man who was inside goes running by the window. "Go," says Dris, pulling Pascual out of the closet.

As they are running down the hall, the Colombian comes out of his room, bare-chested in boxer shorts, blinking in the light. Dris pulls something from his belt, and suddenly there is a gun at the Colombian's head. "Car keys," says Dris, in a tone of voice that discourages dissent. The Colombian backs into his room and Dris follows, gun extended. Over his shoulder he says to Pascual, "Lock the front door."

Pascual hurries to obey. The door is standing open; he closes it and turns the bolt with a solid thump. The Colombian is coming up the hall with a ring of keys in his hand; Dris is behind him with the gun to the small of his back and a firm grip on a handful of his hair. "The garage," Dris says.

"Through the kitchen," says the Colombian in a pained voice.

"Show us." Dris pushes the Colombian into the kitchen and steers him toward a door in the corner. Behind them the front door rattles briefly and then someone pounds on it. The Colombian opens the door in the kitchen to reveal a set of steps descending into darkness. He flicks a switch, and a light shows the hood of a car below. Dris maneuvers him onto the steps, Pascual following. Somewhere somebody is shouting in Russian. At the bottom of the steps Dris releases his grip on the Colombian's hair and tears the keys out of his hand. "Open the door," he says, giving the man a shove. The Colombian staggers to a switch on the wall and presses it. The door begins to rise. Dris has stashed the gun in his belt and unlocked the car with the button on the key fob; he vaults over the hood and tears open the driver's side door. Pascual tumbles in on the passenger side as the engine growls and coughs to life; he has barely managed to get the door closed before Dris rams it into reverse and is backing out at speed, the roof of the car scraping the rising garage door as they go. The Colombian has ducked out under the door and is running for his life.

Dris careens out onto the street in reverse, cranks the wheel, shifts into first and hits the gas. Tires squeal and the car leaps forward. The Russians come around the corner of the house as Dris rams it into second, picking up speed. One of them has a gun in his hand and raises it, but a shot never comes, and when Pascual raises his head above the dash again, Dris has muscled them around a bend and there is nothing but empty street ahead.

▪ ▪ ▪ ▪

"Because he asked you what happens if the police catch you," says Dris, steering one-handed, beginning to relax a little, cruising on an empty motorway as the eastern sky begins to lighten. "That, and leaving the two *gilipollas* to guard us. That's when I knew. They may be grateful, but once the police are interested in you, you're a liability. Unless you're one of them. A thief in law, is that what they call them? Anyway, I don't think we'd have made it out of that house."

Pascual is inclined to agree, and he is fervently grateful he has Dris to make up for his lapses in judgment. "Where the hell did the gun come from?"

"Tangier. I told you I could get one. I had it wrapped in plastic on the crossing, and I took it into the shower with me at the house, because I knew he'd search my things while I was in there. He searched yours, too. You know that, right?"

Pascual shakes his head, in a daze. "I should have. How far are we taking the car?"

"We need to get to Granada?" Dris considers. "We'll ditch the car in Málaga."

"If we had money, we could take the bus from there."

"It would be better to walk. We've got police looking for us, and now we'll have Russians looking, too. They'll check buses and trains for sure."

Pascual muses. "I could call Sara and see if someone at the farm can come and fetch us."

Dris shrugs. "It's just south of Granada? That's at least sixty or seventy kilometers away. Where do we wait in the meantime? Let's see what we might find in Málaga."

In Málaga they find sparse traffic on a wide tree-lined boulevard skirting the port. Dris turns away from the sea and into deserted streets, shops shuttered, cats on the prowl. He makes a few turns, driving aimlessly, then pulls over and consults his phone. Pascual lets his head loll against the window and dozes.

"Ready to do some work?" Dris asks. He stashes his phone and puts the car in gear.

"What kind of work?"

"Good honest labor. If we can find the right man." He drives around the corner, pulls to the curb at the tail end of a line of parked cars, and shuts off the engine. "This is where we get out." He exits, leaving the keys in the ignition. He checks his phone, looks up and down the street, and points. "This way."

Pascual follows, content to be led. The sky has begun to lighten above the rooftops but in the narrow streets the lamps are still on. Dris makes another turn, and a block ahead Pascual can see the corner of a giant structure with ornate cast-iron arches rising above a brick foundation. He recognizes one of the great covered markets found in every city in Spain. This one has a massive Moorish gateway opening onto a main street, but Dris leads Pascual up a narrow lane along the side, crowded with parked lorries and vans. Halfway up is a wide entrance into the market, and men are wheeling handcarts full of boxes in and out. Dris walks slowly, scanning. A short way past the door he stops. A man is hauling boxes out of the back of a Citroën van and stacking them on a handcart. He has white hair and white stubble on a face seamed like a sandstone cliff, hands gnarled from decades of hard labor, and he winces as he takes the weight of the boxes, which are labeled *Embutidos Hernández*.

"Allow me," says Dris, and steps in to drag another box off the bed of the truck. He places it squarely on top of the stack and says, "A man like you should have other people working for him."

The man freezes, glares and says, "Shove off."

Dris raises his hands in a placating gesture. "As you wish. But you could stand by and watch while my friend and I unload the whole truck. Have a smoke, take it easy on your back."

"What's your game?"

"No game. We're down on our luck and need the work."

The man waves him away, shaking his head. "I can't afford to pay you."

"All we want is a ride home at the end of the day." Dris nods at the side of the truck and Pascual notes the inscription there: *Embutidos Hernández – Loja – Granada*. "You won't owe us a *duro*. Just let us jump off the truck in Loja."

The man gives them the eye, standing with his arms akimbo. "I go to all the markets," he says. "After this I have deliveries at Bailén, Salamanca, Dos Hermanas."

"Sounds like a rough day," says Dris. "All the more reason to delegate."

Pascual does his best to look sturdy and enthusiastic, jaw clenched. He has a feeling the deal will hinge on Dris's potential rather than his. Finally the old man grunts. "*Vale.* Get to work then. What are you *golfos* just standing there for?"

"Loja?" says Sara. "What the hell are you doing in Loja?"

"Waiting for my muscles to stop cramping," says Pascual. He and

Dris are sprawled on the rocky earth in the sparse shade of a clutch of poplars on an embankment above a roundabout, a hop, skip and jump from the sausage factory run by the Hernández family on the outskirts of Loja, an old Moorish garrison town on a trickle of a river scoring the valley floor west of Granada. A busy morning of hefting boxes and jumping on and off the back of a truck has given him a finer appreciation of just how heavy *chorizos, morcillas, salchichones, longanizas* and the various types of *jamón serrano* are. True to his word, their employer then duly hauled them back to Loja, which may for all Pascual knows be a charming town; they have seen only the industrial outskirts and the limestone crags jutting up from the surrounding plain. Granada is another thirty kilometers up the road, but Granada proper is not their destination; wherever the farm is, Pascual is hoping it is not far. "Is there anybody there with a car who can come and get us?"

Sara's soft laugh is music to Pascual's ears. "You expect your wife and son to drop everything, throw our lives into confusion and scurry into shelter, and you can't even manage to find your own way here?"

"Forgive me, *cariño,* I'd walk it if I could, but my legs have given out and Dris refuses to carry me any further."

"*Vale.* I'll see if José Antonio can come and rescue you. Where will he find you?"

Pascual gives directions as best he can and signs off. "Saved," he says to Dris. "Maybe an hour to get here. There's a bar down the way there. How much money do you have left?"

"Maybe enough for a coffee." Dris looks around, ill at ease.

"We're probably better off sitting there than here, in case the *guardias* come by and get curious. Say, I've still got your precious flash drive. You still want me to keep it?"

"Why not? You know what to do with it if anything happens to me." Pascual's phone buzzes in his hand. "Hang on." Thinking it must be Sara again with further instructions, Pascual swipes and sees Artemisa's number on the screen. "What's happening?"

"Many things. All of them bad. Are you undercover yet?"

"Almost. Waiting for a ride, the last one we'll need. What's wrong?"

"I got a tip from a contact in the ministry they're preparing to arrest me. I've left Madrid and I'm heading south."

"*Hostia.* How can they arrest you?"

"I'm implicated in an Iranian plot to undermine Western security by discrediting the Saudis and destabilizing Libya."

"What?"

"That's the story they're peddling. They must have been up all night in Tel Aviv and Riyadh cooking this one up. They're telling people you and I are on Tehran's payroll, spreading disinformation about the Saudis to cover up an Iranian operation in Libya."

"Unbelievable."

"Sadly, it will be perfectly credible to a lot of people. It's well known that I've had it in for the Saudis for a long time. As for the man I'm protecting, they have proof of his identity."

"What's that?"

"He's uniquely identifiable by two missing fingers. He's a known Revolutionary Guards collaborator named Bassam Youssef."

Pascual is speechless for a long moment. *"Los hijos de puta,"* he says finally.

"Indeed. You see the position. Once they show a corpse with two fingers missing, it's over. Their version becomes the story, difficult to debunk. Another murky affair nobody really knows the truth about. We're going to have to lie low while we organize our counterattack. Can I come and join you? I can be in Granada in five hours. I'll need directions to this hideout of yours."

"It's a struggle," says Soledad. "I think about giving up two or three times a week."

To Pascual it seems that nothing could be a struggle in this place. To him it looks like paradise, a roughly flagged patio in front of a whitewashed stone house, shaded by orange trees, mountains at his back and the land falling away to the distant plain in front of him. Best of all, he has Sara at his side and Rafa opposite, hair barely contained in a red kerchief, fit, tanned and insouciant, grinning at some joke Dris has made. The embraces on arrival were fierce; Pascual would have held on forever if he could.

They are in the foothills of the Sierra Nevada, a few kilometers up a winding road off the motorway south of Granada, and Soledad is gazing out over her domain. "We have olive trees, of course, and figs and almonds, and vegetables on the terraces. It's a lot of work, even outside harvest time. The terraces need shoring up, the *acequias,* the irrigation channels, have to be maintained. They were built by the Arabs, centuries ago. There's always something to repair." Soledad has the calloused hands to prove it, along with dreadlocks and a trim wiry body in a caftan sashed at the waist. "And we're barely breaking even."

José Antonio comes out of the house with another bottle of wine. He is dark in complexion, raven-haired, lean and angular, *gitano* to his toes and the principal reason Soledad is estranged from a monied family in Granada. "We won't starve," he says, setting the bottle on the table. "It's better to live off the land than beg in the streets."

"Please let us pay you something," says Sara. "All these people descending on you. You shouldn't have to support us."

"Particularly with this woman coming to join us tonight," says Pascual. "That was never the plan."

"Tell me again who this is?" says Sara. Pascual almost laughs at the look on her face.

"This is the woman who figured out what's going on. She probably saved my life. I never intended to bring her here, but now she's on the run, too."

"Then let her come," says Soledad. She puts her hand on Sara's. "You saved my life when I was wandering the streets looking for a way to kill myself. It's my turn now." She reaches for the bottle. "Who needs more wine?"

For a time they are absorbed in food and drink, and then Soledad takes on the topic that has hung brooding over them all afternoon. "So, Pascual. What is all this nonsense, anyway?"

Pascual takes his time answering. He drinks, sets the glass down, shoves it away, looks at each of them in turn. "It's karma," he says.

▪ ▪ ▪ ▪

The western sky is an incendiary orange when Artemisa's silver Audi, coated with dust, comes bumping up the track out of the woods and stops in front of the farmhouse. The sound of the car has brought Pascual, Dris, Rafael and José Antonio out onto the patio. Artemisa gets out stiffly, grimaces, stretches, nods at them. "You found us," Pascual says.

Artemisa comes up onto the patio, carrying a small overnight bag. She is in jeans, riding boots, a denim jacket, hair swept back in the headband. "That was an interesting drive," she says. "Nobody's going to find you here." Pascual makes introductions. Inside, the women stand in the doorway to the kitchen. Soledad's tension eases visibly when she catches sight of Artemisa; Sara appraises her coolly and sends Pascual an unreadable look.

"You must be hungry," says Soledad.

"A little. I had a *bocadillo* when I stopped for petrol. Some water would be good, please. This is an amazing place." Artemisa is looking around the rustic interior, stone walls and exposed beams, fireplace and solid dark furniture. She could be the lady of the manor calling on the tenants. "I am sorry to turn up uninvited like this. If you can give me a couch to sleep on for the night I will be off in the morning."

Soledad shrugs. "We can do better than that. Stay as long as you please."

She settles Artemisa at the table in the kitchen with a bowl of garlic soup and some bread and cheese. Pascual sits opposite her and Dris leans in the doorway. "Nobody followed me," says Artemisa. "I made sure of that. If you're sure you can't be traced here, it's probably as secure as anywhere in the world."

"I can't see how they could," says Pascual. "I left the bugged phone in Tangier. Dris and I have used cash or barter since we crossed the water."

Artemisa nods. "You talked with Salera? Good. He's done amazing work. Together with what I had, it's allowed us to unravel this whole thing. But they're fighting back, and they're fighting dirty. We need a plan. I would not trust any Spanish agency at this point. It pains me to say it, but I don't think we can risk it. At best we would be detained indefinitely. Your Germans may be a better bet. We will have to find a way to contact them. Once they have you in custody you should be safe, and we can lay out the story. For the cryptocurrency transactions we will need to show them the proof. You have it, right?"

"The proof? You mean the flash drive?"

"Of course."

"I have it." He draws a deep breath. "I've been counting on saving it. It's my insurance."

"Saving it?"

"I told Lina that as long as nothing happened to me or my family, it need never see the light of day."

Artemisa frowns at him for a moment and then applies herself to her meal. Pascual trades a look with Dris, who is looking on inscrutably. Artemisa swallows and says, "We have to publish it, Pascual. We have to take it to someone who can prosecute the case. We have to disseminate it as widely as possible. It's proof that the Saudis and the Israelis conspired to steal twenty-two billion dollars from a government supported by the United Nations and struggling to survive. Without that record, all we have is allegations that they can deny and trump with their own fabrications."

Pascual bears her gaze as long as he can, then rises from the table. He goes to a window and looks out into the deepening night. "How am I supposed to protect my family?"

"Once the story is out, they won't bother to come after you. What good would it do them? They'll be too busy running for cover. Once a threat has failed to deter, it is a redundant, wasted effort to carry it out."

"Unless you've got a reputation to maintain. It's all about the next time you want to threaten someone. I think any competent criminal organization is always careful to carry out its threats."

He waits, then turns to see Artemisa push the bowl away. Without looking at Pascual she says, "You will have to trust the authorities. They do have some experience in protecting witnesses and their families."

Pascual paces slowly across the kitchen. He can hear soft conversation in the next room, Sara and Rafael and Soledad and José Antonio. He stops in front of Dris and trades a long look with him. This is now his most trusted counselor, he realizes, a Moroccan-Catalan street tough with a prison sheet for peddling drugs. Dris says nothing, waiting for orders.

Pascual turns to face Artemisa. "I'm going to think about it, and I'm going to talk about it with my family. I'll give you an answer in the morning."

▪ ▪ ▪ ▪

"You went through all that pain to develop a conscience, and you're going to stop listening to it now?" says Sara. "Do what you think is right." In the light from the fireplace she glows golden, a handsome middle-aged woman starting to gray and grow heavy, once a great passion and now merely the indispensable anchor of his wayward life. Pascual has always deferred to her judgment, but now she is forcing him to judge.

"What my conscience tells me is that I owe it to my wife and son to keep them safe."

"That's not your conscience telling you that. That's your love for us. And if that's worth more than your conscience, so be it. But be clear."

She is going to make him work for this, Pascual can see. He looks at Rafael, sitting beside his mother, hair in his face, impetuous and unkempt, the picture of the wild youth he himself once was, except that he has not thrown his life away, not yet. "What do you think?" Pascual says.

Rafael is giving him a look he has never seen before, grave and assured. "I think that if our safety depends on keeping a secret, a lot can go wrong," Rafael says. "Who do you trust to keep the secret? I think we're better off lying low while the law eliminates the threat to our safety."

Pascual stares into the fire. "The law may not be strong enough to do that." He stirs, rises, grimacing as his injuries assert themselves. "Where are we sleeping? Right now I'm too tired to decide which shoe to take off first."

▪ ▪ ▪ ▪

Pascual wakes up in the dark and needs a moment to recollect where he is; too much tumult over the last few nights has permanently disoriented him. He hears Sara breathing at his side and remembers; he rolls to her and embraces her and she murmurs in her sleep. He lies with his arms around her for a time listening to the soughing of wind outside and the faint chirping of the first birds. The square of window high on the wall is beginning to lighten.

Pascual gently pulls free and gets out of bed. Shivering a little in the pre-dawn chill, he feels for his clothes and dresses in the dark. He slips out of the room and pulls the door to behind him, closing it with a soft click. In the living room Dris and Rafael are dark bundles on the couch and the floor. The fire has died down to embers and there is just enough light to avoid the furniture.

Pascual goes into the kitchen and sits on a chair to put on his shoes. He gets the back door open with only a slight creak and steps out into the dawn. Above him the pastures rise toward the distant peaks silhouetted against the sky growing pink. Pascual stands for a moment wishing that this was his life, rising at dawn and struggling to make ends meet on a mountainside farm.

He meanders, past the low stone outbuildings and the well and the rough fieldstone wall of the terraced vegetable garden. Birds are coming awake; a rabbit goes bounding away into the trees. Pascual rounds the end of the house, skirts the patio and the parked cars and ambles downhill toward the view out over the plain, hands in his pockets, musing. How did a city boy like him, a guttersnipe at home in Barcelona, Paris, Brooklyn, Damascus, end up here on a mountain in Andalusia, wishing he could stay here forever?

Pascual stands looking west into the remnants of the night, aware of what he must do, aware that all that has come down on him and his family is his fault, even twenty years after, after remorse and expiation and flight and denial. It is time to stand up, and he is only sorry that Sara and Rafa will be exposed with him.

Pascual listens: wind, birds, faint bleating of goats on a distant hillside. Somewhere far below, in the shadowy oak woods into which the road descends, a car purrs, rolls to a halt and goes silent. Pascual frowns: did he imagine it? A second vehicle whispers, tires on gravel, before it, too, stops.

Pascual listens. There are other farms down there; he passed them on the way up in the truck with José Antonio yesterday. But they were several kilometers distant; does sound travel that far on the cool morning air? Pascual turns and walks back to the house.

Everyone else is still asleep. Pascual picks his way carefully through the living room and back into the room where Sara sleeps. He sits on the side of the bed. Hikers, hunters, bird enthusiasts. There is always somebody tramping through the hills. Is there any reason to panic?

Pascual defers decision by idly reaching down to unplug his phone from the outlet where it has been charging. He powers it up to find there is a text message waiting for him, from Salera, sent late the previous evening:

Be advised Ulitskaya and Landau flew from Tangier to Madrid and then on to Granada tonight.

Pascual flies off the bed, calling for Artemisa.

37

"I heard two vehicles." Pascual points. "Down the road."

Artemisa focuses fast, tousled and blinking as she is, just roused from sleep, sitting up on the narrow bed tucked under the eaves. "What makes you think it's them?"

"Salera texted. They flew into Granada last night."

Artemisa stares at him for two seconds and throws the blankets aside, swinging bare legs under a long T-shirt to the floor. "God help us."

José Antonio pokes his head out of his bedroom. "What's happening?"

"I think we have trouble. Do you have neighbors close enough that you hear their cars coming and going?"

"Never."

"What about tourists, hikers? Do you get many?"

"Not at this hour."

"Well, we have visitors." Pascual makes for the stairs.

Downstairs, Dris has pulled on trousers and shirt and is tugging at shoelaces. Rafael is shirtless, still half-asleep, and the bewildered look on his face stabs Pascual in the heart. "What's going on, *pare?*"

"Possibly trouble. Get dressed and get ready to leave."

"I'll go have a look," says Dris. He hurries out the front door, stuffing something in his waistband.

In the bedroom Sara is pulling on jeans. Without looking at Pascual she says, "Who's here?"

"Nobody, not yet. We're going to have to find a place to hide. Leave everything. Just get dressed and grab your phone."

José Antonio comes down the stairs and fixes Pascual with a glare. "Tell me what's happening." Soledad is behind him, wide-eyed and disheveled.

"I think the people we're hiding from have found us."

"Are we in danger?" The look on José Antonio's face says he knows whom to blame if they are.

"I think *we* may be. I don't see any reason why you should be, if we can disappear. We were never here, as far as you're concerned."

José Antonio says, "How did they find you?"

"That's an excellent question, isn't it?" says Artemisa, coming down the stairs, pulling on a jacket, bag in hand. "Is there another road out of this place?"

José Antonio laughs, harshly. "Where would it go? There are only two directions, up and down. Above us there's only the mountain. On foot you might get over into the next valley and hike down to the village, but it would take you all day."

Pascual has stabilized and begun to think again. "Is there a place up there where we can hide?"

"There are caves."

"How far?"

"Maybe a kilometer."

"How far up can we get in the car?"

"About halfway. After that, it will have to be on foot."

"That's insane," says Artemisa. "You want to let them chase us into a cave? We'll be trapped."

"What I want is to hide."

"What we want is to run. While it's still dark, in the car."

"What if they've blocked the road?"

"What if the sky falls? Look, there are two possibilities. Either this is a false alarm, or they are down there somewhere setting up an attack. If it's a false alarm, we drive calmly down the mountain. If it's them, we catch them by surprise. They won't be expecting us to try to break out. If the road's blocked, we'll see it in time. In the worst case, we leave the car and go down through the trees on foot, slip past them. The point is not to be trapped. And to move fast, before full daylight."

"And I'd say the first thing to do is reconnoiter. Dris has gone to take a look."

"Has he? Well, we'll see if he comes back." She stalks past Pascual and goes outside onto the patio. He follows. The sky has lightened above the peaks. Pascual hears nothing but the birds and the wind. Dris is nowhere to be seen.

Artemisa says, "He's gone to collect his thirty pieces of silver."

Shock strikes Pascual dumb for a moment, meeting Artemisa's accusing stare, and then he says, "No. Impossible."

"You think so?" Her chin rises a degree or two. "Who's got the flash drive?"

Ice in the pit of his stomach, Pascual says, "Dris would not betray us."

"Dris just did. He ran down the hill to deliver what he was hired to get."

"No." Pascual shakes his head. "How? How would they have gotten to him?"

"Were you with him the whole time in Tangier? When he was out taking your phone for a walk, you think they had any trouble finding him? How much do you think it would take to buy the loyalty of a Moroccan street tough? Pocket change for them."

"Why didn't he deliver it to them right away? After I tossed it to him? Why go through the whole charade of crossing the Strait, taking that risk?"

"Once he had it, there was no urgency to take delivery. As for crossing the Strait, if you had both drowned, that would have been just another solution to the problem."

Pascual gropes for an argument and finds none. "You're wrong, you'll see."

"I hope to live long enough." Artemisa strides toward her car. "I'm making a run for it. Are you coming?" She tosses her bag on the seat, gets in and starts the car. The headlights come on. Sara and Rafael come out of the house. Sara says, "Are we leaving?"

Pascual draws a deep breath. "Artemisa is. I'm waiting for Dris to come back. Artemisa thinks he betrayed us."

Rafael says, "That's absurd."

Sara shakes her head. "No, that's impossible."

Pascual nods. "So, if you trust Dris, stay with me. If you think Artemisa's right, the bus is leaving."

Rafael and Sara trade a look. "We're staying with you," says Sara.

Pascual walks to the car and leans down at the driver's window.

"We're taking our chances with Dris. Are you sure you know what you're doing?"

She glares at him. "I know I'm not staying here to be cornered. If they're waiting down there, I'll make them work." She puts it in gear and wrestles it around to point downhill, then steps on the gas and is gone, her taillights disappearing around the bend.

Pascual pulls out his phone. It shows a weak signal. He brings up Dris's number and hits *Call*. Dris's phone rings four times and goes to voice mail. Pascual gives up and puts the phone away. Sara and Rafa are looking at him for guidance and he has nothing. He has failed them again, maybe for the last time. "I think we should find a place to hide until we hear from Dris," he says. "If we don't hear in a couple of hours, we'll try to walk out. I don't know what else to do. We can't stay here and put Soledad and José Antonio in danger any longer."

They are contemplating that when a booming crash sounds, faintly, from somewhere below, and then the shots, two in quick succession and then a short burst of automatic fire. *"Dios mío."* Sara puts a hand on Pascual's arm, horror in her face.

Pascual is paralyzed for a moment and then electrified. "That's it," he says. "Now we know."

José Antonio comes out onto the patio. "Were those shots I heard?"

"Yes. You're finished with us. You never saw us. Call the Guardia, call whoever you need to. We're going to make a run for those caves."

José Antonio hesitates for a couple of seconds. "I think your friend is right. You're better off going downhill."

"Down? But that's where they are. You heard the shots."

"Don't go by the road. There's another way. Go off to the right, through the trees there. Straight down from the house. Follow the *acequia* when you hit it. It diverges from the road, and eventually you'll strike a path to the village. If they're on the road they won't see you, and if you go quietly they won't hear you. Get past them, and then there's cover all the way down to the village."

Pascual stands in indecision for a moment, then says, "All right, we'll go downhill. I think you and Soledad should clear out, too."

José Antonio's expression hardens. "Don't worry, we will. We'll go up to the caves and wait for the Guardia Civil. Now go. *Suerte.*"

Pascual takes Sara's arm, Rafael on the other side of her, tugging her toward the trees. The light is growing, the sky above the mountaintops already a clear luminous blue. In the woods it is still dark enough that they have to slow their pace and go carefully, Pascual leading. Sara stumbles, Rafael steadies her. Pascual carries his phone in his hand, straining to see through the gloom. He hears the *acequia* before he sees it and nearly falls into it when they reach it. It is a narrow concrete-lined channel with a rush of water in it and a path beside it, running downhill to their left. Pascual hops across it onto the path, and Sara and Rafael follow. From their left, uphill, comes the sound of a vehicle moving along a road, not fast. They halt and listen; the sound fades away downhill. After a moment they go on.

The walking is easier on the path, but they go slowly, stepping carefully. The murmur of water in the *acequia* masks the sound of their steps. Pascual's eyes adjust to the dark, and he gets a sense of the topography, the land falling away to their right toward the plain, the *acequia* leading them in a long gentle curve along the mountainside. The light is growing and before long the sun will clear the mountaintops.

The headlights catch them by surprise, snapping on in the gloom under the trees and fixing them in the sudden glare. Pascual's heart leaps, Sara stifles a cry and runs into him. Rafael curses softly. Pascual recovers first and starts to shove Sara back out of the light.

"Just freeze right there, won't you?" Lina calls out from behind the lights.

"Well, Pascual. You have certainly made things hard on everybody, haven't you?"

Lina is dressed for a day in the country, from the windbreaker with the logo of a fashionable outfitter on the breast to the thick-soled leather hiking boots. She has turned off the headlights of the Range Rover now that the sun has risen, and there is enough light to see the rough track the vehicle followed down through the trees, the thicket of juniper that concealed it and the man dressed in black with classic Arabian features holding an evil-looking Heckler & Koch machine pistol, close enough to the Range Rover to keep an eye on Sara and Rafael sitting in the back. Lina shakes her head. "You could have just taken our money and done the job."

"So you could kill me like you killed Pereda?" Pascual finds that *in extremis* he has accessed a sort of desperate calm, knowing his last hope is to keep talking and keep his wits about him. He is sitting with his back to a tree, as ordered, hands clasped over his knees, Lina standing above him.

Lina sniffs. "Pereda had to go because sooner or later he would have tried to blackmail us. It was in his DNA, as they say. We would have been happy to let you enjoy your money."

"You shouldn't have threatened my family."

"You should have just conceded that you couldn't protect them and done the work. Nothing would have happened to them. But now look where they are. Because you had to get cute. You had to involve Mr. Salera."

Stunned, Pascual has to close his eyes for a moment. "No."

"Oh, yes. We know about him. You think we can't detect who's trying to detect us? Once we finally identified him, just yesterday in fact, all it took was a brief visit to that colorful office of his in Gràcia to persuade him to share the location data from those lovely phones he gave you. It turns out he has a child, too."

Pascual engages her arctic gaze for a moment, looking for signs of humanity. "Do you enjoy your work?"

Her chin rises a degree or two. "Call it professional pride."

She turns her head at a thrashing noise from the hillside. The gunman raises the machine pistol, then lowers it. Felix comes trotting along the side of the Range Rover, sweating and panting lightly. He is clad in black like the gunman and wears an automatic on his hip. He gives Pascual a blazing look and delivers a short report in Hebrew to Lina.

She responds briefly and turns back to Pascual. "You'll be pleased to know that he didn't find anybody at the house. Felix is in rather a bad mood, I have to say. Your lady friend disabled one of our vehicles and severely injured a colleague of ours with that car of hers when she rushed us. I'm afraid he's not going to survive."

"My condolences."

"You'll pay," says Felix. "Big time." He nods at the gunman. "I'll let Mustafa have you. He and Karim were close."

Lina raises a hand. "Let's defer all that. That's not what we're here for. What we need from you, Pascual, is that flash drive. We'll make you a deal. Your wife and son go free if we get the device."

Pascual stares for a few seconds and finally starts to laugh. "I don't have it."

Her face utterly blank, Lina says, "Of course you don't. Well then, that's different. In that case somebody's going to have to die. We'll let you choose. Wife or son?"

Here it is, thinks Pascual, the test. "What good is it going to do you? You can't stop the data from being published even if you have the drive. The game's over and you've lost."

Lina trades a look with Felix and takes a step closer to lean over Pascual. "Don't try to bluff me, Pascual. If you had sent the data on that file to someone else it would have been published immediately. Your friend Ms. Pereda would have come up with it when she was making all that noise in Madrid, and she wouldn't have had to flee down here to dodge an arrest. Yes, we know about her, too. She's been on our radar all along because of her father, and when we saw she'd been in Tangier at the same time as you, we knew who your accomplice had to be. So, give it up, will you, Pascual? You haven't offloaded the data, and you've got to have the drive. Now hand it over."

Pascual shakes his head. "I already handed it over. To somebody who will take good care of it. They won't publish the data unless something happens to me, and they don't give a damn about bringing you to justice."

Lina rises to her full height. "Who are we talking about?"

“I gave it to the Russians. In Marbella.”

For several seconds there is no sound but the birds, the wind in the trees and the gentle plashing of water in the *acequia*. Lina says, “Now why on earth would you do that?”

“Because it’s a perfect standoff. We both win. You leave me alone, and as long as I check in at regular intervals, they just hold it to extort what they can from you. All they care about is money. They can’t get the twenty-two billion, but they can make you pay them to keep it under wraps. The negotiations should be interesting.”

Lina steps away, shoving her hands into the pockets of her windbreaker. She walks slowly to where Felix is standing and they confer, again in Hebrew. Felix looks past Lina at Pascual and says, “Shoot the wife and see if he sticks to his story. If he’s lying, he’ll cough it up fast.”

Lina turns, a thoughtful look on her face. “It may come to that. But let’s discuss first. Pascual, I believe there’s a flaw in your scheme. Why would the Russians ever release the data? Even if we do something nasty to you and yours? That would be relinquishing their hold on us. I’m afraid they are a very poor repository for your trust. They will value a chance to extort us much more than they could possibly value a commitment made to you. These are criminals, after all.”

Pascual gropes for a counterargument, knowing as he does that he is playing a losing hand. He assumes what he hopes is a look of quiet confidence as he says, “Vasily Andreyevich’s wife loves flamenco and is quite a fan of my wife, as it happens. And Vasily Andreyevich always indulges his wife. He promised to protect us for her sake.”

It is not much, but it is enough to make Lina's face go completely blank for a moment. Felix makes a dismissive noise, but Pascual can see that Lina has to give it serious consideration, and he hangs his hopes on that. "How fortunate for you," says Lina.

Pascual takes that as an indication that he has won, at least for the moment, but he is not going to have any time to celebrate.

Heads snap in unison as a hollow chuffing noise resounds across the mountainside, accompanied by an eerie orange glow coming through the trees from higher up the slope. The gunman steps away from the Range Rover, raising the Heckler & Koch. Felix swears, Lina takes a couple of vigorous strides toward the spectacle, Pascual begins to get to his feet. Just as everyone focuses on the sight of a car burning vigorously on the road a hundred meters above them, Dris bursts out of the brush. The gunman spins but too late; at a range of two meters not even an unpracticed street-tough can miss with a nine-millimeter automatic. Dris puts two shots in his chest and one in his head before he can bring the machine pistol to bear.

Felix is going for the gun on his hip, but he is thinking cover first, ducking back along the side of the Range Rover as Dris comes around it. As Felix goes into a crouch, bringing up his gun in a textbook two-handed grip, the back door of the Range Rover comes open, knocking him off balance as Dris turns the corner. Rafael shoves hard on the door and Felix has no chance; he looses off three or four shots from the ground, but Dris is practically on top of him by this time, expending the last of his ammunition at point-blank range.

Pascual sees all this in passing, because he is busy springing to his feet as Lina goes for the machine pistol. She manages to get it by the barrel and jumps clear, but Pascual is right behind her. As Lina turns, firming her grip, Pascual delivers the haymaker, breaking his hand and Lina's nose simultaneously and stunning her enough that he can rip the weapon from her hands. She staggers back a couple of steps and sits down heavily, hands to her face.

Suddenly it is very quiet.

Pascual spins to see Dris with his gun hand hanging at his side, a dazed look on his face. Felix is on the ground, clearly expiring; as Pascual watches, he coughs up blood, and then his head falls back on the ground with a thump. Rafael has leapt out of the vehicle to survey the carnage and Sara is climbing out the other side, slowly.

Pascual turns back to train the machine pistol on Lina. She has recovered enough to be shaking blood from her fingers while fixing Pascual with a malevolent glare. Blood streams over her pale lips and onto her sculpted marble chin. "All right, Pascual," she says. "Go ahead and kill me. You never did actually pull the trigger on anyone, did you? At last you'll be able to say you did it, you killed a Jew. Go on, strike a blow for Palestine, or whatever it was you believed in."

Pascual has no answer, no defense, no comeback. Sighting down the stubby barrel of the weapon at Lina's face, he rasps, "And just what is it you believe in?"

If she has an answer, Pascual sees he is not going to get it. He takes a couple of steps backward, holding the gun on her, then wheels to see Rafa wide-eyed, Sara with her hand over her mouth, Dris sagging against the Range Rover. *"Pare,"* says Rafael. "Dris is bleeding."

"We're not really equipped for gunshot wounds, but even if you could have gotten him to the trauma center in Granada, he might not have made it."

The doctor is bearded, bespectacled and earnest, genuinely dismayed. Pascual appreciates his distress, but it is nothing compared to his own, or that of Sara and Rafael. Sara has seen trauma before and is bearing up, pale and still, but Rafa is new to violent death and is weeping silently, sniffing at intervals. Pascual's hand is throbbing but he has refused any attention, waiting with Sara and Rafael for news.

Dris tried his best as Pascual tore frantically down the mountain roads at the wheel of the Range Rover, Rafael holding his friend and Sara frantically checking her phone for the nearest place likely to have a doctor who could do something for a man with a hole in his torso. Grinning against the pain and squeezing the words out with no breath behind them, Dris exhausted the last of his resources boasting about how he cut the fuel line and ignited a pile of brush under the disabled vehicle, the slow burn giving him the time he needed to creep down the slope to be in range when the distraction went off. By the time they reached the clinic at Padul, a scant fifteen kilometers south of Granada, he had fallen silent.

"What is going on up there in the mountains?" the doctor says. "This is the second gunshot case we've had this morning. We just had a woman come in driving a car full of bullet holes, bleeding profusely. She'd had her ear shot off."

Artemisa is barely recognizable with her head wrapped in bandages, but the luminous brown eyes are unmistakable. "You're still alive," she says. "I'm glad."

"Some of us are," Pascual says. "Dris is dead."

Artemisa's eyes flick to the curtain closing off the alcove. "Talk fast. The Benemérita is on the way. Who else?"

"Felix is dead. Two Saudi hit men as well."

"Two? I got one of them with the car."

"And Dris got the other. We left Lina up there to find her own way out."

"Mother of God. This will give the Guardia something to scratch their heads over. What about the device?"

Pascual could not care less at this point about the USB drive, but he knows other people will care a lot. "I've got it. I had to wipe Dris's blood off it."

"And have you made a decision?"

"Yes," says Pascual after a time. "I have."

"Because you are about to be at the center of an international street brawl. I hope you're ready."

"Me, too," says Pascual.

The curtain of the alcove is pulled aside and a broad, gruff-looking man in the gray-green uniform of a Guardia Civil *subteniente* stands glaring at them. "What's all this, then?" he says.

"There's irony for you," says Artemisa. "A separatist firebrand like you, saved by the Guardia Civil." Today she looks a little less frightful, a dressing over her surgically salvaged ear the only sign of recent trauma. The shaved side of her head looks almost fashionable, and it will take more than a maimed ear to rob her of her looks. "Once we were in custody and part of their investigation, nobody could just make us disappear."

"Hardly a firebrand and duly grateful," says Pascual. "But are you quite sure they haven't disappeared me?" He raises his hand in its plaster cast to wave at their surroundings, the cramped kitchen at the back of a third-floor flat in some unidentified corner of Madrid through which he was whisked at night. He and Artemisa sit at opposite ends of a small table shoved against the wall, coffee cups in front of them. Somewhere toward the front of the flat a couple of security gorillas can be heard muttering over a game of *brisca*. "My minders won't even let me go down to the corner for a *café y copa.*"

"Oh, you haven't disappeared. You're all over the news. Three bodies and a burned-out vehicle up in the Sierra Nevada will get people's attention. The media are calling you a 'shadowy figure with a dubious background.'"

"At least they got that right. I wonder how my wife and son are taking it."

"They've gone to earth in France, it seems. The press can't find them."

"It's good to be a Gypsy sometimes, Sara says."

"No doubt. Meanwhile, the word is, you're cooperating with the authorities. There are those who are hoping to see you charged with a variety of crimes. I've gotten myself designated as your attorney, which is why they're letting us have this little chat."

"Nice of them."

"Yes." Artemisa's eyes are flicking about the kitchen, searching. She stands, steps to the counter opposite and reaches to turn on a small portable radio. She twirls the dial until a manic Europop beat fills the kitchen. She ups the volume slightly and returns to her seat. Pascual raises his eyebrows and Artemisa, leaning closer over the table says, "This is a CNI safe house. You think they're not going to try to listen?"

Pascual shrugs and Artemisa resumes. "The Guardia Civil has all it needs, three bodies and an accounting of how they died. I've been cleared on grounds of self-defense, since there's indisputable evidence I was shot at, and your Moroccan delinquent conveniently takes the rap for the other two."

Pascual considers letting that pass but finds he cannot. "He was as Spanish as I am, and he was less of a delinquent than the toffs you've represented in court."

Artemisa grants him a nod. "I'll concede that point. Anyway, the Benemérita is happy to kick the case upstairs, which is where the real infighting is taking place. Villafranca's calling for an investigation of Israeli meddling in Spanish security policy, which is why the cloak-and-dagger people have given up trying to gag me. But that's a bit of a two-edged sword, since Villafranca's a right-wing crank and I risk being tarred with the same brush, to the detriment of my credibility." She pauses for an instant, lips parted. "My association with him was never more than tactical, over a shared concern about the Saudis, just in case you're wondering."

Pascual shrugs. "If we're to be judged on unsavory associations, I will be the loser every time."

"In any event, the outlines of the story are out and rumors are rife. Everyone is going into coverup mode. My colleagues think that if this ever was a Mossad operation, they've certainly disowned it now. It would be interesting to know if Lina made it out of the mountains."

"She had the look of a survivor to me."

"Yes. The Israelis are hard at work selling the idea that this is all Iranian disinformation. Najib's man in Geneva has come forth, and there's talk of a FATF investigation. But if we're going to haul anyone in front of a judge, we're going to need that blockchain data. In fact we should publish it the first chance we get. Once it's out, Lina and the Saudis can't keep the lid on." Artemisa leans a little closer, lowering her voice. "I don't suppose you have access to a computer here."

Pascual shakes his head. "They won't even let me have my phone."

He can barely hear her as she murmurs, "You could slip the thing to me. I'll e-mail the data to the FATF and the International Consortium of Investigative Journalists in Washington within the hour."

Pascual raises his hands. "I don't have it anymore."

He has shocked her, he sees. She says, "Who has it?"

"Dris's mother, I hope. After some reflection, I slipped it back in with his effects when the Guardia released them to be returned to her along with the body. I will retrieve it from her and surrender it when there's a criminal prosecution underway and I'm invited to testify."

Artemisa's eyes are blazing. "That's crucial evidence in the crime of the century."

Pascual sighs gently. "I wish I could be so optimistic as to believe that this is the worst thing that is going to happen in this century. But if it's important, that's all the more reason to put it where nobody will think to look for it."

Artemisa's eyes narrow, and eventually her look softens. "You have a subtle mind. I'm beginning to see how you've survived all these years." She stands. "I should be on my way. I've got another session with the inquisitors this afternoon." She pats at what is left of her hair with a vexed look. "They'll be coming for you again soon, I'm sure. I don't think they're done with you."

"No," says Pascual. "I don't think they ever will be."

From the window of the conference room Pascual can see traffic on the A-6 speeding through the western excrescences of Madrid, Castilla la Nueva disappearing under the Castile of the twenty-first century. Somewhere out there over the horizon are poor benighted Andalusia, a mountain valley, a rugged coast, the unforgiving waters of the Strait, Tangier. Somewhere out there is a world of people in quiet desperation, slogging to work each day, trying to make ends meet, their fates governed by forces and actors they have no inkling of.

In here, across the table from Pascual, is one of those actors, gray in hair, custom-tailored suit and temperament, and he is not pleased with Pascual. "Exactly what outcome did you have in mind?" he says, scowling.

Pascual shrugs. "I don't know. A few arrests, a trial or two perhaps. I would hope somebody would go to jail. Besides me."

The scowl fades slowly. "That, I'm afraid, is not going to happen. Not the first part, certainly, and if you are lucky, not the second."

"I am sorry to hear that. On the first count, if not the second. So your preferred outcome is to let the Saudis get away with it?"

"That might be better than the alternative. Already there are rumors of discontent among the royal cousins, palace intrigues. The crown prince has made a lot of enemies, and this would give them a club to beat him with. Tanks in the streets of Riyadh would not be a pretty sight."

"No. In fact the prospect is not appealing wherever you look."

The gray man sits back on his chair, a grim smile on his lips. "Indeed. As you may be aware, a number of Greek and Italian banks have made a big move into cryptocurrency. *Greek and Italian* banks, mind you. And what do you think will happen to cryptocurrency markets if it is proved that state actors have pulled off a theft and money-laundering operation of this magnitude?"

"I think it would probably trigger a flight from those markets. Which is probably a good thing. They say it's a bubble anyway."

"Perhaps. But if there is a cryptocurrency collapse, then the dominoes fall. A run on Greek and Italian banks puts the whole eurozone at risk."

"When has the euro not been at risk?"

"Your flippant attitude is not helpful. Exposing this affair would set off a chain of events that could be radically destabilizing. You want that on your conscience?"

Pascual sighs. "None of it will go on my conscience. My sins predate the euro crisis by twenty-five years. You're asking me to choose sides. And there's only one side I favor, really, when things get complicated beyond my *corto entendimiento.*"

"Which side would that be?"

"The truth." Pascual sustains the official glare for a moment longer and says, "You'll get the data when the International Criminal

Court or a similar body opens proceedings against the people behind this affair. Not before."

The gray man smolders, but Pascual is unmoved. "We'll see about that," says the gray man. He pushes away from the table and stands. "There are some people outside who wish to speak with you."

Pascual waits, staring out the window, only mildly curious. He has a feeling there will be no shortage of people who wish to speak with him. The door opens and two people enter the room. One of them is Joachim Wirth. The other is a woman in middle age, gray-haired and verging on plump, in a businesslike tweed pantsuit, clutching a slim leather portfolio. She is unremarkable, hair cut in a conservative pageboy bob, not unfeminine but obviously not especially concerned with attracting male attention, somebody's favorite aunt. She favors Pascual with a smile as she and Wirth take seats opposite him. "Hello, Pascual," she says. "Long time no see."

Pascual blinks in astonishment. It takes him a few seconds, but he finally connects this face with one he last saw in an interview room at a military installation in Barcelona more than twenty years ago. "You grew up," he says.

She takes it good-humoredly, laying the portfolio on the table. "You got old."

Pascual ignores Wirth's bitter laugh. "I don't remember your name."

She frowns. "I think at the time I told you my name was Shelby. We can stick with that for convenience. What happened to your hand?"

"Which one?" Pascual raises them both, the maimed left hand and the right one in its cast.

She looks amused. "Let's go with the more recent one."

"I broke someone's nose with it."

She waits for more but doesn't get it. Giving up, she says, "You've met Joachim, I understand."

Pascual nods. Today Wirth is in a different suit, but it still looks as if he slept in it. In creditable English he says, "Yes, you got old. Too bad for Yossi Peled and his wife. They never got the chance."

Pascual draws a deep breath. Here it is at last. He thinks of Sara, thinks of Rafa, thinks of the things he is going to have to give up. "I'm willing to do the time," he says. "I assume that's why you're here."

A silence follows as Wirth and Shelby trade a look. "Tell him," says Wirth finally, with a gesture of dismissal. "It's your operation."

Shelby nods once. "All right. Pascual, I don't know how you did it, but you seem to have foiled a major criminal undertaking here." She still has the slight trace of accent betraying her origin somewhere on the southern part of the Great Plains.

"None of it was my idea," says Pascual. "All I wanted was to be left alone."

"I can believe that. Unfortunately, you made that kind of hard when you chose the path you took forty years ago, or whenever it was."

"I understand that. What I don't understand is what you're doing here."

Shelby frowns again. "Well, let me explain the situation to you. The Germans want to prosecute you, and the Israelis and Saudis want to keep you quiet. These two goals are at odds. That's where we got involved. We hate to see our allies squabbling, particularly at such a dangerous time in world affairs. Now, we see this blockchain data, which I'm told is in your possession, this evidence of this significant theft, as . . . well, I guess you'd say we see it as leverage. Kind of priceless leverage, actually." She smiles.

"Against the Israelis and Saudis. Your gallant allies."

"That's right." The smile vanishes. "In our business, it's always good to have leverage."

Pascual steals a look at Wirth. The German is looking sidelong at Shelby with an expression of distaste.

Shelby continues. "The fate of the twenty-two billion is kind of up in the air right now. Nobody can find this Ulitskaya woman. The Israelis are claiming she was off the reservation on this and she's not reporting in as ordered. I don't know how true that is. Anyway, they say nobody but her and maybe somebody in Riyadh knows how to get their hands on the twenty-two billion. Their main concern now is not to get blamed for the theft. They're sticking to their story that the Iranians are behind this, and until they can be connected to that twenty-two billion with hard evidence, nobody's going to be able to prove they're wrong. That's what makes that little device you have so valuable. Whoever has it can whistle a tune and make the Israelis and the Saudis dance to it. So we're willing to offer you a good deal in exchange for it."

For a moment Pascual just stares at her. "What kind of a deal?"

"The Germans won't prosecute you and the Saudis won't kill you. As long as you keep your mouth shut, you'll be protected."

Here we go, Pascual thinks, more decisions. He looks at Wirth. "What do you get out of this?"

Wirth's jaw muscles ripple. "Nothing. The decision was made at a higher level than me. It seems we still have to defer to the Americans when they want something."

"I'm afraid that's true," says Shelby. "And we want this pretty bad. Let's just say the Israelis and the Saudis aren't always the most cooperative allies. We'll take all the leverage we can get."

Shelby and Wirth sit staring at Pascual until he realizes they are waiting for his answer. He rises and goes to the window. The traffic on the highway is jammed. Away in the south there are clouds on the horizon. Pascual wonders what kind of view he would have from the window of a German prison. He says, "I think I would rather publish the data and go serve my time in Germany." He turns to face them. "Rather that than depend on the CIA for protection."

Shelby frowns. Wirth, in contrast, smiles. He says, "You're quite right. They will own you."

Shelby says, "Nonsense. We'll provide protection as per the agreement. In exchange for the data."

"They'll own you," says Wirth again, no longer smiling.

Pascual looks at Shelby. "I'll publish the data and take my chances with the Germans. Then at least my conscience will be clean."

Shelby leans back on her chair, her face a perfect blank. She crosses her legs and clasps her hands in her lap. Looking Pascual in the eye, she says, "In that case, I'm afraid we wouldn't be able to restrain the Saudis. We have assured them that if we have the data, it is secure. If we don't have it, I'm afraid they will do whatever they have to do to prevent its publication, or make somebody pay if they can't stop it. And you've seen how they operate."

The silence goes on for some time. Pascual searches Shelby's face and sees nothing but the same brutal professionalism he saw in Lina's. Wirth is giving him a pitying look. Quietly, Shelby says, "Think of your family. Give us the data, keep your mouth shut, and the Saudis have no reason, ever, to go after them. Publish it, and all bets are off."

Pascual stands motionless, staring at the floor, hands in his pockets, probing the depths of his defeat. Wirth rises and comes around the table. He claps Pascual on the shoulder and says, "You tried. I'll give you that. Take the deal and go back to your family."

Pascual cannot look at him. "I've had Peled on my conscience for thirty-five years."

Wirth's voice hardens. "May you have it on your conscience for many more. It seems that's all the punishment you're going to get. Goodbye."

When the door slams behind Wirth, Pascual finally looks at Shelby. She is still sitting patiently, hands clasped. "It's a tough business, Pascual, what can I say? Now, can we make arrangements to take delivery?"

Pascual sits up late on his rooftop terrace after Sara and Rafa have gone to bed. He has put a dent in another bottle of cheap Spanish brandy and listened to his neighbors settling down for the night; he has watched the moon crawl across the sky and thought about people living and dead.

This is my prison, Pascual thinks. I have everything a man could ask for, and none of it is deserved, and all of it is precarious, eternally. He raises his glass to all the people he has sinned against and all the people who wish him ill, and drinks.

acknowledgments

Thanks are due most of all to Adam Dunn, for resurrecting Pascual and giving him a mission. The author's education in the arcane world of cryptocurrency was undertaken by Martin Allen, and his technological flights of fancy were overseen by John Salter. Any and all mistakes and implausibilities are strictly the fault of the author.

Dominic Martell was born in the United States and has spent most of his life there, but he has lived and traveled extensively in Latin America, Europe and the Middle East. He has worked as a teacher and a translator. The first three novels featuring repentant ex-terrorist Pascual March appeared in the 1990s, chronicling Pascual's quest for atonement in the chaotic early years of the post–Cold War period. A quarter of a century later, in the transformed landscape of the even more chaotic post-9/11 digitally connected world, Martell began to wonder what had become of Pascual and decided to bring him out of retirement. *Kill Chain* is the first of Pascual's twenty-first-century misadventures.

PHOTO: KEVIN VALENTINE

about the type

The main text of this book is set in Hofler Text Roman, an old-style serif font designed by Jonathan Hoefler Foundary, released in 1991. A versatile font designed specifically for use on the computer that is suitable for body text, it takes cues from a range of classic fonts, such as Garamond and Janson.

Hoefler Text raised awareness of type features previously the concern only of professional printers. *New York* magazine commented in 2014 that it "helped launch a thousand font obsessives."